ABOMEY

RANSOM SMYTHE

ABOMEY
Copyright © 2022 Ransom Smythe

All rights reserved. No part of this book may be reproduced in any form or by any means—whether electronic, digital, mechanical, or otherwise—without permission in writing from the publisher, except by a reviewer, who may quote brief passages in a review.

Alpha Delta Omega Publishing LLC
For contact information please email info@ransomsplace.com

Cover design by Patrick Knowles Design
Interior formatting by KUHN Design Group | kuhndesigngroup.com

Library of Congress Control Number: 2022922341

ISBN: 979-8-9869760-0-6
eBook ISBN: 979-8-9869760-1-3

Printed in the United States of America

Thanks be to God, who has become my Locksmith.

Thank you to my wife, Shannon, my partner in life,
who patiently waited alone while I wrote.

Thank you to my children,
Tyler, Erin, Austan, Genevieve,
Kelsie, and Cameron for their inspiration.

They are my Abomey.

CONTENTS

PREFACE

There is an interesting insight that is revealed when one realizes the difference between hearing and listening. It is a truth that I believe holds consistent across many of, if not all, our senses. There are differences between *seeing* and *having* vision, between *touching* and *feeling*, between *tasting* and *savoring*. It is not a foregone conclusion to think that when a person has an ability, that person will use it in the manner that will maximize its benefit. The difference is comparable to *surviving* and *thriving*.

I recall, though not well, a short story called *The Hospital Window*. I am not sure with whom the credit for the story lies because I have heard more than one version of the story, and none of them identified the author. It is the story of two friends, I will call them Barry and Larry, recovering in a hospital room following a serious accident. One man, Barry, was lying in the bed by the door unable to see the view out the window—either because of location, positioning, or traumatic loss of vision. The other man, Larry, was lying in the bed next to the window and could easily see outside.

The men had been in the hospital for weeks when Barry, the one near the door, became discouraged and began to despair at his lack of improvement from his injury, which signaled he might not return to the productive life he had previously enjoyed. Larry, the man next to window, attempted to encourage his friend with a visual report of what was happening as he looked outside the window. He told of lovers walking hand in hand. He spoke of children running and playing games in the park. He asked, "Can you hear them, Barry?" And indeed, when the man by the door became really quiet and focused, he could hear the sounds of life coming through the window. Though Larry couldn't attend to his friend's broken body, his colorful narrative of the joyful sounds of life that faintly filtered through the window was carefully nursing his friend's broken spirit and the despair began to fade.

The day came when Larry was released from the hospital and the bed became vacant. All alone, Barry, who still remained in the bed by the door, began to realize how much he had come to count on his friend's vision as his despair began to return. Days later, another individual named Terry occupied the bed, but he never gave any report of what he saw out the window.

After several days of not being informed, Barry finally couldn't contain himself any longer and asked, "What is happening in the park?"

Terry was taken aback at this question. If Barry could have seen Terry's face, he would have found a nonplussed and uncertain roommate. "What park?" asked Terry. "There is no park out there. I only see a brick wall."

There are several aspects I find interesting in this story. Clearly, the second man to occupy the bed by the window could certainly see with his eyes—but only with his *eyes*. Larry, the first man to occupy the space, had a vision that saw with his ears. But the point that resonates most with me is the power his "vision" had to heal the man in the bed by the door. Though the point maybe subtle, it is true nonetheless; seeing with the eyes alone doesn't ensure the power or accuracy of vision. A quiet perch in any crowded room quickly reveals the fact that many can see, but not all of them have vision. This is particularly true when it comes to the spiritual realm. The world is filled with people who can read the words of the Bible but miss the voice of God in those passages.

I know one shouldn't mix metaphors, but this book is meant to encourage people to open their spiritual ears and receive a vision for the realities of God. Spiritually speaking, many people see the world through the eyes of someone else, like Barry did from his friend Larry in the bed by the window. Perhaps it is true what a mentor of mine once told me: "God's portal to the spirit of man is through the ears while Satan's portal to the spirit of man is through the eyes."

This is a book that is at least in part about spiritual warfare. Now obviously, spiritual warfare has a different meaning for different people. You might even say some *see* spiritual warfare while others have a *vision* for it. In the latter group, these people have vision to see what others can't, won't, and—for whatever reasons—don't.

In the 1980s Frank E. Peretti introduced a broad range of young Christian readers to the world of spiritual warfare. His broadening of a vision for what spiritual warfare meant was very helpful in opening people's minds to the reality of darkness and light battling around us, and for that we are indebted to Mr. Peretti. But I believe this labeling has done some harm as well. In the process of getting people to understand that there is an interplay between the spiritual and the physical world, it has caused too many believers to see spiritual warfare from a perspective that overly emphasizes this warfare in terms of demonic activity.

Though I do believe spiritual warfare has at its core an element that is rooted in supernatural beings—meaning I believe they play a role in cause and effect in the physical realm—I think this perspective limits the vision for many believers regarding what the issues and battles really are in the spiritual realm that are manifesting in the physical. As a result, they are greatly hindered in their ability to wage effective spiritual warfare; therefore their spiritual growth is impeded.

I wonder how many times a believer has prayed to bind Satan, or one of his demons, but neglected to have a support group with whom they could confess their sins. Yet confessing our sins one to another is a spectacular example of how a believer takes away high ground from the enemy. Confession takes away a position from which Satan can lob guilt or shame, or instill fear, all of which are deadly to the spirit and threaten to kill, steal, or destroy what God longs to develop and cultivate in His people. I wonder how many times a believer has prayed a hedge around their loved ones while being unaware of the ungodly perspectives, values, and passions they allow to seep into their home via the media they consume through their auditory and visual senses. They usher it right in through the use of their computer, smart phone, television, radio, or various other portals that present a near-constant barrage of streaming stimuli that is specifically designed to stir up dissatisfaction with what is and a lustful longing for what might be.

It is my hope to broaden the vision of some believers to the realities of spiritual warfare. To do this, I have selected two topics that I think are traditionally avoided by believers: voodoo and human trafficking. There is significant risk in attempting a story using these contexts. Those who only see with their physical eyes may be repulsed and abandon the story without obtaining a vision for what I am trying to portray. Nonetheless, I think there will be some who see the metaphors for what they are—descriptors of something much more significant, important, and fundamental—and come to realize that what they have been calling reality is just an illusion. Perhaps they will realize they have been looking at a brick wall all their life, missing the evidence of things that are infinitely more valuable and substantial, by choosing to not tune their ear to the *sounds* of *life* being lived in the park because there is no visual evidence to confirm their existence.

A word to the reader: attention should be given to the glossary provided because many of the names of people, places, and things are in a foreign language. These names and places are outlined there to help rescue the reader from certain frustration and confusion in the very opening pages of the book.

To them who have ears let them see something new.

—Ransom Smythe
Nampa, Idaho,
July 2022

GLOSSARY

Places:

Abomey: capital of the Dahomey Kingdom

Ajama: small village of the Dahomey Kingdom forty-five miles from Abomey

Dahomey Kingdom: West African Kingdom in modern-day Benin

Ouida: port city captured by Ahosu Agaja, important to slave trade

Oyo: West African Kingdom in modern Nigeria, east of the Kingdom of Dahomey

Names:

Ahosu: King of the Dahomey Kingdom

Agaja: King of Dahomey. Grandson is Kpengla: 1718–1740

Tegbessou: King of Dahomey. Father is Agaja: 1740–1774

Kpengla: King of Dahomey. Father is Tegbessou: 1774–1789

Aloisio: West African slave of Francisco Félix de Souza

Ehioze: minister of oil production to Ahosu Kpengla

Ekaghogho: a N'Nonmiton warrior under Ode

Ewanisha: wife: Wara; children: Ima and Nourbese; aunt-in-law: Ira

Francisco Félix de Souza (Chachá): eighteenth-century slave trader from Brazil

Imarogbe: (Ima) parents: Ewanisha and Wara; sister: Nourbese; great-aunt: Ira

Irawagbon: (Ira) retired N'Nonmiton commander; aunt to Wara

Nourbese: parents: Ewanisha and Wara; brother: Ima; great-aunt: Ira

N'Nonmiton: a group of legendary female fighters of the Kingdom of Dahomey

Ode: commander of the N'Nonmiton during the reign of Ahosu Kpengla

Omorenoniwara: (Wara) aunt: Ira; husband: Ewanisha; children: Ima and Nourbese

Yoruba: tribal people of the Oyo Kingdom

Vodun:

Asogwe Mambo: highest female member of the Vodun religion

Ason: ceremonial rattle

Fetish: objects used in Vodun ceremonies for their spiritual value; made of animal parts

Gris-gris: a vodun charm or amulet

Guinee: spirit world

Hounsi: attendants of a Vodun ceremony who perform mundane tasks (serving tables)

Horse: person possessed by a Loa

Initiates: devotees of Vodun who are learning the ceremonial practices of their religion

Kanzo ceremony: initiation ceremony into the Vodun religion

Loas: spirits in the religion of Vodun; referred to as Iwa

Ayido-Weddo: the female Loa associated with the rainbow; wife of Damballah

Damballah: the male Loa associated with snakes; husband of Ayida-Weddo

Erzulie Fréda: the Loa of beauty, creativity, and love

Ogoun: the warrior Loa; crafty and powerful

Papa Legba: the Loa who attends the crossroads between the physical and spiritual

Mambo: female high priest

Peristyle: ceremonial gathering place for Vodun worship, much like a courtyard

Poto Mitan: sacramental post in the center of a peristyle, used in Vodun worship

Food:

Acarajé: meal of peeled beans formed into a ball and deep-fried in palm oil

Languages:

Fon: Language of the Kingdom of Dahomey and currently spoken in modern-day Benin

CHAPTER 5

Dress:

Dhuku: an African headwrap

CHAPTER 1

KINGDOM CONSIDERATIONS

Dahomey Kingdom, West Africa
June 17, 1776

The sky was clear and moonless. The air was warm, and the absence of reflected light caused the stars to shine brightly in the night sky as a gentle, salty breeze blew over the cresting waves and across the beach that formed the broad bight in the West African coastline. Wave after cresting wave brought a crescendo of roars, ending with the tinkling fizz across the sands, the rhythm of which easily mesmerized the majority of those standing around, or leaning against, the carriage. Inside sat two occupants, neither of whom were drowsy. One fidgeted restlessly as if he were anxious about being caught in the act of something inappropriate. The other sat calmly, rarely shifting, and when he did so, it was only to inspect his expensive clothing for the invasion of an errant piece of lint or to correct the lay of his lapel. His wig completed the aristocratic appearance while his patience displayed great confidence. He was a king with a slave, yet a king without a throne.

Unlike his companion, the unsettled one was as black as the darkest crevice, where the forest that sat behind them met the beach, or as dark as the night sky if the stars were not there to emit their majestic light. The regal one believed the Black man to be exactly like all the others who had accompanied them that night, valuable for their usefulness. Each had taken up stations in varied positions of slumber around the carriage. Though the skin of the unsettled one was as theirs in color, his dress was not. They wore a mix and match assortment of tribal attire that featured worn-out shirts without collars and either slacks or, more commonly, knickers. None of them wore shoes. He, on the other hand, had been forced to dress like his companion in the more recent European fashion: a wig, stockings, shoes, and a collared shirt. Yet it was the white wig on a black head, combined with the expression he wore on his face, that made anyone watching realize he didn't belong to either group. And with this particular White man, it had likely been done on purpose.

"Relax, Aloisio. You are as restless as the sea," said the sole White person.

"Yes, master," said Aloisio. He did his best to hide his discomfort yet was unsuccessful.

They spoke in Portuguese, but the master did so with great ease as if it was his mother tongue. The slave, though, spoke in a broken manner, as if it were a skill he had been forced to learn with great effort. The master sat tall and straight with a walking stick between his knees, with his hands resting one on top of the other. He was a young man in his early twenties, fit of mind and body. He had only recently come to West Africa from his home in Brazil to strike out on a venture he had seen as a once-in-a-lifetime opportunity. It wasn't just slavery. The transatlantic need for cheap labor had made that a lucrative venture for well over a century. But not everyone understood yet the nuances of how to put into motion the wheels of slavery to maximize profit. Few could see how to integrate the hunger for the products of the new world and the usefulness of the products of the old, let alone how to make them feed one another and change what would be the grinding out of a profit from one or the other into what could be a well-greased mechanism that made a profit at the turn of each cog, leveraging a small investment into a fortune to fund an empire and, ultimately, a throne. Francisco Félix de Souza not only saw it, he could also feel the very reality of it coming into being. This knowingness fed not only his confidence; it had begun to feed his ego as well.

There was a faint call above the crashing waves, causing both men to look out toward the sea into the darkness. A black face peered in through the open window of the carriage and spoke in Fon to Aloisio, who responded with great ease.

Returning to the hampered Portuguese, the man whispered to his master, "They are on the beach, Chachá." The young man again looked to his chest and brushed a nonexistent thread off his coat as if making final preparations for his entrance to a stage. He glanced up and looked into the eyes of his slave with a grin and nodded him out the door to his appointed task. Aloisio hesitated for a brief moment and then, as he returned the grin, opened the carriage door and stepped onto the footstep. While craning his body over the top of the carriage, he gave two short whistles and then exited the carriage.

He spoke in Fon to the men, who instantly came to attention as the jingling of horse and wagon could be heard approaching. Half the men followed him and the wagon toward the beach. The jingling of the wagon tack faded into the sound of surf while the others took up positions around the carriage. Every man had a weapon, either a pistol or musket. As they stood with their back to the carriage, each was peering into the darkness that surrounded them more with their ears than with their eyes.

Twenty minutes passed, and the same jingling was once again heard. Chachá exited the carriage, stretching himself to his full height. The wagon came alongside the carriage with its retinue of security as a handful of torches were lit. Aloisio looked to his master. In the flickering lights of the torches, Chachá raised one finger and pointed to the sand. Then, after jabbing the same finger back at the wagon, he flicked it toward town. Everyone assumed it was a convenient way to overcome the language barrier. In reality, the man's face revealed it was pure condescension stemming from the arrogance that had taken root in his enlarging ego.

Aloisio dismounted the wagon and called out in Fon to his men.

One crate and one small barrel were pulled from under the canvas tarpaulin and placed on the sand at Chachá's feet as the wagon and half the men set out in the direction of town.

Chachá smiled at the crate and barrel for a moment as if lost in thought, then his smile faded as he looked up into Aloisio's eyes and quietly asked, "Any questions?"

The slave stared at his master for just a fraction of a moment too long, but it was enough time to plant a seed of doubt into the mind of his master. He responded, "No. No questions. I know what I am to do."

Chachá tucked his chin to his right collarbone and raised his eyebrows as if to ask his question again while at the same time expressing his own unconvinced state. "The terms? Do you know what I want?"

The large Black man swallowed either to moisten his vocal cords or to stabilize his voice, then replied, "Yes, Chachá. I know the terms." His attempt to steady both his face and voice betrayed more than he desired. The words were true, and though he could state them accurately, he struggled to hide his true fear of what he was about to face.

"And what will you give the witch?"

The Black man winced at the word. "You have determined she may have one." He knew the Brazilian was aware of these legendary women. Yet there was no way this man could fully understand the fear they stirred in the hearts of all the men standing around the carriage. They were the products of the culture built by those legendary women by the wielding of that very same fear. These warriors would not like to hear him referring to them as witches, nor the patronizing disdain the term was cloaked in. He set his face firmly and held back a swallow so as to hide his own fear. "I know the terms. I know what must be done."

It seemed to have the effect he desired as his master seemed to relax and said, "Very well then. Let's get to it." The White man grabbed a pistol from the lad standing next to him, then, looking at each man in the circle, cocked the hammer. Every man did the same as he turned in the sand, strode to the carriage, and silently reentered.

Aloisio looked into the eyes of his men as he singled out his most trusted, and with a flick of his head the group broke up. Shortly thereafter, three men returned with wood, and as the torches were extinguished a fire was started several yards from the crate and barrel. The slave opened the crate, revealing twenty British-made Long Land Pattern muskets from Farmer and Galton in Birmingham, England. These latest editions were intimidating at one hundred yards but deadly within fifty. They were likely the finest Europe had to offer. The weapon had an overall length of 62.5 inches of which the 0.75 calibre smoothbore barrel made up 46 inches The first cog in the machine of fortune, being put in motion by Francisco Félix De Souza, was the obtaining of the means to equip a small army. Tonight's shipment completed the full allotment of these state-of-the-art weapons, along with the needed gunpowder, musket balls, and the means to make more.

Chachá knew that the Ahosu, the Fon word for the King of Dahomey, was in a delicate position. The Ahosu wanted to secure his realm and advance his borders. He was also trying to exploit the various trade opportunities that lay before him—from gold, to slaves, to palm oil—but he had a significant problem: He could not maximize those opportunities while under the tributary status with the Kingdom of Oyo. His ancestor, Ahosu Agaja, had secured the coastal town of Ouida nearly fifty years ago. Now one of the major ports of the West African slave trade was under his control to feed the ever-growing need of the New World for cheap labor. With this city the Ahosu had what he needed to become a cog in someone else's mechanism. It just happened to be De Souza's. The Oyo, however, had no desire to see their subject kingdom make a profit without paying a heavy price.

The Ahosu just had to find a way to deal with Oyo and its cavalry. Oyo's cavalry had repeatedly been able to subdue Dahomey and ultimately force tribute from the kingdom, which in turn robbed the Ahosu of his much-needed wealth and seed money. The only thing that had been successful in dealing with that cavalry were the firearms he could procure and the trenches he could dig. There weren't many armies that could match the fierceness of the standing army of

Ahosu Kpengla. If they could be sufficiently armed, then perhaps he could finally break free from the Oyo Kingdom of the Yoruba people.

Chachá knew there was money to be made in helping Kpengla with the difficulties he faced. But tonight, he had to instill courage into the hearts of his men as they were about to stand face-to-face with the dreaded female soldiers of the Ahosu, known as the N'Nonmiton, which meant "Our Mothers" in their native language. These women were considered the wives of the King, but their ferocity and ice-cold ability to behead an enemy had become the subject of nightmares for many men near and far to the Kingdom of Dahomey. Those nightmares were most intense just beyond the borders of Dahomey. The training the N'Nonmiton endured was notorious. Their bodies, over time, became covered in scars from running through acacia thorn thickets. Their commitment to the Vodun traditions caused them to be greatly respected, if not feared, by their male counterparts and had earned them the moniker of "witches" by Chachá.

Tonight, the slave and servants of the Brazilian who had come to traffic in the lives of their countrymen would face the feared N'Nonmiton of the Ahosu of Dahomey. Their fear was rooted in their uncertainty of whether they would be seen as friend or foe to the fierce warrior women.

Aloisio finished looking over the British-made weapon and knew the quality of the pieces would not be lost on the warriors. They were as familiar with muskets as they were the traditional clubs, knives, and swords. He was about to set the long musket down when he heard a fluttering whistle. He looked into the darkness in the direction of the whistle and waved the whistler into the light.

Four women, dressed in their traditional uniforms, stepped into the radiance of the fire unarmed, as did their escort, who obviously also felt uncomfortable.

"Who speaks for the Ahosu?" asked Aloisio in Fon.

"I do," said the shortest one to his right.

He cocked his head to the right, raised his eyebrows, and gave a condescending frown and replied, "Very well." He extended the musket to her and continued. "Two hundred muskets with four-hundred-gun flints, one hundred cases of ten cartridges each, and one hundred twenty-five barrels of gunpowder for three hundred fifty slaves. Plus, a commitment to replenish the same amount of gun flints, cartridges, and gunpowder for an additional two hundred slaves every other month for one year. Additional guns or supplies can be negotiated in the future."

The warrior took the weapon, examined its mechanism, and used the fire to illuminate the barrel as she inspected it for defects. She then passed the weapon to her companions, who each took a turn to inspect. "Two hundred would be too much to commit based on a single musket."

"Examine the others, if you like. I am sure you will find them all in excellent condition," the man quickly responded while leaning down toward the crate with arms extending an invitation.

Each of the women began examining the remaining crate, and though they tried to hide it, they were obviously pleased with what they were examining. "You still ask too much," replied the leader.

"I am very saddened to hear that." Aloisio looked crestfallen. He received the weapon back and examined it. "These are not satisfactory?" he queried as if he wasn't sure he had fully understood.

The leader raised her eyebrows, shrugged her shoulders, and stated matter-of-factly, "Perhaps worth one hundred slaves."

"One hundred? I had no idea these weapons were so inadequate. If I had only known, I would never have offered them to Our Mothers." He appeared distressed. "My master has instructed me to either get three hundred fifty slaves or accept the offer of three hundred from Oyo."

The women bristled at the name of their enemy, and the three glanced to the tallest woman present in the group, who fastened her narrowed eyes on Aloisio. Now he knew who the real leader was.

"I do not want to give them to the enemies of my people. That is why I had asked my master to offer them to you first," whispered the Black man as he locked eyes with the revealed leader. "I would never … offer you … such inferior weapons. But I could love giving them to our enemies at such a price. A double vengeance, wouldn't you say?" he asked with a bright smile on his face. "This I would be happy to do." The man said in a slow solemn whisper, then he snapped his fingers and briskly added, "Box them up!"

The women looked between themselves without speaking. They were carefully trying to consider their next move, knowing they would be the ones expected by the Ahosu to round up the slaves. "Wait!" said the tall woman more as a command than a request. "You still ask too much."

"I understand your hesitancy to commit such a price for such inferior weapons." The slave paused. "If you can get the Ahosu to agree to two hundred fifty slaves and commit to moving his palm oil through my master's markets, I believe I can get him to agree to two hundred fifty slaves. I want one hundred seventy-five men and seventy-five women. And they must be of a stock expected to survive the voyage—none of the feeble or dying."

"Agreed," said the tall leader.

"Then this is our gift to you as a token of good faith," he said, extending the musket to the leader. "And though it isn't of the quality you are used to, I hope you can make it roar like a lion and then"— she took the weapon—"may the enemies of our people feel it bite like a lion also."

She cradled the musket against her long frame. "We will return with the response of the Ahosu in four days. If the answer is yes, the first group of one hundred fifty slaves will follow two weeks later. We will take eighty muskets and ammunition in exchange. The remainder will follow a month later." She backed away from the fire before he realized the other three were already gone. In the next moment, he found himself alone by the crackling fire, exhaling deeply.

"They are gone, sir!" called one of the men from the darkness to Aloisio.

"We are clear, Chachá!" called the slave to his master.

In the next moment de Souza was behind his slave and uncocked his pistol. "Well?" asked the Brazalian. "One hundred seventy-five slaves?"

Aloisio smiled, "No, sir." He turned to look into the face of his master, who looked up from his pistol, squinting. "Two hundred fifty slaves, a part of the action on the palm oil, and they appreciate you not giving the guns to the Oyo."

His master chuckled and nodded. "Very good," said Chacha. "You have more than earned your keep this day." Both men chuckled as they climbed into the carriage. Upon taking their seats, de Souza tapped the top of his walking stick against the roof of the carriage twice, and the entourage started their return to Ouida.

* * *

Two days later the four women arrived in Abomey and approached the Palace of Ahosu Kpengla. Inside the Palace the Ahosu was standing around, hovering over a broad table with his advisors.

"You must increase the production of palm oil," said Kpengla. "You are not producing at the rate you should be. What is the problem?" he asked as he looked to his advisors in obvious annoyance.

"You are aware, Ahosu, that we are in the middle of the first rainy season," stated Ehioze, his minister in charge of production. The Ahosu just glared at him. Ehioze tried to explain. "What is easy in the dry season becomes difficult in the rainy season."

"And dangerous," offered another advisor. The forest is filled with many creatures, but few of them are feared more than the Western Green Mamba, *Dendroaspis viridis*. The snake is not particularly aggressive, and their nervousness makes them rather shy, causing them to flee and hide. That is … unless they are cornered, which happens more frequently when the rainwaters chase the snakes into the trees where the harvesters of palm fruit could easily surprise them, leaving no place for either to escape. This is a fact so well known by the people of the region that the minister was surprised the Ahosu wasn't aware of it, unless it wasn't an issue of ignorance but one of apathy. "But I am sure the harvesters will be happy to provide the Ahosu with what he needs to build the Kingdom."

"I am beginning to wonder just how committed my ministers are to their tasks. It can't be that I haven't made the goals and objectives clear, can it?" He began looking around the room. In order to display their own personal resolve, not a single man dared to look away from the Ahosu. "Perhaps it is a problem of competence." There was a pause as he let that thought sink in to the minds of his men. "Or perhaps you enjoy being a goat for the Yoruba Kingdom of Oyo to milk."

The men did not dare move.

"Over the past fifty years, we have faced the Yoruba on our own soil and defended our people. Battle after battle, seven in all, we have faced them, and each time we were on the tipping point of victory. Our weapons, warriors, and tactics were superior." He paused for effect. "We have always thought it was the arrival of their reinforcements at the last moment that tipped the scales back in their favor." Another pause created a tension-filled silence as he looked out a window into the distance. "But maybe that is not right. Maybe it was the lack of resolve in the hearts of our fathers and our brothers." He turned back to look into the eyes of his men. "Maybe that is the same lack of resolve I am seeing in your eyes this day." The Ahosu extended himself to his full height and towered over his ministers.

It was quickly becoming uncomfortable in the Palace. Kpengla had ruled since the passing of his father two years ago. His grandfather, Agaja, had expanded the territory of Dahomey to include securing the port city of Ouida. But there was no doubt who ruled the Kingdom today, nor was it uncertain that he longed to surpass his fathers in expanding the Kingdom.

"Speaking of the Oyo . . . " He turned his eyes to the lone woman in the room who had stood quietly at the edge, enjoying the discomfort of the men—not that you could tell it from her face. "My wife," he said, motioning her forward. The woman stepped into view with such confidence that it stood in stark contrast to the posture of the others in the room. "How go the excursions?" the Ahosu questioned.

"We continue raiding the lands of the Yoruba and have taken, on average, two hundred fifty slaves per month. Nearly seventy-five percent remain in good, marketable quality. The remaining twenty-five percent are used as fodder for various activities as forced marches, target practice, honing of hunting skills, and"—she hesitated as she glanced at the minister of palm oil production then continued—"to drive away snakes."

The minister looked to his fellow advisors, none of whom would give him any regard.

"However, we have run into difficulties." The posture of the men in the room relaxed ever so slightly. "We have saturated our markets for slaves. Our weapons are aging, and more and more of them are becoming unreliable in battle. Our first strike at a distance has always given us an edge in battle, especially against cavalry forces. We need more weapons, and we need to expand our markets for more slaves."

At that moment a steward entered the room and approached the N'Nonmiton leader. He halted three paces away until recognized by her. She flicked her head up, inviting him to approach. He completed the last few paces and leaned in to whisper into her ear, then he stepped back. She glanced at the Ahosu and then back to the steward. "Send her in to me."

The Ahosu grasped his hands behind his back and rocked on his heels with a slight air of impatience.

"But we have a solution we would like to offer," she continued. "The issue is how to obtain not only more weapons but more ammunition to ensure our ability to secure your objectives and bring you results—not excuses." At that moment the tall warrior from the beach entered the room. She walked directly toward the Ahosu, gave a slight bow, and stepped to her commander. "Success?" asked the commander. The tall warrior nodded. "Inform our husband."

The tall woman turned to the king. "My husband, we have secured an opportunity for two hundred new British muskets, one hundred twenty-five barrels of gunpowder, and a source for monthly supplies of powder and ammunition through a new Portuguese market for slaves—and potentially for more palm oil."

"New markets for both slaves and palm oil?" asked the Ahosu.

The woman gave a quick and decisive nod.

The Ahosu smiled a broad-toothed smile. "See, boys, what Our Mothers have brought to us?" He looked around the room at the others. "How soon can we begin to make use of these new markets?"

"If the terms are acceptable to you, my husband, then we can finalize the arrangement in two days. We'll need one hundred fifty slaves for the first installment in two weeks, with another one hundred in a month, for a total of two hundred fifty slaves—roughly two-thirds male and one-third female, all market-worthy. We will also need to begin finalizing arrangements for the palm oil," completed the tall warrior.

"If it is obtainable," added the commander of the N'Nonmiton as she glanced at Ehioze.

What had once been the faint hint of relaxation across the room of men was rapidly replace by rigid discomfort once again.

Kpengla smiled. "That won't be a problem, will it, Ehioze?" The name meant "who stands above envy," which fit him in an ironic way.

"Certainly not." Ehioze feigned offense at the thought. He continued, "I just hope this new market can accommodate our supplies. I would hate to have to build additional storage for all the oil."

"I agree to the terms. Secure the deal and see if we can begin to negotiate for more weapons for my wives," said Kpengla to the commander, who nodded to the tall N'Nonmiton.

"Now leave me!" Kpengla commanded, and all turned to exit. "Not you, Ode. I want to speak more with both of you." The N'Nonmiton commander and her subordinate approached their Ahosu. In a matter of moments, the three were alone in the Palace room.

"Yes, my husband," said the commander.

"I have been thinking of how you were named, *born along a road.*"

"Yes," she replied.

"I wonder if it was at a crossroad," said Kpengla, half to himself.

"Oh," said Ode, more to fill in the silence than as a response.

"Your ability to anticipate the future is one of your greatest talents," Kpengla said, then walked to the window and looked into the distance. "I believe you are very familiar with the crossroads. Or, more to the point, those who abide there."

"I see," said Ode.

The Ahosu was referring to the Vodun religion, which the women of the N'Nonmiton excelled in both practice and knowledge. Specifically, he was referring to the Loa Papa Legba, one of the most widely served African deities. He is considered to be the one standing at the crossroads of life and death, the physical and the spiritual, and is the one who grants or denies permission to speak with the spirits of Guinee, or the spirit world. He is always the first and the last spirit invoked in any Vodun ceremony as he is the one who grants permission to speak, then opens and closes the doorways. In ceremonies, when he mounts his horses, the people he possesses assume his character and passions. He prefers to be adorned with wide-brimmed straw hats, the colors red and black, brown pants, and a crooked cane. Upon his arrival he is offered gifts of candy, tobacco, toys, and alcohol. He is known to be quite a trickster and likes to play games. In Vodun, those who are familiar with the spirit realm are very familiar with Papa Legba. Those with whom Papa Legba is familiar have special access to knowledge and opportunities that are necessary for every crossroad in life.

"You speak of our religion and my practice thereof."

"I do," said the Ahosu. "I have come to expect great things from you, Ode. I have no doubt in your abilities, nor in those of the gods of our religion."

Ode was unsure where this was all headed.

Kpengla could see he needed to get to his point. "How many slaves do you have today who will be available to march and meet the trader in Ouida in two weeks?"

There was an awkward pause.

"Not enough," replied Ode. The point he was making quickly sunk in.

"How many do you have?"

"Forty-seven. Of whom only thirty are of the quality he will want."

"How many do you expect to arrive in the next week that are not committed to any other of my markets?"

"Seventy."

"And how many do you expect to arrive next month who are not committed to any other of my markets?"

"Another one hundred."

"So you were anticipating two hundred, not two hundred fifty slaves?"

The women looked at one another.

Before either woman could speak, Kpengla asked, "Did Papa Legba not give you any insight to this unfortunate turn of events?" It was clear that though the Ahosu was pleased to see his ministers being made off balance by his wives, he also had the ability to do the same to them.

"The traitor called Aloisio wanted three hundred fifty slaves for the cargo and was willing to sell it to the Kingdom of Oyo for three hundred instead," offered the tall warrior. She looked toward her commander. "Ekaghogho complained of the inferior production in an attempt to lower the price. The traitor turned that against us, seeming to be excited to sell them despite the lower price than he was requesting from us, especially if he could sell inferior weapons to the Yoruba."

"They are of good quality then?" the king asked.

"Yes, my husband, they are the newest British productions. They will devastate those who stand against them, whether in our hands or in the hands of the Yoruba," said the warrior to her Ahosu.

Both women looked to their Ahosu and waited.

"Then not only are you in need of another fifty, but you will need more slaves in the coming months," mused the Ahosu.

The commander looked out the window. Her subordinate looked at her feet.

"Which happens when?" asked the Ahosu.

"We need them within a week to be sure we have them in Ouida in two weeks," reported the commander.

"Then you have some work to do. Perhaps you will need to seek out Papa Legba for some more help," said the Ahosu. "You might as well get to it." As the women turned he added, "You might have to do things you are not comfortable doing." Both women knew what that meant, but neither liked it. With a look of distaste that each tried to drive away from one another's eyes, they turned to exit the room, leaving the Ahosu to his own thoughts.

* * *

Two days later in Ouida the deal was struck. That same night, an African king and a Brazilian slave trader began to dream of wealth and power in vivid color. Simultaneously, a palm oil minister had nightmares of how he was going to inspire his countrymen into forced labor, in dangerous circumstances, without them feeling like the slaves they were becoming.

* * *

Early the next morning, in the small village of Ajama, which is a forty-five-mile journey from Abomey, a young mother was squatting on the ground that had been saturated by recent rainfall, preparing breakfast outside her hut. An older woman slipped up beside her and squatted in front of a basket of beans, while the former continued her task of preparing dendê oil for the beans.

"Acarajé?" asked the older woman, whose name was Irawagbon and meant *the enemy tried to kill her*. She went by the shortened version of her name, Ira.

The younger woman's name was Omorenoniwara, which meant *not intended to suffer*. She went by Wara, the shortened version of her name. She gave a quick nod and then glanced toward the sky. "And hopefully before the rain begins again."

"Then I will light the fire and help peel the beans," said the older woman, smiling.

"I am thankful for you, Ira," said the younger woman. Ira was Wara's aunt.

"Wara, you are my family. You know your mother was always good to me and supported me through tough days. It is good for me to be the help I can, while I can," remarked the older woman as she rose to the fire pit, filled it with dry wood, bent over, and began lighting the fire.

Wara's mother, Ira's younger sister, died years ago from a mysterious illness none of the witch doctors could treat. Families were hard to raise and care for alone in this village. It often took the assistance of a small clan. Wara was the only surviving child of her mother, and when she died, Wara was forced to care for her own family alone. Alone, that is, until her aunt Ira came home from the N'Nonmiton at the passing of Ahosu Tegbessou, father of Kpengla. She had been a fierce warrior of renown and had even been the commander of the corps for the last half of his reign. But as she aged, it quickly became clear that making war was not for the aged. Through it all she had remained a virgin and was now in her twilight years without children of her own. When her sister died, Ira and Wara each found a need that they could only fulfill with the help of one another.

"It is I who am thankful for you, my dear. Without you, I have nothing." Ira returned to the baskets of beans and began peeling them into a wooden bowl in which she would later mash them. At this time a lovely young girl emerged from the hut, silently wiped sleep from her eyes, and raised a clay pot to her head as she set out to the well for water.

As the young girl headed off, her mother realized that every member of her family needed the other, then she smiled at the strength of family unity this generated. "We can make some extra acarajé, and I will take it with some chicken to Ewan in the forest," she said. "And Imarogbe can go with me. He wants to begin work with them soon." A peel of thunder cracked out from the sky overhead. "Only after this rainy season." Imarogbe was the fourteen-year-old son of Ewanisha, Ewan's full name, and Wara. His sister, Nourbese, was sixteen months his junior and already being positioned for marriage.

"The gods have blessed you, my niece," said Ira as she looked down the path toward the well.

"Yes, I am very blessed," remarked Wara, smiling again as she, too, looked down the path toward the well. She added the oil to the woklike pan and placed it on the fire to bring to a boil.

"I have a request of you, Wara."

The younger woman looked up. "What's that?"

"I intend to seek out the Asogwe Mambo in Abomey for assistance in obtaining a blessing for Nourbese, and I need some of her hair."

"You are going to have a gris-gris made for her?" Nearly dropping the pan, the mother squealed as she grasped the arm of her aunt, gaining excitement for her daughter.

The aunt smiled. "Perhaps Erzulie Fréda will be generous toward her?"

Wara nodded toward the hut as Ira stole a glance down the path, then quickly got up and slipped inside.

Erzulie Fréda embodied the spirit of love, beauty, jewelry, dancing, luxury, and flowers. The heart was her symbol, and she expressed herself through the colors pink, blue, white, and gold. She enjoyed the sacrifices of finer things, such as jewelry, perfume, and sweet cakes. She represented the fullness of femininity and compassion, yet could also be quite a flirt in the ceremonies she attended. On the flip side, her temperament was always a bit unpredictable and pouty—so much so, that some perceived her as unable to attain the things she wanted the most. When she became petulant, she could change her mind and remove every blessing she had previously given.

"Perhaps … But wouldn't that be marvelous if she would," Wara said, half to herself.

The elder woman emerged from the hut with her treasure.

More through a statement, Wara asked, "That is going to cost handsomely." Wara was thinking through the making of the gris-gris as well as the ceremony itself.

They finished frying the acarajé as Nourbese returned with the water.

Ira watched the young girl as she walked up to the hut, placed the pot inside, and then returned to the women by the fire pit, squatting between them. "How did you sleep, young one?" asked the old warrior.

"Well enough," she said with a smile.

The women were collecting the food when another crack of thunder shook the little village. They rushed into the hut as the rain started coming down.

"The gods continue to smile," whispered Ira to her niece.

• • •

Hours later, Wara and her son, Imarogbe, found her husband, Ewan, with the men harvesting palm oil in the forest. The rain was coming down hard, and men were climbing the trees slowly and cautiously as they did their best searching for the greatly feared green mamba. Wara opened her bag and gave her husband a bowl of acarajé and chicken. Ewan smiled and embraced his wife with appreciation and palmed his son's head.

Just then a scream was heard. Ewan turned to look behind him as his family strained to see everyone gazing at a tree upon which a harvester had climbed. At the base of the same tree was the man who had screamed and was still dancing around. Others were chuckling Apparently, the man in the tree had encountered a snake and, after beheading it, had flung the body onto the unsuspecting coworker below him, who was not aware the green-bodied snake was headless. Others were busily collecting the remains of both the head and body.

Ewan chuckled to himself only to turn back to Wara and see she was not pleased in the slightest.

"Working in the rain is making this a very dangerous job," said Wara.

The husband looked to his son flippantly and raised his eyebrows.

"I don't find the risk funny," she added.

"No. We encounter about six snakes a day in the trees, which is about six times the number that we normally do on the ground in a week." Ewan paused and looked back again to his comrades. "We have lost three harvesters to these snakes so far during this rainy season."

"Why is it so important to work the trees at this time?" asked Imarogbe.

"The Ahosu continues to search out new markets as a way to expand his power," replied his father.

"We never worked the trees this hard under Tegbessou," observed Wara.

"No, we didn't. But things have changed." Ewan nodded back over his shoulder in the direction of the workers. "We have all sensed it. No one is sure why. But it causes all the men to feel as if they are being worked as slaves and not subjects of Kpengla." He paused to take a bite of his lunch. "The harvesters are beginning to talk. Some have walked off the job and into the forest."

"Where are they going?"

"Where I'd go." Ewan looked at his wife with a smile and swallowed a bite of chicken "Home."

CHAPTER 2

A LEGACY REDEFINED

Dahomey Kingdom, West Africa
June 22, 1776

Three days later Ira was arriving in Abomey just as the hot part of the day was peaking. Two days prior, she had arisen early in the morning and quietly rifled through her scant belongings, finding the fine linen wrap she was looking for and placing it in her satchel. She had strapped on her battle blades, covering them with the cloak from her warrior days, and grasped her walking staff before heading off at a faster than usual pace. There was little chance she would be bothered by anyone she met along the way. They would first recognize her cloak, then her face, and then would be uncertain if she were traveling alone.

As she entered Abomey, she went right past the Palace that had been her destination for so many years. Instead, she went to her second most frequent destination. She had traveled past several huts with white flags during the day, but there was one particular white flag she was seeking. This flag wasn't on a stick, like in the villages. This flag was hung from a carved flagpole and run up with a halyard. The flagpole was stationed outside a compound that enclosed a large peristyle, in the center of which stood a poto mitan. The compound had multiple gates that could be opened, allowing for the whole community of the capital to congregate for important national ceremonies. Ira knocked at one of these gates by the flagpole and, after a brief conversation with the gatekeeper, she was ushered in.

At the edge of the compound, between the large peristyle and the compound walls, was a thatched building and lean-to. The lean-to was rather long and filled with fetishes used for various ceremonies in the peristyle or for purchase in private personal ceremonies. Irawagbon walked past the Initiates busily at work, then past the lean-to and into the thatched roof building. She was greeted by the Asogwe Mambo.

"Good afternoon, my dear Ira. To what do I owe this great honor?" asked the Mambo.

"I have come two days' journey to seek your services," responded Ira.

The Asogwe Mambo quietly whispered to the Initiates, who were busy at work in the building all the while stealing glances at the famous warrior. As part of their training, every N'Nonmiton spent many of their years in this compound, studying under the Kingdom's greatest Mambo as one of her Initiates. The Initiates, who were only moments before busy at work, quickly and silently left the room. In no time at all the Kingdom's Asogwe Mambo and it's most famous N'Nonmiton stood looking into the eyes of one another, their minds filling with memories of days gone by.

"Do you remember the day we met here for the first time? So young, so feisty, so determined. I knew that first day you were destined for greatness," said the Mambo.

The pair continued to look at one another as they reflected. "I remember your Kanzo ceremony? I was so proud of you," the elder Mambo reminisced. "Then there was that night, years later, when you so boldly requested a spiritual marriage with Ogoun? I about laid an egg." The elderly woman was smiling as she leaned in to whisper, "And when he said yes, how your destiny began to be realized."

The retired N'Nonmiton just stared into the eyes of her aged mentor, who didn't realize her prized pupil didn't seem to be recalling the memories with the same fondness, let alone satisfaction. Her mind was filled with the faces, bodies, and blood that followed that night and formed the basis of her notoriety. She grinned as she saw how excited the Asogwe Mambo was with the memory. The Vodun queen seemed old to the young women back then. Now she had to be well over ninety.

"What brings my prized initiate back to my peristyle this fine afternoon? Surely it isn't for that which she is more than capable to do for herself?"

The pupil smiled at her teacher. "What I long for is great … and I want no room for error."

The eyes of the teacher narrowed as she mused, "Mm." There was a short pause before she added, "You ask for someone else. For someone special?"

The smile of Irawagbon broadened. "Yes … for the daughter of my niece."

The Mambo smiled back as she grasped the hands of her student.

"As you know, I gave up much through the years I was with my husband, the Ahosu, and fought his battles." Ira's eyes began to well up with tears. "I do not have a family of my own. There is no one for me to give my last years of life to. There is no legacy of my own to nourish … to protect. All that remains is the family of my sister, who is now dead. I do this for her." She paused in reflection, then spoke boldly with a new realization. "I do this for them. I do this for us … I do this for me."

The mentor continued to smile, but the knowledge of what was being pursued caused her heart to swell as well. "Then I shall do it for you at no cost."

The smile on Irawagbon quickly vanished and was replaced with distaste. "I will not ask of you that which will cost me nothing." She reached under her cloak and pulled out the linen cloth. She handed it to the Mambo, who unwrapped it to reveal a solid-gold coiled snake, a symbol of the great Loa Damballah, a gift to her from Ahosu Tegbessou when she became the commander of the N'Nonmiton. It would be hard to know which was more valuable: the gold itself or the gift of a king. Regardless, it would prove more than enough to cover all costs associated with whatever Irawagbon wanted, and they both knew it.

"Tell me what you want, and it is yours."

"I need for Erzulie Fréda to be so pleased with my offerings that she will bless a very powerful gris-gris that will prove to be a blessing to my grandniece and our family from this day on."

"I see."

"It must be powerful. Not just for one girl, but for generations to come."

The older woman said nothing but looked deep into the eyes of her friend as she began to realize just what was being asked. It was a request to transcend time and permeate the future. She knew this required a level of Vodun that had never been asked of her before, a level she knew her pupil didn't possess. She wasn't even sure she possessed it herself. "Then we have a lot of work in front of us."

"Today is Wednesday. Tomorrow—" started Irawagbon.

"I know. Yes, tomorrow is Erzulie Fréda's sacred day," interrupted the Mambo with a flick of her hand. "We can be ready. We will be ready. Do you have a token to perform the contagious magic upon?"

"Yes." Irawagbon handed the Mambo the hair collected days before.

"Now leave me. I have much work to do. Your fee is more than enough. Send in my girls when you leave. Be here tomorrow night, and I will be ready."

"I will be here. I knew you would be able to help me." Then she turned with a broad smile and left as candles were being brought in from another building.

The next day Irawagbon spent the daylight hours walking about the city, retracing routes she had taken many times before. There were more than a few wrinkled faces that recognized her cloak and her face, and they gave her a slight bow or nod of respect. The older ones of this city knew who this warrior was. They knew what it had cost her, and they were appreciative. The old warrior received their admiration with uncharacteristic meekness. The years of battles had changed her. Few were aware of the spiritual marriage between she and Ogoun that had been the strength of her life as a warrior, and none were aware of the dark emptiness that her experiences eventually brought into her life.

She returned to the compound of the white flag just after the sun had set, but she stayed out of the way as the Asogwe Mambo and her Initiates remained, collecting the necessary fetishes, gifts, and sacrifices of the various Loas that were anticipated. The cornmeal was being poured out in the great design of veves of Papa Legba and Erzulie Fréda at the edge of the compound and served to notify the worshipers of which spirits were being invited. A fire had been stoked near the peristyle, and the drums and the dancers were congregating. A goat, a chicken, and a bull were within the peristyle, unaware of their fate. The Asogwe Mambo kept scampering about the peristyle. The Hounsi in white were busy at work making their preparations as well. The person who would be the master of ceremonies of the event was receiving his final instructions.

Over the course of the next couple of hours, the disorganization of preparations gave way to the organization of a ceremony, and the faithful Vodun practitioners of the region began to gather at the invitation of the Kingdom's foremost Mambo.

A feast had been prepared and would begin the evening's events.

Irawagbon was taking it all in with amazement as the Asogwe Mambo slipped up behind her without her notice. "What are you thinking, my dear?"

Startled, Irawagbon jolted a little. "I am not sure whose ceremony I am at tonight," she said with a smile.

"You are not pleased?" asked the Mambo, afraid she had either underestimated the expectations of the warrior or overestimated her own abilities.

"No, Mother, I am very pleased." And she was. No detail appeared to have been missed nor skimped on. "It just brings many memories to mind."

"Please, follow me. I have your seat all ready."

The warrior fell in step behind the old priestess and found the seat of honor just at the edge of the large peristyle. From here, she would be able to see it all from a table of honor. Irawagbon took her seat, and the Hounsi began attending to her with food and drink as the feast began.

The first hour and half was like many feasts. There was food, drums, singing, and dancing, along with copious joking and laughing. The Hounsi made sure plates and cups were full—bringing and removing, bringing and removing. There was a rhythm to the work of the Hounsi. A rhythm driven by the beat of the drums, the singing, and the dancing that was intended to mesmerize.

The emcee kept people entertained with stories of attendees and stories of the guest of honor. Stories that were obviously revealed by the Asogwe Mambo to him and contained just enough fact to give a firm base of support to the legend that continued to grow since her retirement and was being added to this night. The palm wine was starting to have its effects, attested to by the fact that many appeared to be struggling to sense the difference between fact and exaggeration. As the feast progressed, one could see the great Mambo working the edges of the feast as she began moving the gathering toward the ceremony portion of the evening.

The tableware was removed, and the Initiates began to replace the Hounsi as they assumed their more sacred roles of moving the gifts and tokens for the arrival of Papa Legba near the edge of the peristyle. The animals for sacrifice were brought into position as well.

The drums became silent for a moment, and within seconds the party became a solemn ceremony. At a signal from the Mambo, the drums began to pulse out the sacred rhythm of Papa Legba, and the Initiates began to dance, each secretly hoping to become his horse that he would ride by possessing their bodies upon his arrival, being the one through whom he would manifest himself in this ceremony.

The master of ceremonies began to lead the worshipers in celebrating and praising the child-like fertility god, Papa Legba, the guardian and trickster of the crossroads. The role as guardian Loa meant he was able to grant or deny access to the inhabitants of the spirit world, or Guinee. Therefore, as per the majority of ceremonies, he was the first Loa to be invoked.

As the sacred dancing and drum rhythms reached a fever pitch, the master of ceremonies melted back into the crowd, and from within the peristyle next to the poto mitan stood the aged Mambo, who began the invocation for Papa's presence. As she began with prayers of adoration and requests that he come, the Initiates began to move his gifts to the base of the poto mitan. Gifts that flowed from the New World as result of the slave trade. Gifts she had learned that he liked: candy, rum, and tobacco. The Initiates also placed more items at the base: a crooked cane, a broad-brimmed straw hat, a pipe, brown pants, a red-checkered shirt, and a black vest. Papa Legba's sacred veve that had been drawn at the edge of the compound was being redrawn with fresh cornmeal within the peristyle.

As the Mambo prayed and the worshipers danced, a young girl who had been sitting at the edge of the peristyle jumped to her feet with a loud, deep laugh and began to jump and dance with surprising strength and agility. Within seconds, the worshipers moved to the edges to allow room for the Loa as he possessed the little girl as his horse.

The little girl promptly went to the poto mitan and dressed in the clothes provided. "He" took a huge swig of rum and crammed some tobacco into a pipe, which he promptly lit, and took a huge draft as if it he hadn't had a drink of alcohol or smoked a pipe in years. He stretched the little girl's arms and squatted while winking at the boys along the periphery. He touched, sniffed, and tasted between great drafts of rum and tobacco. Given the size of the girl, combined with the quantity and speed of consumption of the alcohol and smoke, it was amazing she could remain functional and not become intensely sick or inebriated.

The Loa tipped his hat to the Mambo and with a smile meandered over to her, twirling his cane and grabbing the old woman seductively. "What is it you desire, my girl?" he said as he bounced the young girl's eyebrows.

"We have called to honor you, my lord," said the old woman coyly.

"You have brought my favorites, I see," he said, looking over the gifts. "But I suspect you have requests to make and are not just here to celebrate. Am I right?" He looked slyly out of the corners of the little girl's eyes, searching the faces of the crowd.

"Yes, my lord. It is well known that you guard the crossroads between the living and the dead, and in addition to celebrating you, we long for permission to speak with another."

"Oh, I'm sure you do," said the Loa as he glanced at the guest of honor, and a broad knowing smile broke out across the little girl's face.

Ira shifted a bit uncomfortably in her seat under his gaze.

It took some time for the congregants to adjust to hearing such a rich, deep bass voice coming out from such a little girl, and to see her act so out of character for her age and gender. It was even harder for her parents, who were trying to appear thrilled with the visitation of the Loa upon their child.

"Whom shall I call for you? Shall we call for Damballah? Or perhaps Ayido-Weddo?" He glanced again at the warrior in the seat of honor, who was finding it more and more uncomfortable. The Loa Ayido-Weddo was the wife of Damballah, and they were both connected to the snakes of Vodun. But Ira was seeking the Loa Erzulie Fréda, and she was Damballah's concubine. The uncertainty of this particular combination in the service—wife and concubine—was unsettling and undesirable for the agenda Ira and the Mambo had determined. Papa Legba glanced around the peristyle and spotted only a couple of pythons. "No, I think you are not prepared for either of them," he said with a smile, again glancing at the warrior. "Whom shall I call for you, my dear?" he asked as he whispered into the ear of the Mambo while looking at the warrior.

"Erzulie Fréda, my lord," they whispered together.

The Loa leapt back from the aged Mambo with eyes locked on the warrior. "Then Erzulie Fréda it shall be." The Loa moved about the peristyle, whistling and twirling his cane, still locking eyes with the warrior. "But first, I have a surprise!" The girl bent slightly at the waist and extended her arm and cane to direct the attention of everyone gathered to the far side of the peristyle where one of the Initiates instantly extended her neck and back with a thrust that bolted her to her feet.

There was a booming, thunderous laugh that echoed against the night, and Ira's blood ran cold. She looked with a fear at the Mambo, who was now panicking. Each knew this wasn't Erzulie Fréda. The

Asogwe Mambo shook her sacred ason to get the attention of her Initiates, who, having anticipated the Erzulie Fréda, were bringing in the three wedding rings and her sacred colors of pink, blue, white, and gold. Her sacred veve was being drawn in cornmeal.

"Ogoun! Ogoun!" she whispered fiercly, fighting back her desire to scream. One Initiate dropped the gifts of jewelry and stumbled all over the place to gather them back together while at the same time trying to exit the peristyle. Fortunately, the sacred perfume was not spilt. The brighter Initiates began to switch to the sacred colors of red, black, and green, then to the sacred gifts of blades, swords, and metals. Another scrambled to bring in a fresh jug of rum, and the drums switched to the sacred rhythms of Ogoun, the Loa who had entered unexpectedly.

"Ahh-haaa!" the warrior Loa screamed. "Is this the best you have done for me, my dear?" boomed the possessed Initiate, her arms spread wide as she looked about the peristyle. He looked at the warrior guest and said, "I would have expected more, my dear!"

The Mambo bent low, "It is my fault my lord. I—"

"Silence! This is between me and my wife!" yelled the Loa as he stared wide-eyed daggers at the Mambo and slowly turned to look at his spiritual wife. "Do you remember our marriage night, my dear?"

"Yes," whispered the warrior, nodding.

"I thought we had committed to one another that night." What he really meant was that he expected more from her. No one was allowed to expect anything from him which might resemble commitment. As a Loa, he had his own set of expectations, and to say they could be whimsical was truly an understatement.

"I remember," returned the warrior.

"I remember the battles we fought from that night on."

"Yes."

"I made you the most powerful woman in the kingdom. None could face you in battle."

"Yes."

"And how have you repaid me?"

The warrior was silent.

The Loa began to meander about the peristyle, eyeing the warrior and the congregants.

"Huh?" he asked

Silence.

"You forsook me!" he charged. "You neglected me and my desires." The warrior was fully aware of the Loa's desire for blood. She felt the return of humiliation at the realization that she had been a tool for death and destruction in the physical realm. A tool she thought she was wielding for patriotic reasons, only to realize—too late—that she had been the tool being wielded by the Loa.

The warrior looked at the Mambo, who was busying herself with the Initiates to finish the transition from a peristyle fit for Erzulie Fréda to Ogoun. It was unclear if she was trying to do her best to appease the Loa or to avoid the warrior.

"I gave you the strength and agility of twenty young men, and the blood of your Ahosu's enemies soaked the ground. Thousands died by your hand."

Her mind was filled, and her soul was chilled as she recalled the multitude of men she had met in battle whose eyes, once full of fear and longing for mercy, became cold and lifeless as they slowly dilated and became fixed, as if looking into the distance. It was true, none could stand before her in battle. Many an impossible situation changed when she stepped foot on the field. She had reveled in it initially, but with the passing of her parents and then her sister's death, it all became personal to her for the first time. Life that had once been cheap became extremely valuable, and the Loa who now stood before her, who once was a source of strength, she now saw as a thief. And the thought that he might sense her true feelings for him caused her to fear for all those she had come to love.

"Well, it matters not, my dear. I am not here to demand my due. At least not from you."

Again, silence. The warrior sat, trying to grasp how her plan had gone so wrong. But this was the story of her relationship with Ogoun. He gave and took. Though his initial gift was lavish, he took more from her than he ever gave.

"You think you can just retire from me and be done with us?" the Loa sounded disgusted as if the very words were distasteful and ripe with condescension.

She stared at him quietly.

"I will have my due. And if you won't give it to me willingly, as you should, then I shall take what is mine."

The warrior began to tremble.

"I know why you are here. I know who you are here for better than you do."

Tears began to well up in the eyes of the woman as she took in what he was saying and wondered what it meant.

"You have no idea the depth of what I am saying, do you?" said the Loa as he embodied his horse, slinking about the peristyle without breaking eye contact with the warrior.

She was afraid to move. She just wanted him to go and leave her to her hopes, dreams, and longings. Hadn't he taken enough? She had no family of her own. No one to hold her. No one to care for her. No one to cherish her in her fading years. He had taken her youth, and now he still wanted her as if he didn't see her failings, or he chose to look beyond them. As if he was unable to see her in her current state. As if he were trapped in the thought that she was forever young. He either didn't see her vulnerabilities or was choosing to look past them. Either way, she said nothing.

"You and I have an agreement, and if you won't fulfill it, then I will see that your adopted descendants will," said the Loa with a voice of determination and pride as he worked his horse around the peristyle and he nodded toward the little girl in a final glance.

"Wait!" yelled Irawagbon.

Papa Legba smiled and nodded back with a chuckle as the Initiate—the horse of Ogoun—collapsed into a weakened, confused state.

"Whoops! He is gone, my dear," said the guardian playfully as he took another swig of rum, emptying the bottle.

The warrior and the Mambo looked at each other, searching each other's eyes to try and learn what the other knew that could help them each understand what had just happened.

"Oh well." The remaining Loa shrugged. "Shall we move on, or are we done?" quizzed Papa Legba.

"No!" they yelled as the warrior slapped the palms of her hands on the tabletop and leaned forward in her chair, while the Mambo leaned toward the Loa as if attempting to stop him from leaving. They glanced at one another fearful they would lose their chance and then in unison they turned back to the Loa and earnestly requested, "Erzulie Fréda!"

"I will see what I can do." He smiled again.

The Mambo turned to the drummers and nodded. The drummers began to beat out the sacred rhythm of the Erzulie Fréda. Some of the Initiates began switching out gifts and sacrifices, while others began switching out the sacred veves.

Within moments a middle-aged man at the edge of the peristyle began to laugh playfully and seductively. The man would gesture to those around him, regardless of their sex, while he made his way to the poto mitan. Onced there the Loa began dressing herself in her fineries and partaking in the gifts that had been brought to her. For several minutes, giggles and flirtatious engagements with the crowd were punctuated by self-absorbed indulgence with the articles at the center of the peristyle. The Mambo would periodically attempt to draw the Loa toward her, only to be interrupted as the elderly horse was redirected to someone else in the crowd as she slyly switched between a simple saunter and a seductive promenade. One couldn't help but noticed the frustrating glances between the Mambo and the warrior.

However, when the Loa came by the warrior, she stopped in her promenading right in front of the warrior and locked her eyes with a pause. The Loa looked the warrior up and down. "What have we here?"

"Good evening, my dear Erzulie Fréda. You are welcome."

The Loa continued to look the woman over, and at one time a snarl flashed across the right corner of the old man's mouth. After a pause made awkward by being slightly too long, the Loa weakly said, "It is a lovely evening. Though it is becoming rather tiresome." The Loa looked out the corner of her eyes, glancing at the Mambo and then fixing her gaze on the animals staked nearby.

The Mambo instantly knew what was not being said, and she looked to her Initiates. The quicker-witted in the group were watching the Mambo very carefully and saw her nod toward the goat, the chicken, and the bull. Within moments the animals were ceremonially executed, and the dirt began to soak up their blood as the life ebbed away, flowing from the beasts into the dust. The Loa began to slowly contort his body as if he was enjoying a warm shower. His eyes first closed to savor the moment, then were wide open as new vigor caused the face of the Loa to be more animated. The older man began to look different, as if the life waned from the beasts while it waxed in the human.

The old man clasped his hands and brought them to the side of his face. And with a pursing of the lips the Loa narrowed her eyes.

Without a word of thanks, the Loa said, "That's better, isn't it?"

The warrior had seen blood many times in her life. She had spilt the blood of thousands of her Ahosu's enemies, her enemies. But at some point in the journey, the blood had become precious, and seeing the slaughtering of these animals evoked a sense that did not allow her to agree with her god. Irawagbon just forced a smile toward the Loa. The Loa allowed a brief, condescending snarl to again flash across the face of the old man.

The Mambo noted the brief exchange and interceded with a shake of her ason toward her Initiates, who promptly began flooding the base of the poto mitan with food and more gifts, known to be favorites of the Erzulie. The man sprung to the gifts and began to consume the sacred food. The Loa seemed to enjoy the sensations provided by its commandeered horse.

"We would humbly ask a favor of you, most venerated Erzulie Fréda!" announced the Mambo as Initiates continued to resupply the tables surrounding the base of the poto mitan.

"What is it you ask of me? Perhaps I shall grant it." The Loa seemed to only be half listening as she continued to revel in the sensations provided by its host.

"Most gracious Erzulie Fréda, we ask your blessing and your favor through the endowment of influence, power, and protection on the bearer of a most-powerful gris-gris. We ask that the bearer be irresist-ible to those who encounter her." Loa stopped her consumption of favorites and glared at the warrior, then at Papa Legba, who was lean-ing against an outer post of the peristyle, smoking his pipe, smiling a knowing smile at the Erzulie as if the two were in on a little secret.

The Mambo never lost her stride in her cadence. "The ability to woo and attract the finest of suitors and situations. The power to cre-ate, manage, and, if need be, manipulate through the complexities and subtleties of conversations and relationships. We ask that all who wear it be blessed to have the command of elegance, poise, graceful-ness, finesse, and agility in stature and station that you yourself have."

"That's it? That's all you request?" the Loa mockingly asked as she returned to promenade about the peristyle while eyeing the warrior.

"From generation to generation," stated the warrior, who was finally able to articulate her greatest desire. Asking for the power to do good for multiple generations was an attempt to undo the death and destruction she had ushered into the lives of others. There was no way in the remaining years of her life that she could undo the destruction she had brought, but perhaps Erzulie Fréda would allow a power for good be lived out through her family for generations long after she was gone.

The Mambo eyed her older Initiates, who responded with bring-ing more gifts to the peristyle, which seemed to please the Erzulie.

"This would require a token to establish the necessary link. Sym-pathetic magic just won't work. It must be contagious. You know of what I speak?" As the Loa was explaining the requirements, the Mambo nodded to her senior Initiate, who brought in the piece of cloth in which was folded the hairs the warrior had obtained just days before. The token was laid before the Mambo, who extended her ason toward it as she looked at the Loa with a smile and a bow of the head.

The old man looked toward the warrior with a knowing glint in his eye. Their eyes locked for a lengthy and indeterminate amount of time. He glanced over at Papa Legba, who was still smoking and smiling. Erzulie Fréda looked to the dark sky and took a deep breath. "It's my night. You've showered me with gifts and brought my favorites.

You've enlivened me with your offerings." She took another deep breath and let it out slowly. "I am of a mind to grant your request." She turned to the Mambo. "Prepare your best, and I will grant it." She looked to the warrior, becoming tearful before letting out a sob. With a shaky voice, she added, "I know she will need it." With a nod she glanced at Papa Legba, who chuckled, then both horses collapsed with fatigue, completely unaware of what had happened.

There was a flurry of activity as the family and friends of the horses began to gather around their loved ones, questioning them on how they felt and answering questions in return. The wonder of the honor of being a horse was replayed in their minds. The other Initiates gathered around the one who had been the horse to Ogoun, and they began talking of the lave tet, the initiation rite after a servitors first mount. The other older Initiates began clearing the peristyle.

The Mambo and the warrior gathered at the edge of the peristyle. "I don't think I like how that played out, my dear," said the Asogwe Mambo to her previous pupil.

"Nor I. But we got what we wanted." The warrior gazed into the eyes of the Asogwe Mambo. "A blessing for my family… a blessing for Nourbese." She bit her lower lip as she bobbed her head, trying to reassure herself.

"I don't like the unexpected presentation of Ogoun. He did not seem delighted."

"He never seemed delighted with me. Only with the chaos I could create."

"I thought you loved him."

"Love him? I do not think the Loa experience love."

"But Erzulie Fréda is the embodiment of love," whispered the Mambo.

"I do not think love is what that was. I don't think … " The warrior paused as she fought back tears. She swallowed hard, glanced away, and in a few moments looked back at the Mambo. "I am not sure I know what love is. But I sure hope that wasn't it." She smiled at the Mambo and received a smile in return, then put her hand on the arm of the warrior, who looked a bit older now than she did yesterday.

"You need to rest, my dear." She embraced her pupil, her friend. "Now leave us. We still have work to do and only a few hours left of this sacred night."

"When would you have me return?"

"First thing in the morning," the Mambo whispered with a smile. "It will be ready, and you may have it. Then you need to begin your journey home. I am sure you will want to present such an amazing gift as soon as you can." The Mambo turned and walked toward the thatched roof building, shaking her ason and calling her older Initiates.

The warrior was left standing alone and thought to herself, *I just hope it is the blessing I want, not just the gift I am given.* The warrior exited the compound through the gate under the white flag.

The next morning the warrior returned to the compound just before sunrise. The sky was red and foreboding. It caused the warrior to wonder if this day the sky might be warning of something more than just bad weather.

She used her walking staff and knocked at the gate under the white flag, which was promptly unlatched by an Initiate who was pleased to see the warrior. "Good morning, My Mother. Follow me, please."

Ira entered, and as she followed the initiate, she could see the compound was once again emptied and had been tidied and swept clean of the debris from the night before. There was a mound of dirt over the place where the lifeblood had drained from the sacrifices. She couldn't help but wonder if the Loas' appetite for blood and carnage could ever be satisfied. In those times, when human sacrifices were made, it was clear the Loas were thrilled as if they could sense the life leaving the body. It seemed more like an addiction that could not be satisfied.

They arrived at the thatched roof building. The Initiate opened the door, stepped aside with a bow, and gestured the warrior in. Ira stood for a moment, looking at the girl, wondering who her family was and what they thought of her participation in this craft. Like most of their people, she was sure they were pleased with what they at least thought she was experiencing. But at the same time, she was certain they had no idea of the slow, constant drain it put on her soul. It was like a hope that is never satisfied, like an itch that never goes away, even after it is scratched.

The warrior nodded her appreciation and entered into the building. The Mambo was standing at the center of the room next to a table on which a lamp sat. Many of the older Initiates stood around the periphery. "Good morning, my dear," said the Mambo.

"Good morning, Mother."

"We worked through the night. Every attention was given. All sacredness maintained." She extended her hands toward the table on which sat a fine piece of cloth. And upon that cloth sat a small leather bag embroidered with a gold snake. "It is ready. It is perfect."

The warrior stepped forward and quickly, almost unceremoniously, folded it in the underlying cloth and deposited it beneath her cloak. "I cannot thank you enough, My Mother. I knew of no one else who could have helped us." A bit quieter, she barely whispered as if correcting herself, "No one who would have helped me."

"It was my pleasure, my dear. I hope to see you again."

The warrior smiled at the aged Mambo and glanced around the room. After a brief pause, she stated, "Fair skies and warm fires." The Mambo nodded her appreciation, and the warrior turned on her heels and promptly left the building, crossed the compound, and exited through the gate beneath the white flag. She glanced up at the flag, which hung rather limply, only twisting slightly in the gentle breeze. Given her years of battles, she couldn't help but wonder just who was surrendering what under this flag.

CHAPTER 3

FLICKERING HOPE

Dahomey Kingdom, West Africa
June 27, 1776

It would usually have been another long two day return trip back to Ajama, but along the rain-saturated trails it took a full day longer. The determination on her face ensured she wasn't hindered on the path by fellow travelers. The determination in her heart ensured she kept as quick a pace as possible. She kept checking her cloak to make sure the cloth wrap was where she had left it. Her only fear now was to lose the gift along the long muddy trail. She had traveled these trails countless times, crisscrossing the Kingdom. Always they had been with urgency, always with determination, always to deliver something to someone not expecting the warrior's gift she delivered. This trip was significantly different.

As with the other journeys she had made in the past, she felt the rhythm of her feet slapping the water. She felt the rhythm of her breathing. What made this trip different was that previously, she had brought gifts of death and destruction at the urging of her spiritual mate and through his power at the direction of her Ahosu. Today, she was bringing what she thought was a gift of life, a gift of hope, a gift of great beauty and value. Today, she was delivering a gift that would not bring death and destruction but instead would bring the means for life and prosperity for generations to come. Today, she brought the very things that undergirded the reasons she had fought.

She had spent a lifetime plowing the fertile fields of this kingdom with death and destruction. Now was the time to plant the seeds of life and prosperity, and she would do it in what remained of the only family she truly loved and trusted. She would have died for her previous family of warriors, but this family was one she wanted to share her remaining days with and cultivate the wonderful and beautiful fruits of life.

She couldn't help but feel a change was in the air as even the memories of the unexpected Ogoun couldn't swallow her hope. Her feet raced to the rhythm of her pace, the rhythm of her breathing, and her mind raced with the rhythm of alternating hope and fear. A hope of a life full of joy and happiness for her grandniece filled her whole being, which was followed by a brief moment of fear until she again touched the cloth under her cloak and hope returned, then the process repeated.

Hour after hour she ran, she breathed, she hoped, she feared, and she touched. And with each passing moment, she was closer to home.

When she was about one mile from her family's village, she slowed her run to a trot, then a walk so as to arrive appearing causal and relaxed. As anticipated, it worked. She rounded the last bend in the path, slipped into the clearing of the village, and began whistling a cheerful tune that caused others in the village to turn and greet her. This acknowledgment filled her heart with even more gratitude until she was all smiles as she approached her family's hut.

Nourbese spotted her first and shouted with joy to her mother at the arrival of their matriarch, their warrior. Nourbese jumped to her feet and bounded like a deer into the embrace of her great aunt.

"Momma said you would come back!" said the young woman. "I have missed you."

"And I have missed you, too, my dear," said the older woman, fighting back a tear and wondering if there had ever been a time when someone missed her with such longing.

"Where have you been? Momma said you were on a special trip."

"I was, and I shall tell you all about it." The warrior put her arm around her grandniece's shoulder as they walked on.

"Where did you go?"

The elder one laughed. "Ha! I will tell you *all* about it."

The younger woman put her arm around her great-aunt's waist as they walked back to the fire.

"But first let's help your mother finish up dinner." The older woman looked around the fire. "Where's your brother?"

"He has joined father in the palm groves. He wants a job there, and Momma isn't happy. He hopes that by being present they will offer him a job. So every chance he gets, he runs errands to the region of the groves for whomever wants him to."

"Welcome home, dear one. Was your journey fruitful?" asked Omorenoniwara, who stood, embraced her aunt, and frowned at her daughter as if a secret had been told.

There was a brief rush of fear, causing Ira to feel for her cloak. The fear faded as she felt the wrap once again. Her face broke into a grin of relief as she said, "Yes. Yes, it was."

Ira turned to Nourbese and looked her in the eyes with a smile. "Dear one, at a young age I found I had an ability few others possessed. Its uniqueness led me in a direction that others have followed, but with less ability and less prominence. I have spent my whole life in service of the Ahosu. I have seen things … " Her voice faltered. "I have done things that I wish I could unsee and undo. Things that have covered my hands and feet in blood. No amount of praise from the people can wash it away." She broke her gaze and looked about the village at the other huts where their neighbors lived each day with a sense of security, knowing the warrior of renown lived nearby. "In the process, I have lost much. I have lost years of being with those whom I would have loved and would have loved me in return. Those years are now gone." She reached out and touched the chin of the young woman. "And I am on the verge of leaving this life having missed out on things of much greater value."

Wara drew her aunt's arm close to her side, embracing it as she looked into the fire near their feet.

Nourbese was silent, unsure where this conversation was headed.

Ira could see she was losing the young girl. "Well, that part doesn't matter. What does matter is that here with you I have found the home I never had. As I near the close of my days, I want to give back to you all a token of my deep love and appreciation for all that you have given me." The warrior began to feel a lump forming in the back of her throat as she again fought back a tear. She realized it wasn't fear or shame she was fighting; it was love. And with a bowed head, she let the tears flood her eyes.

The two younger women embraced the elder as they all reveled in the realization that they held on to something more than just one another's physical closeness.

For the remainder of the evening, the three women worked the fire and prepared dinner as Ira relayed to them her journey and the details surrounding it. She even shared with them the surprise visit of Ogoun, which still left within her a sense of uneasiness. She told of her younger days and her spiritual marriage to Ogoun and how the union had given her an ability that none of her companions had possessed. An ability that formed the foundation and had opened the doors to her embodiment and reputation as a warrior. She also explained how making that decision so long ago had closed so many other doors that now she wished had been opened, and remorse filled her voice.

Ira talked through dinner and into the evening, laying the background story that led up to the moment she had been waiting for. "Wara, will you stoke the fire? I have something I want to give Nourbese."

Within moments the fire was burning afresh, and in its radiance their faces glowed and their bodies were warmed. The warrior reached into her cloak, withdrew the gris-gris, and displayed the prized possession to mother and daughter. "This charm is enchanted. It was fashioned by the Asogwe Mambo in Abomey under the direction and blessing of the great Erzulie Fréda. It is a token of the great Loa's blessing on your life," she said, handing the token to the mother.

Wara looked at the bag and realized this was not a small token and immediately began trying to estimate its cost. The more her mind contemplated, the quicker the smile left her face. She looked to her aunt and said, "This must have cost a fortune. Where did you…" her voice trailed off as she extended the bag toward her daughter while glancing into her aunt's eyes, who was looking for a reaction from Nourbese. Nourbese was overcome with the realization of what had been done for her, and she reached out to take hold of the bag.

"It's for me?" she asked.

"Yes," said the older woman. "It is for you and your mother—and your brother and your father. And yes, it is for me as well…just in a different way. You could say it is for all of us."

"It is for the family," clarified Wara. "It is a symbol of hope and longing of those who have gone on before—"

"And those who will soon follow," interjected the warrior.

"Yes, and those who will soon follow," repeated Wara. "It is a symbol of all the hopes and longings of those who have gone before that rest on you and your future."

"May your life be blessed with fruitfulness of not only the womb but in bountiful joy and laughter. May the richest blessings in life be yours, and may you be the custodian of those riches for the family to come. I want for you to hold all the things I could only grasp for but will never hold for myself," offered Ira. "And perhaps, with the blessing of Erzulie Fréda, you will grasp it and hold it closely." Ira took the bag and tied it around the neck of her grandniece as a tear began to slide down her cheek. "I hope to see the day when you begin to hold those blessings. But if not…" She finished tying the bag and sat back, her eyes glistening and a smile spreading across her face. "I rest in knowing I have done all I can to secure it for you. And when your days are coming to a close, then you are to pass it on to the one you trust to be custodian of our hopes in the next generation."

Wara was startled at the realization of what was being said. "It is a transgenerational blessing?" It was clear the cost of this gift was beyond calculation. To call it priceless was offensively inadequate.

The two younger women leaned in and embraced the elder, who patted both their arms with her hands. This became the moment where the warrior felt she had secured the most important victory of her life.

. . .

Four days later the three women awoke to a beautiful, clear morning. And for the first time in a long time, there was neither the pitter-patter of rainfall nor the roll of thunder. They busied themselves in corporate activity about the fire, preparing the morning's meal of the staple acarajé. The sun was warm, the sky was clear, and Imarogbe had reluctantly returned home—to his mother's relief. Wara longed to provide her husband fresh supplies for his stay in the groves but couldn't bring herself to send them with her son out of fear he would stay. Instead, she asked her aunt to take them.

After breaking the night's fast, the warrior collected the supplies and set off for the groves. She was nearly halfway to the groves when the forest trail grew eerily quiet. The birds stopped their chirping, causing the hair on the back of her neck to prickle. Acting on instinct, she dropped to her knees and slipped off her cloak, freeing herself from any bindings that could hinder stealth movement, then felt for her blade, grasping the hilt.

She heard the chirp and *cha-ka-tah* of a single blackcap babbler, which confirmed her suspicions as the bird usually dwelt among a flock of four to twelve other birds, raising their young communally. There were no other birds chirping. The sole sound seemed awkwardly inappropriate in the silence. There were others in the forest with her, and she had been seen. She closed her eyes to enhance her hearing, awaiting the shrill of a battle cry and the rush of an enemy, but heard nothing. Within twenty minutes the natural sounds of the forest returned, and the sense of danger passed. She remained where she was for another ten minutes before she dared to move. Whomever it had been, they had seen her first and worked hard to not be seen, desiring only to pass by undetected.

An hour and a half later she arrived in the groves. There was the usual buzz of activity as the fruit of the oil palms were being harvested, collected, and brought to a central location for initial processing before being shipped to Abomey. She stopped a worker and asked for the location of her nephew-in-law, Ewanisha. The worker glanced about the grove and pointed to a tree one hundred yards off where Ewan was starting his ascent. The worker gave a whistle, and everyone looked to see the warrior, causing Ewan to wave her over to his area. She smiled as she set off in the direction of his tree.

The other workers smiled and waved their recognition toward the well-known warrior as she passed by. Just as she was arriving at the tree, she heard a scream and a machete fell from above. She looked up to see a large green snake repeatedly striking Ewanisha in the leg. His attempt to escape the snake caused him to lose his grip on the tree, and he tumbled to the ground, eyes wide in terror as others came rushing to his side. The snake was quickly bludgeoned to death by the workers.

Ira knelt at his side as fear creeped across his face. "It burns!" he cried out.

"Shh, don't talk," said the warrior. "Help me get him to the shade," she instructed the workers. The man was lifted and carried to the side of the grove as the warrior drew a flask of fluid from her pouch and gave him a drink, trying to reassure him. "Perhaps it didn't have much venom," she consoled.

But a glance at the leg showed multiple puncture marks with slight bleeding and the start of red streaks and swelling. The look of terror and pity began to fill the eyes of the workers who stood nearby. They had seen it before. As always, it left them feeling helpless. The warrior shooed them back to work. She didn't need their knowing glances darting Ewan's way in this moment.

"It will be fine," she said soothingly, using a cloth to wipe away the blood oozing from the openings. "I'm certain the snake didn't release much venom."

The man chuckled. "It burns … and burns a lot."

The woman kept blotting the wounds, trying to think of something to say.

"Wara …" Ewanisha's voice trailed off as he grimaced. He looked at his leg, then at the woman he had so much respect for. "I had hoped for so much more." His eyes shifted back to the bite. "Not this."

Ira kept blotting the wounds, unable to make eye contact with her nephew-in-law. He was a good man, who loved his family and did all he could to provide for them. It just seemed the gods were against them.

The swelling was beginning, and hope was fading. There had been enough venom released into his system. This was now certain. Her eyes began to fill with tears, so she began to blot harder and faster to look busy. "There, there I'm sure—"

The man chuckled as he interrupted, "When was the last time you saw someone survive strikes like this?" He grimaced again.

Within ten minutes no amount of reassurance could help. The leg was swelling remarkably, and the pain was becoming hard for the man to bear. He was starting to break out in a sweat and trying to stand. "Help me, please." He reached out to her, already on his feet, but he was unsteady, and a pain in his head was starting to throb. "It won't be long. So much to do. So much left undone."

"Shh. Shh, just rest."

"I can't rest. There is no time to rest." Tears began to fill his eyes and he became dizzy. "My Mother, you must care for my family." Within minutes he was struggling to breathe. "Tell them how much I love them." His knees buckled and gave way, causing him to collapse back to the ground. "I can no longer provide nor protect. I didn't want it to end this way." The warrior sat next to him and cradled his head. She looked at his eyes, which were now swollen with tears. "I will never see them again. I won't see my son take his place in the village, nor my sweet Nourbese…" His voice trailed off with a sniffle.

The warrior sat silently, trying to comfort the dying man. So many times she had ushered the living into death and Guinee, and she had done it with such speed and finality that there wasn't any time available for the poor souls to reflect on the sum total of their lives. They had been unable to assess the value of their history. Unable to ponder the hopes and dreams they had held for the future. Unable to fully realize that the ones they had been blessed to journey with were of far greater value than they had sufficiently acknowledged. Now, she sat trying to prolong life while this man reviewed his years, his achievements, and his folly.

As Ewan choked out quiet sobs and utterances of pain, she noticed the fasciculations starting in the musculature of his leg and his abdomen. She wiped his brow free of the sweat that had mingled with dirt and swatted away the flies that sensed what was coming.

His grimaces grew more intense, and he was clearly uncomfortable as his breathing was becoming more constrained. "What will they do, Mother? Will you look after them? Will you be there? You have been so good to us, and for that I am thankful."

"Shh," whispered the warrior. "I know." She was no longer trying to reassure, only to comfort.

His eyes began to dart around in panic as his body grew limp.

"I will do my best, my son." She again brushed a fly from his face. "I will do my best."

The eyes of her nephew-in-law were wide with fear as his breathing came in shorter, shallower gasps. Within thirty minutes of the first strike of the green mamba, Ewanisha breathed his last. The light faded from his eyes as the last tears spilled out from the corners.

Ira sat, holding him close as his body went completely limp, feeling certain he was dead. She left the corpse for the other workers to tend to and quickly set out to inform her niece of the tragic events. She would need to begin preparations for the arrival of the body and its preparation for mourning. The coming days would require much planning and execution to ensure a proper ceremony to usher him into Guinee, the spirit world.

She spent the next couple of hours running toward home, soothing her grief with the in-and-out rhythm of breathing and the thumping of her feet, trying to think of what she was going to say to Wara. There had been such excitement and enthusiasm about the future these past couple of days. She knew that Wara had seen a brightness as she looked into the eyes of her family. But now what would she see? Her husband now lay cold and lifeless. With every thump of her feet, with every breath in and out, she pondered how to word the heartbreaking news, but nothing came to mind. The darkness that seemed to have faded away over the past couple of days seemed to be crashing back down upon them.

Her mind was racing with thoughts she was unable to control or direct, and they came as fast as her legs were racing. Then, all of a sudden she smelled it. The aroma caused her to stop abruptly. Between pants, she inhaled deeply through her nostrils, confirming the old familiar aroma of death and smoke. In that instant, a new fear overwhelmed her like a flood.

"Nooo!" She shrieked as she again began to run, ignoring her breathing, sprinting the last several hundred yards without hardly taking another breath.

It wasn't long before her fears were confirmed. As she burst into the clearing in the forest, she found the village in flames and bodies strewn about. There was no one in the hut of her family or in the nearby surroundings. During these first few minutes of assessing the situation, that felt like hours, she searched the village and eventually found her niece at the edge of the compound lying facedown in the dirt in a darkened pool of drying blood seeping from her pelvic area and her upper thighs.

"No! Please, no!" she screamed again. She rolled Wara over with ease, but doing so only confirmed the light of her life had already been extinguished. "No, no, no," whispered the warrior, overwhelmed with her world crumbling. She cradled the head of her niece as she had the head of Wara's husband just hours earlier. The wound to the right thigh was singular, severing the femoral artery. It was obviously quick and fatal. A blow delivered by someone who knew what they were doing. A wooden stick lay next to her; apparently, Wara had used it in defense, which was clearly inadequate against the blade. The lifeblood likely drained out quickly, causing her to become unconscious in seconds. From her estimation, all life was extinguished in less than a minute or two.

No time to reflect, no time to assess, no time mourn.

The children! Her mind raced. *Where are the children?* There was carnage everywhere. The village had been home to several families and amounted to eighty or more people. She glanced around and recognized many by their shape and dress, quickly deducing none of the dozen or so bodies were the children. In fact, there weren't any children among the dead. She jumped to her feet and tried to look beyond. She glanced in the nearby huts, whose thatched roofs were now nothing but embers. Some huts had remains of those who had ineffectively sought shelter there. But no signs of Nourbese or Imarogbe. No signs of anyone under the age of thirty. She quickly surveyed the remainder of the village and found no trace of the young ones.

She went to the middle of the village and began to work her way out to the edge, searching every corpse, every hiding place. None remained alive. All had been executed with great precision and speed. Then it struck her. *This was a slaving raid!* But so deep into the Dahomey Kingdom? It didn't make sense. How could the Yoruba penetrate so deeply without a word? She recalled that moment earlier this morning on her way to the palm groves. She *had* stumbled into a raiding party. That's what had made the forest grow so quiet. But why didn't they attempt to silence her? They obviously knew she was aware of them. They easily outnumbered her. Why didn't they strike her down? Upon reflection, she almost wished they had. The Yoruba would not pass up a chance to eliminate her. Some had probably recognized her. It didn't make sense.

After the raid, they would want to return home with their booty as quickly as possible. It would be too easy to track them down and recover the captives if they weren't quick. That is why they killed everyone in the village. They didn't want any witnesses. She looked back into the forest the way she had arrived. They would have attempted to return to their lands by the route she had just come. But she would have seen or at least had heard them. A band of slaves cannot move through the forest without a sound.

She stopped again, deep in thought. They would have rounded up the captives, killed the wounded, and selected out the ones who were sick, too young, or too feeble, then separated them to the kill zone to be eliminated while the strong and healthy were bound at the wrists and shackled at the ankles. She had actually done it many times while marching slaves down *La Route de l'esclave*. If she could find the kill zone, she could find their trail and then should be able to catch up to them and perhaps free the children. She began the frantic search just ten yards out of the clearing and into the forest. She searched both sides of the trail she had just come down but couldn't recall anything that could help her locate where they had gathered the children. She had come through so quickly and with such haste that she hadn't given enough attention to her surroundings. Nothing seemed to make sense. She went another ten yards into the forest, then another. After nearly half an hour she had thoroughly searched this edge of the forest.

Then it struck her. They didn't come this way. She ran back down the trail and into the village. She spotted the trail headed out of the village toward Abomey, deeper into Dahomey. She raced to the opposite edge of the village and quickly found the kill zone. She searched the bodies of the undesirable ones and, as expected, did not find her grandniece and grandnephew. Strewn amidst the bodies of the unwanted lay discarded clothing. *Why the discarded clothing? Why here, on this side of the village? Why not on the other side in the direction of the land of the Yoruba?*

A queasy sensation came over her as she realized these weren't Yoruba raiders. She recalled the events from earlier in the morning. These were N'Nonmiton. These were her own people. No wonder they had left her alone that morning. They either feared wasting time or the loss of a couple of troops. Either way, they had preferred to go around her than through her.

But if these were N'Nonmiton, they would likely be headed back to somewhere near Abomey to sell the captives as slaves to the traders. They wouldn't want to do it in Abomey; it would be too risky. The taking of captives from their own people to sell as slaves was risky enough for the N'Nonmiton because it would damage their reputation among the people. Instead of being cherished, they would be feared and scorned.

She had to focus. Now was not the time to ponder the reputation of the N'Nonmiton. She had to find her family and, if possible, rescue them. It would be easier to get ahead of them and await their arrival. It was too risky to approach them from behind. They would be moving slower than she could. If she set out quickly and ran through much of the night, resting only briefly, she could make up for their head start and might be able to intercept them before Abomey. Then she would follow them to their rendezvous point with the traders and during the night free the children without being noticed.

She set out again, running to the rhythm of her breathing. She ran the rest of the afternoon, stopping only briefly to refill her water at a small brook. At night her pace slowed to allow for the small amount of moonlight to light her path. Well after midnight she lay down for a brief moment and rested, only to be back on her feet before the break of dawn. That next day the rains had returned and the path become slippery, slowing her pace a bit more. Nonetheless, she continued pacing her breathing to the rhythm of her feet. And so it continued, breathing in and out pairing with the slap of her feet on the wet ground as she ran through the rest of the day.

Sometime in the early hours of the following morning she arrived at her destination, comfortable that she had outpaced a raiding party on its way to the area of Abomey. This location would most likely be the last place they would pass before options would begin to open up for them to take the captives to meet with traders and be out of the way of prying eyes.

It is amazing what a culture will tell itself when faced with its own dark truths. It will begin to rationalize, compromise, or refuse to acknowledge the darkness it finds. And as Irawagbon waited she began to realize she had done the same thing. How many of these raids had she participated in? How many mothers and fathers breathed their last from the very same wounds that had ended Wara's. Wounds she had herself inflicted, all the while convincing herself of her duty to her Ahosu, the protection of her family and people, the accumulation of wealth and resources that never seemed to satisfy. How many families had she destroyed by slaughtering or selling into captivity? She did not like this new revelation.

She settled in her spot from which she could see the trail and waited.

As hard as she tried to think of something else, her mind kept coming back to the terrible sensation that she was guilty of some great crime. A crime that was bigger than any one act, or series of actions. She had always believed there was good and evil. But she was not always certain the perspectives on good and evil she had been given by her parents, her profession, her people, or her religion were accurate. She had seen too much to not believe in the existence of the Loas. She knew there were supernatural beings with great power, yet she couldn't help but think everything they offered came with strings. If only there were a Loa who didn't need the gifts, who didn't require the offerings, who didn't relish the blood and death. If only there were a Loa who wanted to be valued for who they were and not just what they did. That would be a Loa who was worthy of her esteem. The Loas she knew always seemed to be bargaining, always wanted more in return.

It was what finally drove her away from Ogoun. He was never satisfied with what she had, never satisfied with what she offered, never satisfied with who she was as she was. She began to sense the betrayal, the loss, and the pain until she became numb and fell into a restless sleep.

She awoke with a startle to the chirping of several birds. It was already morning and the sun was quickly rising in the east. Where was the raiding party? Was she really that much quicker, or were they really that much slower? Could they have passed in the hours she slept? She glanced at the path. It looked undisturbed. There were no footprints in the fresh mud. She could not think of any place along the way where traders would have been willing to meet them. No, if the party were to meet traders near Abomey, as was customary, then they had to come across this path and then set off in one of a hundred different locations. But if they had beaten her to this point and had already passed, then why wasn't there any evidence of the party's passing in the mud? It didn't make sense.

She waited another three hours and still no raiding party. It was well after noon when she concluded that waiting any further here was fruitless, and she set out for answers in Abomey.

She arrived in the capital well after dark and sought lodging with the Asogwe Mambo, who was very gracious and hospitable but didn't like the conclusions the warrior was drawing after she told her story.

"Why would Our Mothers do such a thing?" asked the Mambo.

"I don't know. But it is the only thing that makes sense."

"I think you presume too much," said the aged woman.

"Do you? Do you really?" Irawagbon couldn't hide her sarcasm, but the Mambo ignored it, writing it off to the passion of a distraught family member.

The old woman had seen much in her day, and times were changing since Kpengla took the throne of his father. The atmosphere in the capital had become more secretive, more sinister, and comments made in public by officials were less direct, more abstract, as if people were becoming more afraid of being trapped in their own words; therefore the capital preferred being vague and obscure. It was affecting the culture of the city, the culture of the Kingdom.

The Mambo attempted to change the subject. "How did your niece like the gift?"

"Mother, I appreciate all you did for us. But to be honest, I have had an uneasy feeling since seeing Ogoun the other night. I fear he intends evil where I have intended good." She paused, staring into the candle that lit the room while they spoke. "I confess, I no longer trust him."

The Mambo was obviously unsettled and not sure the change of subject was a good idea. "Be careful, my daughter. Ogoun is very powerful."

"Sorry, Mother. I do not intend to offend. But I am losing the ones I have loved." Tears began to swell in her eyes. "If I lose the children, I will have lost everything I hold dear. And I am sure he is part of it."

The Mambo made her way to her side, embraced her, then whispered, "Get some sleep."

The next morning the warrior arose just before the sun, gathered her things, and slipped out of the compound to head toward the Palace. She stationed herself along the street at a point that gave a great advantage to seeing both up and down the street from which she could easily see who was coming to, and who was going from the Palace.

Within a couple of hours, the street began teeming with people, and the warrior had to adjust from sitting to standing in order to survey the whole street. By late morning she spotted the N'Nonmiton commander coming up the street with an aide toward the Palace. Ira slipped into the foot traffic and began to make her way on an intercept course. In the blink of an eye, she stood in front of the commander and her aide.

"Good day, My Mother," said the commander. "To what do we owe the honor?"

"Good day, Commander Ode," said the older woman. "How fortunate it is to find you."

"Oh?"

"Yes, a curious thing occurred this past week, and I have been pondering it ever since."

"Yes?"

"I was visiting my nephew-in-law in the palm groves near Ajama." The aide glanced at the commander, who betrayed nothing.

"Go on ahead. Tell the Ahosu I have been delayed," said the commander to her aide. Then, turning back toward the older warrior, the commander said, "The palm groves near Ajama, you say? I hear they have been disgruntled with the Ahosu over his request for more oil to advance the concerns of the Kingdom." Ira ignored the veiled attempt to intimidate her.

"Oh, I know nothing of that. I know of no misgivings. I am sure they are pleased to offer their service to the Ahosu and the Kingdom." The elder warrior sufficiently brushed off the attempt at misdirection and hiding her growing contempt. "The misgivings that concerned me were brought to my attention by a woman who reported seeing a band of N'Nonmiton pass her in the forest, only later to see the small village of Ajama decimated by a raiding party. She expressed concern that it was Our Mothers who did it." The older warrior watched carefully as the younger warrior betrayed nothing. "I told her she must be mistaken. Our Mothers would never betray us like that."

"Indeed, to accuse Our Mothers of such an act is very grievous. Did she offer proof?"

"No, just a curious connection between acts of war and the presence of warriors in the very area." Ira noted there was no direct repudiation of the claim. "I told her that it doesn't make sense. Our Mothers would never do such a thing, right?"

"It concerns me that she would consider such a thing possible."

"If there were raiding parties in that area of the Kingdom, you'd be aware of it, right?"

"I would, and I am." The commander chose her words carefully. "There have been raiders in that area of the Kingdom. We believe them to be Yoruba raiders, and we have bands of N'Nonmiton in their pursuit. We intend to pursue them all the way to the border of our lands and to slay them if we catch them. Perhaps that's what she saw?"

"*If* you catch them?"

"No, I said *when* we catch them." The commander corrected the elder warrior. "Now you must excuse me. These raids have placed a lot of concern on the Ahosu, and I must not delay him any longer. Good day, Mother."

"Good day, Mother."

And with that exchange, the commander set off for the Palace, and Ira headed out of the capital, thinking, *there is no doubt the N'Nonmiton performed the raid. But where will they make the exchange with the traders? It will have to be quick. They won't want anyone to catch them in the act of selling their own people.* The pieces began to fall into place. *That is why they discarded the clothes.* She went on to rationalize in her mind that they likely dressed the captives in the clothing of the Yoruba and began marching them. Therefore, if they were dressed like Yoruba and were marched far enough and fast enough, then they could march them right down *La Route de l'esclave* into Ouida to the market, and no one would be the wiser. Everyone avoided the slave marches anyway. It was easier to overlook the brutality of the whole affair if you just looked the other way and distracted yourself for a few minutes. The distaste of the reality was easier to bear if you rationalized its existence at a distance.

"That's it! That is why I can't find them. They never came this way. How stupid! I misjudged the whole thing. I tried to head them off on a trail they never took. They aren't meeting the traders in Abomey.

They're headed to Ouida, and they now have nearly three days' head start!" said the warrior in near disbelief.

Within moments Irawagbon was at a sprint, headed toward *La Route des l'esclave*, hoping against all hope that she wasn't too late. If she couldn't intercept them in route, it would be nearly impossible to intervene after they entered Ouida. And once they passed through the Gate of No Return, it would be impossible to reach her family. It was named the Gate of No Return for a reason. She was so determined in her gait that she did not see the two warriors who had just exited the Palace in pursuit of her.

She was hours into her journey when she realized she was being followed. She figured they would try and take her in the middle of the night, hoping she was resting. But she formulated a simple plan that would likely hinder their goals. She wouldn't stop for the night. So she ran. She ran through the night and into the next day.

As she ran, she pondered what needed to happen. She was still a day's journey away from Ouida, if she could keep this pace, and she needed to catch the group before Ouida. Even though they would move slower as a group, she knew they would be pushed rather quickly, and they'd had a significant head start.

She knew if she could get to Ouida before her pursuers did, she would have the safety of numbers in the city. They would never dare to attempt to injure her in the city, in front of so many witnesses. But she had to catch the raiding party in route or risk losing the chance to liberate her family altogether. Her pursuers were already risking so much of their reputation in this act of cultural betrayal. They would likely let her live if she couldn't get the proof she needed of their betrayal. Plus, they would not risk being caught killing one of their own. But out here on *La Route des l'esclave* no one was watching. No one cared to watch. If they caught her here, and if they could kill her here—which was an even bigger if—they could cover their actions and no one would ever know.

If she was able to get to the city first and free her family and others just before they were entering, then she would have her proof. The possibility of this becoming a reality gave her more determination and the strength to keep going: running, breathing in, breathing out—*slap, slap, slap*. Within hours after sunrise of the second day, she could no longer see the ones chasing her, and she felt a bit relieved. But there still was no sign of the raiding party.

CHAPTER 4

LOST AND FOUND

Ouida, Kingdom of Dahomey, West Africa
July 1776

A few hours later she knew she was closing in on Ouida, and she knew she was close because she had picked up the fresh trail of a large party. Time was running out, and the timing had to be perfect. If she were too early, she would either catch the party too far from the city and be vulnerable to attack by the N'Nonmiton pursuers. Too late and they would reach the city and be in the clutches of the traders before she could get there and rescue them. So she ran on with hope fading as she crested each hill, only to see the raiding party was not in sight.

Another thirty minutes had gone by as she crested the last hill and found the muddy trail to Ouida empty except for the footprints of a large party entering the city. They had already arrived. Out of breath she dropped to her knees and began to sob. The growing possibility that she would never see her family again filled her with a lonely desperation. She sat with her tears steeping in anguish, when suddenly two N'Nonmiton warriors burst through the forest and were upon her in a moment.

She jumped to her feet and tossed aside her cloak, grasping the hilt of her blade. The younger of the two rushed impatiently at the retired warrior and paid for it with her life. In a flash, the elder dropped to her knee, and with a single slash she severed the femoral artery of the young warrior, who squealed in pain and fell to the ground, grasping at her thigh as her clothing filled with blood. She tried frantically to stave off the bleeding but without success.

Ira slowly rose to her feet and faced the remaining warrior. They paced in a circle, sizing one another up. The younger one never drew near enough to strike, as a crack from a distant British musket rang out, and the front of Ira's tunic flushed red. Her legs buckled, and she collapsed to her knees into the grass. Her vision slowly darkened, and as it did she heard the low laughter of a familiar voice. Then she saw him … Ogoun.

"No, no, no! Why are you here?" she whispered.

"I have come to collect my own," the Loa said.

"But I don't want you. I never did. I only wanted what I thought you would have offered. I wish there was someone else."

The Loa hesitated. "What did you say?" He seemed annoyed.

"I never wanted you. I regret that day we wed. I had nowhere else to turn. The day we wed was the day I began wishing there was someone else. Someone who valued me for who I was, someone who saw the true me and loved me anyway. If only there had been another, someone different whom I could have given my life to."

"Silence!" shrieked the Loa.

She had never sensed fear in his voice, but there was no mistaking it.

"You're afraid, aren't you?" she whispered.

"I forbid you to speak, human!"

"Be still," said a new voice, deep and steady. The Loa wilted and shrank like a flower in extreme heat. The new voice continued. "Speak on, Ira," and in the closing seconds of her life, Irawagbon the N'Nonmiton warrior held a lengthy conversation.

"I had so much that I longed to see … to feel … to experience. I wanted to feel safe, and I wanted others to feel safe too." Her voice faltered as the memories of her childhood came flooding back. Memories of her father. Memories of when she and her sister had been so small. Her father had gotten drunk, as he often did. "And so, I entered the N'Nonmiton. I wanted to be the best I could be, so I allowed myself to be talked into marrying Ogoun."

The Loa glanced up with a sneer, but he kept his silence.

"Why was that important, Ira?" the Loa glanced to her right, and it caused her to look as well. About fifteen feet away to her right stood a man with an olive complexion wearing a white tunic. His face was scarred with patches of a stubbly beard projecting out through the scars. "Come, tell me. I'd like to know." It was strange to hear a non-Black man speak such fluent Fon.

It wasn't his looks that were attractive. It was his voice. He spoke with a tone of kindness. But even in his kindness his voice demanded respect. You could see the power and authority he held over Ogoun without raising his voice. Even Ogoun sensed it and responded. She glanced back at Ogoun, whose eyes were full of contempt and disdain as he watched her.

"Don't mind him. Come talk with me," said the man, as if Ogoun were a poorly behaved servant. She looked back at the man who was extending his hand out to take hers. She couldn't resist. She took his hand, and he turned with her to face Ouida and the sea beyond. A gentle breeze was blowing onshore, fresh and inviting. "Pretty day, isn't it?" He extended his free hand to point her up the trail. "Shall we?"

"Yes," she whispered. They began walking.

"Tell me of your family … of your father." His voice was so inviting and curious, as if he was truly interested and had all the time in the world to listen.

She hadn't wanted to talk of her father for a very long time. He was the source of a lot of pain. "He drank too much. It caused him to say and to do things. Things that should never have been said … or done." As they walked on, she could hear the seagulls squawking overhead.

"Like the night your brother died?"

She stopped and looked at the man. "How do you know about that?" There were tears welling up in his eyes as he looked out at the sea.

"Believe it or not, I was there. It was a terrible, terrible night." He paused for a moment. "It was a terrible night for everyone when they found out the truth. For you, your sister, your mother … and your father." He looked at her and smiled a small, knowing grin.

"It ought to have been different," she whispered as a lump formed in her throat.

"Oh, my dear one, you have no idea of how much truth you speak in those six words." They continued walking. "You're not alone in your longing for things to be different." He gave her hand a little squeeze, then lifted her hand to his cheek, wiping away a tear with the back of his hand. As he did, she couldn't help but notice the scars on his wrists. She craned her neck a bit to get a better look, then looked into his eyes as he looked back.

"We all have scars, my dear." He smiled. "We all have scars from our battles in the struggle for what ought to be." She looked again at his wrists and his face.

"It's why I joined the N'Nonmiton, isn't it?" she asked.

"Yes, it was a very big part of it." He nodded in agreement.

"Whatever the reason for going, it didn't work out the way I wanted."

"Why do you think you joined?" he asked.

She paused as they continued to walk. "I think I needed to feel strong. The women of the N'Nonmiton were strong, capable women."

"Even men are afraid of them," he said with a smile.

"Yes, they are. But I didn't realize my peace and security would come through others losing theirs. I wanted to be respected, not feared. I wanted to live, not bring death. I wanted a place of laughter and joy, and to not bring him"—she nodded toward Ogoun— "pleasure by tearing others down." She was getting worked up as the reality of what had happened came into fuller view.

"A heavy price to pay," the man whispered. They continued walking, and the old warrior was quiet as she reflected on the ways in which she paid that price. "Was it ever worth it?"

She stopped and turned to look back at Ogoun. "It was never worth it."

The man turned and looked as well. "He resents the value I have in humanity." He paused as his statement sank in. He looked back at Irawagbon and said, "It's why he resents you."

She was lost in thought when all of a sudden it struck her that an olive-skinned man with disfigured features whom she had never seen before said he valued her. *How could he value— Wait a minute!* She looked him in his eyes as he stood there, looking into hers, quietly waiting for her to process. This whole time she felt like they were just talking. It was so casual, carefree, and easy that she hadn't realized how much he seemed to already know about her. He hadn't so much asked her questions to learn about her as he had asked to help her learn about herself. She didn't feel as violated as she thought she should.

After a few moments she asked, "Who are you?"

He looked back at the sea and closed his eyes, inhaling deeply and exhaling slowly. "For now, let's just say I'm a friend."

She looked back at Ogoun, who watched them from a distance, not daring to move, not daring to speak. "Where have you been my whole life?" she whispered.

He chuckled and opened his eyes, then looked at her again. Smiling, he asked, "How would you guess I know the things that I know?"

He did know a lot. He seemed to know everything. But she was certain she had never seen him before.

"There is so much I want you to know. So much I'd love for you to learn, to see, to feel … to be." He paused. "It can't happen all at once or it would destroy all of the beautiful things I have in store for you. And I couldn't bear that."

She watched him, stunned, trying to take it all in.

"Would you believe I know you better than anyone else does?"

She was afraid to respond because he might stop sharing. Up until now, he had her talking and thinking about herself.

"I know things about you that you don't even know about yourself."

She kept watching him.

"I know the night you married Ogoun you weren't happy about it, were you?"

She shook her head.

"Everyone seemed happy for you that night, but no one saw you cry before—or after—the ceremony." He smiled as he spoke, then he paused and his face turned serious. "You felt it that night, didn't you? You felt that sense of something not being quite right, that sense of foreboding. I know you did."

"Yes," she barely whispered as she glanced at Ogoun, who continued to watch them, still afraid to move, afraid to speak. "I wanted to run away, but I didn't want to lose my chance at having strength and power, so I wouldn't feel..." Her voice trailed off.

"Vulnerable?" he asked.

She nodded in agreement. "Vulnerable."

"I think you hoped you were trading fear and vulnerability for power and safety. It's not a good trade, Ira. Fear is not fought with power, nor with strength of arm. One cannot ever be safe by generating fear in another person. They might feel safe, but they are actually further away from safety."

She nodded again. "I know now."

"You know those are not the weapons that conquer fear. But you also do not know how to defeat fear. You've experienced fear's defeat, but you haven't realized what the most effective weapon against fear really is."

She looked back into his eyes.

"What is the weapon that works against fear, Ira?"

She was drawing a blank.

"You experienced it this week. You've experienced it many times before, but you didn't realize how strong it could be. You felt it made you vulnerable."

Still she was drawing a blank.

"Do you remember how you felt a few days ago when you presented the gris-gris to Nourbese?"

"I was happy. I was joyful. I was excited."

"Yes, yes, yes—and more. Do you know why?"

"I was... I was..." She looked around while she tried to pinpoint whatever it was the man wanted her to recall.

"It was love, Ira. It was love. And your heart was so full of it that there was no room for fear. You showed it again as you went looking for their captors. Not a drop of fear, only love. Love is very powerful.

I can tell you Wara had no fear in her closing moments for the same reason."

She looked back into his eyes and it hit her. She hadn't been fearful of anything at that time. "I am fearful that I have lost them forever."

"Yes, but believe it or not, that's because even though your love is powerful, it isn't powerful enough to change what is into what it ought to be. Despite this fact, love is still the answer. It is just that the most powerful love isn't the love you have for them."

She looked at him again.

"If you love me and listen to me, then the love we have for one another will cast out all of your fears and you will never have to fear again."

She started to get excited. "You can save them?"

"No, not in the way you think."

"No, you can't, or no you won't?" she asked.

"Actually, for me it's both. I won't because I can't, but at the same time I can't because I won't."

She was struggling to understand.

"You see, for some people it is easier for them to believe I am not able to do something because I lack strength, or I lack know-how. But it's just the opposite. Because of what I know and the strength I have, I am willingly unable. The truth is closer to this: I won't do what others want me to do. That is because of what would happen if I did. When the things I could do stay in the realm of things that never happened, people struggle to understand why."

She was still struggling.

"Understand that I love them just as much as I love you. I know them as well as I know you. And if you believe that, then I hope you can believe that there is a very good reason why what is happening to them must play out. It must be as it will be. And it is just as true for me to say, 'I will be whom I will be.'"

She squinted at him, then looked at Ogoun, who hadn't moved but was still looking intently as if to see how this conversation would end and whether he was going to be in trouble or not.

"I hope you can trust that I love you and them, even when the appearance of things makes you want to be fearful. When you know and trust this truth, you will notice the fear beginning to fade. Humans can be very connected to outcomes. The more we are attached to outcomes, the more vulnerable we feel; therefore the more fearful we become. You will know you trust me when you are comfortable with any outcome. Even the ones that used to make you fearful."

She was still looking at him, trying to take it all in. She looked again at Ogoun.

He followed her glance. "Perhaps it is time to start heading back."

She took his hand again, and they started walking back up the trail.

"Before we get back, I need to know something."

She looked up into his eyes, signaling a desire to know what it was he had to share.

"Ogoun is going to want to make his claim on your life."

She swallowed hard to choke down the lump that was forming. "Is there nothing that can be done?"

"Yes, I have done everything that is necessary, but there is something I need from you."

"Anything! I don't want to go with him."

"I think it is going to be fine. Just answer with all the honesty your heart can manage."

"I will try." She swallowed hard again.

He smiled, and they walked the rest of the way in silence.

As they approached the spot where they met earlier, the man said, "Well, Ogoun, I think she wants to come with me."

"Noooo!" he shrieked. "You can't have her. She belongs to me. In the moment of her death she has not chosen you. She still belongs to me."

"That's not quite true. The shadow of death has not finished crossing over yet. There is still time."

"No!"

"Ogoun, there is still time." He didn't raise his voice, only stated a fact.

The Loa cowered. "There's time, but she has chosen me."

"Well, let's ask her. Irawagbon?" He and the Loa looked at her.

She looked from the Loa to man. "Yes?"

"Ogoun has laid claim to your life on the basis of the choices you have made, and I don't only mean the spiritual wedding. You have chosen evil when you ought to have chosen differently. Those choices will not allow me to exercise my longing for you, and he knows it."

She looked back at the Loa, who was sneering with disdain at her, and she felt the old familiar chill run up her spine.

The man smiled. "Do you remember what I told you about fear?"

She looked back at the man and recalled only seconds ago what he had said: *I hope you can trust that I love you and them, even when the appearance of things makes you want to be fearful. When you know and trust this truth, you will notice the fear beginning to fade.*

She nodded.

"Do you want to go with Ogoun?"

"No," she said.

"But she has already said yes!" countered the Loa.

"Some time ago, Ira, I made it possible for you to join me. What I did was for this very moment, and the moments to follow. Are you interested in going with me?"

"Very much," she whispered.

"She can't!" screamed the Loa as he jumped with a start.

"Silence, Ogoun! I'm not speaking to you." The man spoke calmly but with such authority that the Loa could do nothing but wither further until he became silent.

"Do you agree and confess that your choices in word, thought, and deed have separated us?" the man asked.

"Yes," she confirmed.

"Do you regret and repent from ever making those choices?"

"With my whole heart. If I had known of you sooner, I would have chosen sooner. I just never knew."

"I know. Let me ask this last question. I have told you that I made it possible for you to come with me. Do you believe that I have done this for you?"

"Yes, I believe you have," she whispered as she looked into his eyes. "It is why you have the scars, isn't it?"

He smiled and said, "Yes, and I would do it again because I love you. Goodbye, Ogoun, you may go."

And in that same instant the Loa disappeared, and the warrior felt different. "I'm going to die, aren't I?" she asked.

The man smiled. "Yes, but I tell you it doesn't mean what it would have meant just moments ago."

"Will it hurt?"

He looked at her with a smile. "Does it hurt?" he asked.

The red spot that had started to form on her cloak had returned and was again increasing in size. She dropped back to her knees. "A bit." Then she fell from her knees onto her chest.

"Are you scared?"

"I have no reason to be … I have love." And with that, the warrior breathed her last breath.

In the next moment, she was standing alongside her dead body. Beside her stood the olive-skinned man she had been talking to, and a second man who was dark-skinned like she was. Her new husband spoke to the dark-skinned man. "Be with her, and help her to understand what she is about to witness."

"Yes, my Lord," said the man. He turned to Irawagbon, held out his hand, and said, "Hold my hand, Ira." She took his hand, and the meadow and her dead body began to change. In the distance she could see two N'Nonmiton; one was holding a British musket, and the other was the surviving member of the team who had been tracking her. They were walking toward her, and it caused her body to flinch.

"Relax, Ira. Stay right here," said the man standing with her.

The two warriors walked toward them, causing her to tense even more. The man wrapped an arm around her and steadied her. As she watched, the two warriors appeared strange. They looked thinner, or lighter. She couldn't quite put her finger on it. As they approached, she began contracting herself to take up as little room as she possibly could to allow them to pass. But in what appeared to be the wisp of a vapor, they passed right around her and her companion. It felt as if a breeze had just blown across her body. She and her companion turned and looked as the two warriors each grabbed an arm and began dragging the dead warrior's corpse away. With each passing moment the scene she was witnessing was fading, and she was able to discern a different scene permeating through the meadow she believed herself to be standing in. She quickly turned to her companion, who was looking at her.

"Do you see it?" he asked.

She looked away and saw the two figures dragging away a dead body and could easily see what appeared to be a great hall. She nodded her head but said nothing. She leaned into him a bit. With each passing moment one scene became thinner and transparent, and the other took on a fuller, more distinct appearance. She was finding it harder and harder to see the scene, or environment, she had just recently been a part of. Before long, she could barely see them.

"It's still there," he said. "It is just as real now as it was when you saw it more fully."

She looked at him, uncertain of what he was saying.

"But there is something more important for you to see." He kept his arm around her shoulder as he turned around with her, facing the opposite direction. She, however, kept watching as her body was drug away by the N'Nonmiton. They never completely faded away, but it was becoming harder to see them and harder to not notice the other scene of the great hall.

"They are taking the body away to hide it in an attempt to cover their shame."

She nodded her understanding. Shooting her had been an act of deep treason. They would have fewer questions to answer if the old warrior was simply never seen again.

"Ira, let them be. There are more important things at hand," said her companion.

She twisted her head back to look at where he was directing her.

In the distance she saw a dais upon which sat two thrones. In front of the one on the left stood the olive-skinned man she had come to know. Upon the other larger throne sat a pillar of fire. It did not appear to be burning anything; it simply revolved slowly upon itself.

"He always stands as His own are passing through the valley of the shadow of death," said her companion.

"Valley of the shadow of death?" she asked.

He smiled. "In battle, have you ever had the shadow of a club, or bludgeon, or other weapon pass over you?"

"Yes."

"How did it feel?"

"It didn't strike me, but I felt the rush of my heart skipping a beat, then starting up again faster. I felt the tingling in my arms and body."

"So it is with death. It is a bit more complicated, but let us just say that the shadow of death just passed over you. It didn't strike you, but you felt its effects."

"Passed over?"

"Whether you passed through it or it passed over you depends only on what the witness sees." He paused just briefly for his words to sink in. "You witnessed a passage through the valley of the shadow of death. I saw it pass over you. Regardless, it was only a shadow. It is a shadow of something much denser, something much more substantial."

"Like what?"

"That is why we are here. Watch," he said, pointing toward the dais.

In the next moment Ogoun appeared before the dais.

"Why is he here?" she asked.

"He still believes he has a right to you and has come to claim that right," said the man.

"I don't want to go with him!" she blurted out.

Her companion smiled. "It will be all right."

"How do you know?"

"Because He isn't sitting. My Lord always stands when his own passes through the valley." The warrior and her companion looked at one another, and he smiled. "Ogoun is going away empty-handed this day."

She seemed somewhat reassured by this stranger.

"Unfortunately, Ogoun's claim is usually honored, and he leaves with one of our people. When he comes to stake his claim and then leaves with them, my Lord is sitting. Every time he has left with a soul in his hand, my Lord was sitting. Today, He stands."

"Our people?" Her faced demonstrated her confusion.

"I am like you. I, too, have passed through the same valley. I was an orphan and found myself in the care of a missionary woman who introduced me to my Lord and taught me His ways. Like you, on the day the shadow of death passed over me, He was there. Then when I watched Ogoun approach the dais, my Lord was standing." The man was smiling as if it was the greatest event in all of history. "Here it comes. Let us listen."

Irawagbon listened as Ogoun pleaded his case. He was accusing her of every wrong word, deed, and thought. Every dark action, evil deed, or wrongdoing in Irawagbon's life was being paraded before the thrones that sat at the dais. There were even things she never realized were evil, wrongdoings that were being attributed to her. The olive-skinned man just stood there with His arms crossed, looking down at Ogoun, patiently listening. At times the man spoke either to Ogoun or to the pillar of fire, whom He referred to as Father. A few times there was a voice that came from the pillar of fire. The whole conversation was carried on in Fon.

"They are speaking in Fon."

"Are you sure?"

"Yes, I am sure it is Fon."

"No," he said. "I was wondering if it was Fon they were speaking or Fon you were hearing. Since arriving here, I have met a multitude of people, many of whom I had no idea spoke Fon. When I commended them on their Fon, they were taken aback and instead complimented me on how well I spoke their native tongue. It seems we all speak and hear our native language here."

They again fell silent. Irawagbon watched as her former husband tried to claim her from her new husband. The claims mounted, and mounted, and mounted. Everything Ogoun claimed she had said, she had done, even the thoughts of her mind and longings of her heart were laid bare before the throne of the Great Judge.

The process seemed to be unending, and Ira lost track of time. She was unable to determine how long it had been. But the point came when Ogoun had finished.

The voice from within the pillar of fire stated, "Ogoun, you could have stopped at one offense." The Loa said nothing. "The verdict would have been the same, and yet you seem to take pleasure in being the accuser." Again, the Loa said nothing.

The olive-skinned man with the scarred face, wrists, and feet moved to stand between Ogoun and the pillar of fire and said, "Father, all that Ogoun has brought forth is true. Each and every one is true and accurate, and I expect nothing less from him. I stand here not to refute the accuracy of the accusations."

Irawagbon shifted nervously and glanced at her companion.

He was smiling, then said, "He is standing, dear one. There is nothing to fear. He is our Prince of Peace."

The olive-skinned man continued. "The accusations are complete, and each and every one is worthy of the penalty of death. There is no offense remaining that he has not brought forth."

The Loa was smiling but continued to hold his silence.

The voice from the pillar of fire spoke again. "The judgment is guilty. Before we pronounce judgment, do you have anything to add, my Son?"

Now Ogoun shifted nervously.

"I do, Father."

"Proceed."

"Father, the only thing I have to add is a request. I believe you remember the promise you gave me regarding the days I walked this land."

"I do."

"I have spoken with Irawagbon. She has confessed that she is guilty and has repented of these sins, trespasses, and the iniquities that lay within her. She has asked that my authority be spread over her, and I have done so."

"I accept your offering, my son. Mercy is granted. That will be all, Ogoun."

And with that, Ogoun exited the life of Irawagbon forever.

The voice from the pillar of fire addressed the old warrior. "Irawagbon, your sins are forgiven, and your iniquities have been atoned for. You may enter My rest."

Her companion embraced her. "Welcome home, dear one,"

As the olive-skinned man approached her, the pillar of fire faded away, and her companion stepped back.

"You are free, my dear one, freer than you have ever been, and you never have to fight for it again."

The warrior Irawagbon felt something she had never known before. It was a warmth that covered her against every cold she ever felt; it was a coolness that dispelled every heat she had ever felt. There was a peace she had always sought but had never held. Without realizing it, she released the blade from her hand, and it fell. As it fell toward the ground it faded rapidly, just as everything else had.

Later that afternoon, on the Fourth of July, Nourbese and Imarogbe finished their examination by the slave-trader physicians, and both were selected as sturdy and fit for the journey. Others who weren't as lucky were separated out and led to a secluded spot, and instead of being returned to their homes, they were executed. Within the next hour, brother and sister passed through their own Gate of No Return and were chained in place to a ship bound for the New World to meet their new master. The N'Nonmiton left with their installment of weapons and ammunition, continuing to pursue the plans of their Ahosu. De Souza, on the other hand, looked over his merchandise as he began planning how to expand his empire.

CHAPTER 5

CORRUPTION OF POWER

Outside New Orleans, Louisiana
Mid-April 2018

The night was bordering on complete darkness as the late-model Mercedes sedan edged its way southeastward from Baton Rouge toward New Orleans on Interstate 10. The passenger glanced out the window at the faint crescent moon thankful that it reflected so little light as to essentially allow them to travel along unnoticed. They sat quietly, not speaking, but each man's mind whirled, playing out scenarios and considering strategies as they sat in their own solitude for nearly the whole hour it took to drive to their destination. Just before reaching New Orleans, the driver pulled off the interstate and began to work his way back toward the mighty Mississippi River. They quickly entered an area with more of a rural feel and drove on for a few more miles.

"Sir, I'm not sure about—" said the driver as he glanced at the black leather duffle bag sitting beside him in the front passenger seat.

"Not now, Maurice," interrupted the man sitting in the rear passenger seat. He craned his neck to get a good view out the front windshield. "This is it."

The driver craned his neck as well as he pulled into a broad driveway up to a large wrought iron gate with a guard booth outside. He pulled the car to a full stop, slipped it into park, and began rolling down the window as the large guard approached the sleek vehicle. The driver looked at the passenger in his rearview mirror one last time to see if he could discern any evidence that might suggest an opportunity to, again, attempt to persuade him from his determined course. The passenger looked out the windshield at the approaching guard as he arrived at the car and bent down, looking at the two occupants.

"*Bonswa*," said the guard in Créole.

"Governor Boudreaux to see Madame," said the driver.

The guard looked them both over carefully and glanced at the black leather bag before saying, "*Jis yon ti moman.*" He straightened up and walked back toward the booth, whispered into his sleeve as if he were some kind of secret service agent, then put his hand to his ear. A second later he removed his hand and nodded toward the booth, and the gate began to slowly open as he waved the Mercedes through and he began walking away from the vehicle.

The driver raised the window and slipped the car back into gear as he quietly said, "Talk about making a deal with the devil."

"That's enough, Maurice. Not another word about it," said the passenger.

"Yes, sir." The assistant shifted in his seat as the car slowly slid up the long driveway.

The estate was a large plantation with impeccably manicured lawns and large beautifully sculpted gardens. The headlights of the car revealed the magnificient beds of flowers. The red and blue cardinal flowers were coming up and would bloom later in the summer. But the stunning Bonnie's Pink Prairie Phlox rimmed by different colored Louisiana Irises were an alluring contrast to the green grass of the lawns and the dark earth of the beds. In the distance up a slight incline stood a magnificent two storied, expansive, white-brick, black-shuttered Antebellum-style plantation house, lit up with flood lights. As the car crested the top of the incline and came around the circular driveway, the Mississippi River could be seen in the distance, with the faint crescent moon well above the horizon but still adding to the mezmerizing view.

The front of the manor had several trellises on each side of the porch that were covered by Carolina jasmine. Their beautiful yellow petals created a soft contrast against the white walls, and their delightful fragrance wafted into the vehicle, creating a dreamy, soothing feel that caused the driver to shake off the vulnerability these sensations generated, leaving the governor shaking his head in disdain.

On the grand porch stood another large, muscular, well-dressed Black man. As the car came to a stop, the man came down the steps and opened the rear passenger door. "*Bonswa*, Governor. Welcome back to the Plantation." The deep, sultry Creole accent added to the hypnotic setting.

"*Bonswa*. And thank you, Henrí. It is good to be back." The governor stepped out and buttoned up his suit jacket, straightening the edge as he looked over the front of the stately manor. "It's as beautiful as ever." He smiled at the behemoth Black man. "Maurice has come with me. I assume he can wait in the parlor?" The assistant grabbed the black leather bag, exited his side of the car, and walked briskly around the front.

"*Sètènman*," said Henrí, unfolding his hands as if to say, "But of course!"

The three men ascended the porch. At the top Henrí opened the door and stepped aside so the other two men could enter into the foyer. Henrí followed them in and closed the door behind all three of them. The governor and his aide walked to the entrance of the parlor and turned around to await Henrí, who arrived on their heels. He extended his hand toward the parlor and said, "*Mesye*."

Maurice glanced at the governor, who nodded him into the room. As the aide entered the room with the bag, the giant of a man closed the door behind him and addressed the governor. "Fodow me, please. Madame eazen her study." Henrí started down the hallway toward the northern wing and the governor joined in step behind him.

The estate was beautifully decorated with Antebellum-themed paintings ironically featuring Black masters with White slaves. The furnishings of the estate were period specific, and no expense appeared to have been spared in obtaining them. At the end of the hallway, Henrí came to a stop in front of a set of double doors and turned toward his guest. "*Jis yon ti moman, Mesye.*" He quickly rapped at the door and immediately stepped in. Seconds later he reopened the door and ushered the finely dressed gentleman into the study.

At the far side of the dark room were two sets of French doors separated by a large fireplace with a broad mantle and large floor-to-ceiling windows that looked out onto the back lawn. It gently sloped down all the way to the river, yet partway down the slope a large, flat gathering area had been meticulously carved out of the hillside. In the center was a carefully laid out peristyle with a poto mitan. At the edge of the gathering area stood a large, beautifully carved flagpole, depicting snakes crawling up a stick. Upon its top sat a broad, white flag gently tussling in the night breeze. The surrounding lawns were well manicured like the front, and though the lawns were lit like the others, the peristyle sat in darkness.

Along the wall to the governor's right, facing the windows, were a series of shelves and cabinets that held various fetishes for the Vodun religion that could be sensed more than seen in the darkness. To the left of the room on the far wall was a broad bookshelf filled with books that showed the effects of time and use. In front of the books sat a broad desk that faced the center of the room, allowing its sole occupant to glance up and greet her visitor.

"*Bonswa*, Pierre." The woman was beautiful and appeared much younger than the eighty-plus years he knew she must have been. The sole light in the room was lit by the oil lamp that sat on her desk. By that light one could see the woman was elegantly dressed in a bright-yellow print dress with matching dhuku that stood out brilliantly against her mulatto skin. Around her neck hung a very old leather bag embroidered with a gold snake. From under the back of her head wrap, one could easily see strands of her black hair sprinkled with rare strands of gray. She closed the book she was reading and stood, extending the book to her assistant.

"*Bonswa*," said the governor.

Henrí approached the desk, took the book, and returned it to the shelf as the woman frankly stated, "I believe we shall all have tea, Henrí. And we shall take ours here at the table."

The man nodded to his mistress. "*Wi, Manman.*" The giant took two steps back into the dark and whispered into his sleeve.

The woman came around the desk and brought the lamp with her to a table that sat in the center of the room while extending her hand to an open seat across from the one she was about to slip into. Before sitting down, the woman bent over and picked up a python roughly measuring three and a half feet that had been resting on the seat. As she picked it up, the snake began to uncoil, and she whispered gently to it, then carefully draped it around her neck. The snake seemed right at home on its new perch, and its beady eyes appeared to glare at the visitor, who unbuttoned his jacket and sat down after taking just a quick glance to make sure his seat was unoccupied.

"It has been a long time, Pierre," said the woman as she picked up a deck of tarot cards that had been sitting near the edge.

"*Wi, Manman,*" said the governor. He watched her smile as she began to spread the cards out on the table. "It has."

"Roughly eight years, I believe." She glanced up with her grayish blue eyes as she continued laying the spread. The man shifted uncomfortably in his chair, not sure which set of glaring eyes bothered him the most. She continued to smile. "Shall I read the cards for you?"

He did not reply as he shrugged his coat jacket to loosen its grip on his body. The whole night seemed to be closing in around him.

"Perhaps later"—she looked up from the cards—"we will spread one for free."

There was a quick rap at the door. Henrí stepped out of the dark and opened it as a gorgeous young woman in her mid-twenties entered with a silver tea service tray, which she set on the edge of the table. "Governor, I believe you know my granddaughter." The young woman's shapely form was dressed in a bright-red print dress with matching dhuku. She had the same soft mulatto coloring with the same memorizing bluish-gray eyes as her grandmother.

The governor couldn't help taking a slightly deeper sniff of the familiar smell of cocoa butter while the lovely woman served the Madame. He shifted in his seat, craned his neck out of his collar, and he shrugged his shoulders while clearing his throat, which caused him to quite nearly come completely out of his seat by the sheer awkwardness of his movements. This not only failed to relieve his sense of discomfort; it seemed to intensify it. The young woman smiled coyly.

They had met. It was just a few years earlier, in the bar of the finest hotel in New Orleans. He had been celebrating his reelection as governor for his second and final term. She had been one of his campaign staffers, and though he hadn't really noticed her before, he had noticed her several times that night.

They had each caught one another's glances on multiple occasions throughout the evening, and he had stolen enough glances on his own to notice she had turned away more than one potential companion for the night. As the party wound down, he had retired to his room but couldn't stop thinking about her. He ended up returning to the bar several hours later and considered it his good fortune to find her still there, sitting alone at the bar. Given whose granddaughter he now knew she was and what had happened over the course of the next few hours, he at least knew why his discomfort was intensifying. One thing was certain: it wasn't good fortune that sat dressed in yellow and was smiling at him now.

"I believe all have now been served, *Manman*," reported Henrí.

"*Mesi*, Henrí," said his mistress as she glanced from one man to the other. The man gave a quick nod and slipped back into the shadows on the far side of the room. The woman in yellow flicked her finger toward the door, and the woman in red left the tea service and exited the room with a shallow curtsey. The older woman offered the governor the sugar bowl, which he declined with his hand before picking up his cup and saucer from the desk between them, then sat back a bit farther in his chair away from those eyes, both sets of them. "Shall I continue with small talk, pretending this is a social visit, Pierre? Or would you like me to tell you why you wanted this visit?"

The man again shifted uncomfortably in his seat as he placed his cup and saucer back on the desk. He cleared his throat to speak but couldn't find the words to follow. The length of the pause was punctuated by the ticking of a mantel clock positioned on some dark shelf.

The woman flipped one more card, set down the deck, and picked up her own saucer while lifting the cup to her lips and taking a sip. Again, she smiled and said, "Okay, let's start with what I know." She took another sip and set down the cup and saucer. "I know we sat in this very same room a little more than eight years ago and came to an understanding." Her cold, bluish-gray eyes locked on to his and her smile vanished. "An understanding I lived up to, and you did not."

The man shifted once more, then cleared his throat again, but afterward remained silent as he looked out the window as if to find inspiration. Though he saw the darkened peristyle, it wasn't enough to cause him to lead out.

She tilted her head and raised her eyebrows in question. "Do you not agree?"

The man glanced back at his cup and said, "Well…" When he looked up, the woman had widened her eyes, finding it hard to believe he was even going to try. The snake had lifted its head and flicked its tongue at the man as if it was just as surprised as the woman.

He glanced once again at the peristyle and chose his words carefully. "Eight years ago, I started out on an ambitious course and made some sound decisions. One of those decisions was made here in this room and proved to be particularly prudent and very fruitful." He leaned forward and picked up his cup and saucer, raised it to his lips, and took a solid sip. "However, it wasn't long after that my diligence wavered, and I neglected…specific obligations of that arrangement."

The woman was listening but looking at the cards. "And tonight, you are here to attempt a similar arrangement for an even more ambitious course?"

The man took another solid sip, closed his eyes, and gave a subtle sideways nod.

"Come now, Governor. You and I both know your two terms are up and you must decide whether to retire at the young age of fifty-four"—she paused to take a solid sip—"or count the costs and launch into a campaign against a formidable three-term incumbent United States senator, steal the primary away from said senator, and hope to win the general election soon after." She set her cup and saucer aside a second time. "Is that about the size of it?"

He shifted again, realizing that his clothing was beginning to feel tight and stick to his body from the heat and sweat. The room was slightly facing the west, so it captured the afternoon sun, but he was equally certain she'd set the thermostat on the warm side for the precise purpose it was now having on him. "Yes … quite nearly."

"I think it is quite clear that I am capable of performing my obligations." The woman paused ever so slightly and then resumed by emphasizing his title: "Governor." Her eyes gave him a look of restrained haughtiness and she continued. "And I know my abilities would be more than capable of securing something as easy as a senator's seat. The pole we both are dancing around tonight is contaminated by the blood of your inabilities, isn't it?"

There was nothing left to do but stop looking at the floor and start dancing with the only other partner present. He shifted one last time, then leaned forward in his seat as he set his saucer and cup down one last time. "I prefer to think of them not as inabilities, but as incomplete acts. Acts I intend to fulfill tonight." Unnoticed by the governor, Henrí put his hand to his ear. The woman looked at her aide, who stepped forward and whispered into her ear. "I have brought with me tonight the remainder of the unpaid balance for previous services rendered, as well as payment for the next—"

Henrí stepped back as the Mambo held up her hand, silencing her guest. "The $400,000 you brought in the black bag with you tonight will complete your obligations for previous services, but it only covers the first half of what will be needed for the future services." She was no longer smiling. "Unfortunately, if I am correct and we are looking at a run for a seat in the United States Senate, then this will only suffice for all the preparations. We won't be able to begin scheduling the ceremony until we have been paid up front. I'm not accepting half as down payment this time, Pierre. I require payment in full upon agreement."

The governor sat upright in his seat, and his discomfort gone. Perhaps he had found his inspiration. "You want an additional $250,000?" he said with a brazen strength manifesting from his voice.

"What! You thought you could just call me up and say, 'Hey, Madame D'Souza! I've got the $125,000 that I owe you. Would you work your magic, and get me a US Senate seat for the same price as a governorship?'"

"Well, I—"

"No! There is no 'Well, I thought this' or 'I thought that.' We had an agreement for $250,000, Pierre, and I honored my commitment. You, on the other hand, did not." The snake was starting to sway a bit. "Did you think you could just bring me the rest of *my* money—money you already owe me—and hope that by tossing in an extra ten percent as interest I would just say, 'Shew, Govena, it be mi onna'?" He couldn't help but feel she and the snake were both swaying. She stood up, and the python looked up at her. "No, that isn't going to happen." She pressed down the dress covering her thighs as she took a deep breath.

The governor leaned forward onto his elbows, brought his hands together in the reverse hand steeple, and opened his mouth to speak but was interrupted.

"Save it, Pierre! I taught your staff everything they know!" said the woman, widening her stance and placing her hands on her hips. For added effect, she arched her back a bit and raised her chin. Her grey eyes locked on his, and he saw a flash of self-righteous power that bolted forth. She crossed her arms and turned her body slightly, pointing one foot toward him and the other foot toward the door. "I'm tired of dancing with you, Pierre. Let me bring you to your point and inform you of your two options."

The man again sat back and slouched just a bit.

"You are here because you know you need me to get that seat. You've tasted power and, like everyone else, you enjoy its flavor." She walked back to the table and leaned forward, placing her hands flat on the surface. "You have two choices. You can choose to go ahead and find the rest of the quarter-million-dollar fee my services are going to cost you. Or you can try and find someone else to help you get that seat. Either way, the $400,000 stays here. You can think of it as either a down payment for my role in a successful campaign, or shall we call it 'incentive money' to not introduce my granddaughter to your wife and family."

There it was, the hook, and it was set good. That introduction would be painful for his family, but manageable. Though his wife had her suspicions, she liked her lifestyle well enough to overlook a little unfaithfulness. What they called a marriage would likely survive, but the damage it would do to his campaign would likely be fatal. Once he announced his candidacy for the US Senate, his opponents would begin their research looking for just this type of scandal, and they were likely already digging around. He knew he had nothing to leverage the witch with, and even though he did not like being forced into it, he'd worked with this team before, so he knew he could count on her not making that introduction just as much as he could count on her making it if he tried calling for a substitution partner at this point in the dance.

He thought of Maurice and the reservations he had tried to raise. The governor knew what the aide had been wanting to say. "There will be no living with him now, will there?" said the Mambo as if reading his mind. He grinned slightly and shook his head. "I never liked him, you know," she added. "He is sleeping in the parlor. Apparently, he can't hold his tea. But don't worry, my granddaughter has been, shall we say, keeping him company."

"Poor ole boy won't even remember the pleasure."

"No, he won't. But don't worry, the encounter was thoroughly documented with such care that if he should ever get a little too *ensousyan*, then you can just let me know, and I'm sure for a fair price we can make a similar introduction for his wife and family."

"You don't miss any opportunity, do you, Mother."

"We are a full-service establishment. In fact, just say the word and instead of Henrí having the boys put him back in your Mercedes, he could take a boat ride into the bayous. You were raised in these parts, Pierre. You know how beautiful but dangerous a place like the bayous can be."

"The bayous are not the only thing both beautiful and dangerous," he said, causing the Mambo to give him a coy sideward glance. "No, Mother, he is still useful to me. Besides, he has a solo in the church choir he needs to deliver this next Sunday." The

Mambo nodded to Henrí, who again whispered something muffled into his sleeve.

"Oh, now isn't that delightful." The Mambo smiled as she returned to her chair and sat down. "Now, Pierre"—she held the snake close—"do we have an agreement?"

"*Wi, Manman*, we do. And I shall not fail you this time."

"I should think not." She was stroking the head of the snake. "What's the saying? 'Cross me once, shame on you; cross me twice, shame on me.'"

The governor stood, buttoned his suit jacket, and gave a parting thought to the black leather bag as he moved toward the door, which Henrí opened for him with a broad smile. As he stepped over the threshold without looking up from her spread of tarot cards, the Mambo called out to him, "Pierre, as you leave, allow me to point out what I hope is very clear. I am a powerful woman who can just as easily destroy you as I can help you!" She looked up and added a final statement. "And I won't need to charge a fee to destroy you, though I am sure I can easily find someone willing to pay me handsomely to do just that."

The man swallowed firmly and said, "*Wi, Manman. Bonswa.*" He nodded to Henrí, who smiled with a nod back.

Moments later, the Mercedes was winding its way back to Interstate 10, but this time it was headed back toward Baton Rouge, and the driver and the passenger had switched places.

Back at the Plantation, Henrí had taken the governor's seat at the table and was quietly watching the Mambo work the spread. "I think we now know why she hasn't called Henrí." The giant of a man said nothing as he waited patiently for the explanation. "No matter how I inquire, the answer is still the same. She isn't at the university." The man bit down on his upper lip.

"What do you want to do, *Manman*?"

"Gather her sisters and question them carefully. See if any of them have heard from her. Even if did she contact them, she is not likely to have said anything that would reveal where she is. But we could get lucky."

"*Wi, Manman.*"

"Don't frighten them. Be casual and inquisitive."

The man nodded.

"I must know where she is. She has been acting strangely over the past few months, and at her last visit she was standoffish."

"She did seem different, *Manman.*"

"*Wi.* She did. She was careful to avoid me most of the time she was here. Something was brewing in her then, and likely well before. The look in her eyes had changed."

"Shall I question them in the morning?"

"Yes, first thing while they are gathered. Then I want you and François to take the car up to Baton Rouge and check with her friends and classmates at the university. See if they know anything.

"*Wi.*"

"Henrí, it bothers me less that she is missing than it does that I can't see her. It is as if she has left my sight." She gathered the cards for yet another spread. "I will see if anything—or anyone else—is amiss. I want you back before vespers. So plan accordingly."

"*Wi, Manman.*"

"I don't have to tell you, Henrí, how important this child is to me, do I?"

"*Non, Manman.* I know how important the babe is to you."

"Yes, yes," said the woman, somewhat perturbed. "But I meant both of them. Santana and her unborn daughter are both very important to me."

"*Konprann, Manman,*" said the man, his brow furrowing as if he was hurt to have been misunderstood.

"Ogoun has revealed to my mothers and confirmed to me that the seventh time a seventh daughter was born to a seventh daughter in our line, then that daughter would be gifted as none of her ancestors had. It…" her voice trailed off. She had just flipped the last card of the spread and was not pleased with what she saw. Henrí watched as she slowly sat back in her chair as she withdrew her hand from the table. "Wait." She sat quietly, looking at the spread from a slight distance as if it would help her see everything more clearly, and then as if it had worked she looked into the air behind Henrí. With a nod of her head she said, "Forget about tomorrow morning.

Grab the candy ledger." The man stood up from the chair and went to the shelves behind him where she had been staring at and pulled out a large leather ledger. He handed it to her as she handed him the snake. After the exchange, she opened the book, flipping to the last entries and worked her way back." Under her breath she said, "Stupid girl." Then she closed the ledger firmly. "Take François and head into New Orleans and pick up Fréda. See what she knows."

"*Wi, Manman.*"

Forty minutes later the two men were cruising up and down the streets, starting in the French Quarter and working their way out. After the first couple of passes through the Quarter, the men stopped their black Cadillac up from the corner, where several of Madame D'Souza's girls were gathered, and flashed the lights. As one of the girls approached, François rolled down the window.

"*Kisa w'ap fè la*, François? *Manman* no like yon coming down here, trying to sample da merchandise."

Henrí leaned toward the window and pointed his finger at the girl as François sat slouched in the passenger seat. "*Fèmen moute ti fi!* We working. Where is Fréda?"

"How should I know. She no work this strip. She sell candy," said the girl as she stood up and crossed her arms, not pleased with how she was being talked to.

"I know what she do, and I know where she should be. I know where all you suppose to be, and she is not dar!" A small sports car came to a stop across the street and honked twice.

"I have ta git back to work," said the girl, who smiled and waved.

Henrí leaned forward just a bit more as he got in the last word. "Yon text me if you see her, right?"

The girl gave a quick nod as she flicked her wrist, signaling him to move on. The Caddy driver pulled out and made two or three more stops with similar responses before François interrupted. "Hey! Hey, dar she is!" he said as he flicked Henrí's arm with his left hand and began pushing the button to roll up his window with his right, all while sitting up straight in his seat.

"Where?" asked Henrí as he pulled the car into traffic.

"Ovah dar! Udder side of da street up a block."

The girl was approaching the next intersection as Henrí gunned the engine. When she finished crossing the intersection, he rounded the corner and honked his horn. The girl pretended she hadn't heard the honk and kept on walking. François hopped out and gave a short whistle as he opened the back door. The girl glanced over her shoulder, trying to be discreet, but François locked eyes with her and said with a nod, "Git in."

The girl reluctantly climbed in as François climbed in beside her. Henrí punched the gas and the car sped away to a quiet street where it was dark. Henrí shifted into park and asked, "Where you bin, Fréda? We bin lookin' for yon."

"Workin," said the girl. She was in her late teens with dark skin and dark brown eyes and a gap dead center in amidst her crooked teeth. She obviously didn't look like the other girls.

"Not don here yon not. Dis where pretty girls work. Yon too ugly to work here," said François.

"I workin," insisted the girl.

"Sho me da junk," said Henrí as he adjusted the rearview mirror so he could see her.

"I sold it all," replied the girl.

"Din sho me da money," said François as he started feeling her pockets.

The girl slapped his hands and stared out the window into nothingness.

"Yon not working, Fréda. *Manman* know dat. She checked the books," said Henrí. "Yon selling for someone else?" He watched her as she kept looking out the window. "Hey!"

"No," she whispered.

"Huh?" he asked again.

"I said no!" she emphasized with a small shake of her head.

"Look at Henrí when he talk to you," said François as he grabbed her chin and forced her face toward the rearview mirror. She just spun herself farther away and looked out the back window. François slapped her hard across the face.

Her cheek stung, and a tear started to well up in her eyes. François saw weakness and pounced. He slapped her again and shoved her so hard the back of her head struck the driver's side rear window. The girl began to cry.

Henrí looked at François. He didn't mind him being rough; he just didn't want his job complicated by a sniffling little girl he needed to interrogate.

"Where da junk, Fréda?" demanded François. The girl just shrugged. "Where da money?" She shrugged again.

"Where's Santana?" asked Henrí. The girl glanced a look of fear at the big man. She had been caught off guard, and she knew it was obvious.

"I dun know where she went," she said, frightened.

"Who told you she went anywhere?" demanded Henrí. "She not in Baton Rouge? She not in school? Tell me where she is, Fréda!" Henrí yelled.

The girl was shut up tight now. For the next several minutes the men berated and beat the girl, trying to get her to talk. She knew that if she opened her mouth now, she would betray her cousin, and she wasn't going to do it. Something had happened to Santana the first semester she was at LSU. She was different. All the other girls told Fréda she was ugly and stupid, and they mocked a father she had never known as if they had any better knowledge of their own. Fréda didn't know how or why, but Santana had changed. Yet she had a way of making her feel worth something when no one else did; therefore she would do everything she could to protect the only one who had ever been nice to her.

After a while, the men realized they had all they could get out of her and they weren't going to be able to learn anything new. So they decided to take her to the plantation and see what *Manman* could learn.

By the time they had arrived, the young girl's lip was swollen and split, with a trail of dried blood on her chin. Her right eye was glassy. The sclera injected. There were tears welling up while the left eye had swollen shut. Bruises were beginning to show on her face. The men handled her roughly as they forced her into the Mambo's study.

"Why Fréda, are you doing your makeup different? I say there is something different in your presentation, and I can't quite put my finger on it." The Mambo's voice was dripping with sarcasm. "Sit down, dear."

The girl didn't budge.

"I said to sit down!" screamed the older woman. The men pulled out a chair and thrust the girl in it. The younger woman appeared to be in a different place, almost like she'd disassociated, and ignored the other three.

"What have you been doing, my dear granddaughter?" The term of endearment was so obviously out of place it failed to induce cooperation.

The young girl said nothing.

"Where is my money, Fréda? Where is my candy?"

Fréda remained silent.

The old woman dug her nails into the swollen tissue of Fréda's left cheek until the young girl screamed in pain.

"Oh! There you are, my dear. I thought perhaps you had fallen asleep." The sarcasm had returned. The Mambo's voice became deep and firm. "Where is Santana?"

The young girl was reliving her most recent memories of her cousin and was surprised at how she was able to remain focused in the face of her angry grandmother. This was something she had never experienced before, and she figured it was because of Santana. From this she drew inspiration to fight on, to not reveal anything.

The Mambo nodded to the men, who each grabbed one of her arms with one hand, and with their other hand they held her shoulders against the chair. In a short bit of time she was secured to the chair, and her grandmother pulled out a syringe and needle.

"Have you been sampling my candy, dear?" her grandmother asked as she prepped a dose of heroin to inject.

The girl looked on in horror, and though she screamed, she still said nothing. By now there was little she could do to fight off her fate. She wrestled briefly while her grandmother began to access a vein, but once the men stepped in, it wasn't hard to overpower her. After injecting the drug, the Mambo looked at the arms of her granddaughter and said, "Well, those look like pristine arms. Perhaps she hasn't been sampling the candy after all. Uh-oh, that may have been too much."

Within just a few moments, Fréda began to sense her mouth going dry as a warm, flushed feeling spread across her torso. At this point, the drug had activated, and the pain in her face started to dissipate.

"Fréda, where's Santana?" asked the Mambo soothingly.

"Huh?" asked the girl.

"Where is Santana?"

"Gone."

"Gone where?"

"I won tell yon."

The sing-song voice combined with the soothing effects of the drug were beginning to blend together.

"Come on, Fréda. Where is Santana?" This dialogue went back and forth for several minutes, but it wasn't long before Fréda began to get very sleepy and was soon unable to focus on the mesmerizing voice she had been hearing. Soon thereafter, her breathing began to slow down. She started to snore, and her lips and fingertips turned blue. Her final words were, "Who is that?"

"Who are you talking about, Fréda?" The others glanced in the direction of her gaze.

Fréda was never heard from again by the woman or the two men who stood in the room. But she did have a lengthy conversation with an olive-skinned man who had entered the room, unbeknownst to the other three. When their long conversation was over, the man was standing, and the body of Fréda D'Souza had died, but her spirit had found home for the first time.

"Stupid girl," said the Mambo. "Feed her to the gators. I have work to do."

"*Wi, Manman,*" the two men said in unison.

CHAPTER 6

MEMBERS OF ONE BODY

Meridian, Idaho
Early May 2018

Okay, everyone! Be on the lookout for the Wolves!" Margaret Smithson had just pulled into the parking lot of Meridian's foremost shopping venue, The Oasis. The Oasis housed several trendy retail shopping spots and upscale dining establishments, and the group of girls had planned a day of girl talk combined with shopping and eating. Margaret's late model Jeep had its top off and was filled with four other girls, all from Pacific Northwest Christian University, where they were students for only a few days more. Finals were over, and they were celebrating the close of another school year. The group was meeting up with four other girls from nearby Ribley's College—who together had formed a small Bible study group, which alternated weekly gatherings at each school.

Margaret was the oldest of the group and had enrolled at PNCU after serving for five years in the Army as a military police officer. This fall would start her junior year studying criminal justice. She was really the guts of the group in more ways than one. The other girls acted like she was their big sister. They enjoyed being around her because of her no-nonsense personality. She had wicked fighting skills that had more than once been applied to several sexist male students on each campus. She quickly became the group's champion in any competition between the sexes because Margaret seldom lost. This resulted in the boys being drawn to her like moths to a flame. Her top-notch good looks and athletic abilities, combined with uncommon intelligence, was attractive, which ultimately led to each of the guys finding themselves competing in their favorite event, then losing in a most humiliating way.

No one called her Margaret though. In her younger years she earned the respectful name of Max, which seemed to personify her in every way. She was a stickler for following the rules that were clearly marked, but also had a way of making authority figures fix the rules that weren't as clear.

"Ooh, check him out!" yelled Brook Luxuria. There was a twenty-something guy out for a jog who had just crossed the entrance they were pulling into. She yelled out the Jeep, "Hey, watch out, man. She'll kick your butt!" He looked over his shoulder as Brook held on to her hat. Then, with the straightest face she could muster, she nodded her head toward Max. She had hoped that would set a hook and he would soon be winding his way back to find an opportunity to connect up with her later.

This would complete Brook's first year at PNCU. She was studying business and had an eye for the boys. There were also some rumors floating around that she had learned how to use her looks to entice guys and had racked up several fines from the resident hall staff this past year for her indescretions. She was once fined twice in the same night.

Max smiled, directing the Jeep in toward the parking lanes while shaking her head and quietly hoping she wouldn't have to do just that. The other girls laughed.

The occupant directly behind Brook was Madelaine Dé Bauche, also a freshman, and an education major who came from a long family line of teachers. She was being groomed to enter the "family business" of teaching, and she wasn't excited about it at all. She had been pressured into it, and as of yet she hadn't found her way into anything different, nor a voice to express it to her family even if she had. She and Brook were the closest of friends. Maddy idolized what she saw in her friend. More accurately, Maddy's alcohol habits, born from family challenges, distorted her ability to properly assess her self-worth and Brook became a mirror with which Maddie could evaluate herself. Because if Brook liked her then she must be an okay person.

The occupant behind Max was Ashley Van Gloria, a sophomore marketing major. Ash tended to have conflicts with the other girls whenever she felt she had been slighted or was being ignored. Max often felt that Ash had come to school to major in a coping skill to help her with her sense of inadequacy. It was part of what drew Ash to Max. She longed to have the strength, beauty, and status of Max for herself. She didn't necessarily want to take it away from Max; she just desperately wanted to be seen in the same way.

In the middle rear sat Hope Couture, the fashion queen of the group. She not only had an eye for fashion; she had a craving for it. Hopey was a junior art major. Her specialty was charcoal drawings, and she constantly sketched out clothing ideas with her ever-present sketchpad.

Max believed most girls spent their lives dreaming about their future but never getting around to living it. But she actually believed Hopey had one of those not-so-common combinations where her natural ability and giftedness aligned with her desire and dedication and would likely result in greatness. Max fully expected to see some designs by Hope Couture in some prominent fashion magazine in the future. When Max saw Hopey, she thought of the phrase, *Fashion is for those who have no style.* What guaranteed Hopey would be successful in her chosen field was that she didn't need fashion; she had her own sense of style, which was so classy and unique that it ensured her brand of uniqueness would always be fashionable for others.

"Oh, I see them," said Ash.

The girls from the Ribley's College seemed to have arrived at least a few minutes earlier, as they had already spotted the well-known Jeep, it's occupants, and had begun heading over even as it was edging into its parking space.

"What up, Wolves?" yelled Brook.

"You Peregrines are late as usual," said Erica Uberis as the groups met up and shared their ritual hugs. Erica had driven her group because she was the only one who had a car. This status had earned her the nickname Uber. The fact that she drove a sporty late-model BMW convertible with blue exterior and creamy leather interior only enhanced her status. Erica was a freshman with an undeclared major, which was probably a good thing because she came from a family with lots of money and spent more of her time spending it than she did figuring out how to earn or make it. And while Ash had conflicts at times with her own PNCU group, no one could get under her skin like Uber could. At least, this is how it appeared to Max, who thought Ash resented the fact that Erica didn't have to major in marketing to promote herself; instead, she could just pay cash for it.

"Let up, Erica. Don't you know Peregrines are never late," said Lindsey Avaritia as she leaned in to hug Max. "They're just early to the next event." Lindsey was the official leader of both groups. She was a senior at the Ribley's College and was majoring in economics.

The third girl in the group of four Wolves was Sandra Acedia. Sandy was a sophomore, also studying criminal justice but was a bit on the slow side. Not mentally though. She was a very bright student who could quickly assess a situation and distill it down to its essentials. Her slowness showed up in her physicality. She didn't give much attention to her looks and seemed to neglect the basics of personal hygiene and fashion. She didn't wear any makeup, and her clothes never appeared to fit right. She seemed to have more reason than Ash did to get caught up in appearances. It was easy to see she could benefit from additional attention to both hygiene and fashion. She just seemed to lack the energy. She would rotate between depression and anxiety almost all the time. She also may have been borderline anorexic, but the bagginess of her dress caused everyone to be uncertain. The rest of the group wasn't sure how to handle her awkwardness, and none of them felt comfortable leaving her alone, which meant staying inside most of the time because Sandy hated the sunlight.

The fourth and final girl of the group was Jasmine D'Silva. She was a junior international business major with hopes of working overseas for a Fortune 500 company but would settle for working overseas for anyone willing to hire her. Jaz was the only African American of the group, and her speech sounded Southern to the others. She claimed to have been born and raised in South Texas, but her accent didn't sound particularly Texan. Another fact: Jaz was thirty-eight weeks pregnant.

"Where do we start, girls?" asked Lindsey.

The chorus of ideas that erupted all at once was quickly interrupted by Max. "Wait, wait. This is our last outing together as a group for the year. And for some it's the last outing."

"Forever!" said several girls with Max at the same time. Everyone looked at Lindsey, and several made sad frowny faces. "Let's break up into groups of three and spend some time with each other. Find out what one another's plans are for the summer. Make sure you also allow time to give one prayer request, and then spend a little time praying for each other. We will then meet up at the fountain in an hour and a half to switch up groups." Though Max was not the official leader, she was the de facto leader, and everyone, including Lindsey, liked it that way.

"Good plan," said Lindsey. "And there needs to be at least one Wolf and one Peregrine in each group."

"Agreed," said Max.

And with the final instruction, Brook, Maddy, and Sandy headed one way. Max, Hopey, and Uber headed another. Lindsey, Ash, and Jaz were about to head out when Lindsey cried out, "Wait!" She bent down and began tying Jaz's shoelace that had come untied. "I don't want you to trip and fall. I'm not sure if we could get you back up again."

"Hey, I'm pregnant, not fat."

"It would still take at least both of us to pick up both of you," chuckled Ash.

Lindsey stood up. "What are you doing this summer, Ash?"

"I'm trying to get an internship with the Idaho State Department of Agriculture for marketing."

"What would that entail?" asked Jaz.

"I'm not sure, but I'm hoping it will satisfy a graduation requirement and will let me live near home. If I don't get it, I'll go home and work for my dad. It makes him feel like he is teaching me hard work and dedication while he pays the school bills."

"Your dad is paying your school bill to a private liberal arts university?" asked Jaz in amazement.

Lindsey just listened.

"Ha!" Ash burst out laughing. "Well, the majority of the bill is paid by grants and scholarships, but he is putting in more than I am, and this makes him feel like he is paying for everything."

"Are you taking out loans, Jaz?" asked Lindsey.

"Some, but my grandmother is helping me out with the rest. She has a janitorial business she had handed down to her that was started in Houston, and she expanded from there. Her business is in San Antonio and goes up into Dallas. She has several wealthy clients who allow her to bring in a lot of money." She bent her head and looked over the rim of her sunglasses. "She has high hopes of me joining the business. But I really don't want to make my living on helping other people clean up their messes."

"There is something about family that makes them possessive. They say they want all these things for us, but they can't admit the majority of the reason is so they can feel needed or important. It's as if they are giving us a great gift by passing something on to us. And perhaps it is. Perhaps it is part of the fullness of life. I wonder if they really do see this business as a gift. Like a fruit tree that they planted, nourished, and cultivated, and it gives them a good feeling to offer something they believe will shelter and feed their descendants after they are gone," offered Lindsey.

"Sure, perhaps? But I'm a hurdler, and I'm not interested in running a leg in her relay," countered Jaz.

"Sounds like you and your grandmother are not on the same page. But I think it is sweet that she wants you to be part of her life," said Lindsey, trying to change the focus of the conversation.

"I'm sure it sounds sweet. But you don't know my grandmother. She has issues." The other two girls had a feeling Jaz wasn't going to get into the details about how she truly felt about her grandmother, as she often "painted" her with a dark onyx, highlighted with shades of vagueness.

"Families can be just plain weird," interjected Ash, trying to expand the conversation without really changing topics.

"You can say that again," said Jaz.

"What do you mean, Ash?" asked Lindsey.

"I think families end up being the place where you dance between a deep desire to belong and a deep desire to stand out and be unique. It takes something difficult to change the dynamic, which then makes it rather complicated when you put a history of changing your diapers into the mix."

"Exactly! It's like the very glue that holds the family together also tends to be the force that tries to push it apart," offered Jaz.

They entered a shoe store and spent the next several minutes trying on shoes until Jaz gave up, complaining that she wasn't spending any money on something that wouldn't fit her swollen feet properly. And since it would still be several weeks away before her feet would return to her normal size, she saw no reason to waste any more time forcing her foot into something that was cramped and made her feel like one of Cinderella's stupid step-sisters. It wasn't long before they were back out, walking the alleys between shops.

"How about you, Lindsey? What are you doing after graduation?" asked Ash.

"Yeah, girl, whatchu gonna be doin'?" piped in Jaz.

"Oh boy, here it goes." Lindsey shook off a smile. "Well, I'm going to work for my mom and my uncle. They own several sandwich shops together, and I'm going to manage some of them for a couple of years, then work toward buying my own. We have a business plan already mapped out. They know all the ropes and have been doing it for several years. Between the two of them they have made all the mistakes, and they say by the time I'm thirty-five I will be set. They spend most of their time now traveling, doing mission trips, setting up orphanages and the like. I want to do what they're doing. And since they have already done it, it seems like the perfect internship with the perfect mentors."

There was an awkward pause broken a few seconds later by Jaz. "You should have gone first." Her eyes met Lindsey's. "No, really! You should have gone first!"

All three girls started laughing.

"Sounds like the perfect family situation," said Ash.

"It does sound like it, doesn't it?"

"Some girls have all the luck, huh, Ash?" quipped Jaz.

"They sure do."

Lindsey smiled. "Maybe it's true in my case. Who knows? Time will tell."

"What does that mean?" asked Jaz. Then she sarcastically repeated, "Maybe it's true in my case?"

"I'm sure your family life has many challenges that mine does not." Lindsey paused and went silent.

"And ... " coaxed Ash.

Lindsey grinned a shallow smile and looked at the other two, then briefly paused before saying, "But I never knew either of my grandmothers, and my father died when I was a little girl." Now the other two went silent. "Where you have challenges, I have emptiness. Where you are frustrated with those in your family who generate the tension between bonding and independence, I have an emptiness. It feels a little strange, wishing I knew firsthand what that tension and pain was like."

"Hey, let's stop in here," offered Ash, in what ended up being a intentional change in the topic.

They had found themselves outside a "baby and me" store and thought browsing for late maternity and earlier childhood items would be a nice distraction. They spent the next half hour to forty minutes holding up different clothes against Jaz's protruding belly and looking through newborn clothes and toys. Jaz never talked about the baby's father, and ever since the night the topic came up and she started crying, no one ever got up the courage to ask again.

With about fifteen minutes left before their scheduled time of arrival at the fountain, the three ladies found some shade and sat down for their quiet time together. One of the things that kept the group together was the fact that even though they were obviously different, and each was broken in their own way, they longed for the best in one another. They found among their kindred spirits enough to connect them in ways that otherwise would never have happened.

In the following minutes the three girls prayed for each other. They prayed for the summer plans they had discussed, and each of the hopes and dreams they felt they had seen and heard about from the other. They confessed the pain they endured in their lives and the longings they had for their friends. They prayed that God would reveal to them the mystery of *family*. There was so much pain and frustration they each uniquely held, and they were cautious of its potential negative effects. They knew resentment could easily take root in the cravings they had for intimacy in their families. So they asked for His help in getting past their challenges; expressed their thankfulness in celebrating the goodness that presented itself so fruitfully at times; while requesting patience for those times when goodness seemed absent or hidden. They wrapped up their prayers as the other groups joined them at the fountain.

"Okay, let's do this!" bellowed Brook.

"I'll go with Max," Ashley said.

To which Sandy added, "Me too."

"Then I'll go with Brook," chimed in Jaz.

"Hopey, do you want to go with Brook or Lindsey?" asked Erica.

"I'll go with Lindsey."

"That puts you with Brook and me, Uber," calculated Jaz.

"Then that puts the EY triplets together. Hopey, Lindsey, and Maddy," said Maddy, pointing each out with her finger.

And just like that, the deck had been reshuffled, and each girl fell into her group as she either declared or was chosen.

"Same instructions as last time," directed Max. "Share your summer plans and one prayer request. Meet back here in an hour and a half for the final grouping. Remember, tomorrow night we will have our final Bible study at my place in Nampa."

"Ready … Break!" said Brook. And the three groups broke apart and set off in different directions.

"Hey, can we head back this other way? There is a store I want to check out," Ash said, running ahead before hearing an answer.

Max looked at Sandy and said in a fake whisper, "I don't really think she was asking, do you?"

Sandy snorted a laugh as they started out at a slow pace to at least follow Ash, but it definitely wasn't any pace with which they would catch up with her anytime soon.

Sandy used the moment with Max to ask a question. "What's up with Ashley? Why is she so insecure?"

"You noticed, too, huh?" Max smiled and looked at Sandy, "I have been wondering the same thing."

Before Max could ask Sandy what she thought, Sandy beat her to it. "So what do you think it is?"

"A mentor of mine told me of a guy who was a famous singer in the day but who is also an amateur photographer," started Max.

Sandy glanced up as they slowly walked along.

"He says that what he enjoys most about taking photographs is the very same thing that people say they find intriguing about the pictures he takes."

"What's that?"

"When he photographs his subjects, he likes to get three poses. The subject can pick the setting, the clothes they want to wear, and even the location. He just has one request."

"Yeah?"

"Each of the three poses must be done in the same setting, same clothes, and the same location."

"Okay, I get that," said Sandy, trying to see where this was all headed. "What, like standing, sitting, and laying down?"

"Nope, he wants one pose to be demonstrating how the subject sees themself, the second pose is how the subject thinks others see them, and the third pose is how they want others to see them."

"All three are the same person clothed in the same outfit, using the same setting in the same location—all the visuals are the same? Except you see what ends up being three different people?"

"Right," said Max.

"So Ash is suffering from an internal conflict between three different people?"

"Well, more accurately, we all suffer from an internal conflict between the me I see, the me I fear you see, and the me I want you to see. It's not just Ash." Max looked around the shops and their patrons. "Everybody here, Sandy, struggles with the same thing." Max stopped and gestured to the meandering crowd. "Look at 'em."

"All the dirty little secrets they are hiding, the longings they are craving, each of them is on a journey to become someone they know they aren't?" Sandy wasn't sure she was following, but she sure was trying.

"They aren't that person today."

"But they long to be one day," said Sandy in a clarifying statement that sounded more like a question.

"Right. That desire to become someone else is the motivation we all deal with in the journey from today to tomorrow. The journey from the person I was, the person I am, and the person I hope to be all mixing together."

"So how does that fit with Ash?"

"It wouldn't be right for me to point at the splinter in Ash's eye while ignoring the log in my own."

"What?" Sandy had confessed early in joining the group that she wasn't raised in the church and was still trying to figure this God thing out.

"Sorry," said Max. "That's a reference to a scripture verse in the Bible. It's in a section called the Sermon on the Mount. There, Jesus essentially tells His listeners to not be a hypocrite by finding the one issue with your friends and family that annoys or irritates you when you yourself have your own list of issues that are just as annoying or irritating."

"So you don't want to rat out Ash. I get it."

"Well, not quite. I really don't want to talk about specific issues we both see in Ashley when I know that I have several of my own issues."

"Ahh," said Sandy. "You just don't want to talk to me about it."

"Some of us have issues with pride, some with lust, some with greed. Sometimes we just care too much about what other people think. These issues distort our perceptions of what we see in ourselves and what we think others see in us. Eventually, we say and do things in an attempt to manipulate who we are becoming, or who we want others to think we are becoming. I mean, we are all doing it."

"All of us, huh?"

"Yep, each and every one of us, to some degree or another. That's why we need God. That's why we need Jesus. To sort it all out and help us see our worth in the mess. By obtaining the means to be gracious with one another as we all go through the process."

"So, you're saying we are all screwed up?" Sandy stopped and looked at Max. "Not just Ashley?"

"Right." Max looked at Sandy. "Not just Ash.

"And not just me."

"Sandy, we are all screwed up. The good news is, we don't have to stay that way. He wants to mold and shape us into an image of who were meant to be."

"I think it would be easier for me if God just automatically changed me into the way He wants me to be."

Max pulled down her sunglasses and tried to look really hard into the eyes behind the other pair.

"What?" Sandy retorted in a whiney *don't judge me* voice. "It's true! I do!" The whole time she kept her glasses on.

Max smiled and said nothing.

Sandy looked away, then said, "*Becoming* is a lot harder than *became*, or *completed*."

Max remained quiet and let the silence draw Sandy out.

"The journey itself is so full of pain and struggles and growth, while the destination … " Her voice trailed off as if she either couldn't find the words to complete the thought or simply found them too hard to say out loud.

Max knew the silence couldn't draw Sandy out any further, so she gave her a nudge. "While the destination … what?"

Sandy shrugged as she looked around the complex. "The destination sounds so much more enjoyable, so much more peaceful than a long, drawn-out journey marked with pain and suffering."

"You've described the very essence of Sabbath," said Max.

Sandy looked back at Max, who had more to say. "After the fall of humanity, God cursed the ground, and it no longer just gave Adam and Eve its fruit. They had to work for it by the sweat of their brow, and so it continues on to today."

"And you're saying we have to work hard for more than just our food?"

"Yeah. Think about it. What if the things that used to not require any cultivation to come to fruition now require that we participate in the process of the cultivating. And the real curse isn't just that we have to cultivate; it's the fact that we cultivate with futility. We have to cultivate again and again. We have to return to fields every day to either plant, or water, or pull weeds, or fertilize, or weed again and again, or we risk the strangulation of the plant that yields the fruit we long for. And in the end, the fruits of our labor are either consumed or rot, only requiring that we start that process over again next season. It's a never-ending process that never satisfies."

"It does sound futile."

"It is futile. At least, it is in our own strength. It is impossible for us to cultivate in our own lives the things we need most, and I'm not talking food. All the love we experience, all the joy we experience, all the peace we experience, all the patience we experience, all the—"

"All the kindness, gentleness, faithfulness and self-control, right?" interrupted Sandy.

"You got it! The fruit of the Spirit is a great example of the very thing we can't cultivate in ourselves in any meaningful or lasting way." Max was surprised by Sandy. Not surprised that the girl was insightful. She had displayed plenty of evidence of that, but Sandy had never engaged at this level or intensity before. "We are all seeking the manifestation of the fruit of the Spirit as part of our final destination, and the Sabbath is a promise that one day we will no longer need to be cultivating. There will come a time when we can truly rest. It is so important that He wants us to remember it every week. In the meantime, however, we are in the middle of the work week and, like you said, the journey is much more difficult."

"And this is the journey we are all on? The journey of finding and cultivating the things of God?"

"Yep. We are all on a journey to that destination. It is just that some of us are struggling to find our way. Instead of love, we are cultivating lust. Instead of joy, we are cultivating happiness. Instead of peace, we try to avoid conflict. Instead of patience, we cultivate efficiency—and on and on it goes. Many are constantly striving but never step back to realize this truth."

Sandy seemed to be soaking it in and processing it.

"A mentor of mine likes to use the word *ought* to describe the draw we have on our life toward the destination God has for us." Max kept on feeding the hunger she felt she was sensing in Sandy. "Our lives ought to be filled with the fruit of the Spirit; unfortunately, most of humanity can't or won't hear the voice of God in their lives. They do not yield to the activity of the Spirit as He attempts to cultivate the very things people are longing for. Instead, we end up doing our own spiritual cultivating without His guidance and end up damaging our garden. We pull up those things we consider spiritual weeds, which might just be the early sprout of a plant that would bear not physical fruit but spiritual fruit … if we left it alone. Or we don't spiritually fertilize our lives with the proper spiritual fertilizer. We definitely don't use enough of the water of the Word. That's evident in the way we neglect our devotional life by spending time physically living our lives doing physical things."

"Why?"

"Why won't people let God cultivate in their lives?" Max was attempting to clarify what she thought Sandy was asking.

"Yeah, why do people resist God?"

"For lots of different reasons. The most common reason is that they are lost and confused."

"What do you mean?" Sandy almost sounded annoyed. "That just sounds religious. All you are saying is that people are lost and need to be saved."

"Then let me be more specific. The most common reason people won't let God cultivate the good things in their lives isn't because they are not saved, though that causes people to struggle for obvious reasons. No, most of humanity struggles because they are distracted by the world and its perspectives. They see the similitude but miss what it represents. They get caught up in the similitude of life and miss the reason for life."

"Wow, Max, you just took a left turn and lost me!"

"Well, think of it this way: We have been using the metaphor—or let's use the word my mentor uses, the *similitude*—of cultivating a garden. But what we are trying to discuss is actually not a physical garden; it's the spiritual reality represented by the garden. And our responsibility to develop our spirituality is represented by us being a gardener."

"Yeah?"

"If we continue to use this garden as our similitude, then the reason people struggle is because they get caught up in the similitude as if it were the reality. Then they try to fix their spirituality by actually going out and pulling weeds in their physical garden."

Max figured the door into Sandy's life was opening by the direction of God. This poor girl seemed to be an individual who was always so depressed and anxious, and perhaps God was using Max to do some spiritual cultivating today. If so, then Max wanted to be intentional and not rush. So she sat down and motioned for Sandy to join her.

"Sandy, what if everything you experience in this physical life was actually not your real life? What if the physical realm of life is really a shadow of something much, much bigger and more substantial?"

Sandy looked hard at Max and was beginning to wonder if this whole discussion would actually end up somewhere helpful. "Are you trying to tell me this place we are sitting in"—she pointed around the complex—"isn't real?"

"No, I am not saying it isn't real. I'm saying it's a similitude of something more important and something more substantial. Our physical experience serves the purpose of helping us understand spiritual truths. It helps us more fully understand the way things ought to be."

"Ought, huh?" the girl asked as she squinted into the sun. "What else does this cryptic mentor of yours say about *ought*?"

Max sniffed a shallow laugh. "She says oughtness was one of first things created."

The young girl now squinted at Max, and this time she used the silence to draw out Max for further explanation.

"She says there is something called the theology of creation, and it is so important that the Bible begins with it as the creation story. 'In the beginning God created the heaven and the earth. And the earth was without form, and void; and darkness was upon the face of the deep. And the Spirit of God moved upon the face of the waters. And God said, Let there be light: and there was light. And God saw the light, that it was good: and God divided the light from the darkness. And God called the light Day, and the darkness he called Night. And the evening and the morning were the first day,'" quoted Max.

"Ooookay. Like I said, she's cryptic."

Max again snickered. "One of her favorite points to make is about 'the principle of expositional constancy.' A principle she claims leads to a lot of revelations from Scripture. She says the Spirit of God tends to use certain terms for the same purpose over and over again. Even though different authors are credited for having written the Bible, it is her belief that the true author is the Holy Spirit, and He uses these metaphors consistently."

Sandy seemed uncertain as she stood up, and they began to follow after Ash. "You're losing me. Why is this important?"

"It is how God teaches us what is important."

"So, you're saying understanding this principle of expositional constancy helps us see what God is telling us is important?"

"Yes."

"How does that work?"

"Take this as an example: In Scripture the *stone* is a metaphor for Christ. He is the stone the builders rejected. He is the cornerstone. He is the stone that topples Nebuchadnezzar's statue in the dream interpreted by Daniel. And he was the rock from which the children of Israel drank from while wandering the desert, as recorded in the book of Exodus chapter seventeen, and then again in Numbers chapter twenty."

"Okay, wait. I'm lost. I got my first Bible a year ago, and for most of the year I've had no idea where to start."

"Well, what have you read?"

"Let's just say I haven't read those parts, okay?"

"Okay, then let me fill in some blanks."

"Yeah. And talk to me like I'm a fifth-grader."

Max chuckled. "Alright. The first five books of the Bible are called the Pentateuch and were written by—"

"Wait!" interrupted Sandy. "Like I'm a first-grader."

"You know about the story of the children of Israel leaving Egypt, right? Can I start there?"

"Yeah, that will work. God sends the plagues. Kills the firstborn. They split, and then they wander through the desert for like fifty years or something."

"Well, about thirty-eight years, but you got the highlights."

"Okay, go on. I'm actually in first-grade mode."

Max smiled and said, "I'll try." She took a deep breath. "Okay, they leave Egypt and travel the desert where there is little food and little water, which caused the children of Israel to grumble and complain. Ultimately, God tells Moses to take his staff and strike a rock, and when he does, water comes out that is enough for them all to drink. That's in Exodus chapter seventeen. Then later they are at a different place, again needing water, and this time God tells Moses to speak to the rock, and it will give water. But Moses doesn't speak to it; he strikes it twice. And let's just say that God is not pleased. He is so upset that He decides Moses will not be allowed to enter the promised land, claiming that Moses didn't act in a believing way and did not act in a way that would set God apart as special and unique. Now when you read through the passages, it can seem as if God is being a little overly sensitive about it, like the punishment doesn't seem to fit the crime."

"No, I agree. It seems as if God is overreacting."

"Right, but if you think about the similitude of the rock, you realize God wasn't upset that people got water from a struck rock. He was upset that His similitude had been damaged. When Jesus came to

Earth the first time as the Lamb of God, He was smitten and killed just like the prophets said He would be. But when He comes back the second time as the Lion of the Tribe of Judah, He won't be smitten and killed. And that was the point God was making with the way He wanted the two rocks to be addressed."

"Well, why didn't He just say that then? Why didn't He say, 'Look, you need water, but you also need this guy named Jesus even more, and I'm going to send him to you twice, and the first time I am sending Him to be killed. But the second time He won't be killed. So to help you remember what I just told you, Moses here is going to strike the rock this time, and next time I will just have him speak to it.'" Sandy was shaking her head. "Why all the cryptic language of metaphors?"

"Great question! I asked the same thing, and it is another interesting story that I plan to talk about at my house tomorrow during our Bible study. Something for everyone to think about over the summer. Then we will see what everyone thinks when we start back up in the fall."

"So what does this have to do with what your cryptic mentor says about *ought* being created."

"Oh yeah, back to the similitude of creation and what God wants to teach us." Max paused to reorient her thoughts and then started again. "So on the first day God created light. Then He separated it from the dark. She says that when you go through the Bible and find all the things the Bible calls good, they are often associated with terms such as 'being in the light,' or 'deeds of the light,' or 'walking in the light.' Light is the similitude for all the things that God determined 'ought to be,' and they were created on the very first day. And when He called it good, He put His stamp of 'oughtness' on those things. For this very reason they can't be wrong or bad because He separated the 'ought' from what we might call the 'ought not.' Those are all the things we would call sin, or trespasses, or iniquities. The things 'ought not to be' are all the evil and dark things in life."

"I have a feeling this may be a topic we need to put on the schedule for next year, after our talk on the purpose of cryptic similitudes.

But for now, let me see if I have this much straight: we are all screwed up while on a journey of becoming someone we are not."

"Someone we are not … yet."

"Right, and for some reason the journey is vitally important; therefore we can't skip to the end."

"Yeah, my mentor says that's part of the point of the parable of the wheat and the tares Jesus talks about in the New Testament." Sandy shushed her hand at Max as if to say, *Don't go there, yet. I'm still trying to get the first stuff.*

"Some on this journey are trying to determine for themselves what they're becoming, and they keep messing up. They're using wrong cultivating techniques or focusing on counterfeit fruit."

"Right, and it's not some of us, it's all of us. We're all trying to determine for ourselves what we're becoming, and we keep messing it up. Some of us are just further along in the journey and getting better at letting the Spirit do the cultivating."

"And the Spirit does all the cultivating by the use of similitudes He has placed in the Bible, right?" asked Sandy.

"That is essentially it. I think you have it. And Ash is on her journey, like us, but she's just stuck in areas we aren't."

"While we are stuck in our own."

"Exactly," concluded Max.

They had finally caught up with Ash and found she was actively trying on outfits that looked wonderful when worn by a mannequin, but they didn't have the same effect when worn by her. The sad thing was you could see her trying to convince herself that she looked as great in it as the saleswoman claimed. They were both working the dress. The saleswoman was looking to make a sale, and the girl was looking for the approval she felt people gave to the mannequin and she heard from a saleswoman. They were both marketing the dress.

For the rest of that rotation, Max's group went much like Brook's group did the whole time. The girls shared, to some extent or another, their plans and dreams for the summer. There were actually very few surprises from then on, with the exception of Jaz telling her group about learning that Lindsey's father had died when she was little and how awkward it was to continue discussing their own struggles. Ash, after the others caught up, gave the same revelation in her own group. The fact that Lindsey had kept this so quiet for so long intrigued all the girls. They began to talk about what other secrets sat tucked away in each girl's heart. Secrets that, if revealed, would take each of them to a new level of awkwardness but also a new level of growth and self-awareness.

Later, when they shuffled the deck one last time, the same topic of conversation continued much as it had the previous rotation, only this time it was Maddy and Hopey, who had no idea about Lindsey and her dad. The realization that they were the last to learn this little tidbit left them with a certain level of hurt. Especially after they had just spent the last ninety minutes with Lindsey, and she had said nothing about it to them.

While Maddy and Hopey were debriefing and processing the "Lindsey revelation" within each of their own groups, Max, Lindsey, and Brook had already made it back to the fountain. Max and Lindsey had been discussing the close of another year together for about twenty minutes when Hopey and Jaz came running up from behind. Hopey fell gracefully into Lindsey's chest in an attempt to slow herself down and whispered, "We gotta get Jaz outta here!" Jaz just kept on running as fast as her fat little feet and pregnant belly could move. "Let's go! Let's go!" There was a sense of urgency in her voice that got the other three up and moving in the direction of the cars.

CHAPTER 7

HOUNDS OF DARKNESS

Meridian, Idaho
Moments later

What's going on?" asked Max.

"Sandy saw two large Black guys and started joking with Jaz about how Black people really stand out in Idaho. Then when she pointed them out to Jaz, she just freaked," explained Hopey, who was nearly out of breath. "I've never seen her so distressed. I swear she went six different directions at the same time trying to hightail it back to the car."

"Black guys are people, too, Hopey. That doesn't make them evil or bad," said Lindsey, trying to lighten the mood.

"Jaz said they looked like guys who worked for her grandmother," explained Hopey.

Lindsey looked around the complex but didn't see anyone standing out. Even though there were one or two dark-skinned guys walking about, none of them appeared to be together. "Did they see you?"

"I don't think so. But we weren't waiting around. I'm telling you; Jaz is about to pop a vessel. It can't be good for the baby."

"Hopey, you go with Jaz immediately and hide in either the Jeep or in Uber's BMW." Max then had another thought. "Preferably the BMW, if Uber gets there soon enough. And see if you guys can get the top up before anyone shows. I think her windows are tinted, and that will help hide you. Brook, you go find the others, and we'll plan to meet up back at the vehicles. Lindsey, how about you and I head back that way and see if we can spot those guys? That way, if need be, we can distract them so Jaz and the others can get away." The two leaders turned to head back the way Hopey and Jaz had come from.

"Right, and Brook, please text me when everyone else is back at the vehicles!" directed Lindsey. The team broke up with Brook headed in the direction she last saw the rest of the group going, and Hope began quickly shepherding the frazzled Jaz toward the lot where they had parked and left the cars.

"Come on!" called Max

Sandy was right. It didn't take them long to spot to the two men. They were giant-sized men, dressed in expensive suits. But they were headed away from where the girls had parked the vehicles earlier. So it wasn't hard for Max and Lindsey to spend the next several minutes nonchalantly monitoring the two men as they tried, unsuccessfully, to blend in with the crowd, surveying the comings and goings of everyone. It did seem that they were looking for someone in particular. And while Max always thought approaching these issues head-on worked best, she felt that for now, Jaz was safest while these guys were on the opposite side of the complex, searching in the wrong area from where their friends were. Max knew if she overplayed her hand, then she and Lindsey would be marked. They could actually lead these two suspicious-looking gentlemen back to Jaz, and for right now, the guys were just plain lost.

About ten minutes later Lindsey got a text, saying, "All present and accounted for." And then, as if to break the tension, a second text came through, "Package is safe and sound. Return to extraction point alpha!" Lindsey snorted and showed her phone to Max, who just smiled as they both headed back to the vehicles. "I wonder what emoji one puts with that?" asked Max.

Twenty minutes later they were on the freeway headed back to Nampa, where everyone stopped at Max's place. It was decided that it would probably be the safest for Jaz to just stay in Nampa with Max for the night while the others scouted their respective campuses. They would all meet up back at Max's the following night for the Bible study as scheduled, and the Wolves would make sure they weren't followed. Everyone agreed that if Jaz's grandmother had men at The Oasis in Meridian, then it was certain that they were, or soon would be, on campus in Caldwell looking for her there as well. In fact, they probably started in Caldwell earlier in the day and had found someone who told them Jaz had gone to Meridian. They might know all her friends' names as well, though they doubted anyone else at Ribley's College knew where Max lived or that the other PNCU girls all lived on campus.

That night, the whole group of girls, regardless of where they stayed, started out having trouble sleeping, but one by one they all began to drift off, starting with Max and ending with Jaz. To everyone's surprise, Sandy had talked Uber into the two of them staying at Jaz's place. Sandy said she felt bad for having played a part in what had scared the poor girl. She had told them she actually thought it might keep Jaz safe if she and someone else were there all night with the blinds open enough to let someone see in. They figured the guys wouldn't bother them if they knew at least two other girls were staying there without any evidence of Jaz being in the house.

And it appeared to have either worked as planned, or the guys had yet to learn where Jaz lived, which everyone felt was unlikely. Either way, the night ended up being quiet. The next day had started out with a little more anxiety than usual for this time of year, but in the end, it remained uneventful as well.

* * *

The following night the group had gathered as planned at Max's without any of the three other Wolves. They waited fifteen minutes before Max allowed them to begin to worry. By the time they were a full fifteen minutes beyond their start time, anxiety was growing, and people started texting Uber, Lindsey, and Sandy. But it was to no avail.

They knew the night had been uneventful because Max had talked with Lindsey, who had seen Uber on campus and she relayed as much to Lindsey. The group of girls were about to go from reasonably stressed to irrationally freaked when Uber's BMW pulled up and Lindsey and Erica stepped out.

"Where's Sandy?" asked Max.

"We have no idea," replied Lindsey, somewhat annoyed. "She didn't show up at the rally point for the ride, and she wasn't at her place or Jaz's. Then we made a quick run around campus. That's why we're late."

"She was acting a little weird last night, all sullen and withdrawn. She spoke very little and seemed distracted. She still felt somewhat responsible for Jaz being a wreck yesterday," Uber shared.

"Why didn't you respond to our texts? We were freaking out!" interjected Hopey.

"It's that stupid Do Not Disturb function on our phone that automatically kicks in when you start driving. We all swore we'd use it, remember?" Uber was a bit defensive, which just added to the irritation. Then she said in her most sarcastic voice, "Remember when you said to not text and drive? It was your idea, Hope."

"Oh, yeah." Hope snorted, then added goofily, "Glad your safe."

"When I got up this morning Sandy was gone, and all I found was a note saying she had a paper to turn in and would see me at our usual rally point tonight."

Within a few minutes they had pretty much convinced themselves that Sandy must be okay and had really just missed her rally point. It wasn't long before the topic naturally switched to Jaz. She was still a little shaken. She shared that she had given it a lot of thought through the day and figured she would ignore her grandmother's agents and cancel her summer traveling plans. Then, in the next couple of days, she would just head home for the summer and face whatever music her family, especially her grandmother, was playing. She knew if she could get back on her own home turf with her family, then she could make right whatever was wrong with her grandmother and all of this would fade. Lindsey offered to stay with Jaz at her place so she wouldn't have to be alone. They all wished Jaz well and said they would be praying for her.

It was nearly forty-five minutes later when they finally decided to get started. They sat down on the ground around the living room.

"Now before we get going here, I want to preface tonight's study with a word of caution," stated Max. Everyone froze in the act of what they were doing and stared at her. As the *de facto* older sister of everyone in the circle, she immediately had everyone's attention. "Well, no, not like that." There was a slight chuckle. "What I mean is, I have been leading Bible studies for quite a while, and what we are about to do can at first be rather difficult. When we approach the Word of God, we can easily give ourselves too much credit for what is about to happen." The girls were loosening up a bit out of their frozen state, but they were still not sure what Max was trying to say. "Don't just listen to the words being read. Hear the voice of God as the Holy Spirit interprets those words and applies them to your life. Here is my point in a nutshell. Pay attention to what you read, but be even more sensitive to what the Holy Spirit is specifically teaching you through the words you read: one is a task; the other is a relationship."

And with that, Max had Lindsey open in prayer.

At the conclusion of prayer, Max continued, "I had hoped Sandy would be here tonight to help open this up, cuz yesterday she and I had a great conversation about how God transforms us by the way He talks to us. I thought our conversation would fit in nicely with what I have been studying. In sharing our example, it will provide us with significant insight into how God speaks to each and every one of us. I think it will also give us something to ponder over the summer. So let's get started. Please take your Bibles and open to the Old Testament book of Hosea."

Brook and Ash started racing one another trying to find the passage and noticed all the girls were struggling to find it. Nearly all of them admitted they had never read any passage from the prophet.

Max continued, "While you are all searching for it, I'll give a brief overview."

Rrrrrrip! Everyone looked at Ash.

"Not only did I beat you, Ash," Brook said as she thrust her hands toward the ceiling, "but, I'm pretty sure a person can go to hell for defacing the Bible."

"Real funny, Brook," was the only retort Ash could come up with.

"Yeah, and that Bible belongs to Max. She *will* kick your butt!" said Brook as she easily parried.

"Besides, Brook, you should find it quicker. You and Maddy just finished Bib Lit this term." All the Peregrines were required to take a Biblical Literature class to graduate. The shortening of the seven-syllable title of the course down to two-syllables corresponded to what most students desired to do to the overall length of course as well.

"Old Testament was last semester."

"At least you had Bib Lit," bemoaned Jaz.

"Just be careful," said Max as she looked at the Bible. "For those of you who aren't required to take a Biblical Literature class"—she looked at the Wolves—"or have since forgotten about the old prophet." She looked at Hopey.

"What?" Hope shrugged her off. "I found it," she said as she pointed to the open page.

"Hosea was one of the prophets to the Northern Kingdom. He lived about the same time as Isaiah and Amos, and he was really the same type of prophet to the Northern Kingdom that Jeremiah was to the Southern. This was during the time leading up to the Assyrian Conquest of the Northern Kingdom."

"Do you know about what year, Max?" asked Lindsey.

"Somewhere around 790–780 BC by most of the sources I checked," informed Max.

"The message delivered by Hosea gives a very heartfelt perspective of the way God interacts with His people here on earth. He suffers when His people are unfaithful because it places Him in an excruciatingly painful position. He cannot condone sin, but He will never stop loving His own—"

"That was cute, Max. I see what you did there," interrupted Brook. "*Excruciatingly painful position.*" Everyone glanced at Brook. "You know … The cross that Jesus died on. Crucifixion is the root meaning to the word *excruciate* … Oh, never mind."

Max tried to emphasize the point without letting everyone get too distracted. "This ex-cru-ci-a-ting-ly painful position causes God to try and woo back those who have become lost to Him." Max looked at Brook and spoke, "And yes, Brook, that was the point of the cross, wasn't it?"

Brook smiled knowingly.

"What many commentators mention about this era is that it was a prosperous time for the Northern Kingdom, and from their perspective life was good. They were experiencing wealth and prosperity not unlike the 'good ole days' under Solomon. But despite all this apparent blessing, they were lost on the inside. Not unlike the beginning of *A Tale of Two Cities* by Charles Dickens—"

This time it was Uber's turn to chime in. "It was the best of times, it was the worst of times."

"Right. It appeared great from the outside, but the inside was rotten," explained Max.

"And God was suffering," chimed in Jaz.

"Okay, so how does this tie in with your talk with Sandy?" Lindsey wanted to know.

"It ties in this way, Hosea is a book with a puzzle that has the solution on the inside." There were a lot of blank stares. "Kind of like that question, 'Who's buried in Grant's Tomb?' God delivers His message in the metaphor of a marriage."

"Wait, this is the prophet who married the prostitute, isn't it?" asked Maddy.

"Bib Lit is paying off, I see," said Brook as she held up her hand for the no-look high five Maddy gave enthusiastically.

"Word!" replied Maddy.

"God's Word!" followed Brook. Some of the girls just rolled their eyes, while others shook their heads at the shameless self-promotion of the two.

"The King James Version calls her 'a woman of whoredoms' and the NIV calls her 'a promiscuous woman,'" clarified Max. "I think you split the difference, Maddy. Regardless, the Bible is clear she is adulterous, and God tells Hosea to marry and have children by her, saying, 'For the land hath committed great whoredom, departing from the LORD.'"

"Ouch!" remarked Ash.

"God was having Hosea live out what He Himself was experiencing in the unfaithfulness of Israel. He was having Hosea live out a metaphor, an example that was similar to what God Himself was experiencing," said Max.

"Is that the puzzle or the solution?" asked Lindsey.

"The metaphor is the puzzle. The solution is found later. Turn to chapter twelve verse ten. Here, God is talking about Ephraim and Judah when He drops this tidbit that is a solution—and the point I want to make tonight. In the King James it says, 'I have also spoken by the prophets, and I have multiplied visions, and used similitudes, by the ministry of the prophets.' Ash, what version do you have?"

"NIV," she replied.

"Would you read verse ten, please?" asked Max.

"Sure, 'I spoke to the prophets, gave them many visions and told parables through them.' Just verse ten?"

"Yep, that is perfect, thanks." Max began to try and make the point she thought God had wanted her to share. "This is the point I want to make, and it can leave us with something to think about for the summer." She paused as she prepared to summarize her point.

"First, the puzzle, or ... the metaphor. Each of us has been living in a relationship with God, much like Hosea's wife: we have been—and I think to some degree still are—spiritually adulterous. He was specifically using it as a metaphor to speak of Israel and her relationship with her God, and I believe it is also a metaphor that applies to us today as well. We are not yet fully who He has called us to be either. 'We all, like sheep, have gone astray.' We are still in the process of becoming that person. And for some reason many of us struggle with the becoming part and are still a long way from being whom we ought to be. Now I'm not pointing fingers at anyone in particular, other than pointing out what I think we can all clearly see is true about me. But how many of you right now feel you are a perfect example of who God longs for you to be?"

No hands went up. "Anyone?" asked Max. "One day we can be singing 'I Love You Lord,' and later that same day we have become distracted by our own concerns, desires, and cravings. We begin to exhibit the evil inclinations in our lives, and they get expressed as falling short of what He has for us, even though we try. Sometimes we are flat-out acting in ways that we should not. It doesn't matter what it is we are doing, and it likely isn't the same action for each of us. Some of us get caught up in our own pet sins of lying to protect our image, coveting to make us look and feel bigger and more important than we really are—and on and on.

"Sometimes it's a feeble attempt to do the right thing, but our heart isn't in it. Sometimes we hope that by not saying something mean it will be just as good as saying something loving. And sometimes we tend to judge others by what they do and judge ourselves by what we think we would do."

"You're saying sometimes we do wrong and sometimes our doing good isn't good enough?" Brook wanted clarification.

"In essence, yes, that is what I am trying to say. I'm just giving examples of the different ways each of us flubs it up every day," said Max.

"Okay, I will buy it," conceded Brook.

"Now let's look at the solution, the use of metaphors, or what my mentor calls *similitudes*. It's been said that God loves us the way we are, but so much so that He doesn't want to leave us that way. God is still in the business of transforming lives, but for most of us it isn't something that He does immediately."

"Yeah, but some people seem to have found a shortcut." Erica had been pretty quiet until now.

"It's true, some seem to either be on a faster track than others or they know a shortcut. I've met some. But I don't think there are any of them who would tell you they have already arrived," countered Max.

"You're saying it's a journey we are all on, not a destination any of us has arrived at yet?" This time Lindsey was looking to clarify.

"I know I haven't. In fact, this is precisely what Sandy and I were talking about yesterday and why I was really hoping she would be here tonight to share any thoughts she might have had since then."

No one seemed to want to argue with her.

"So the solution?" asked Ash.

"For some reason, the journey seems to be very important to God. Therefore He has given us His Word, the Bible, to guide and direct us. But if we aren't careful, we can miss what He is saying. And we had better pay attention to his ... What does King James call it? His *similitudes*?" Max could see there were still some blurry looks.

"I get what you're saying about the puzzle. I do believe none of us can say God is finished with us, and I do believe some people seem further along in their journey than others. But I'm not sure I see how what you call the solution actually helps solve the puzzle." Lindsey was just being honest and asking what was on everyone else's mind. "How do similitudes and metaphors help us in our journey? Why isn't God more direct so He doesn't have to use metaphors?"

"Sandy basically asked the same thing yesterday," responded Max. "There is a verse in Jeremiah chapter twenty-nine verse thirteen, 'And ye shall seek me, and find me, when ye shall search for me with all your heart.' Now here He is talking through Jeremiah to the Southern Kingdom, but can we take it as a metaphor for us?" Again, some blank stares ensued, so Max pushed a little to keep them thinking. "Do you think that when God was speaking to the people of the Southern Kingdom about going into captivity, there is something we should take to heart today, or is it only to be read as history?" There was a pause that Max felt was too long. "Come on, ladies. Can we take the book of Jeremiah and apply it to our lives today?"

"Yes, I think we can," said Erica, and others agreed.

"Can we take part of it, or all of it? When God says through Jeremiah to the people of the Southern Kingdom, 'You will seek me, and you will find me,' I think He is talking to me just as much as He was to them. Do you agree?"

Again, the group seemed to agree as they nodded their heads.

Max continued. "But you know what scares me about this passage?"

"What follows the word *when*?" offered Brook.

"Yep, how many of them, and how many of us, are searching for God ... but not with our whole hearts? And is there any reassurance in this passage, or anywhere else in the Bible for that matter, that people can find God with a halfhearted search?" Max could tell she was starting to win some over just by the looks on their faces. "How many people are searching for God but aren't doing so wholeheartedly?

"I tend to think that the reason we are all on this journey—yet have not quite arrived—is so that our hearts can be refined. The Bible refers to the process of refining as 'trying,' and it is the process of purifying. God is purifying our hearts through a process. And part of the refining process is a round of spiritual hide-and-seek. And as we seek, He is found. But then we have to seek Him again, only this time it requires a deeper longing of our heart." Eyes were once again glossing over.

"Hide-and-seek? Really, Max?" asked Hopey incredulously.

Max folded her hands into her lap and lowered her eyes. "The year before I enlisted in the Army"—she looked up and into Hope's eyes—"I was assisting my mentor in her classroom. One day after recess, when all the kids came in and had taken their seat, my mentor noticed one of the girls was missing. She asked me to monitor the class while she went looking for her. Twenty minutes later Miss Nelson found the girl sobbing. 'What is wrong, Britany?' she'd asked.

"The kids had been playing hide-and-seek. I had seen her running after the other kids, trying to be a part of the group from which she had been outcast. They would run and laugh, and each child had a chance to hide and be sought. Every child, that is, except Britany." Max's voice cracked and she swallowed hard. "'Let me hide!' requested Britany. 'Sure, you can hide,' said the snotty, popular girl. 'We will give you thirty seconds.' The popular girl hid her eyes and began to count. As the others did the same, Britany ran to hide. When they had finished counting, the kids looked up as the popular girl was headed to the building. 'Are we going to look for her?' asked the others. 'Why?' she said, without looking back. The others just followed her in, and no one went to look for Britany." Max's eyes welled up with tears.

"What did Miss Nelson do?" asked Lindsey.

"She followed the Spirit and left the ninety-nine. And when she found Britany, she just embraced her and told her how worried she had been. How happy she was to find her. How much she loved her and how happy she was to have her as one of her students."

The group was silent as each thought of the times they had been the outcast and how often they had also been the snotty, popular girl.

"So the God of the universe hides?" said Ashley, hoping someone would complete her thought.

"Just to see if we care enough to come searching," finished Hopey. "I think I get it now."

"What does Jesus tell us in the Sermon on the Mount?" Max continued.

"If you think lustful thoughts, then you've committed adultery?" winced Brook.

"Yes!" responded Max, acknowledging the truth but also insuring the group didn't linger there. "But I was thinking about the verse that says, 'Blessed are the pure in heart: for they shall—' What comes after that?"

"See God," finished Ash.

"Right. Now hang on with me. I am not saying this is the case. But I want to challenge something I think will make all of us a little uncomfortable." Max paused, considering if she really wanted to put this next thought out there. Figuring it was the last time they would meet for the year, she decided to go for it. "Like Erica mentioned earlier, I think each of us knows at least one person who seems to see God more clearly than others. They seem to have found a short-cut. They just seem further along in their journey. And if that is true here on Earth, then what if when we all get to heaven, the refining process directly correlates to the clarity in which we see God when we get there as well?"

"What do you mean? In heaven some will see Him more, or better, than others?" asked Ash.

"I didn't say more; I said clearer," clarified Max.

"Eww. I'm not sure I like the sound of that idea," stated Hope.

"Yeah, me neither," Jaz chimed in.

"I'll have to think on that one, Max," added Lindsey. "It sounds like you're saying God plays favorites."

"Believe me, I'm not trying to convince you of anything, or persuade you to agree with me. I'm just asking you to consider if it might be a possible explanation for why God has us all on a journey? Why we are all at different points in our journey. And most importantly, what if there really is a shortcut, and the key to growth, or purification, is in hearing and trusting God as He tells us His stories with similitudes. What if there is a design in the process of the journey? What if God designed the journey as a way to not only woo us back to Him, but also as a way for us to prove, try, or—better yet—refine our love for Him?"

"Give us an example of this metaphor, or similitude, at work refining us," requested Brook.

"Let's look at the one we have already been studying. Do you know who else was called Hosea?" Max posed the question, but no one wanted to risk being wrong, so they said nothing. "Hoshea, son of Nun, was the real name of the man Moses called Joshua. Now maybe it's just coincidence, but the Greek word for Joshua is *Jesus*. I find it interesting that God tells a story of a man named Moses, who is the symbol of the Law. He is called the lawgiver. But the symbol of the Law can't bring the wandering children of God out of their desert and into the promised land. He has to die before the man—whose Hebrew name is Hoshea, called Joshua, and the Greek version of which is Jesus—can lead them into the promised land. And then in our passage tonight God tells a story of the Hebrew prophet, Hosea, a variant of Hoshea, and therefore a variant of Jesus, who is married to an adulterous wife. Is it possible that God was refining Israel as His bride, and our Hosea, Jesus, is refining His bride? I'm just saying there are similarities between the stories, which causes me to stop and think. As I ponder these similarities, or similitudes, I sense something in my spirit that stirs, and I feel closer to God as I sense Him revealing these thoughts. I can't help but wonder if, in that process, my heart is being purified, and God is allowing Himself to be found and seen."

"I thought we were a glorious church without spot or wrinkle?" Lindsey pushed back.

"Look at what it says in Romans chapter eight somewhere near the eighteenth verse." Max flipped through several sections. "'I consider that our present sufferings are not worth comparing with the glory that will be revealed in us.' Sounds a little like what we were just saying about the journey and the destination, doesn't it? And a little later, at verse twenty-two, 'We know that the whole creation has been groaning as in the pains of childbirth right up to the present time. Not only so, but we ourselves, who have the first fruits of the Spirit, groan inwardly as we wait eagerly for our adoption to sonship, the redemption of our bodies.' Again, sounds to me like the journey and destination."

And with that, Max stopped and allowed the silence to work its magic.

"Wow, that is a lot to think about, Max," said Lindsey.

"Yep," said Brook as Hope and Ash nodded. You could see Jasmine and Maddy were still thinking but unwilling to disagree openly, at least not yet.

Lindsey followed up her last comment with, "It still sounds like God has favorites. Like, He reveals Himself to some more than He does others. I'm not sure I like that."

"I don't think I am saying God plays favorites, Lindsey. As much as I am saying some people see, or hear, God more clearly than others. I'm not sure He is playing favorites if He makes the condition the same for all people," explained Max.

"So all people have to seek Him passionately or He won't be found?" clarified Ash.

"He is only going to let Himself be found by people who want to see Him—who really want to see Him. He will be found, or discovered, to the degree that He is being sought," Max clarified further.

"It sounds like you're saying God is intentionally cryptic. He is intentionally not being clear for the purpose of seeing who really wants to hear from Him." Maddy was still trying to distill it down.

"Funny, Sandy used the same word yesterday: cryptic. But yes! Otherwise, why use similitudes and visions at all? It seems to explain why some things are harder to understand than others. I think there are things God says outright, and then there are things God delivers in a metaphor, or similitude," explained Max.

"So God intentionally takes a riddle, wraps it in a mystery, and places it inside an enigma, like Churchill stated?" asked Maddy.

"Look at Proverbs chapter twenty-five verse two. It says, 'It is the glory of God to conceal a thing: but the honour of kings is to search out a matter.' I think the thing of greatest value that He conceals is Himself, the greatest treasure in all of creation." Max was pulling out all the stops, and it was clear this wasn't something that she had just thought of; it was something that had been percolating for a while.

"I don't think I like the idea that God is…" Jasmine pursed her lips and shook her head slowly before saying, "Cryptic."

"Why not? Jesus was." Max was willing to talk with anyone willing to engage.

"What?" This time it was Maddy who was incredulous.

"I have heard several people say Jesus spoke in parables because it was the strategy of an oral culture to help people to remember what was being said. They say parables were to help His listeners remember. But that isn't what Scripture says."

"Where does it say that?" asked Maddy.

"Matthew chapter thirteen starting at verse ten." Max flipped to the passage. "'And the disciples came, and said unto him, Why speakest thou unto them in parables? He answered and said unto them, Because it is given unto you to know the mysteries of the kingdom of heaven, but to them it is not given. For whosoever hath, to him shall be given, and he shall have more abundance: but whosoever hath not, from him shall be taken way even that he hath. Therefore I speak to them in parables: because they seeing see not; and hearing they hear not, neither do they understand.'"

"I need a second opinion," interjected Brook.

But even after reading from different versions of translations and even a couple of paraphrases, it was hard to escape the fact that it was God's intention to hide the truth of the Kingdom from some people while allowing others to find it while Jesus was actually carrying it out. The part about people who have a lot getting more, compared to people who don't have much and then getting what little they have taken away seemed to challenge Lindsey's favoritism concern.

"Yeah, a lot to think about." You could tell Ash was pretty much done. You could hear it in her voice and see it in her posture. Everyone started to get up and move about. Some went to the kitchen to get something to drink and find refreshments in the fridge and pantry, which consisted mostly of protein bars, fresh fruit, and bottles of water.

Max chuckled. "You have all summer. Well, some of you have more than the summer." She looked at Lindsey.

"You may have to hook me up over the Internet for the first couple of sessions next year as everyone unpacks this," said Lindsey, only half joking.

"Max, what's going on in your backyard?" asked Brook.

"Yeah, I hear drums," commented Ash.

"What?" Max could also hear what sounded like distant drums.

"It looks like a baby woolly mammoth is having a seizure on your lawn," said Brook through a scrunched-up face.

"What is that?" Maddy stared out, confused.

"I have no idea, but I'm going to find out," answered Max.

When the group of girls had left the living room and entered the kitchen, Brook had come to get a glass out of one of the cabinets next to the sink and just happened to glance out the window that looked into the backyard. In the middle of the yard was what looked like a haystack. In fact, it was a Zangbeto mask often found in West African countries, such as Benin and Togo, and it was bouncing and spinning and dancing to the rhythm of drums that could be heard but without an apparent source.

In the center of the yard stood a column that wasn't supporting anything, around which were piled various objects.

"Is that a dead cat?" asked Maddy.

"Looks like road kill on a leash," quipped Brook.

Max went out her back door as the light began to fade from the setting sun. None of the others were willing to leave the house before Max, and neither did any of them want to stay inside once she left. At first the group just stood and watched as the haystack continued its rhythmic gyrations and spinning for several seconds, then Max began to move toward the object. But as Max got closer, it stopped and spun around in what appeared to be an attempt to face her and then came to a complete stop. Just as quickly the beating of the drums stopped.

The haystack-like figure tipped on its side, and out stepped a sweaty, frazzled Sandy.

"Sandy! What are you doing?" yelled Max.

The girl raised her arms and in Creole began shouting something none of them understood. But from the tone of her voice, it appeared to be not very nice. It lasted about fifteen seconds, and then she turned and went to the column in the middle. She reached into a pot that sat leaning against the column and pulled out a fistfull of whatever was in the pot.

She raised her arms to the sky with one fist closed and the other open as she hollered something at the sky. Then, with her open hand, she reached down and grabbed an ason and began to shake it as she moved about the column. After three passes, she moved to one side of the back porch where she used the substance in her closed fist to make a circle as she allowed it to slip from the bottom of her fist. She continued talking in Creole while periodically glancing toward the eastern horizon.

The girls tried to call out to Sandy to stop whatever it was that she was doing because it was creeping them out. But Sandy just ignored them, and it created the sense that the girls weren't even there. She kept gliding and dancing and singing, then began chanting. She would stop every now and then to shake the rattle at Max, or the column, or the circle she drew. The only one who seemed to get her attention was Max.

It wasn't long before she went back to the column and grabbed another handful of what ended up looking like corn meal, then went to the other side of the porch and drew an intricate design in the same manner as she did the circle. Then she went back to the column and threw what was left of what was in her hand at the base of the column. She bent down and picked up a string, which was tied to the dead cat, and slung it toward the design she had just completed.

Then she turned on her heels and went straight to Max and said, "Who do you think you are? You have no authority over me. You have no right to sit in judgment over my life. You no longer have any say in what I do with my life. I reject you! I reject your authority! I denounce the day I met you. I reject any claims you might have on my life. I renounce any agreements we have between us. I no longer submit to your direction or manipulation."

Max looked stunned, unable to take in what was going on. The others were just as speechless. Then a cold and oppressive sensation came over them.

"I never wanted this! I never wanted you! Go back to wherever it is you came from."

At this point Sandy was in a dither, standing within inches of Max, who reached out to touch her. But Sandy slapped Max across the face with a force and a sound that caused all the girls to gasp. But Max restrained herself.

"I love you, Sandy, and I always will." Sandy reached out and promptly slapped Max on the other cheek.

And with that, Max turned on her heels and went inside with tears streaming down her face. Sandy immediately turned on hers as well and strolled out of the yard with her face, body, and clothes soaked in sweat.

The rest of the girls stood in utter amazement for several minutes, struggling to grasp and make sense of what they had just witnessed.

Finally, Brook said, "What … in the world … just happened? Where has she been all day? Practicing voodoo? And what language was that? French?"

Hopey was the next to try and find her voice. "Is that …? Was that …? Did I just witness a voodoo curse or something?"

"That was creepy," whispered Erica.

Ash just stood there with her mouth open.

"I'm going to check on Max," Lindsey said.

They all entered the house but found Max had retreated to her bedroom with the door locked. There was no coaxing her out. The group of girls returned and straightened everything up in the kitchen and the backyard before they silently locked the doors and left.

CHAPTER 8

A MOTHER'S LOVE

Nampa, Idaho
later that night and early the next morning

Max couldn't get out of her head what she had seen. It made no sense. What had happened between yesterday at the Oasis and just now in her backyard? She had been so invigorated by her conversation with Sandy and the apparent progress she had made in grasping what they had talked about just the day before. What caused her to go all jungle on the group? What was the dance all about? And what was the verbal dressing down at the end? She couldn't think of anything that would have led to her deserving that. Again, it made no sense.

She felt shock. She felt betrayed but didn't know by whom. She wasn't angry, but she was hurt. But more than anything, she was confused. She ended up going to bed earlier than usual, but her mind continued to race, making it hard for her to fall asleep until well after 11:00 p.m.

Sometime after 2:00 a.m. she roused from a deep sleep with an eerie sense that she was not alone. She threw back the covers from her body and sat up in bed, her mind instantly awake and her sense tingling with an urgency to detect the reason for her arousal.

"Relax," said the voice. "I won't hurt you."

"Sandy?"

"Just take a deep breath. Yeah, yeah, it's me."

Max rolled toward the light.

"Please don't. I would prefer to not have to look you in the eye, at least not yet." Sandy's voice was calm. "I also don't want anyone outside being suspicious that I'm here."

Max swung around and put her feet on the ground. "What are you doing here?"

"I need to explain." Sandy paused. "And I need your help."

"You sure have a weird way of asking for it."

"I know." Max could hear Sandy sit back in her chair and could sense her exasperation.

"What happened, Sandy? What did I witness last night?"

"A show … of sorts," she offered. Her voice was tight, and she let out what sounded like a deep sigh.

"It looked like some voodoo mumbo jumbo, and you freaked everyone out."

"Well … that was the point." Sandy was quiet, and Max decided to let silence do its work. Sandy had chosen to come here, and it just made sense that she would lead when she was ready. "It wasn't real Vodun. The rhythms weren't sacred. The poto mitan wasn't sanctified—nor anything else, for that matter—and the veves weren't legit."

"What language were you speaking?"

"The language I was speaking last night was Creole, and that was real. But I knew no one would understand what I was saying."

"Why, Sandy? What was the point?" asked Max.

"My real name is Santana D'Souza. I come from a long line of Vodun priestesses. Those guys that freaked out Jaz are actually looking for me."

"What?" Max shook her head, though it couldn't be seen in the dark.

"I didn't just meet Jasmine D'Silva when I came to Ribley's College. I followed her, though she doesn't know it. She does have a grandmother who is a crooked business woman in South Texas. She runs a lucrative money laundering business that my grandmother uses every now and then. I found out about Jaz once while I was in Texas on an errand I was given." Santana paused and said, "Wait, let me start at the beginning." She stood up and began pacing.

"My grandmother is Madame Marie Laveau D'Souza. That name does not mean much up here in Idaho, which is partly why I came here. In Southern Louisiana and all along the Gulf Coast, there are many who fear her name. She is into prostitution, drugs, blackmail, and several legitimate businesses that she has for various dark purposes."

"We all have some black sheep in our families."

"Ha! Yes, I am sure that is true. But like I said, I come from a long line of Vodun priestesses. It is black magic kind of stuff, and it is also truly demonic. You could say we are a special kind of Black."

Max thought it best to just let the story unfold.

"I was six when I remember witnessing my first Vodun ceremony. I watched as my grandmother called forth various spiritual beings, and then I saw my cousins becoming possessed by these same beings. I would watch as my grandmother struck deals and made arrangements with the dark side, then watched in fear as those arrangements were realized."

Max shuddered at the thought of a young girl exposed to such dark activities so early in life.

"I will spare you the parts of ritual sacrifices, initiation rites, and what all. The important part is that over a hundred twenty years ago there was a prophecy that the seventh time a seventh daughter was born of a seventh daughter, the Loas would endow her with very special and powerful gifts."

"What's a Loa?"

"The closest thing for you to think of would be a demon." Santana straightened up, placed her hands on her hips, took a deep breath, and blew it out slowly before continuing on.

"Are you saying you have seen real demon possession?"

Santana laughed. "Of course! Lots of times. Some of the times it was just funny, and we would all laugh. Other times it was embarrassing. You didn't have control when they would possess you, and you wouldn't remember anything that went on while they were using your body. But after a while I began to realize these Loa weren't just using us to communicate. They were using us to mock and humiliate us. They really hate humans. For some reason they especially hate females."

"The seed of the woman," Max whispered to herself.

"Well, Madame has made a small fortune from selling rituals for favors and making charms and amulets that grant spiritual favors and blessings. But she made a very large fortune selling her daughters and granddaughters for sex. Her prostitution ring is all across the Gulf Coast now, from Florida to Texas."

"Which is how she became familiar with Jasmine's grandmother?"

"Yes … likely. But to be honest, I really don't know how they met."

"You said she was into drugs as well?"

"Yep, mostly heroin, but also designer drugs."

"I'm not sure your grandmother and I would get along."

"If you just met her on the street, you probably would at first. She has a very winning way about her. But it wouldn't take long to realize she has been working some angle to get something from you. And if you weren't careful, you could be deep into something before you ever realized what had happened. In fact, if you crossed her, they would likely find your body naked in some hotel with a syringe and needle hanging from your arm."

"What about this seventh daughter thing?"

"Oh yeah!" Santana stopped pacing and breathed through her teeth again.

"Are you all right?" Max asked.

"Yes, but we are running out of time. My grandmother has been obsessed with this prophecy of the seventh daughter of the seventh daughter. The whole idea is like an urban legend. But she is obsessed with it and has convinced herself that it's true, and given what I know of my grandmother, it very likely has some validity to it." Santana fussed with the bedroom curtains to make sure they were drawn tight over the window, then moved toward the master bathroom. "Anyway, I am the seventh daughter of my mother, who is the seventh daughter of my grandmother and—" She took another deep breath and blew it out slowly. "Guess what is about to happen in your bathroom tonight."

"Whoa, wait! Are you in labor?"

"Yep."

"And that's why those guys are here?"

"You're catching on. And I can't let them have my baby, Max. There will be no end to the horrors she will know, and be taught to inflict, and that is not what life … How would your mentor put it? It's not what life *ought* to be about."

"I have to get you to the hospital. They can protect you both." Max was feeling a sense of urgency and had begun to panic.

"Not gonna happen, Max. They can't protect us."

"Sure they can. Those guys can't just come in and steal your baby."

"Maybe not. But think about it. How am I going to protect her once I leave? They will have found me. I have no family to turn to. They very easily could kill me and take the baby whenever I left. Unless you know a hospital I can move into for the next eighteen years or so."

"Surely your grandmother would never let them do that?"

"Ha! You really don't get it, do you, Max? Think of the most self-centered, narcissistic, male-bashing, hedonistic, money grubbing…" Santana, stood straight up, put her hands on her hips, and breathed through the labor pain again. "If you can conjure up that image, then you're getting close. Don't get me wrong, Madame cares deeply about me… right up until this baby is born, then my usefulness to her is over. She plans to pass everything to this baby, and none of it is good."

Max was still trying to sort out options when she realized Sandy, or Santana, had moved to the bathroom and was taking off her clothes and running a tub for a warm bath. "What are you doing?"

"We are going to deliver a baby. But like I said, I need your help."

"I've never delivered a baby before."

"That's not the help I need. Remember, this is my seventh." Max had followed her into the bathroom and closed the door before she turned on the light.

"Then what help do you need?"

"I need you to protect my baby. I need a safe place to deliver. Once my baby is here, I need you to protect her until we can find a safe place to hide her. I can't let them find me while I am laboring or recovering from the delivery. They will take the baby, and I will never see her again." At this point, Santana sat on the commode and held Max's hand. "More importantly, I can't let my daughter grow up in the way I did."

Tears were forming in her eyes. "Max, you of all people should understand. I have lived my whole life in a household built one yard from the gates of hell, and they will never let me have her, nurture her, teach her, mold her, or shape her. I will never be allowed to be the mother I long to be. The mother I never was to this one's siblings. She needs to be raised in a home built one yard away from the gates of heaven. We need to find a way to get her into an adoption agency without my family finding her. If Madame finds her before she is adopted, she will literally mobilize all the forces of hell to get her back. Once she is adopted, my daughter should be safe. Madame won't risk exposing herself to any scrutiny. Madame doesn't have the connections up here in the northwest to pull off any shenanigans to find her, or to whisk her away if she did. It would take a legal battle, and she can't risk it."

"What do you want me to do? I really think you've overestimated my abilities, Sandy, or Santana," Max said.

"I prefer Sandy. It reminds me of who I ought to have been, not the person I was." Sandy smiled. "First, you need to help me deliver this baby, then get her dried and keep her warm. I will clean up in here. Afterward, I need you to help me get back home. Over the next couple of days, we will see what happens. I'm sure they know where I live and are likely watching the place. Once they know I'm there, they will come in to check on the baby or take her if they find her. If for some reason they leave us alone, then I will come and get her from you, and I will put her up for adoption in Portland. But if they do show up, they will do everything in their power to find the baby. I know I won't give her or you up. And anyone who gets asked about possible friends or associates who might help me out—"

"That is why you put on the show last night. You just bumped me down the list of likely helpers?" Max interrupted.

"Yeah, something like that," Sandy confessed as she climbed into the tub of shallow warm water. "The English part wasn't directed at you; it was directed at the spiritual forces who have dominated my life. You have been nothing but the sister I always wanted but never had. You've been a mentor and friend, and I wish we had met under different circumstances." Sandy winced and doubled over. "Oops. I think my water just broke. It will happen fast."

"I thought labor took longer." Max was beginning to feel more uncomfortable.

"Maybe for some women. But remember, this is my seventh, and a few hours ago I took a special tea that induces labor. After I saw Henrí and François the other day, I knew I needed to execute plan B. Plan A went out the window."

"Plan B?" asked Max.

"Plan A was to deliver in a local hospital with my new sisters around me. But I knew I needed a plan B. I knew of Jasmine's fears, and knew I could use them to create a distraction."

"I bet offering to stay in her house wasn't an accident either," Max said.

"Nope, I knew they would likely be watching my place, and they likely had no idea who Jasmine really was, at least not yet. I figured it was the safest place to stay. Then I got up early yesterday and prepared for the fake Vodun ceremony and purchased the ingredients for the abortifacient herbs."

"I don't think I want to know how it is that you know about all these things."

Sandy smiled. "I don't think I want to tell you." She cupped warm water and poured it over her body. "Ooh, this feels good."

"What do I do?" Max was just beginning to realize her role, and though Sandy was over twenty-four hours into her plan, Max was just minutes into realizing she was part of it.

"There is a bag of stuff in the hallway just outside your door. Please turn off the light before you open the door." A few minutes later Max was back in the room with the bag, the door shut, and the light back on. She rifled through the bag and found towels, a change of clothes, a blanket, bottles of premixed baby formula, a little outfit for the baby to wear, as well as a large manila envelope and several black garbage bags. Max began unpacking and organizing the contents out onto the countertop while Sandy got busy doing her thing. The contractions were clearly coming quicker and quicker, and Sandy was breathing like a pro.

"Don't lose track of anything. You won't want anything incriminating left behind." Max looked at Sandy, who just shrugged. "Do you have a hard ball, like a softball or baseball?"

"What?" Max wasn't sure she heard correctly.

"Do you … have a … softball or something firm? I will need it to push on the uterus to stop the bleeding after I deliver."

"Are you sure that's a good idea?"

"No, I'm sure it's not. But it has worked before."

Max turned out the light and slipped out again only to return a few minutes later with a boxing glove. After she returned to the bathroom, closed the door, and turned on the light, she showed Sandy the glove and said, "Don't ask."

Over the course of the next twenty minutes, Sandy got to work, and with Max's helping hand she promptly delivered a beautiful baby girl. Sandy had packed the necessary equipment to clip and severe the umbilical cord, which she asked Max to do the honors with. Max took the newborn in her arms, then proceeded to clean the baby and swaddle it. Sandy got to work with the glove, pushing it into her uterus to help it contract. It also took Sandy a bit to get her strength together, and she opened the drain to the tub, pulled the shower curtain closed, and opened the valves to start a shower. The warm water felt soothing but also zapped her strength. It wasn't long before the two ladies had cleaned up the bathroom so that it was back in its previous state. Sandy had begun nursing her baby, and the bag was repacked.

"What now?"

"Now we see if Henrí and François are worth their salt. I want to get back to my place. I'll have you drive me to within a half mile or so, then I'll walk the rest of the way. You head home with the baby. If all goes well, then I will contact you tomorrow or the next day, and I will head to Portland to find an agency that can take my baby."

"I know someone who likely has connections in that area, and I can get in touch with her tomorrow and start looking into an agency. And I'm coming with you." Max was already getting her mind into gear when she stopped and asked, "What are you going to name her?"

"I was thinking Abomey. Family tradition says my ancestors came from Abomey, in West Africa, and I think it just fits. A name is all she will be able to take from me." She was getting teary-eyed again. "The rest is up to whomever raises her, and with that I need your help."

"What if Henry and Frank are there?"

"You just let me worry about that. They aren't getting my baby, and I will see to it. I will do whatever it takes to ensure her safety. If they are there, your job will be to get her to the people who have the home one yard from the gates of heaven. I will be busy making sure I cover both of your escapes."

"I don't like the sound of this, Sandy."

"Listen, imagine hearing on TV someday about a young prostitute found dead in an old hotel somewhere from a drug overdose, and it happened to be someone you had known in high school. Some lonely girl, bullied by everyone else, someone who just needed a friend, someone you could have helped avoid that life. What would you do if you had a chance to spare her of that fate?"

Max was silent. She believed Sandy was only telling her the PG-13 parts of her family life, and Max knew Sandy was right. She would never be the same if she didn't act now. Besides, if Sandy was lying or exaggerating, then in a couple of days, in the light of day, Max knew who she could trust to sort this all out.

"Okay, I'll do it."

"Thank you. Thank you so much," said Sandy as she began to redress.

"How in the world did you hide this pregnancy from all of us?"

"It's not that hard when you wear big, baggy, ill-fitting clothes and hang out with a girl who is pregnant and not trying to hide it. You tend to fade into the background, and people see what they want to see," Sandy explained with a shrug and a smile.

The ride to Caldwell was one of mixed emotions. Max drove while

Sandy had a moment with her daughter. She spoke to her sleeping baby in Creole, and every now and again tears would form in the young mother's eyes. Max couldn't help but wonder how young Sandy must have been when she delivered her first baby. It was the age-old question: What is the world coming to when babies are having babies? She wondered what a mother says to her newborn when she isn't sure if it might be her last words to share. How do you boil life down into a couple of sentences and bestow them on one who is sleeping? It seems that sometimes the fact that something needs to be said is more important than the fact that it is heard.

"Sandy, I really feel the need to pray for you right now."

"Pray for *us*," directed Sandy.

"Dear God in heaven, I can't help but think that I am meeting some new people for the first time. I have never known of the pain and the injury that has been inflicted on my friend. It makes me wonder who else in my life I really don't know. But none of this is new to You. You have known my friend Sandy and have had longings for her that You have had since before she was born, before the foundation of the world. I know that You have a plan for her and her baby. Please, Lord, let her know how much I love them both, and help me to do what You would have me to do for them, amen."

"Amen," said Sandy. Then in a whisper while brushing away some tears, she added, "See, Abomey? There are people in the world who love us."

It was sometime between 3:30 and 4:00 in the morning when Max pulled into the side streets of Caldwell where Sandy had a house that she was renting. Sandy kept having her change directions, and it was confusing Max.

"Sandy, what are we doing?"

"Limited traffic cams. It will be hard to associate the Jeep with getting me home. Turn here, please," said Sandy. "You can pull in just up there and turn out the lights."

"Are you sure about this, Sandy? Why can't we just call the cops and get them locked up?"

"They haven't done anything illegal that can be proved. Then they will be on my tail, and I'll never shake them. At least now I have the upper hand, and with your help I can put Abomey beyond their reach forever. Please, Max. Trust me. If I'm wrong, and they don't come after me, then I will call you in a couple of days and we can do it your way. But for now, believe me when I say you can't trust these guys."

Max had always thought Sandy was bright and perceptive, and maybe these guys were as bad as she said. If they were, then what would be the harm of giving it a couple of days? "Okay, but call me," Max relented.

"I will. I will. But I will also do whatever it takes to keep my baby safe. I wasn't able to before. I've lost six to that witch, and I won't let her have this one. Not now. Not when I know there is something different. Abomey needs what she ought to have, and this is the only way I can ensure she gets it."

Sandy handed her sleeping baby to Max. "When I'm gone, put her in the seat, and then drive home. I will hide in the shadows for several minutes, then make my way back to my house." Sandy pointed to a car seat already strapped into place in the rear seat of the Jeep. Sandy had thought of everything. She reached up and flipped the switch off the dome light, reducing the risk of drawing attention. Then she opened the door and, before she climbed out, opened the duffle bag one last time and took out a large water bottle, guzzling it down. "Got to stay hydrated, you know?" She smiled, then placed the bottle in one of the black bags. "Now if anything goes wrong, pack up all your stuff and leave for the summer as if you were too upset with the events of last night. There is an envelope in the bag that I want to go with Abomey. But dump everything else except the car seat and the envelope in some rancid dumpster behind an old apartment building, like in Emmett or Payette. If you double-check the bathroom and throw everything away in these bags, then there won't be anything left to connect me to either you or her." And with those last words of instructions, she leaned across the Jeep, kissed her baby, hugged her friend, and was gone.

A few minutes later Abomey was tucked safely into her car seat, and Max slipped the Jeep into gear and pointed it back toward Nampa while saying a silent prayer in hopes that this was all just a bad nightmare. That mom and baby would be safely reunited in just a couple of days.

Once the Jeep took off, Sandy waited in the shadows for another ten minutes before she stepped out and walked to the end of the block and started the half-mile walk to her house. As she got close, she took the alleyway at the back of the property that served as a service road, giving access to the garages situated at the rear of all the properties.

She stayed pretty much in the shadows, moving from one garage to the next, stopping with each couple of steps and listening for any noise that could help her know where her pursuers were at. She also knew that one of the neighbors had a dog, and if she wasn't careful, it could easily give her position away. As she moved from the shadow cast by a neighbor's garage two houses down from her own, she accidentally kicked a small copper pipe, about four inches long, in the dirt. She quickly bent down, picked it up, and placed it in her pocket. After she stood back up, she felt something warm running down her leg, and she figured she had better hurry.

It was another twenty minutes before she made it to the back of her own property, then went to the back of the house where she found the electrical panel. She turned off the power to the house as quietly as she could before she silently let herself in.

She could sense that they had at least been in her house, or perhaps still were. Things just didn't seem to be how she'd left them. Letters that had been carefully scattered were now stacked neatly, and she was sure they had been read and everything photographed as well. She walked through the rest of the house and found every room was too tidy. She had intentionally left certain drawers partially open that now were not as they had been.

Sandy had learned early in life that the best way to know if your things had been searched was to neither leave them too straight nor too ruffled. Those conditions could easily be approximated. It was easy to completely close or completely open a drawer after it had been rifled through, but no one would keep track of a drawer being left two finger beadths open. They could approximate it, but with her two fingers she could easily tell if it was in the position was where she left it or not, and these drawers were not in the same position. She returned to the kitchen, pulled out a chair, and sat down to wait.

It wasn't long before she could hear the faint creak of wood buckling under the weight of something heavy on the stairs leading up from the basement into the kitchen, then the slow release of the latch of the door, and finally the sliding of the hinges of the door as it was eased open. Within moments the door was wide open, and the large silhouette of a man could faintly be distinguished against the far wall of the kitchen.

"*Bonjou*, Henrí. Is that François on the stairs behind you?"

The silhouette froze. "*Wi, madmwazèl. Tout bagay anfòm?*"

"*Wi*, Henrí. All is good, for now."

"Let me turn on some lights so I can get a good look at you," offered Henrí. He reached for the light switch near the stairs, but the flip did not illuminate the stairwell as he had hoped.

"I don't think so. Let's keep things the way they are for now, shall we?" She shifted slightly in her chair. "Just so you know, Henrí, I have a 9mm, and I am not afraid to use it."

"*O, mwen renmen anpil.* Would you really shoot your old friend?"

"No, Henrí. I could easily put a bullet through François's head for the things he has done to me and my sisters. But you have always been good to me." She shifted again. "But this morning it isn't at either of you that I am pointing the gun. Would you believe that I am pointing it at my pregnant belly?"

One could sense the tension tighten in the frame of the giant man. "*Mon pitit mwen.* Don't joke with your old friend. Why you want to hurt yourself like that?"

"Oh, let's not play games, Henrí. We all three know why you are here, and I am not going back to *Manman*, and I am not letting you have my baby. Not this one. This one is mine, and when she is born, I shall care for her. My grandmother will not have the satisfaction of ever seeing her. And if I can't raise her, then no one will."

"Let's talk 'bout this, *mon pitit mwe*. You know your grandmother—"

"No, no, no, Henrí. You know my grandmother," Sandy interrupted.

"You know the plans she has for my baby, and I will not let her have this one and raise it for her purposes. It shall be mine and no one else's."

There was a creak on the stairs as François shifted his weight.

"Now, now, François. Don't move. You're tempting me to kill you."

There was just enough light for the men to see the reflection of the barrel of a gun in her raised hand. François gave a slight whimper and didn't move again.

"Santana, you know how important you and the baby are to Madame."

"Henrí, you know how unimportant the two of you are to me and the baby. And I am not at all interested in seeing my baby live out her life in the ways my grandmother feels are important. We do not see eye to eye on what is important for the baby." Sandy was starting to slur her words ever so slightly and again she shifted her weight.

Henrí began to sense something wasn't right. The end of the game didn't make sense. "What shall we do, *cheri*? Do yon want us to stand here until morning? Or perhaps you plan to make us stand here all day long?"

"I haven't decided yet. I haven't calculated how long it will take the police to show up when I pull the trigger. They might save me, but I'm sure the baby will be dead. Either way, once the neighbors hear the bang, I'm sure it won't be easy for you to escape without being seen. And do you realize one … one of the reasons I came to Idaho is that … is that there, uh … there just aren't that many Black people here. You won't be hard … hard to find."

Something was going terribly wrong. Henrí knew it but just couldn't put his finger on what it was, or why. François was growing restless, and if something didn't change, they could have a bloodbath on their hands. Wait, bloodbath? Henrí inhaled deeply through his nose. That's it! He smelled blood, and just then there was a crash at the table and the clanking of a hollow pipe.

Henrí sprang toward the table and slipped on something wet on the floor. "*Jwenn limyè yo!*"

François slipped twice as he went for the light switch by the back door. But after flipping it up and down, nothing happened.

"Outside, outside! The box!" screeched Henrí, trying not to yell.

Seconds later there was a *thunk* and the back porch light came on, as did the one in the stairwell. François came back into the house, and in what little light there was, he saw Henrí sitting next to Santana in a large pool of dark-red blood that wasn't coagulating like it should.

"No! No! No!" moaned Henrí. He felt Santana's limp belly. "She has already delivered. Search the house again!" François searched the other rooms to see if she had deposited the baby in one of the rooms after arriving. Henrí pulled off a glove and felt for a carotid pulse. It was fast but very thready.

There was a faint smile on the young woman's face. "Where is she, Santana? Where is your baby? I can protect her. I can shield her. Please, *mwen renmen anpil,* where is your baby?"

"She is truly safe. Safe in a place you will never find her." And the bluish-gray eyes of the young mother went lifeless.

François burst back into the kitchen. "Nothing. No baby." He looked around him. "What a mess. Do we clean it up?"

"No. There's no time. The baby must be with someone she trusts." Henrí gently laid Santana's head on the floor. "We must find that baby. We can't waste any time. Once the girl is found missing, things will get heated, and we can't waste the time cleaning up. She will still be missing. Let's get out of here."

They exited the house by the front door, and with a quick trot they headed up the road to their parked black Mercedes sedan with tinted windows. In the car, Henrí promptly called Madame and explained the situation to her. She was not pleased.

"Bug the house and stay put! Watch who comes in the morning. Whoever has the baby may return later this morning. Whoever does come may lead you to my baby." There was obvious tension in her voice, and she was fighting to control her anger. "Bring me back my baby!"

"What about Santana?" asked Henrí.

"Who?" replied the Mambo, and the connection went dead with a beep.

François checked the windows and could see the street was clear, so he climbed out as Henrí popped the trunk and rolled down his window. François pulled out a duffle bag, removed a receiver, handed it to Henrí through the driver-side window, and headed back toward the house with the bag as Henrí switched on the receiver and watched the neighborhood. After about three minutes there was a squeal and a test phrase from François. Moments later François was back in the car, and Henrí was pulling out of the neighborhood for a quiet, secluded parking lot about half a mile away where they sat back and slouched in their seats.

A little over an hour later, just as dawn was breaking but before the sun was up, there was a knock at the door, which caused both Henrí and François to sit bolt upright in their seats. Henrí punched François in the arm. He, in turn, grabbed a notebook and pen.

There was another knock on the door, and then the door could be heard opening.

"Sandy, are you home?"

"Go on in, Jaz. What's that smell?" There were footsteps on the wooden floors.

"Whoa! Erica, in here!" There were footsteps racing across the floor. "I'm gonna be sick." A horrible retching sound followed.

"Oh no! No!" Another set of footsteps sounded across the floor. The door slammed shut. About three minutes later sirens could be heard entering the neighborhood: first came a set of police cars, next was a fire engine, and finally an ambulance arrived.

A few moments after the police car past there was a loud banging on the door. "Open up, Caldwell Police! Show yourself!" The door opened. "Dispatch, this is Unit 37. I'm entering the residence."

"Copy Unit 37, 0644."

"Is anyone in here? If you are hiding, you must show yourself right now!" There was a shuffling of feet as someone searched the house.

"Dispatch, Unit 37, I have a body, main floor. Please notify the lieutenant and the medical examiner."

"Copy Unit 37, 0648." There was a distant creak of a door, and the sound of boots descending the stairs into the basement, and moments later they could be heard coming back up again.

"Dispatch, Unit 37. The residence is clear of any other persons."

"Copy Unit 37, 0652." Boots could be heard again marching across the floor, and the front door opened and closed again.

The bug went silent for the next several minutes, and the two men sat in their rented vehicle, watching as two police cars went zipping past them with lights on but sirens off. Some time later, the bug went live again as the first policeman on scene reentered the house with his superior, and they discussed what they knew at this point.

"Apparently, the deceased is a female in her early to mid-twenties who has been a student at the college here in town. Her friends report that everything seemed normal until Sunday, when she and a group of friends went shopping in Meridian. While there, the deceased noticed two Black men looking at her friend suspiciously. One of the gals in the group is from South Texas and felt she recognized them as being strong arms for family she was trying to avoid. The gal's name is Jasmine D'Silva, and she is one of the girls outside. The presence of these guys pretty much freaked the girls out and changed the tone of their outing. Neither of the girls outside—Jasmine D'Silva and Erica Uberis—think the deceased knew either of the guys. Jasmine lives by herself, off campus, two blocks from here, and Erica lives on campus. I have the names of the other girls in the group, which include some from PNCU in Nampa. They say they are all part of a Bible study small group that meets weekly through the school year. They had their last meeting yesterday evening at a Margaret Smithson's house in Nampa. Apparently, the group of girls were having a grand old Bible studying time when they noticed the deceased performing some satanic ritual outside in the backyard. Complete with voodoo curses, dead cats, and dancing round a pole in some grass skirt or something. Anyway, that's what I've got so far."

"All right, give me the list of names and addresses, and let's get some help getting interviews. We will start with these in Caldwell and then work our way to Nampa later today. Then let's get the forensics team in here and process the scene." The lieutenant looked around the kitchen. "I mean, just what are we dealing with here? Was this a suicide or some whack job? Was it a ritual killing?" He shook his head. "What happened?"

"Dunno. But seems really sad. Such a waste of a young life."

"Yep, indeed. A beautiful, young co-ed."

"Okay, LT. I'll stay here and cover the scene. Let me give you the names and addresses."

"Yeah, shoot." And with that the officer notified his superior and two unsuspected listeners of the names and addresses of the group.

The men in the car half a mile away quickly drove to the address where Jasmine lived and bugged her home while she and Erica remained stuck at Sandy's house.

CHAPTER 9

UNWAVERING DEVOTION

Weiser, Idaho
later that evening

I don't know, Dad. I'm not really sure what to think. But I believe her. It is actually the only thing that makes sense of it all."

Max had wasted no time cleaning the bathroom and loading up the Jeep. She had decided on the ride back to her place, after dropping off Sandy, that if Sandy, or Santana, or whatever her real name was, was telling the truth, then she would likely need to stay one step ahead of the guys after her. Besides, if Sandy was only being hypervigilant, then she would be calling by cell phone, and Max could be anywhere, not just sitting at the next place people were going to come looking. Max had laundered the towels and confirmed there was no blood in the bathroom. She gave it all a good cleaning just like she would have when she left for the summer.

The towels were dumped in Middleton, and the boxing gloves were thrown in a dumpster behind an apartment complex in Emmett, and everything else of Sandy's, except the car seat and the envelope, were thrown in a dumpster in New Plymouth. The beauty of going through Middleton, up to Emmet, over to New Plymouth, then back down into Payette on highway 52 was the limited traffic cams. Max arrived in her hometown of Weiser late afternoon and was safe, feeding the baby and watching local programing when her father came home that night from work.

Alex Smithson was a sheriff's deputy for Washington County. He had raised Max in Weiser ever since her mother died in a traffic accident when Max was just a toddler. She had really never known her mother. But the people of Weiser were warm and gracious and, most had looked after the tomboy as their own. Alex quickly decided he wouldn't be able to raise his daughter anywhere else because of the faithful friends and neighbors, teachers, coaches, and everyone else who knew him and Max.

"I don't like holding secrets." Max was back to lamenting her situation.

"I understand, honey. But as of yet, there hasn't been a crime committed. Neither you nor Sandy have done anything criminal, and you can't prove those two guys have done anything illegal either. And it is hard to hold a person with Sandy's background to an expectation we would hold ourselves to."

"Is there any way to check her story? I mean ... What if I never hear from Sandy again? What if her grandmother really is a foul person, and these guys really are hoodlums up to no good. Do I follow through with her wishes?"

"Well, I can do some sniffing around and see what I can learn. If the grandmother is as bad as reported, it won't be hard to find out. Then ... " He bent down and brushed Abomey's cheek. "Keeping this young lady away from her great-grandmother will likely be the best thing for her, though I don't think the courts will see it that way."

"Do you think Sandy is right? If Abomey makes it into adoptive care, do you think the great-grandmother will give up pursuing her?"

"Very likely, because the scrutiny that she would be under in that situation is different than the scrutiny she would be under when the girl is a ward of the state. And the state is looking for family to give the child to. And that's assuming she is able to find her at all."

"Maybe."

"So the plan all depends on what happens with the mother, right?

If all goes well, and Sandy calls in the next day or two, then she gets her baby back. If things go sideways, then you get the baby to an orphanage in Portland and hope the great-grandmother doesn't go looking for her."

"That is the plan."

"Perhaps you should run it past The Locksmith?"

"Yeah, that's what I was thinking. In fact, I tried calling her earlier and had to leave a message."

"Maybe she's in prison." Her father just raised his left eyebrow and shrugged his shoulders.

"That is funny, Dad. Real funny." Max shook her head.

Miss Anna Belle Nelson was a retired school teacher from the Weiser School District. She had never married, yet had a maternal way of treating each of her students as her own child. She was kindly known as The Locksmith.

When Max was in fifth grade, she and her best friend, John Quinton Riley O'Malley, had been students of Miss Nelson. When Jaker, the name John Quinton Riley went by, moved to town, his family moved in next door to Miss Nelson. He had moved in the summer, and he hadn't known who their neighbors were. One night after the moving van was gone, but the unpacking remained, John Quinton Riley was out playing by himself quietly in his backyard. His parents spent the day working at the clinic where his father was a physician, and his mother was a nurse. But they spent their evenings unpacking and putting their contents away. Jaker found it best to stay out of their way.

Jaker was rather pensive and insightful for his age and often spent his alone time lost in his own thoughts. But as the night had grown late and a full moon was out, Jaker quickly became distracted by his new neighbor who was at work in her backyard. He walked over to the fence and through the lattice saw an elderly lady, looking at the moon through a telescope, then making sketches. Every now and again she would quietly hum and sway. He stood there quietly, wondering what it must be like to see the moon through a real telescope.

"Want to look, young man?" asked the woman, who hadn't even looked up or acknowledged his presence.

"Yes, ma'am."

He came through the gate, and she showed him the moon, teaching him about the phases and the interesting things she thought about while she watched the moon. She liked the fact that there were two sources of light in the sky. One that shown bright and gave all the good things to the Earth: warmth, the ability to see such beauty and color. While the other was the source of light in the darkness. She was always intrigued by how the moon provided light in the darkness not by making the light, but by reflecting it. Because of these musings, she felt she had learned something about her relationship with the creator of heaven and earth and herself.

She spoke of a friend who had experienced multiple traumas in her life as a young girl. The woman told him that she had shared her musings with the girl, and it wasn't long before the girl was being awakened early every morning by the Lord to come to the moonlight. As she did, she began to sing and dance through the pain of her life as she, too, began to think about her relationship with the Lord. The darkness was her pain. The amount of light in the darkness was the result of how much of her face she presented to God and allowed Him to be reflected through her. She began to realize there were days, and seasons, in her life when the light was getting brighter, and there were seasons in her life when the light was fading. She began to learn when each was happening and how to live her life like the moon, becoming full and bright in a dark place.

Through the experience, the young girl found a language of hope that led to healing and purpose in a life that had once been filled with great sadness and pain.

The elderly woman was picking a lock in the young man's life, and he never even knew it. He asked a lot of questions, for which she had a lot of interesting answers. When he asked what she did, she said, "I'm a locksmith. I help people unlock chains, doors, safes, and many other things that bind. I help people pick the locks to some of their greatest treasure chests for which they have no key." He thought that sounded cool, until a few months later when he went to school and found out she was his teacher. Through the years that followed, he found out what others already knew. She had a way about her that was very much like a locksmith, and everyone in Weiser, and a great many places farther away, knew it too.

That was the year Max met and got to know Jaker, and they both, in turn, got to know Miss Anna Belle Nelson: The Locksmith. From that year on, whenever there was a question or mystery they were struggling with, she would help them unravel it to a very satisfying solution. So it was only natural for Max to seek her out when she got home.

Just then, Max's cell phone buzzed.

"Locksmith or Voodoo Queen?"

Max looked at the number. "Locksmith," she replied. She poked the green button on her screen. "Hello, Miss Nelson." She paused as the person on the other end of the connection finished her greeting. "Yes, ma'am. Thank you, ma'am." She paused again, then continued, "Let me get right to it. I have a small dilemma involving a newborn and a mother who was raised in the occult…" She paused. "The mother is from Louisiana, a student at Ribley's College and a good friend of mine. Her family is into voodoo and criminal activities along the Gulf Coast. She has asked that if certain situations develop, then I should take the child to Portland to be adopted so her family won't raise the child in the occult." Max paused, and an incomprehensible voice could be made out on the other side. "Yes, ma'am, that is about it. Would you have time tomorrow morning to chat a bit?" Another pause. "Yes, I can make that work. You have to leave by when?" Again, the incomprehensible voice sounded. "Okay, ma'am, I will see you then."

Alex had moved closer to the TV. "Max, you'd better come here."

Max set her phone aside and walked over to the TV as her dad turned up the volume. The local news programming was on, and a banner came up across the bottom of the screen that read, "Ribley's College Co-Ed Found Dead."

"Oh, no," moaned Max.

The woman at the anchor desk began reporting. "Tonight, Caldwell authorities are investigating the death of a young college student from

Louisiana, found dead in her off-campus home. The cause of death has yet to be determined, though authorities say there is some evidence of foul play. Friends and classmates are being questioned, and authorities are looking for two African American males whom they believe may be able to help shed some light on the activities leading up to her death. Everyone with information about the incident are being asked to contact Caldwell Police Department. In other news tonight—" Alex pressed the power button on the remote, and the screen went black.

"Perhaps we should visit The Locksmith tonight?" suggested Max.

"Yep." Alex took in a deep breath. "There went all hopes for a clean plan B, and it does sound like a suspicious death." He paused and scrunched up his face. "I'm headed over to the sheriff's department, and I'll see if I can dig up anything on this grandmother … D'Souza, you said, right?"

"Yes. Madame Marie Laveau D'Souza."

"Why don't you feed the baby, and I will be right back." And with that, Deputy Smithson grabbed his keys and headed out the door, climbing into his late-model Buick sedan.

An hour later Abomey had finished her bottle, endured an awkward burping session, and was just getting the finishing touches on a diaper change when Alex returned with enough information to make them want to hurry. "It's not a good idea to be seen with the baby out in public. It is likely to cause too many people to want to ask difficult questions."

"When I got here, I pulled the Jeep into the garage and closed the door before I got Abomey out."

"It is probably best if you stay here and I go see Miss Nelson. You are not going to want to know what I found out yet."

Max became extremely uneasy. "What did you find out?"

"Let me talk to Miss Nelson first. I'll be right back." The deputy flipped his keyring around his finger and opened the door but was unable to exit the house. "Oops! Well, never mind, Max. Guess who is here?" Alex stepped aside and in walked a pudgy, five-foot three-inch, bluish-gray-haired woman. She wore horn-rimmed glasses and a lace shawl for a collar over a pale floral-print dress, with a white handbag dangling from her left wrist.

"I just haven't been able to rest easy this evening, and I couldn't help but think it might be related to your call, Margaret." Miss Nelson had never used a nickname, or abbreviated form of a name, at least not that Max could ever remember. She rarely used terms of affection or endearment. She was always so prim and proper. "I have an unsettled feeling in my spirit about this." It was uncanny at times how perceptive Miss Nelson could be. She seemed just as upset as they were. Their uneasiness came from the television. Her unsettledness came from her sensitivity to the Holy Spirit which was also likely due to the reason she didn't own a television. In the past Miss Nelson had said that if she wanted honest information, the media was the last place she would look for it.

"Come on in, ma'am. I was about to head over and tell you a bit more that I have found out this evening. But you beat me to it."

Miss Nelson was in her early eighties, but she had a sharp mind and kept physically active to the point that people felt time had begun to slow down around her. She came in and headed for the kitchen.

"How about a fresh pot of tea, ma'am?" Max seemed to be anticipating the next move.

"I think you read my mind, Margaret. I think best with a fresh pot of tea."

"Yes, ma'am. I will get right on it." Max busied herself about the kitchen.

"Why don't you start filling in the details for us tonight instead of tomorrow morning, Margaret. I have a feeling we are about to run out of time."

Max returned from the kitchen and over the next couple of minutes she retold the tale of how the two girls met, her initial impressions of Sandy, what name she had first known her by, and her given name. She spoke of how easily the girl could stand in the background, emitting the impression of timidity and caution as well as a hint of insecurity. Now that Max thought about it, her feigned demeanor was a very effective and powerful ruse. She now felt Sandy was anything but timid or insecure, and even though exercising caution still made sense, it was for a different reason now. Shortly after introducing the main character of her story the teapot began to whistle, and Max began steeping the tea and preparing the cups for all three of them. For the next twenty-five minutes to a half-an-hour, she related the details of her story.

She reviewed the Bible study group topics and dynamics, but the majority of her recitation focused on this week's events from their outing at The Oasis; the dramatics of the two men following Sandy; the apparent engineering of the role of Jasmine by Sandy, and how it appeared to have served as a distraction; and finally, the faux voodoo ceremony. Then she told of Sandy's nocturnal visit, the birth of her baby in the bathtub, the instructions Sandy gave her for the child, and Sandy's request to be dropped back at her home alone— as well as the two contingency plans. Max finished with the tale of the dumpster dump-offs and everything that had happened since her arrival at home including what they just learned from the nightly news. Miss Nelson only interrupted occasionally so she could keep the facts straight, and for clarification purposes.

"Deputy Smithson, I expect you have more to add," stated the older woman in a curious way.

Max's dad had been sitting quietly taking everything in up to this point. "Yes, ma'am. I was able to take the name Margaret gave me and then use connections I have in law enforcement. Madame Marie Laveau D'Souza is considered the Voodoo Queen of the South and is based on a plantation outside of New Orleans. Sources say that her voodoo activities are greatly respected, if not feared, and is not perceived as a charlatan. She has branded her skills and branched out into organized crime through prostitution, drug trafficking, extortion, and murder. Her organization is familial, which she runs through a strong matriarchal system rooted in her voodoo religion called Vodun. Local law enforcement is rather scared of her."

"Why?"

"Many of them claim to have had extensive voodoo experiences, but the federal department believe she has information to blackmail them."

"What else do the federal agents say?"

"They consider the local assets tainted and have struggled to infiltrate her organization. They consider her extremely dangerous and difficult to predict."

"And what is your feeling? Are they just covering for a lazy work ethic, or is Madame D'Souza a legitimate threat to this baby's life? That is what this boils down to, correct?"

Both father and daughter nodded their agreement, and the deputy said, "I am afraid it is the latter."

"Margaret, it doesn't sound like you think Santana was a disgruntled adolescent who was begrudging her loving grandmother. And Deputy, your sources are painting a picture that corroborates Santana's. If we surrender this baby, the courts will have to give her to the great-grandmother. They won't be persuaded by hearsay. They will attempt to be legally impartial to her voodoo religion. You know that the mother trusted you with the life and safety of her daughter. You know it was her expressed wish to have the baby adopted into a family that would raise her in a different environment far from the influence of her great-grandmother. Agreed?"

Again, father and daughter nodded their agreement.

"Well, then there are a few things I want to check, and I will be right back." The older woman stood up and stepped away from the table.

Miss Nelson was not only intelligent and wise, she had an extensive network of contacts. They were contacts that most people would never dream of. Contacts that once you heard of them, you wondered how any one person could develop such a wide network in one lifetime, let alone while simply being a teacher in a town of five thousand people for several decades. But connected she was, and this network allowed her to pick some of the most difficult locks.

Alex pulled some little cookies from the pantry and set them out. "Where's Jaker? Why isn't he here? You guys usually commit your crimes as a duo."

"Yeah, I called his mother this morning."

"What did Cokie say?" her dad asked.

"Jaker has been on an errand and isn't expected back until late tomorrow. I figured it was too much to try and unpack over the phone."

"What errand is he on?"

"You'll have to ask The Locksmith. Since his graduation, he's usually on one of her assignments."

"Do you know where he went?"

"Back east somewhere. The Beltway maybe."

"That wouldn't surprise me one bit."

"His mom said she thought he was under the impression that he would be arriving and then heading right back out again. This time to Africa."

"Africa?"

"Yep. So if I can wait to head to Portland for a few days, we may get a chance to catch up. If not, then I may end up missing him altogether."

"Have you thought more through this Portland gig?"

"No. I'm a little concerned too. I really don't want to get into a situation where I have to try and explain all this to people who likely aren't going to care even the slightest of bits."

"No, Margaret. I agree that wouldn't be a good idea now, would it?" Miss Nelson had just walked back into the room. "I think it best we start thinking this through. I just called a pastor friend in the New Orleans area and asked him about what he knew of our infamous grandmother. He confirms our fears and paints with an even darker shade of black. He said she cannot be trusted and is deep into the occult, conducting rituals on her plantation that she uses to market... What did you call it, Deputy?"

"Her brand."

"Yes. Her brand. I think we should seek the wisdom of the Lord here to confirm what our prudence is telling us."

"Good idea," said Max.

The three of them sat at the table and held hands as The Locksmith consulted the Lord.

"Oh, Great God in heaven. We recognize Your Majesty and Your Holiness, and we lift up Your name as sovereign of the universe. We ask this night, Almighty God, that as we lift Your name, You will sanctify it in our midst. We beseech Your wisdom tonight in a matter that is too difficult for us. We have grappled with its implications and feel we are aware of the facts. We believe that our spirits are being pulled in a direction that normally we would not want to go, but we believe that if we pursue the course our courts would have us pursue, we will be allowing a great injustice to be perpetrated. We need to know Your mind tonight, oh Lord—Your thoughts, Your wisdom. We are aware of the desires of a young mother who has lost her life in an attempt to separate her newborn child from the kingdom of darkness. We are aware that the kingdom of darkness has desires for her to become someone we think it neither prudent nor wise for her to become. Nor do we feel she should be exposed to this evil environment. We ask that You intervene with Your guidance and Your wisdom. We believe it is Your will to intercede for her. However, even though it be prudent for us to intervene, we do not know if it be wise. Lord, we do not expect that You will invite us into Your council chambers, or seek our considerations, or enter into deliberations with us; therefore we recognize that You may have plans we are unaware of. We do not want to presume to work on Your behalf when we are only trampling Your wisdom with our pride. So, we humbly ask, Lord, what would You have us do? We pray for guidance in the name of Your Son Jesus Christ, who shed His precious blood for our redemption and for the life of this little one. Are we agreed?"

"Amen," said the other two.

"I believe I will have some tea, if that is all right with you two." The elderly woman lifted the tea pot, filled her cup, and picked out a cookie.

The deputy wasn't sure what to do at this point. The deepest part of him wanted to pick up where they left off with discussing and evaluating, and perhaps come to some conclusions as to what to do. Maybe make some solid plans. He decided to hold his peace and take his lead from the two ladies in the room, who appeared to be comfortable just sitting there. He knew Max had a close relationship with Miss Nelson, and he figured this wasn't their first prayer meeting, so letting them set the course and pace seemed prudent. Several minutes later he began to fidget.

"You know, Alex, most of the world perceives wisdom and prudence to be the same thing," The Locksmith said.

"Oh?" replied the deputy.

"Yes, but I remember a verse I came across when I was a much younger woman that set my spiritual life on a new course—into uncharted waters, you might say."

"What verse was that?"

"Proverbs eight, twelve. 'I wisdom dwell with prudence, and find out knowledge of witty inventions.'"

"Hmm." It came out like a grunt, but it was unintentional.

"I was drawn to the first phrase, 'I wisdom dwell with prudence.' It sounds like close proximity, but it represents being separate and distinguishable—similar yet distinctive."

Alex knew there had to be more, so he waited.

"Do you know there are stars in the heavens that are so close to one another that with the naked eye, it is impossible to distinguish one from the other. It takes a telescope of sufficient resolving power to allow a person to see that, in fact, what appears to be one is actually two. What we perceive as the same is actually different and unique."

"As in the case of wisdom and prudence."

"Case in point," said the woman with a single nod and a raised eyebrow. "Is wisdom the same thing as prudence?"

Alex sat and pondered, somewhat unfamiliar with the leadings of The Locksmith. "I would say that to many people they are considered very similar, if not the same."

"Agreed. To the world prudence and wisdom are essentially the same thing. But I would maintain that through the lens of Scripture, they are very different."

"Okay, help me to see it," the man requested

"Margaret?" asked the elderly woman with a face that implied, *Would you like to answer?*

"Dad, in the light of Scripture, *wisdom* is a figure of speech for Christ, or the guidance of the Holy Spirit. When you come across the concept of wisdom, you can easily put in Christ or the Holy Spirit, and it makes sense. In this verse, God is making a distinction between the power of reason and intellect, the power of the rational, and contrasting it with truth that transcends the rational. For example, is it rational to pick up a snake by the tail, or strike a rock and expect water to gush forth? Or how about trimming a force of thirty-some-thousand fighting men down to three hundred, then making your selection based on how they lap up water. There are miracles after miracles in the Bible where what God asks someone to do doesn't make sense. Therefore, is it wise to do what God asks? Yes, obviously it is. It is as if the very point He is making is that you can't trust prudence to make the right decision. So do we throw out prudence? Of course not. That is likely the point of the verse we were just talking about. But Miss Nelson has taught me that wisdom comes from the heart and mind of God; whereas prudence is something that He embedded into the fabric of creation itself."

"So basically you're saying that for now we wait?" asked Alex.

"In essence? Yes. But what we are really doing is setting aside prudence and allowing time for the Almighty to insert His wisdom. It isn't easy at first. But it gets easier with time. You will find it is a conscious effort at first. People often start by repeatedly setting aside their attempts at prudence. They find themselves trying to stop an activity over and over again, and the vigilance becomes wearisome. What makes it easier is to fill our mind with something else. Occupy our mind with an activity that keeps it from its thought-monitoring activities."

"Occupy it how?"

"Praise," the two women said in unison.

"Thanksgiving works in a pinch just as well," informed the older one. "Focusing your mind on an attitude of praise and thanksgiving makes it really hard to ponder prudence."

"For how long?" he asked.

"It isn't a length of time. It is the onset of a realization, almost like an epiphany. There comes a moment when you get the feeling this is all a bad idea. Or maybe you get the feeling all is well, and you get the inner green light that it's time to move forward. It is something you feel in your spirit."

"What does that mean. 'Something you feel in your spirit'?"

"For me, whichever indication I get is followed by a sense of calming reassurance that all is well, regardless of the outcome. That calmness is very soothing, very satisfying, very reassuring. Whatever direction the Spirit is leading at the time of that reassurance is the direction of leading," explained the older woman.

"Like now?" asked Max.

"Like now," answered The Locksmith.

"Well, I think I missed it," conceded the deputy.

The two women laughed. "Shall we see?" asked Max.

"Sure," was the reply.

Max went to a nearby drawer and pulled out two three-by-five cards and handed one to Miss Nelson along with a pencil. "Louisiana or Portland?"

"Okay." They both began writing as each playfully hid their cards.

"We are about to see if there is unity in the Spirit, or confusion. Is that correct?" asked Alex.

"Exactly," said Max.

"So what is it to be? Your answers, please."

Max flipped her card. "Portland!"

The Locksmith flipped hers.

"What?" stated father and daughter, shocked.

"Yes!" replied the woman.

"Is that wisdom talking?" asked Alex.

"No. Wisdom said no to Louisiana. Prudence said no to Portland. Remember now, 'I wisdom dwell with prudence.'"

"Okay, please explain." Alex's curiosity was increasing, and he wanted to know how this verse was manifesting in this woman's walk of faith.

"Once I know the direction of His leading, I am more comfortable with prudence planning the course. It isn't wisdom or prudence; it's wisdom *and* prudence. But if you are going to live a life of faith, you must make room for wisdom, and that is hard to do if you lack the resolving power to see the difference between the two. The problem isn't being prudent. The problem occurs when prudence displaces the voice of God in your life so that you never make allowances for Him. You often find after receiving wisdom that prudence still participates, though not always. If wisdom tells you to go to Hawaii, is it prudent to drive your car?"

"So why not Portland?" asked Max.

"I know no one who could help us with this issue in Portland. But I know the perfect person here. I just need to call him to discuss the details," answered The Locksmith as she pointed to her card.

"Then we will forget Portland." Max seemed content. She could not remember Miss Nelson ever being wrong, though she'd said it has happened before on several occasions and tries not to make a habit of it.

"I'll make the phone call. But in my spirit I really believe this is what we are to do. Now is the time to disagree if you think a different course of action is wiser or more prudent." Miss Nelson looked at both father and daughter as each shook their heads. Again, she stepped from the room for several minutes while Alex enjoyed the remainder of the cookies and the tea, and Max fed the baby, who had become restless.

Max had finished giving the bottle and began the burping process when Miss Nelson returned to the table.

"Okay, my contact has been read in. After I explained the details, and we had a time of prayer, he came to the same conclusion. He is in agreement and has made several suggestions on how to pull this off and place our young one in complete, irrevocable safety. Here is the plan, and I think we need to move on this immediately." Over the next hour, Miss Nelson reviewed the plan with father and daughter until each was not only comfortable with the task but comfortable with their roles as well.

Shortly thereafter, The Locksmith said good night and left for home, and the Smithsons talked about the evening and their sense that God's hand was upon the two of them and the baby. Alex noted that it wasn't like they had an assurance that all would go according to plan. Instead, they had a strong sense that regardless of what happened, it was all in His hands, and each could say it is well. This allowed them to sleep soundly through the night.

. . .

The next morning a sole jogger casually paced himself through the early-morning streets of the small town of Weiser when he passed a black Mercedes sedan rental with tinted windows. He passed the car without a second look, rounded the corner, and two blocks later entered the Smithson home.

Forty-five minutes later the Jeep pulled out of the garage with the doors on and the windows up. The moment it was put in gear and had begun moving forward, a large passenger climbed out of the black Mercedes with a duffle bag, after which the car then pulled away from the curb and followed the Jeep.

The large passenger then proceeded around to the backyard of the home, and after successfully picking the lock, entered through the back door. Ten minutes later the same individual exited the home with the bag in hand and began walking up the street away from the home.

While this was happening, the Jeep drove to the local McDonald's drive-through and purchased a breakfast meal, then drove around for fifteen minutes, ultimately returning to the Smithson home. The driver pulled the Jeep back into the garage and closed the automated door. The Mercedes returned to its previous parking place and, after a few minutes, the passenger returned and climbed back into the car.

"It's done. No signs of the girl or the baby. No-ting in the trash outside or in the neighbors' bins either," said the passenger.

"*Bon*," said the driver. Then with a nod of his head, "Check the device."

The passenger turned on the receiver and the clanking around of kitchen dishes could be heard. The occupant of the house was suddenly heard speaking on the phone.

"Hello, Weiser Police Department. This is Deputy Smithson. I need to report at least a breaking and entering." There was a pause as the caller listened to the person on the other end of the connection.

"I'm not sure. Nothing appears to be—" He stopped to listen to the dispatcher, who interrupted him.

"Well, no, things don't look rifled through necessarily. But things are not where they were. The most telling sign is that I have an interior web camera that caught him looking through my house. Will that be sufficient to send a car over? I could ask the sheriff to look into it."

The driver slapped the passenger across the back of the head.

"Nah, I'm just harassing you, Jane. I know he was here, and being that I'm in the city and it's your jurisdiction, I thought I would let you guys have first crack." A pause ensued while Alex was listening to Jane's response.

"No, from the looks of the camera he was wearing gloves. I really can't tell what he was doing or what he looks like. It appears … like he was just poking around, looking in the rooms, checking the garbage. I don't know, but it seems kind of weird. I'll look around a bit more and see if I can find anything missing." The bug went silent. Then the deputy could be heard again. "No, Max was here earlier. But she had to be in Denver for a conference and had already left with a friend. So no, not the Jeep, a red Prius. Better gas miles, I think. They left late last night." He paused again to let Jane speak, then resumed. "Yeah, I know. I think it might have freaked her out. I won't tell her until she gets back next week. Good, I'll wait here for the city guys to come on by." Jane spoke her last instruction, then Alex proceeded to end the call. "Yep! Thanks, Jane. Talk to you later." When the conversation ended, the deputy started whistling.

Through the blinds out the front window, the deputy could see the black Mercedes pull out and head south on its way back to Boise where the occupants would return the car and catch the next flight to Denver. With a smile, the deputy then texted Miss Nelson's number. The text simply stated: "Now should be fine."

Immediately thereafter, a black Buick left Miss Nelson's house and headed west in the opposite direction of Denver.

CHAPTER 10

WRESTLING WITH DARKNESS

Ontario, Oregon
later that morning

Attention in the institution! It's 8:45 a.m. 9:00 a.m. Callouts, line movement, line movement!" boomed the voice over the loudspeaker.

"Let's go, Johnson," said adult in custody #70342588, Mr. Perez.

"I'm ready," said adult in custody #60034895, Mr. Johnson, and the two men headed out of their cell, 1C52. Johnson slapped his chest and jeans pockets before rushing back to the cell to grab a pen to write with. Both men carried notebooks.

"I thought you said you were ready," joked Perez.

"I am." Johnson slipped the pen in his breast pocket and looked at Perez. "Now." Both men chuckled.

Each week Perez and Johnson met with three other adults in custody in Religious Services on Complex One. "Perez, Johnson, where do you guys think you are going?" demanded Officer Bolen.

"We have a religious callout sir," explained Mr. Perez as both men came to a stop.

"Let me check." Officer Bolen looked over the callout sheet for the day and promptly located both names on the list. "Okay, gentlemen, carry on then. And have a good day," instructed the officer.

"Thank you, sir," replied both men.

. . .

Fifteen minutes earlier a white, older-model Ford Escape with low mileage pulled into a parking space of the facility and came to a stop. As the sun shone out of the eastern horizon, a westerly breeze blew across the knoll on which the Malheur River Correctional Facility stood. MRCF was established as medium-security facility and sat on over five hundred acres with over one million square feet of enclosed space. There were three complexes of multiple housing units, which housed over three thousand adults in custody. The facility, in essence, made it the second largest city in the county.

Outside the car stood an elderly woman with bluish-gray hair. The contrast between the woman and the facility caused any who didn't know her to wonder what she was doing there.

She turned off her cell phone, dropped it into her purse, and then locked her purse in the trunk of her car before grabbing her Bible from the back seat and heading for the main entrance.

"Good morning, ma'am," greeted the officer behind the X-ray scanner.

The woman placed her Bible on the scanner and allowed it to slide on through. The uniformed correctional officer just glanced at the screen more out of habit than out of concern for contraband. But in a prison, careful diligence is critical to maintaining safety. A lack of diligence has been proven deadly in these environments.

"Good morning, William. How is your wife?" asked the elderly woman.

"Very well, ma'am. Thank you for asking."

"Tell her I said hello, would you?"

"Yes, ma'am. I will do that." The officer handed her the sign-in sheet, which she dutifully completed, then attached her facility ID on the lapel of her blouse. Miss Nelson had been coming to this facility for so long that they had issued her an employee-like identification card. This was more a badge of honor than a functional necessity. She had been using the laminated generic ones for years before showing up one day and being issued one with her picture on it. The officer stamped the back of her hand with the fluorescent security ink.

The sally port door hissed just prior to it sliding open, and locks clanked into place, holding the heavy door open and allowing her to enter. Once inside there was a softer click, and the same door slid closed while the woman faced the darkened window holding her ID badge so the person behind the window could verify her identity.

"Good morning, ma'am," was heard over the intercom.

"Good morning. Is that you, David?" asked the visitor, adjusting her head as if that would help her see through the dark glass. It didn't work.

"Yes, ma'am! It is good to see you," came the reply.

"It would be good to see you as well, David," laughed the elderly woman, still unable to peer through the darkened glass.

"Enjoy your visit, ma'am."

"Thank you, David. I believe I shall."

The second door of the sally port hissed and in its turn slid open with another clank as it locked into position, and the older woman walked through and headed down the administrative wing as the second click signaled the door returning to its closed position. At the end of the hall, Miss Nelson came to another door, which remained closed until her approach was noted by David on security cameras. The same clicks, hisses, slides, and clanks were heard as she was ushered into another long hallway that forced her to go either left or right. Turning to the right led to the doorway of the visiting room for adults in custody; going left led to the complexes. She turned left and headed for Complex One. The end of this long hall there formed a T-intersection with another hall that ran perpendicular and at which sat a desk appropriately called the T-desk. The officer manning that desk greeted her as the others had, and she returned the greeting as she made another left and ultimately entered Complex One. Moments later, she was sitting in one of six chairs forming a circle in the chapel area for religious services and waited for her cadre of disciples.

. . .

Three minutes after the announcement of line movement, Perez and Johnson joined her in the room, followed moments later by Mr. Hanson, also from Complex One. And for the next several minutes they exchanged pleasantries until the two other adults in custody, Mr. Gascon and Mr. Williamson, both from Complex Two, arrived and took their seats.

"Well, good morning, gentlemen. Thank you for coming. Shall we get started?"

"Yes, ma'am," they all responded.

"Mr. Hanson, would you do us the honor of opening in prayer?"

"Um ... okay," replied the man. "Dear God, please be with us today. Help us to hear what Miss Nelson is going to share, and may we be better people for hearing it, amen."

"Amen," replied the group.

Miss Nelson glanced at the clock on the wall. "My, we always have such a short time together, don't we?"

Each of the men responded their agreement in various ways, from a verbal "yep" or "uh-huh" to a nod with raised eyebrows.

"I believe our requested topic to begin reviewing was the topic of spiritual warfare. Was that you, Mr. Gascon, who expressed the initial desire to discuss this topic?"

"Yes, ma'am. When I was growing up, I had relatives who were always praying against demons and powers of darkness. I always thought it was kind of weird, so I wasn't sure what to think of it. Since coming to prison, I know the life I have been living wasn't leading me anywhere, and now I wonder if I should've paid closer attention to what they were saying," explained Mr. Gascon.

"I see. And I believe the rest of you gentlemen were also curious for what I think are likely to be different reasons. Am I correct?"

"Yes, ma'am. I am interested in getting a better understanding of what the armor of God is about and how it is used in a spiritual battle," followed Mr. Williamson.

Miss Nelson looked around the group and found five men nodding and looking intently at her.

"Very well, then let us start with first things first. I will skip over what most people think of when they think of spiritual warfare. Instead, let us see if we can broaden our views so our faith can grow larger and stronger, shall we?"

Again, all men seemed to agree.

"First, it is of premier importance to establish that every human is a combatant, whether they realize it or not. Make no mistake; there is a war, and battles are being fought every day. This is my belief, and you don't have to agree with me if you do not want to. However, this belief has changed my life, and I offer it to you for your consideration to see if it might change your life as well. Underlying all that you see around you, everything that you perceive as *real* is a cosmic battle in which you are both a combatant and the prize." Her opening remark was met with curious, blank stares. "Allow me, if I could, to use the analogy of a chess match. How many of you either do not play or do not understand the basics of chess?"

No one raised his hand as everyone around looked at one another. "I think we all play some, ma'am," answered Mr. Perez for the group.

"Very good. Then let me put it this way. Spiritual warfare is a cosmic chess match between the Creator God of the universe, whom we shall just refer to as God—if that is okay with each of you—and the despotic, usurper god of the physical realm, whom we shall call Lucifer, or Satan, which means adversary—if you will allow me to use that name. In this chess match each human is a pawn, and the only difference between each pawn is in the mind of the opponent. Satan is using the pawns as tools. He is willing to neglect them, waste them, sacrifice them, and use them in a manner that suits himself best. While God is always trying to advance the pawn across the board to make her the queen of His son the King. To the one, the pawn is nothing more than, shall we say, cannon fodder; to the other, the pawn is a future queen."

"You're calling Lucifer, the devil, a despotic usurper?" clarified Mr. Johnson.

"Yes, the world's primary authority had been granted to Adam, but it was usurped by Satan, who has been the adversary of humanity from the very beginning."

"Okay, I think we all follow you so far," said Mr. Johnson. A look around the circle showed nodding heads of affirmation.

"Let's think about this arrangement for a second. Now what I am about to share with you is a personal perspective that I cannot support with a specific passage from Scripture, but neither do I think it is refuted by a specific passage. The spiritual beings we often refer to as angels were given a role that some of them aspired to exceed and were successful in achieving through what we call the fall of Adam and Eve."

They weren't even five minutes into the meeting, and their faces were starting to lose their curiosity by showing blank stares.

"Let's switch to a different analogy. Imagine a play that is being produced by a family. There are so many roles that need to be performed for a play to be successfully produced. Included in these roles are a producer, a playwright, a director, actors, and stagehands, to name a few. For the sake of our discussion, we won't argue who fits the role of producer, playwright, and director, but let's just agree that our triune Godhead fills these roles in one way or another just as different members of the same family do, and we will specify that Christ also has an acting role, in addition to playing the role of producer, playwright, or director," said Miss Nelson as she laid out her analogy.

"So, the God family is Father, Son, and Holy Spirit, and they are producing a play. The Father produces it as the Creator, Jesus is the playwright, the Author and Finisher of our faith, and the Holy Spirit is the Director. Is that the sum of it?" said Mr. Williamson.

"That will suffice for our purpose, Mr. Williamson, and I won't spend a lot of time developing this part as it goes beyond the purpose for our study. Because in reality, Scripture speaks of each member of the Trinity performing the same roles. In some places the Father is given credit for an act, while in another passage that same act is credited to the Son, or the Holy Spirit. But for the purpose of my illustration, we will grant them differing roles," clarified Miss Nelson.

"So, the actors are—" started Mr. Gascon.

"Humanity," concluded Mr. Hanson.

"Correct," confirmed Miss Nelson.

"And who are the stagehands, Miss Nelson?" added Mr. Gascon.

"The stagehands are the supernatural beings that many believers call angels."

"What do you mean, 'call angels'? Isn't that what they are?" asked Mr. Hanson.

"Mr. Hanson, the term *angel* is really a term that refers to a function, like a job title. Angel essentially means *messenger*, and in that sense, Jesus was an angel, Paul was an angel, and Peter was an angel. It wasn't just Gabriel who brought God's messages to us. So these supernatural beings play the role of stagehands, and their job is to facilitate the play and for the most part remain unseen."

"A good stagehand changes the scenes, adjusts the backdrop, facilitates the props, but does not play the role of an actor?" It seemed Mr. Williamson was catching on pretty early in the discussion.

"Correct. So let's make this our first takeaway point: The supernatural beings we call angels are stagehands to the play of life and were not meant to be actors in the play. That's why Scripture really doesn't discuss them much other than to make mention of them in some supporting role, facilitating the play God has scripted out."

Guys who had forgotten that they had notebooks all of a sudden opened them and started jotting down notes.

"Okay," said Mr. Hanson.

"So good angels know their role and they stick to it, like Gabriel, Michael, or the unnamed angel who rescued Peter from prison. The malevolent supernatural beings we call demons do not stick to their roles and instead want to usurp a role they were not intended to play. Satan did not want to just play stagehand to the frailer, less powerful, and seemingly less important humans. His pride caused him to aspire to something greater, and he was able to exaggerate the role for himself and his followers by compromising the lead actors through what we call 'the fall' in one of the early scenes in the play."

"But what does this have to do with spiritual warfare?" asked Mr. Williamson.

"I think it is important to recognize that there is a tension in this production caused by what we might call a *revolt* of some stagehands.

I think it is also important to realize the revolting stagehands should still be considered stagehands and be treated that way."

"What do you mean?" interjected Mr. Gascon.

"I think many believers are playing into Satan's strategy by giving him the recognition he is wanting but doesn't deserve. When we begin discussing spiritual warfare, we need to keep this in perspective. They exist, they have a role, but they were designed to support a play much bigger than themselves. For this reason, we don't want to give them more recognition than what was originally intended, and definitely not the attention they are seeking," summarized Miss Nelson.

Mr. Williamson again attempted to get clarification and distill this into something he could put into his notebook. "So in our discussions of spiritual warfare, demons play a role, but we should not give them too much recognition?"

"Correct, I think too many believers play right into Satan's strategy and miss the bigger picture of what spiritual warfare is about." Miss Nelson paused for a moment to gather her thoughts, then continued. "When he is successful in this, he is able to get believers to fight a one-front war without realizing there are at least three fronts to our spiritual war. As a result, they become ineffective in fighting any of them well."

"What are the three fronts?" asked Mr. Johnson.

"The front we have been talking about is what I call the satanic front. It is the supernatural beings themselves and their activities. The second front is the world, and the third front is our flesh. The battle is fought differently on each front. We will get more into it in the future when we talk about the armor of God. For now, let us sketch out three different tactics, one for each of the fronts. These tactics are fight, faith, and flee.

We need a strong faith to fend off the perspectives, teachings, and lies the world values and tries to push down our throats. We need to use Joseph as an example for fending off the attacks of the flesh by fleeing the situations that will attempt to entangle us. And we need to resist the devil, as we are told in James, and follow Christ's example in the wilderness, using Scripture to fight off Satan."

Miss Nelson's description was now getting meaty, and the guys were trying to scribble down the nuggets they would chew on and challenge one another with over the next week, though some were getting frustrated at processing this new information.

"It seems to me that there is quite a bit of overlap between these fronts," pointed out Mr. Perez.

"Agreed," stated Miss Nelson. "But let me see if I can describe some of the battles I have seen and heard people trying to fight. Also, I can share my opinion on why they sometimes haven't been successful."

"Okay," said Mr. Perez as he made sure Miss Nelson knew she still had the floor.

"Imagine a person with a fleshly addiction. Let's say a sexual addiction." Mr. Perez shifted a bit in his seat. Every one of the other guys knew he was in prison for a sex crime, and he had a sense that Miss Nelson was aware of it as well, even though she had never asked the guys why they were incarcerated. "How much more Scripture do you think this addict needs to fully understand that his addiction is wrong and not what God intends for him?"

"Well, he needs some Scripture. Isn't it Paul who says we need the law to show us what sin is?"

"Yes, but how often have you seen someone who knows what Scripture says, yet he still wanders into situations that put him in close proximity to the things he is addicted to, causing him to fall into temptation and submit to his addiction?"

"It happens a lot."

"Yes, it does happen a lot. How often have you told a person that he just needs to trust the Lord, or pray, or read their Bible more? I think we have all been guilty of saying 'I will be praying for you,' then forget to do it much of the time. I think we have all shared our favorite memory verse, song, or hymn. The problem at this front is not that Satan is using his tactics of fear or hatred, nor is the world necessarily trying to force a perspective down his throat. No, the problem is his flesh has a longing he must keep himself away from. He can't go where he used to go, see what he used to look at, smell what he used to smell, or touch what he used to touch. Once his flesh tastes those things again, the tendency is that his willpower will be overwhelmed, causing him to fall again. The scripture he has memorized will not come to his mind, and no amount of sharing one's faith perspectives can give him enough guidance to keep from falling yet again. His defense must be set up farther from the battlefield, and he must avoid it before his sensations overwhelm his willpower and cause him to do what he ought not to do. Perhaps the best advice we could give him is the advice Paul gives us, that he should not make any provision for the flesh."

"So, we shouldn't do those things?" Mr. Perez asked, then paused briefly. "We shouldn't do the praying, the memorizing, and all that?"

Miss Nelson smiled. "Oh, no, I am not saying we should not do those things. We should encourage one another with these things. We should definitely focus on Scripture and do our best to connect to God in our weak moments. To not do those things is not my point. My point is that those things are often not enough if they are being applied in the moment of weakness after we have allowed ourselves to linger in the temptation. And the application is difficult when you have allowed yourself to get so close that the cravings from within outshout the longings for God."

"Is there a biblical example in Scripture?" asked Mr. Gascon.

"I think I would submit the story of Joseph and Potiphar's wife as the main example. When she tempted him with seduction, his solution was to flee. Later, you can look it up in Genesis chapter thirty-nine. It seems the approach to address things of the flesh is to flee," offered Miss Nelson.

"Like seeing donuts when you're on a diet," chipped in Mr. Hanson. The others chuckled with recollections of self-realization.

Miss Nelson raised an eyebrow.

Mr. Hanson fleshed out his thought a bit. "Donuts are a weakness of mine. If I am on a diet and I see a donut, it is a huge temptation for me. It is best for me to not go into a room that I know has donuts. It isn't smart for me to go where I know I will be tempted. If I do, the chances are I will fail and give in to the craving."

Mr. Johnson echoed, "In AA we have seen knowledge be insufficient to curb cravings so many times that we have referred to it as 'A head full of AA and a belly full of booze.'"

"Same elemental point," confirmed Miss Nelson. "But there is overlap as we mentioned. It isn't just the flesh, the world, or Satan. The world will present a perspective where true love is often portrayed as a large amount of sex with multiple partners and will present it as carefree and enjoyable by everyone. The sex addict will need to fight this perspective with a faith that is grounded in a deeper covenantal understanding of love. But—and this is the point—this will often be insufficient to fight the battle against his flesh when his senses arouse these carnal desires."

"I think you are saying that many believers approach spiritual warfare as simply praying that Satan and his horde be bound. They then rebuke him and ask that hedges be built to keep him out of something special or sacred while missing the other fronts in the war," summarized Mr. Perez.

"I think you have put elements of my point into the proverbial nutshell," she responded.

Mr. Perez looked at Mr. Johnson and tried to whisper, but in his excitement it came out louder than he intended. "Holy Roley is going to go ape nuggets when I tell him this."

Mr. Johnson snickered as Miss Nelson disapprovingly called him out on his distraction. "Mr. Perez, please?"

"Yeah, man, a lady is present," said Mr. Hanson, ribbing Mr. Perez.

"Oops, sorry, ma'am. No disrespect intended. I really am working on my language, aren't I, Johnson?" appealed Mr. Perez.

"Yes, ma'am. Perez here had a very foul mouth when we became cellies the first-time many years ago. Since then, guys have noticed that there is a difference in the way he lives his life," said Johnson. Mr. Perez smiled at the recognition he received for the change in his behavior, and Miss Nelson smiled at him with a knowing glance.

"Miss Nelson, could you give me a little bit more on the worldly front?" asked Mr. Hanson.

"The worldly front is one that occurs in the mind. It is a war of propaganda. It is a battle for the mind, the prevailing of a viewpoint. It is a front in which Satan uses a specific tactic to confuse the believer into failure and ineffectiveness. Its most effective components are in the blurring of the difference between good and godly, and in the promotion of prudence over wisdom."

"We've talked about wisdom dwelling with prudence before, haven't we?" asked Mr. Williamson. "Prudence is the role of reason, or logic, and it is the rationale that is embedded into the fabric of creation that we use every moment of every day. It is the force that makes mathematics and the sciences hold consistent and reproducible. While wisdom is the heart and mind of God that directs reason and gives it purpose." When Mr. Williamson finished, the room was silent, and every eye was on him for an awkward stretch of at least five seconds. "What?" he asked defensively.

"You've been chewing your cud, man!" exclaimed Mr. Hanson, causing others to smile or snort their agreement. Miss Nelson had previously shared with them her view that contemplative meditation on the things of God is like chewing the cud. She had said to them that, biblically speaking, there were two factors that determined whether an animal was a clean animal. Clean animals had split hooves and chewed the cud. If an animal possessed one factor but not the other, then it could not be considered a clean animal.

To Miss Nelson these were metaphors, or similitudes, for aspects found in humanity that had been made clean by Christ. They had split hooves because they lived in two worlds, the physical one and the spiritual one, not just one or the other. When they were fed the word of God, they didn't just swallow it; they chewed on it to break it down into something they could digest in their stomach, then later burp it back up into their mouth and begin chewing on the same old piece of food again to gain even more nutrition out of it. She agreed it was somewhat disgusting but also had said, spiritually speaking, believers essentially did the same thing. They would take a passage of Scripture and reflect on it until they found something they could apply to their life, then later bring the same passage back to their mind and find something completely different to apply to their life. It wasn't unusual to find a single passage delivering several important applications if one contemplated it long enough.

"Yes, indeed, Mr. Williamson, the world loves to have believers use prudence against God's clear designs and instructions," replied Miss Nelson. "The world also will settle for something that is obviously good to keep the believer from pursuing what is godly. But despite the obvious benefits of prudence, it is a poor counterfeit to wisdom."

"Can you give an example of how this happens?" asked Mr. Gascon.

"Sure. Is it good to give offerings to God?" queried the woman.

"Yes, we should give tithes and offerings," said Gascon.

"Then I think we can use a passage from Mark chapter seven where Jesus quotes the commandment to honor your father and your mother. He then points out to the religious leaders that they had a tradition that if a person committed an offering to honor the Lord, then he didn't have to honor his father and his mother with it. It had been dedicated to God, so he didn't have to do anything to honor his parents. In essence, Jesus was saying that if a person is willing to give an offering to God, it is a good thing, but if the person honors his parents, it is a godly thing. I see this type of issue playing out in a lot of people's lives. It is good and prudent to pay your bills, but it is wise and godly to pay your tithe. It is good and prudent to save the whales, but it is wise and godly to be a good steward. It is good and prudent to spend time with your friends and loved ones, but it is wise and godly to remember the Sabbath Day and keep it holy. There are so many things that are prudent and appear to be good, but we never stop to consider if it is something God has directed for us to pursue. If He has not, then it is neither godly nor wise. Is it good and prudent to laugh and enjoy ourselves? Yes, certainly. But it is not wise or godly the way some people use humor to cut and belittle others. I cannot tell you how many broken hearts, dreams, and expectations I have seen slaughtered on an altar to the god of humor. I think if we stopped and put our minds to it, we could easily find multiple ways in which we have sacrificed something from God of immense value for something that is just good and prudent."

The men weren't really writing in their notebooks anymore. They were staring at their feet, at their hands, or across the room as each mind drifted to the times in their lives when the treasures of God were shunned and ignored to allow them the opportunity to pursue something of lesser value, all the while convincing themselves and others it was a good thing.

Miss Nelson paused and allowed the gravity of the moment do its work, then softly said, "The first sin recorded is the quintessential sin that characterizes all sins. It, too, is a metaphor. It is the taking of the one thing God reserved for Himself. The right to know, or define, what is good and what is evil. Only God has the capacity to call something good, and that something, whatever it is, receives that quality and becomes good. God did not find good things and make them. God made things and then gave them the quality of goodness. God says something, and it is. It is not that God cannot lie; it is not that God refuses to lie. I tend to believe that no matter what God says, His Word becomes truth. It becomes truth the moment He utters it. Goodness is a similar quality that he pronounces on people, and objects, and thoughts. His perspective cannot be compared to an outside standard because there is not one. For most believers the world will never attempt to get us to do evil instead of something godly, especially when it is so blatantly obvious we will readily give up godliness for the things we think are good."

Miss Nelson stopped to allow them time to consider what was being said. It was a few minutes later when Mr. Gascon said, "I don't think I have ever thought of spiritual warfare as anything more than humans fighting demons through prayer."

"Yeah, it's like the sum total of the Kingdom of Darkness were demons that had to be battled," added Mr. Perez.

"Are there only three fronts to the war?" asked Mr. Johnson.

"No, that is probably too simplistic. However, I do believe it covers many of the battles we fight, and it is plenty to chew on," said Miss Nelson with a smile to Mr. Hanson. "Now I want to impress upon you that I am not refuting those strategies against those rogue supernatural beings. But I am trying to make the point that if fending off supernatural beings exemplifies the sum total of your spiritual war strategy, then you are likely living in defeat in many areas of your life. You are inadvertently giving these stagehands more billing than they deserve. Remember that both aspects are just fine with them: one results in your failure and the other in their glory."

"It sounds to me like the three different fronts are a direct approach against Satan, an indirect approach against the world, and an avoidant approach toward the flesh," said Mr. Gascon.

"I think that is a great place to leave it for now, gentlemen," said Miss Nelson as she picked up her Bible. "As you contemplate the things we have discussed, I would encourage you to read Daniel chapter nine and pay close attention to the last ten verses of the chapter. This gives us the fullest description of the stagehands at work and some of their rogue nature as well. If you find extra time, look through Scripture and *Strong's Concordance* to track down the different times and places the word *angel* is used in Scripture. Then read Isaiah chapter fourteen verses twelve through seventeen to get some background of the fall of Satan and the role pride played. But make sure you read Ephesians chapter six verses ten through eighteen to review the armor of God. We will pick up with that portion of Scripture in the very near future."

"Like next week?" asked Mr. Perez.

"Not likely next week, but soon," answered Miss Nelson. "Nonetheless, before we go, I want to pray for you."

The men stood and, as awkward as it can be in prison, held hands. "Oh, God of the heavens, I praise Your name and lift You up, asking You to sanctify Your name. I give You recognition and all the associated glory and honor for the things I have come to treasure. Treasures I sense that also captivate the hearts and minds of these men. I come to You this day to ask a blessing. I ask that You reveal Yourself to them in accordance to their longing, and may they never be the same as a result. Amen."

"Amen," said the men.

"Attention in the institution! It's 9:45 a.m. 10:00 a.m. callouts, line movement, line movement!" said the voice over the loudspeaker.

"Goodbye, gentlemen, until we meet again," said Miss Nelson.

"Thank you, ma'am," said each of the men as they got up, shook her hand, and left.

• • •

An hour later The Locksmith had retraced her steps back through security, driven her car home, and was sitting at her kitchen table when she heard a rap at the front door. The woman stood up from her snack of tea and cookies and went to the door. "Good day, John Quinton Riley. Won't you come in? I have just sat down to a nice cup of tea and a plate of cookies in anticipation of our visit."

"Yes, good day, Miss Nelson. I love the way you anticipate our visits with a cup of tea. Thank you," said the young Mr. O'Malley. John Quinton Riley O'Malley was a protégé of Miss Nelson and had been since the day he met her. Since graduating from Pacific Northwest Christian University a few years ago, he has been either her traveling companion or, more frequently of late, her trusted courier and agent. In recent years, many of Miss Nelson's contacts began to put a face to the name they had heard many times through the years, as Miss Nelson spoke fondly of her student and neighbor.

"What news do you bring from Washington?" asked The Locksmith.

"Senator Agirre-Fernandez sends her greetings and expressed her appreciation for your thoughts and insights. She received the document but did not review it in my presence. The next day prior to my flying out, she contacted me and stated she would look further into the facts you presented. She also asked if she should share your assessment of those facts or if she could keep those to herself."

"I will let her know the facts are for her to digest. She can use as needed and share with whomever she sees fit. However, my commentary is for her alone."

"Yes, ma'am. Sometime I hope to visit Washington in the spring to see the cherry blossoms."

"It is a sight to see. Perhaps someday it will happen."

"What's been going on while I've been gone?" asked Jaker as he popped a cookie in his mouth.

"Well, Margaret had a baby," replied the older woman.

Jaker nearly choked on the cookie. "Wait, what?"

"Ooh, I am sorry, Mr. O'Malley. I really should not start in the middle of a story," said The Locksmith as she smiled and shook her head in apparent self-reproach.

Over the course of the next hour or so, Miss Nelson retold the story of Max and her group's exciting past several days, including the tragic death of her friend, Santana D'Souza, the rescue of her baby from the Kingdom of Darkness, and the hopes of finding her a home one yard from the gates of heaven.

"Wait a minute! I know most of Max's friends, both Peregrines and Wolves. I don't know a Santana," interrupted Jaker.

"No, not by that name. But you do know her as Sandy Acedia."

"Sandy? She's really a Santana? Wow! I will definitely have to get debriefed on that story. Where is Max now?"

"Margaret is on an errand with the baby," said Miss Nelson, and she left it at that. Jaker had learned a long time ago that when Anna Belle Nelson became vague in her lack of details, it was on purpose, and further coaxing would not yield the response one desired. It was best to leave it alone, so he did.

"Well then, what now?" asked the young man.

"I'm sending you to Benin."

"Ah, the Africa trip?"

"Yes, I have a friend who has been trying to organize an evangelistic crusade with other Christian leaders in the country, and he is running into opposition."

"So you want me to dash over to Africa and take a look to see if there are some locks you can either pick, or fashion a key for, to help him move forward. I assume it is the usual routine visit: discuss the plans, sound out his heart, and see if we can find the potential obstacles to his calling, then report back?"

"That is about the size of it," explained the older woman as she gave a shallow shrug with a gentle shaking of her head, implying that it was merely a routine trip.

Though John Quinton Riley had never been to Benin, had never met Miss Nelson's friend, and had nothing to go on in terms of what the details of the crusade were, there was one thing that Jaker knew for certain: nothing about a trip for Miss Nelson was ever routine.

"Okay, when?" was his next question.

"I need you there early next week. Oh, and along the way I want you to meet up with another friend of mine who will be traveling to Benin as well."

"Okay. Are there any instructions for that meeting?" asked Jaker.

"Yes, he is a pastor about to take a new church in Oregon. But before they move, he has agreed to help us out. He will be traveling to provide a resource for the same crusade, but he will be accompanied by his adolescent daughter with whom he is struggling. With their upcoming move, he and his wife are terrified of how taking her from her friends and familiar surroundings might impact her."

"Oh?"

"He feels he is losing her to the world, and he is greatly distressed," The Locksmith replied. "See if you can assess the depth of the infiltration, the types of chains that bind her or him, and—"

"Report back," interjected Jaker.

"You are such a good boy," said Miss Nelson with a smile. "It is nice of you to help such an aging woman with her little issues."

Jaker O'Malley smiled, knowing there was a seed of truth in the fact that Miss Nelson's age was part of the reason he was going and not simply her asking. Twenty years ago it would have been—and was—different.

CHAPTER 11

ON THE FRONTLINES

Paris, France
early the next week

Voyage sûr monsieur,"* said the attractive flight attendant as Jaker approached the exit to deplane the Air France flight that had just landed at Charles De Gaulle Airport.

"*Merci, mademoiselle. Permettriez-vous une question en anglais, s'il vous plaît?*" asked Jaker.

"But of course, sir, how can I help you?" responded the attendant.

"I am meeting friends for a later flight to Cotonou. If we don't connect with one another, is there a place I can leave my luggage while I head into Paris?"

"Certainly, sir. You may store your luggage at the Left Luggage facility in Terminal Two near the railway station on the fourth floor. Head to your left and watch for the signs."

"*Merci!*"

"*Certainement, monsieur, profitez de Paris,*" said the attendant with a smile.

"Thank you! I hope I shall." And with that, he stepped off the plane and headed up the jetway. Jaker had very little doubt that his travel companions would be at the gate prior to their next flight. But based on the need for abrupt adjustments to some of his previous travel plans, he always felt better knowing where he could leave larger luggage and take only his daypack in a pinch, then return later and collect the bulkier items.

Thirty-five minutes later, he had navigated his way through airport security and was standing at the departure gate for his outbound flight to Cotonou. He was plenty early, and the current flight boarding at this gate was headed to Florence, Italy, so he found a seat off a way from the podium, made himself comfortable, and pulled out his Bible to catch up on some reading.

Many years ago he had made it an attempt to read through the Bible at least once a year and was about to continue on in Judges. Sometime later, he was lost in the story of Ruth when his attention was drawn to a father-daughter duo just sitting down across the center aisleway. The man tossed a large backpack into the chair next to them.

Jaker set his Bible aside, determined to see if they might be his traveling companions. He made his way over to the couple and asked, *"Excusez-moi monsieur, parlez-vous anglaise?"*

The gentleman looked up and said, "Sorry, I don't speak French." The girl was wearing H&M cotton-twill jogging pants tied with a drawstring, a light blue Hollister T-shirt, and canvas flats. She sat with her knees up, feet on the chair, and heels tucked under her bottom, never looking up from her phone.

"Well, that just increased the odds that you are the right people." Jaker offered his hand. "Jaker O'Malley. Reverend Truesdale?"

"Ah, yes. I thought your name was John," said the man, smiling as he stood up to gave Jaker's hand a quick pump.

"Heh, yeah … Not even my parents call me John. My friends shortened my full name from John Quinton Riley to the initials JQR, and I've been Jaker ever since. Except to Miss Nelson, who has never called me anything other than John Quinton Riley since I was in her fifth-grade class. So Jaker will probably work best for us."

"Michael Truesdale, and Mike works for me." Pastor Truesdale stepped to the side, extending his hand toward his daughter "And this is my daughter, Cherish."

"How do you do?" Jaker offered his hand to her as well.

"Hey," said the girl quietly, never changing position or looking up from her phone as if it were her usual way of returning a greeting.

"Cherish, can you properly shake hands?" asked her father.

There was a shallow eye-roll as she let out a disgruntled, "Fuff, fine." She stood to her feet, shook his hand, and said, "How do you do?"

"I am well, thank you," responded Jaker with a smile.

"Dad, I'm going to go look at the shops," she said, heading out from the alcove of seats.

"Okay, but please stay on this end of this terminal, agreed?" he stated as the girl trotted off.

Once she was out of hearing distance, he said, "There are days that I am not sure we will all survive to see her fourteenth birthday."

"I understand thirteen is a tough age for kids. I know it was for my generation, and that wasn't very long ago. I mean, I still remember flip phones and multitap texting, thinking it was the latest and coolest thing on the planet, but few kids now would put up with that ancient technology. They are so much more connected to the Internet and the world. I think the digital world has made life a bit tougher in many ways."

"Yeah, who'd heard of cyberbullying when you were that age, right? What, ten or eleven years ago?" asked the father, realizing he was barely talking to an adult.

"It wasn't very long ago. But I guess that is my point. I think my great-grandfather had more in common with his great-great-grandfather than I do with my grandfather. When my dad was young, getting a car was a rite of passage. That was how you connected and interacted with your friends. But now"—Jaker nodded up at Cherish, who was taking a selfie next to a Prada store-front sign, likely to post it on her favorite social media account—"it's not a car but a phone, and a smartphone. Seems this is the new rite of passage."

"She does spend a lot of time on that phone. Texting, posting, surfing, chatting, and whatever else kids can do on it. I'm not sure when it happened, but somehow, someone took all the telephones, all the televisions, and all the computers, threw them into a blender, and now we have smartphones," mused Mike.

"And watches," added Jaker.

"Yes, and watches," said Mike with an agreeing nod.

Jaker smiled and asked, "Do you have other children?"

"We did." Mike paused and his countenance got serious. "Cathy and I lost Rishy's younger sister, Lacy, a few years ago to leukemia."

"I'm sorry to hear that."

"Yeah, well thanks. It was rough on everyone. Rishy suffered as collateral damage while Cathy and I fought through all of our own pain and suffering."

"I think the most difficult part of losing a family member is that it causes a family identity crisis," mused Jaker. "Was coming on this trip her idea, or you and your wife's?"

"Heh, well … good question. Early on she seemed excited about the trip, and I think I would have said it was her idea. But now I wonder if it's more of a desperation play on Cathy's and my part. You know, to shake things up a bit." The father sat staring off down the terminal at his daughter, not really intellectually aware that the physical distance was closer than the emotional distance. "I guess we will see if it works," he offered quietly, turning his head and smiling at Jaker.

Jaker returned his smile. "I will be praying for you two on this trip. Then I'll be expecting that God will do what God alone can do … transform hearts."

The intercom overhead snapped to life as the gate agent rattled off the gate announcement in French. "Oops, that's our flight!" exclaimed Jaker as he began gathering his things. The announcement repeated in English: "Good afternoon, ladies and gentlemen, this is the pre-boarding announcement for flight 217 to Cotonou. We would like to invite those passengers with small children, and any of our passengers requiring special assistance, to begin boarding at this time. Please have your boarding pass and identification papers ready. Regular boarding will begin in approximately ten minutes time. Thank you."

Mike was flagging down Cherish, who was already working her way back to the gate. When she approached, she helped lift the large backpack onto her father's shoulders.

While lining up for boarding, Jaker intentionally stayed farther back not only because his seat assignment had him later in the queue, but he wanted to watch how father and daughter interacted when they thought no one was watching. He knew he needed to have a better idea of how each carried themselves, how they interacted with one another, as well as how they interacted with other people in order to give a thorough report to The Locksmith. More importantly, he began to pray for transformation in a young life that already had experienced one of life's more intense tragedies.

The flight to Cotonou was uneventful and the weather was clear, allowing for a great look at the Saharan Desert. It was impossible to not reflect on how life can be so barren and lifeless without water, and how true it was spiritually as well. He found himself looking for the rare places where water could be found springing up out of the desert but found none. He knew there were at least ninety known oases, ranging from just a few acres to much larger, and again his mind wondered to the spiritual similarities. It struck him that at times it can be as hard to find pockets of faith in a person's life as it was for him to find the oases on this flight. But hope can be powerful, and sometimes survival means loaning those who are about to die of thirst some of the water you have brought with you while you search for more. He wondered just how thirsty the daughter, father, or entire family might be.

The flight arrived on time later that evening, and upon gathering the checked luggage and clearing customs, the small band met up with their host, Solomon Nosakhere, who was waiting for them just beyond customs.

Mike walked right up to Solomon, and they embraced. "It is good to see you, my brother," said Mike.

"The Lord is good to bring you back safely to us. Who have we here?" asked the pastor.

"This is my daughter, Cherish." Cherish had to pocket her phone while navigating customs and had not had the chance to reengage it.

"Welcome, young lady, to my beautiful country."

"Thank you," said the young girl, more from the knowledge that it was the expected thing to say than it being a heartfelt response.

"And this is Miss Nelson's protégé, John Quinton Riley..." Mike was struggling to recall Jaker's last name.

"O'Malley, sir, but please call me Jaker," he instructed as he offered his hand.

"Right! I'm sorry, Jaker," apologized Reverend Truesdale.

"That's all right. I am sure we will get to know one another very well before the trip is over," said Jaker, waving off any perceived offense and shaking hands with the African pastor.

"Well, I am pleased to have you both," said Pastor Nosakhere as he started gathering bags. "Let me take you to your hotel. I thought it would be nice to let you stay in a hotel tonight for a couple of reasons. First, this is where the committee for the upcoming crusade is going to meet tomorrow morning, and I thought you might like to sit in on that meeting. But I also thought you might like to rest up in a more modern setting to catch up on your sleep or adjust your internal clocks. Yes?"

The new arrivals nodded. "Sounds fantastic," said Mike.

"Then tomorrow after the committee meeting, we will head out to the orphanage. There we have a few rooms you can stay in. We will also have some more quiet time to discuss the crusade and explain the work we do with the children."

"Sounds great," agreed Mike. Jaker, again, gave a nod.

"How about we get you settled for the evening as it is already getting late, and I will meet you here in the morning with the hotel staff to show you around the facility where we can talk about what we have planned. Yes?"

After all were found in agreement, Solomon Nosakhere helped them load their belongings into his van. On the ride over he told them a little about Cotonou and its history. It wasn't long before they arrived at the hotel where he helped get the group registered and settled into their rooms. It had been a long day of travel, and everyone needed some rest.

After Jaker had closed and secured the door to his room, he quickly took a refreshing shower and placed two calls. The first was to his mother, letting her know he had arrived safely and had met his host. Then he called Miss Nelson.

"Yes, ma'am, arrived about an hour ago."

"Did you meet up with the Truesdales?"

"Yes, you could have given me a heads-up on their tragic loss."

"I could have. But I didn't want to hinder your ability to assess Cherish without a bias."

"Uh-huh," he reluctantly agreed.

"Initial thoughts?"

"She is a typical teenager in many ways. She acts somewhat aloof. Self-absorbed. Hesitant to engage and likely to exhibit a high degree of anxiety if she misplaces her phone."

"Highly dependent upon others' perceptions of her? Is she heavily rooted in how she is perceived by others in general, or someone specific?"

"I'm not exactly sure, but she does seem to be more concerned about social media status than she does her status with her parents."

"That is a common problem. What is her dress like?"

"She is well-kept, not dark in either mood or presentation, makeup is light and complimentary. She seems neither bold nor outspoken."

"Try to get to know her. What does she like? What music does she listen to? How much influence does the world have in her worldview? How much of her fleshly side—"

"Check out her spiritual warfare fronts, right," said Jaker more as a statement than as a question. "As always, there is the spiritual component, but I don't sense any interest in the blatant dark side of spirituality. I believe she is going to have more going on in the worldly and fleshly fronts than in the demonic or occultic. I think the spiritual side appears more of the neglectful and apathetic type than as a foothold in the occult," posited Jaker.

"Well, then I think we at least have a place to start our praying," concluded The Locksmith. "Did you meet with Solomon?"

"We just met. Seems nice, but we really haven't had time to get to know one another yet. He is meeting with us here tomorrow morning when we will have the chance to sit in on the crusade committee meeting, then head out to the orphanage."

"I think you will enjoy that. It will be interesting to see the effect the children have on you, and on Cherish."

"Yep, I was wondering the same thing."

"Alright then, Mr. O'Malley, please be safe, and contact me after you have had a discussion with Solomon. I will be interested in how the warfare is established in his life and work as well."

"Yes, ma'am. I will check in tomorrow or the next day."

"Very good, John Quinton Riley. I will look forward to hearing from you."

"Goodbye, ma'am."

"Goodbye." The connection went dead, and Jaker climbed into bed for some much-needed rest.

The next morning Jaker easily found his way to the hotel's restaurant for a Mediterranean-style breakfast.

"*Bonjour, monsieur, votre numéro de chambre s'il vous plait?*" asked the attendant.

"*Bonjour, le numéro de chambre est duex cent quinze, merci,*" replied Jaker.

"*Bonjour, monsieur et mademoiselle, votre numéro de chambre s'il vous plait?*" asked the attendant again, causing Jaker to look behind him.

"I'm sorry?" asked Pastor Truesdale.

"He is asking for your room number to put the meal on the tab," interceded Jaker.

"Oh … umm." He looked to Cherish.

"Two forty-five," she offered.

"*Deux cent, quarante cinq,*" offered Jaker to the attendant.

"*Je vous remercie.*"

"*De rien,*" said Jaker as he led the party past the buffet toward a table and offered some subtle instructions to Cherish. "Like a lot of places you eat at while traveling, you will find plates and flatware at one end of the serving line. After grabbing those, you make your way through and take a little bit of anything that looks good to you and put it on your plate. I think you will find the dishes labeled in French with an English translation underneath. You will recognize most of the food and fruit, but some may surprise you in their size or color, maybe even the taste." Jaker smiled as Cherish sheepishly raised her eyebrows. "Also, watch out for seeds. Some of the fruit you're used to having without seeds will surprise you, and finding a dentist in a foreign country can get tricky."

"That sounds like good advice," she said.

"Now you will want to hit the table behind you, as the French influence is not only in the language…" Jaker turned slightly and nodded to the serving table behind them. "It is in the pastries as well."

"Even better advice," said the girl with a nod, looking over the table of pastries.

The trio made their way through the lines and got settled at their table where an attendant brought them beverages.

"You seem to know your way around the international breakfast line," remarked Mike.

"Hah! Since graduating from college, I have been working with Miss Nelson almost full time, and she has me traveling quite a bit."

"What did you study?"

"I was a history major."

"Is that where you learned French?" asked Cherish.

"Well, I was exposed to French while at college, but it wasn't until I started using it while I travelled that I felt I really began to learn it. But I guess that is like a lot of things, isn't it?"

"Uh, I don't know?" she replied with a disturbed shrug, obviously not anticipating engaging in conversation beyond a simple yes or no.

"It has been my experience, limited as it may be, that it is one thing to read and study something and quite another to know and apply it. I found the same was true with my faith, my studies… Well, with a lot of things," he explained.

"Isn't that the truth?" chimed in Mike.

"Sometimes it is a key experience that can cause a radical transformation from what we think to what we become." Jaker looked up. "There's Solomon!" He waved their new friend to the table.

"*Bonjour*," said Solomon.

"*Bonjour*," replied the three guests.

He exchanged pleasantries and then asked about the restfulness of the evening and how well they slept. He answered questions about his country and his people, but specifically about his congregation. The conversation naturally drifted to the meeting.

"There are several pastors I have been meeting with for some time now who I have hoped will begin a coordinated evangelistic effort in each of our communities," shared Solomon.

"How is that going?" asked Mike.

"Honestly, not well," said Solomon, shaking his head. "In fact, some of them have told me recently that they won't be able to be here today."

"Why?" asked Jaker.

"I'm not sure. I am hoping you might be able to help me gain insight. If it is the Lord delaying the effort, then so be it. But if there is something that can be addressed, then I don't want it to fail on my part, or our part."

Jaker smiled to himself, realizing the pastor was at least asking the right wisdom versus prudence questions. "I will let you two sit at the table, and I will sit back and watch from a distance and see if the Lord will help us discern what is happening. It may be that he has brought all you pastors together for a purpose other than the one you are expecting," said Jaker. He and Mike signed off on their tickets with the attendant and made their way to the meeting hall.

Pastor Nosakhere opened the door to the room and ushered the trio of guests in, then began making introductions.

Once the introductions were made, Jaker and Cherish made their way to seats at the side against the wall, while Mike and Solomon sat at the table. Before long, all the seats were taken and the meeting began. Solomon once again made introductions to everyone around the table, then opened in prayer. As the meeting progressed, Jaker took several mental notes and tried to keep Cherish informed as to what was going on. Eventually, though, it was clear Cherish was not interested in the conversation at all. It didn't take long for Jaker to identify a couple of signs of why the conference was struggling in the planning stages before it ever started.

Jaker leaned over to Cherish. "I've seen enough. I'm going to go for a walk. Do you want to come?"

"Sure."

The two slipped out quietly. Once outside, Jaker asked, "Is this your first time out of the country?"

"No, I've been to Canada a couple of times," stated the girl, acting as if going to Canada made her an international traveler.

"Very nice. Anywhere else?"

"We took a mission trip to Mexico a couple of years ago."

"Oh, what was that like?"

"We went to a YWAM mission and built homes for poor people. It was pretty cool."

"Tell me about it."

"The team went to Tijuana and stayed for about a week or so."

"Probably the San Antonio Del Mar campus. Pretty stucco buildings with a big soccer field in the middle of the campus?"

"Yep, that's it. Have you been there?"

"Sure have. What did you do while you were there?"

"We fed the homeless. We did a refugee experience. We built a home for a family that didn't have anything."

"Did the house look like a shed you might find in someone's backyard?"

"Yeah, it did."

"Were they pleased to have it?" Jaker could see she was reliving some of the experience. Cherish nodded. "What I remember is seeing people with nothing, who then received something and acted like it was everything." Cherish remained quiet. "Were there any children?" Jaker knew full well there were. Cherish nodded again.

"A girl, about my age, with a sister a little younger."

Jaker waited and let the silence do its work as they walked. After a few minutes he asked, "Did they speak English?"

"No, we had an interpreter."

"What did they say?"

"Not much. They were pretty quiet."

"What did their faces say?" he asked.

"What do you mean?"

"I have found that when you don't know the language, you can still learn a lot by watching the faces. I was able to speak to my family when I went—"

"Because you speak Spanish too," interrupted Cherish.

"Well, yeah, I do. I find even though you can learn a lot through body language, I can still miss a lot unless I ask."

"What did they say?"

"Well, like your experience, they didn't say much—in the beginning. They communicated first with their eyes, watching us very carefully. They were embarrassed that rich Americans who had everything came to where they lived, and saw it was basically a cardboard box with pallets."

"And you could see it in their eyes?"

"Oh yeah. You could see them stealing glances at us and then kick the dirt as if none of it mattered."

"What did you say to them?"

"I asked them about their friends. I asked what they liked to do, what they wanted to do when they got older. You know what I found out?"

"What?"

"They were a lot like me. They worried about their family. They liked to be with their friends. The girl wanted to go to the university and be a teacher, and her older brother wanted to be a mechanic. The boy ended up showing me his prized possession."

"What was it?"

"A pair of new tennis shoes."

Cherished stopped and looked at Jaker. "You're kidding."

"Nope, they were brand new, never worn." He looked back into her eyes, "And they no longer fit."

"He never wore them?"

"Nope."

"Why?"

"He knew what it had cost his mother. He knew all that she did for as long as she did it just to raise the money. In a way, they were too valuable to actually end up wearing." Again, he waited for time to do its work, then said, "I think it was then that I realized he had a better sense of what was truly valuable than I did."

They walked around the compound, and Jaker asked about her

friends, her activities, her likes, her dislikes. It wasn't long before he felt he had made a new friend, and they understood one another a little better.

The meeting lasted about an hour and a half, then broke up. After the pastors had left, the trio brought their luggage to the front desk. While Solomon packed the van, Mike and Jaker cleared their bills.

Within an hour of the meeting concluding, the group of four were headed out of town toward the orphanage. Solomon was rather quiet in thought as the trip got underway.

"I was getting the impression that the meeting wasn't going very well," said Jaker as he interrupted the African pastor's thoughts.

"No, it was like every other meeting. Did you pick up on anything?" asked the bewildered pastor.

"Yes, I will review my thoughts with Miss Nelson tonight. But I think you are experiencing a common problem." Jaker changed the subject. "Tell me about the orphanage."

"We have fifty-three children staying at the orphanage, from six years of age to eighteen."

"Are they able to enter any earlier or stay any longer?"

"Rarely. We try to keep it to these specific parameters. But at times it is hard."

"Like when you have four age appropriate siblings and a younger one who is five?" asked Jaker.

"Exactly! Or one who is just turning eighteen, but their internship doesn't start until three months after their birthday."

"What is the cause of them becoming orphans?" asked Mike.

"You mean beyond losing their parents?" asked the pastor with a chuckle.

"Yes, beyond losing their parents. War, disease … Why?"

"We have very little war in Benin beyond some tribal type issues. More like family issues. We have some children whose father killed their mother, then the mother's family killed the father. A real mess," said Solomon. "Africa is a desperate place for the vulnerable ones."

"Africa strikes me as being a lot like the rest of the world but without all its makeup on," commented Jaker.

Solomon smiled and nodded. "Benin is a very interesting place. It prides itself in being the birthplace of voodoo and the birthplace of modern slavery."

"Modern slavery?" The concept puzzled Mike.

"Slavery isn't new, as you know. It has been around for thousands of years, but it's usually activated when nations conquer other people, and taking them into slavery is a way to pacify and provide for them. In many ways it was a welfare system. In Benin we sell our own to make ourselves better off. More accurately, we sell them to keep ourselves from getting worse."

"How?"

"Families struggle to feed more than four children, so when more children are born, the older ones are trafficked to slavers for a price. The families perceive it much as they do in the States when a child graduates from high school or college and it is time for them to move out and make their own way. Here, they just have to do it much sooner. The problem is they are still so vulnerable that they are almost always taken advantage of, and sometimes in the most inhumane ways."

"How much voodoo is there these days?" asked Cherish.

Jaker wasn't sure if it was her discomfort with the trafficking question or her curiosity about voodoo that caused her to change the subject.

"Very prevalent," said Solomon. "There are those who still perform the animalistic practices of our ancestors in various ceremonies and sacrifices. They still seek the favor of their gods. Even those who will tell you they are Christian still practice some of the same traditions their families have for centuries."

"How much of it is a cultural perspective?" asked Jaker.

"It is very much so. Voodoo has been ingrained into the culture for generations. The generational implications of these connections are deep and wide. Decisions made several generations ago are still being felt. Most are just simple folk who are trying to live life the best they can, following the advice and leadings of their elders. You can still see huts with white flags. You still find people preferring the witch doctors over the Western medical doctors. People still are frustrated, worrisome, and feel vulnerable, and they seek assistance from the supernatural much like they do in every culture. They don't have Jesus or a biblical worldview to help them address those cares. That is why the crusade is so important."

There was silence as each person was lost in their own thoughts for a while.

Solomon broke the silence. "I think it may be interesting for you to know that the orphanage is receiving a new child. She is a thirteen-year-old girl who will be returning from Nigeria where she was trafficked four years ago. We were able to get word to her of the death of her mother, and she has become worried about her younger siblings who stay at the orphanage. Currently, she is working with our contacts to come back to Benin."

"How exciting," said Mike from the back seat.

Solomon adjusted the rearview mirror so he could see Mike. "Yes, you would think so."

"It isn't?" asked Jaker.

"Often the child who left has returned a … shall we say … a different child. Their experiences often change them in fundamental ways. She should arrive in the next couple of days."

Everyone wanted to know what that meant, but also wanted to remain in the dark. Without seeking the answer, they sat quietly the rest of the way.

It was late afternoon when the car arrived at the home, a five-acre compound with several buildings that served as a boys' and a girls' dormitory, a common shelter for group gatherings, a building with a kitchen and dining area, and a building for visitors and class-rooms. Upon arriving the children began to gather to see who their new visitors were and chatter among themselves at the funny-looking White people. Even with their intimidating eye-scans and sizing up, the children were friendly and playful, fascinated by the hair on the men's arms and their pale skin. The trio of travelers were able to get settled in their rooms and rest a bit before their dinner of rice and chicken with slices of pineapple.

The evening was spent playing with the children and getting to know them, but they still had a bedtime curfew in order to be able to get up for school the next day. The academic year was in its closing days, but it was not over yet.

After the children went to bed, Jaker placed a call to Miss Nelson to update her on the day's events. He gave her a brief overview of what he had learned.

"What was the meeting with the pastors like?" asked The Locksmith.

"Each came invested in their own agendas and couldn't rally around a common one," replied the protégé.

"A conflict of *me faith* versus *we faith*?"

"Exactly! Each pastor was passionate about the elements he felt God had specifically revealed to him, which prompted an interjection of his priorities, hopes, and expectations. They ran circles around one another and couldn't come to a common agenda. They each knew what God was revealing to them in their own walks, their own congregations, and expected others to affirm those expectations. These were augmented by some subtle tribal differences as well. They each brought their own faith but couldn't find a common faith in which to journey together and see what God wanted to do with them as a group."

"I didn't know you knew Fon."

"I don't. Several of the pastors were from the north—"

"So there was Fulfulde, Bariba, as well as Yoruba and Fon. Therefore they spoke French."

"*Exactement!*" emphasized Jaker.

"So, a me faith/we faith conflict. Well, at least we can pray. How about Cherish?"

"We had a chance to talk a bit today. She is appearing to me to be a confused young lady, not an angry one. She isn't resentful toward her parents. She is just in a place where the environment she has grown up in has become so familiar that she is seeing the polished veneer of other environments, and it has her attention."

"As if she is tired of the same old nutritious meals and likes the taste of the frosting on the cake for dessert."

"Yes."

"Watch for opportunities to point out the benefits of the well-balanced diet she has been raised on."

"We did a little today talking about mission trips. I think she has had some limited travel that has allowed her to have some insight into the benefits of God at work in families."

"Well, again—" started Miss Nelson, and she was joined by Jaker in concluding the statement.

"At least we can pray!" They both laughed at the shared sentiment.

"Ma'am, what can you tell me of Max?"

The Locksmith explained the errand she had been vague about previously and followed up on what had happened since. "Margaret stopped at a yard sale in Yakima, on her way to Seattle, to buy a different car seat, hoping to put an extra level of protection between Abomey and the grandmother. She was concerned that there might be residual fingerprints or DNA on the car seat Santana had purchased, and she believed whatever car seat she had would have to be left with the infant. Once she had Abomey safely strapped in the used one, Max dropped the new one off at a Goodwill station."

"Ahh."

"Then she drove to a small community north of Seattle, during evening traffic, where two nights later she dropped off the car seat and baby at the community police station. Three minutes later, as an officer was leaving, the baby was noticed and taken inside. Two mornings after that, Margaret left with morning traffic. I have since heard from my contact in Seattle that the appropriate social worker was contacted. Abomey is in the system where there is a shepherd to guide our little lamb. The police have been searching for who might have delivered an infant recently. They have searched what few camera feeds they have, but it appears Margaret has successfully moved Abomey from one environment to another in a miraculously untraceable way. I expect her to return to Weiser via Portland later today."

"How about the Caldwell Police?"

"The news channels have announced that Santana D'Souza had delivered just hours prior to her being found. They believe the delivery may have occurred elsewhere, but a search of the local hospitals has been unrevealing. They have several theories. They believe she may have botched an attempt at a self-abortion. Herbs were found in the home she had been staying in that could have been used. They think whoever was there in the home with her was likely trying to help her, then became frantic and fled."

"Any suspicion toward Max?"

"The police want to question her, but the girls in Margaret's Bible study group have shared consistent stories of the attack against her by Sandy the night before, and everyone believes she was so hurt by the event that she has taken a road trip. She is not a suspect, but she will have to answer some questions, to which I don't think she will honestly be able provide any answers."

"Any news on the grandmother?"

"She is in contact with the local police departments hoping to find an abandoned infant, but to no avail. I also know she is looking in Denver, which we expected. But she isn't looking for a baby in Seattle, and Seattle isn't looking for a grandmother out of the Pacific Northwest. The belief is that if Abomey can get into a solid foster care environment, she will ultimately be adopted, and we expect that the grandmother will not risk the scrutiny it would take to get Abomey back."

"She has too much to lose?" asked Jaker.

"Presumably," responded Miss Nelson.

"It sure would be nice to hear she made it safely to a home that is one yard from the gates of heaven."

"Very true, John Quinton Riley, but I have found that heaven and hell are actually only two yards from one another. The only difference between being one yard from the gates of hell and one yard from the gates of heaven is where you put your face and where you put your back."

"Good point."

"I believe it is good night for you, Mr. O'Malley."

"And I believe it is good morning for you, ma'am. I will call again later."

CHAPTER 12

THE ARMOR OF LIGHT

Ontario, Oregon
a few days later

Consistent with previous visits, the sally port door hissed as it slid open and then clanked into position. "Good morning, ma'am," declared the officer in the master control room.

"Good morning, David," replied The Locksmith. The first sally port door clicked again as it began to slide closed.

"Ma'am, how long have you been coming to this facility?" asked David.

The Locksmith held up her ID that in previous visits had been attached to her lapel. Today, it was attached to a lanyard, a transition she had made since last week. She let it drop as she spoke. "I have been coming for about seven years now."

"Are you seeing the same guys?"

She smiled as the past seven years flashed through her mind. "Yes, for the most part. I have had only one change in seven years."

"Ma'am, if you don't mind me asking, why do you keep coming?"

She paused as she pondered not the answer to the question but to consider the rationale behind the question. "David, I find a lot of personal value in coming. I truly enjoy my discussions with the men I meet with in the 9:00 a.m. callout group, and I have been pleased in the transformation I have seen. I have met people on the street locked in tighter chains than those worn by the men I meet with in here. True freedom cannot be bound with bars, cuffs, and chains. And I know true bondage can occur in the privacy of one's own home."

This time the officer behind the darkened glass paused as he pondered the rationale behind the answer. "I guess you're right," said the voice through the intercom. "Keep up the good work, ma'am."

"Thank you, David, you too."

There was another click and hiss as the other sally port door slid open and Miss Nelson began to make her way to the Religious Services room when the voice on the overhead intercom called out, "Attention in the institution! It's 8:45 a.m. 9:00 a.m. callouts, line movement, line movement!"

There was the usual bantering back and forth as the men entered. Once the group had assembled Miss Nelson opened with her usual greeting. "Good morning, gentlemen! It is good to see each of you. Shall we get started?"

"Yes, ma'am," the men responded.

"Mr. Gascon, would you do us the honor of opening in prayer?"

"Dear God, we come to You today to ask for Your guidance. Please open our hearts and our minds to what You have for us today. Amen."

"Amen," said everyone else.

"Thank you, sir. I believe today we are picking up our previous discussion of spiritual warfare with the armor of God. But before we do, I think you were also going to read from Daniel and Isaiah. Did you get a sense of the stagehands at work?"

"Interesting perspective, ma'am," said Mr. Hanson. "After reading those passages, I get the feeling that a lot of what we see at work in the world, say on the political front, is being influenced by supernatural beings." The other men nodded their agreement.

"But are they involved in only geopolitical activities?" asked The Locksmith.

The men were quiet and uncertain of what was being asked.

The elderly woman tried a different approach. "Have you ever been involved in a disagreement with someone and felt the tension rise in the conversation, then afterward you found yourself antagonistic against the person you had the disagreement with?”

“What do you mean?” asked Mr. Williamson.

“Imagine an argument with another person in which an agreement is not arrived at. Have you ever experienced the tension roll over into your interaction a bit later where you find yourself either saying out loud, or at least in your mind, some sassy remark or using a condescending or confrontational tone, perhaps not even toward the person you had the disagreement with?”

“Are you saying sometimes when we are at odds with one another, and if we aren’t careful, there is carryover of the hurt or bad feelings we are having into other interactions?” Mr. Williamson seemed to be catching on.

“Who has experienced that?” asked The Locksmith. She could see in their eyes that they each felt they had, but no one was willing to admit it until they had a better idea of where this was going.

“Are you saying these supernatural beings are involved in ways other than the geopolitical activities we read about in Scripture this week?” asked Mr. Williamson.

“Someone look up Ephesians chapter four verses twenty-six and twenty-seven.”

“I will,” Mr. Johnson offered.

“When Mr. Johnson has found this verse, we will have him read it aloud. As he does, ask yourself why Paul has given us this advice?”

“Got it,” said Mr. Johnson. Miss Nelson nodded toward him. “‘In your anger do not sin, do not let the sun go down while you are still angry, and do not give the devil a foothold.’”

“The supernatural beings are at play in our emotions?” asked Mr. Williamson.

“You tell me. What does it mean to give the devil a foothold?”

“It sounds to me like there is something in our emotions that we have to be careful about or the devil will use it,” said Mr. Perez.

“I think I can see that happening at times,” followed Mr. Williamson. “There are times when the emotions of the moment can feed the emotions of the next, and if you aren’t careful, they can be negative emotions.”

"Don't you think the same is true of positive emotions as well?" asked The Locksmith.

"You mean being loving or joyful and having it spill over into future interactions?" asked Mr. Gascon.

Miss Nelson raised her eyebrows and gave a nod.

"I think that is also true," announced Mr. Johnson.

"What does this have to do with the armor of God?" interjected Mr. Perez.

"Before we enter that discussion, I want to reiterate an important point. Do you remember our previous discussion about the three fronts in spiritual warfare?" she asked

"Yes, the world, the flesh, and Satan—or the supernatural beings," responded Mr. Perez.

"The point I want to reiterate is that it is never a one-front war, and seldom a one-front battle. It is often a multifront attack. The rogue supernatural beings can use the flesh or the world, as we have discussed here. The Enemy can use our fleshly emotions and our thoughts, which are formulated by the perspectives of the world, to do us harm."

"And we use the armor as our defense?" asked Mr. Perez.

"I will say we can only effectively engage in spiritual warfare if we fight in the armor of God."

"Okay, so how do we do that?" queried Mr. Gascon

"First we must realize this isn't our armor," began Miss Nelson. There were some blank stares.

"In Isaiah the fifty-ninth chapter, we read of the Lord's displeasure that there was not any justice on Earth. There was no one who was intervening on behalf of those who were suffering the injustice so 'He put on righteousness as a breastplate, and a helmet of salvation upon his head.' This is the very armor He uses in the analogies of when He fights His battles. So when we put on His armor, we are fighting in His righteousness and through His salvation." Miss Nelson could see the blank faces of uncertainty. "Let us say you are being confronted by an accusation of having said something that you did say, but in a way that you didn't mean, and it is tending to make you angry because you are not being understood. More accurately, you are being misunderstood. There is an injustice in your cause. The injustice results in a righteous indignation because you have been wronged. However, if you aren't careful, Satan can use this as a foothold and drag you down a path you never intended. How is this best defended in spiritual warfare?"

"Realizing your righteousness doesn't depend on you being right in this situation?" asked Mr. Johnson.

"Correct. What does your righteousness depend on?" followed up Miss Nelson.

"On the righteousness of Jesus Christ?" Mr. Johnson said, beaming.

"On the righteousness of Jesus Christ," Miss Nelson smiled back as she parroted the response.

"What about the helmet of salvation? How does that fit?" asked Mr. Gascon.

Miss Nelson turned toward him and nodded. "Much the same way. Remember the story of David and Goliath? David is heard through the camp asking about what Saul was offering for the one who would remove Goliath. Saul hears about it and summons David to his tent. Saul questions David and becomes persuaded to allow the lad a chance. So David is allowed to put the king's armor on. David ultimately refuses, but why?"

The men were looking around group, but Mr. Williamson spoke up first. "Because they didn't fit."

"In essence that is true. But I wonder if God is instructing us that David cannot fight for a spiritual truth using physical armor. He understood that this physical battle represented a spiritual battle. He believed in the cause of God. You can hear it in the way he talked to Goliath. He believed in the truth that God had a design and a purpose for the people of Israel, and he knew that trusting in the armor of a king was like trusting in his horses and chariots. Mr. Williamson, would you read the first three verses of the twentieth chapter of Deuteronomy?"

It took a moment, then Mr. Williamson obliged. "'When you go out to war against your enemies and see horses, chariots, and an army larger than yours, do not be afraid of them; for the Lord your God, who brought you out of the land of Egypt, is with you. When you are about to go into battle, the priest is to come forward and address the army, saying to them, Hear, O Israel, today you are going into battle with your enemies. Do not be fainthearted or be afraid; do not be alarmed or terrified because of them. For the LORD your God is He who goes with you to fight for you against your enemies, to give you the victory.'"

Miss Nelson followed up, "The seventh verse of the twentieth Psalm says, 'Some trust in chariots, and some in horses: but we will remember the name of the LORD our God.' Part of the reason so many believers struggle in their spiritual walk is because they keep trying to fight a physical, worldly, or fleshly battle in physical, worldly, or fleshly armor. They can't believe, or trust, that victory and righteousness come from the Lord. They keep putting on physical armor and trusting in horses and chariots, all of which are symbolic of worldly strategies and tactics—or better yet, armor."

"What do you mean, physical armor?" asked Hanson.

"I mean trusting in the usual defensive strategies of the world and the flesh. Strategies like advocating and fighting for your rights, getting angry, and using physical force or invoking a legal defense if necessary. Can you think of others?"

"Undermining others' credibility," offered Mr. Williamson.

"Lying or cheating," offered Mr. Hanson.

"Ridiculing or embarrassing your adversary," said Mr. Perez.

"Sometimes you have to fight for what is right," said Mr. Johnson

Mr. Williamson brought it back full circle. "You're telling us that by using these strategies we are trying to fight a spiritual battle with earthly armor and weapons?"

Miss Nelson sat there, allowing time to again do its work.

"Are you saying we shouldn't speak the truth and advocate for it? That we are to never get angry when the truth is being trampled on?" asked Mr. Williamson.

"Remember in the previous verse it says *in your anger do not sin*. We have spoken before about prudence and wisdom living together.

Advocating for the truth and promoting justice is prudent and wise. Lying, cheating, and embarrassing your adversary may be prudent by worldly standards, but it isn't prudent according to the wisdom of God to do those things, which is why God has instructed us that in our anger we shouldn't sin. Because in our emotional anger Satan is going to be at work trying to defeat us by leading us into prudent but unwise worldly or earthly strategies to fix or overcome our problems. When we fall victim to this, we are living defeated lives and never get the chance to see God show up arrayed for the battle He has said He is going to fight for us. We must remember what we have been taught in Ephesians chapter six verse twelve: 'We wrestle not with flesh and blood, but against principalities, against powers, against the rulers of the darkness of this age, against spiritual hosts of wickedness in the heavenly places.' It is the rogue supernatural beings who are trying to twist a normal response into an ungodly response that is based in a worldly or fleshly perspective." The Locksmith paused again.

The men sat there, thinking through what was being said. "What about the belt of truth? How does that fit in?" asked Mr. Gascon.

"I think it very interesting how the belt of truth is the first thing mentioned. I think it has to do with how important it is," began Miss Nelson. The men listened patiently. "The importance of truth is where it comes from and how it is determined. We all live in the post-modern era where individuals claim for themselves the right to interpret the reality they are experiencing and expect that perspective to be as equally valid as everyone else's. For example, Mr. Hanson here may state his belief is that I am fat. I might find the statement to be a harsh overstatement, while Mr. Perez might think it brutally honest, and Mr. Johnson might consider it a fanciful joke. The question is, where is the truth?"

"For the record, you're not fat, ma'am," said Mr. Hanson. The others chuckled.

"Too late, sir, you have already offended my honor." Miss Nelson feigned hurt. "The problem lies in the fact that we exist as what I call subjective beings. All our statements are based on our perceptions, which are fallible. But it isn't true with God. God isn't like human-ity because He is an objective being. He doesn't learn; He knows. When He expresses Himself, things come into being. The first les-sons of the Bible are that He speaks and therefore things come into existence. God's knowledge isn't like our knowledge. What was the one thing God reserved for Himself and didn't give Adam and Eve a right to obtain?"

"The Tree of Knowledge of Good and Evil," stated Mr. Perez.

"Correct. And why did He do that? Was He saying we couldn't know good from evil?" She looked around the group. They appeared to be following but were quiet. "I doubt that. I think He was say-ing we humans are incapable of knowing … the *way* He knows. The reality of this life we experience as human is that when something is discovered, then we know it. But for God, when He knows some-thing, *it becomes.*"

The guys were starting to struggle again.

"Imagine a baseball game where it is the bottom of the ninth, the game is tied, there is the winning runner on second, the count is full, and there are two outs. The pitch is a fastball down the middle of the plate, and the batter slaps a line drive over the shortstop's head. The second base runner has a great jump and is waved home for the scoring run, but the centerfielder has played it near perfectly and is going to make a play at home. The throw is perfect. The catcher is perfectly positioned, and the ball is on-line to the plate. The runner slides and the dust settles, then both teams are celebrating their ver-sion of the truth, along with the fans of both teams. But this is a very special game in that it is being umpired by the man Abner Doubleday.

"One cannot say that it was a tie and give it to the runner. One cannot say the ball made it first and therefore give it to the catcher. Is the runner safe or out? It really doesn't matter what any of us—the players or the fans—think. The only thing that matters is what Mr. Doubleday thinks, and he is the only one who can declare the runner as safe or out. Only the umpire—and in this case, he is the one who authored the rules of baseball—is the one who can make the call regardless of what others may say after the fact because his is the only opinion that is going to get registered. He alone will decide the verdict, and there is no one else to appeal to. And every reality of truth has its foundation in this: God alone decides what is truth and what is not, what is good and what is not. God Himself separated light from darkness and called the light day and the darkness night."

The men seemed to ponder this point with a bit more clarity as she could see the processing at work on their faces.

"When we begin to search for truth and cling to it with this perspective, I think our spiritual walk begins to change. When we have become convinced of what God has said is true, then what other people say, what the world says, or what our flesh says really doesn't hold the strength it used to. Combine being clothed in His righteousness with His helmet of salvation, and you begin to see how the defense against each of the fronts begins to take place."

"I like the idea that truth is rooted in the person, or character, of God," said Mr. Williamson.

"It is important to realize it is not the other way around," pointed out Miss Nelson.

"What do you mean?" asked Mr. Perez as he looked up from his notes.

"I think people believe God has to do what is just. But in truth, God doesn't have to consider what is just in order to do the just action. That would be characteristic of a subjective being. Remember, God is an objective being. He is incapable of doing anything other than to act justly, and this relates to why Jesus had to die. If God was going to act justly, then He had to solve the problem of how to call something unrighteous righteous and to do it in a just way."

Again, there were some tortured looks on the faces of the men.

"I think a good place to try and understand this is through act of forgiveness. How can God forgive? Socrates is attributed with having said, 'It may be that the Deity can forgive sins, but I do not see how.' If God is an objective being who defines justice and righteousness, then He is incapable of acting outside of His own character, which is why we can't stand in His presence in our own righteousness. Our own righteousness is insufficient. I believe this is one of the reasons God must be a triune God. The essence of forgiveness is in the taking upon oneself the pain of the offense and not shifting it back onto the offender, or a different person. This is why so many people struggle in seeing God as a Father who would kill His only Son as payment for the unrighteousness of humanity. It begs the question of how does an unrighteous act, or state, or sin get forgiven by an unrighteous act of killing someone else who isn't guilty in its place? And I agree it sounds like the Father is killing the Son, and that knowledge is hard to attribute to a holy God. But if the Father and the Son are the same God, and in essence the same being, then that God can take on the pain and penalty of the offense and not hold the sinner accountable for their sin."

The looks on the faces of the men were just as tortured as they were moments ago. "I don't think I'm getting anything about what you are saying," said Mr. Johnson.

The Locksmith smiled and decided it was indeed getting complicated. "Let us leave that seed planted as a potential thought and water it with this: How does God show His immense, transcendent power as a Designer, Architect, and Creator?"

"We see His supreme power as Creator in the majesty of His creation," reported Mr. Perez.

"Yes, by allowing humanity to see it in the majesty and complexity of His creation," said Miss Nelson. "How does He show His supreme love as God?"

"Ew, I don't know," responded Mr. Perez as the other guys chuckled.

"What does the Bible say about love?" asked The Locksmith.

"I don't know," repeated Mr. Perez, again receiving chuckles. "It doesn't take long to find the limits of my knowledge." The Locksmith smiled back at his honesty.

"Someone read John chapter fifteen verse thirteen," asked Miss Nelson.

"'Greater love hath no man than this, that a man laid down his life for his friends,'" read Mr. Williamson.

"But what does the Bible state about Jesus' love?" asked the elderly woman.

"'For when we were yet without strength, in due time Christ died for the ungodly.'" All eyes turned to Mr. Hanson, who had closed his eyes and was quoting from memory. "'For scarcely for a righteous man will one die: yet peradventure for a good man some would even dare to die. But God commendeth his love toward us, in that, while we were yet sinners, Christ died for us.'" As he opened his eyes they were moist, and tears were welling up, but he continued on. "'Much more then, being now justified by his blood, we shall be saved from wrath through him. For if, when we were enemies…'" He began to get choked up and his voice cracked. "'We were reconciled to God by the death of his Son, much more… being reconciled… we shall be saved by his life.'" The others sat silently absorbed in their own thoughts now, staring at the floor or across the room.

Moments later Mr. Williamson whispered, "I was a horrible person. The damage and pain I inflicted left me feeling separated from the rest of humanity. When I came here, I knew I would never be going home." He sniffled to clear himself. "Not because it was a life sentence, but because I knew that home no longer existed. The home that should have been filled with love was instead filled with hate and resentment."

He looked across the circle at his brothers, who were affirming that they understood and what he was saying was resonating with them. He smiled at them and finished his thought. "This meeting time we share is the closest I will ever come to being at home again until the day I go to Him or He comes to get me."

The group was silent for a long time.

"God shows the extravagance of His love by allowing humanity to get itself into such a precarious and vulnerable condition that nothing but the death of God Himself could liberate them," she explained. "Many of those who struggle with a Father killing His Son to facilitate forgiveness instead cling to a view of a Messiah who is victorious over sin, death, and all the rogue supernatural beings. Which I also believe is true but not because of His death. I believe it to be true because of His resurrection. And I struggle to see how the brokenness of the relationship between God and humanity can be fixed without both. The death of God Himself in the person of Jesus Christ allows God to truly forgive and allows the relationship to reset to one that is right every time a relationship that is damaged by sin is made new from God's perspective. The fact that He is able to reenter the relationship is because He was resurrected. He is killed by the damage in the relationship but keeps coming back because He has triumphed over sin and the grave."

"Is it okay to say hallelujah?" asked Mr. Johnson.

"I think it is more than appropriate. If not at this point, where would one ever appropriately say hallelujah?" she said approvingly.

"Hallelujah!" said several of the men.

Miss Nelson noticed Mr. Williamson seemed lost in thought. "Is that not good news Mr. Williamson?"

"Yes, ma'am, it definitely is. I was just wishing the ones I have wronged could forgive me the same way. I wish I had known then what I know now. I tend to think things would have been different," he mused. The room was silent for several seconds as each person in the room reflected on how that applied to them as well.

"Amen," said some of the others.

"Well, I think this leads us to having our feet shod with the preparation of the gospel of peace," continued The Locksmith.

"How does this help us fight the three fronts in spiritual warfare?" asked Mr. Perez.

"I find it interesting that this is the only piece of armor that is one of readiness, or preparation. It isn't the gospel of peace it is the preparation, or readiness, of the gospel of peace. I also think it is an interesting type of gospel when talking of warfare. In my life it has played out in a few different ways, but I think the most helpful way to consider this is in realizing how important it is to have your heart motivated for advancing the kingdom of God according to His plan." Miss Nelson paused briefly, then added, "I think this is our invitation to have our own moment in Gethsemane."

"Uh-oh," said Mr. Williamson. The others chuckled again, and many were writing notes.

Miss Nelson smiled as well. "Anyone who believes there is another way to heaven other than through Jesus doesn't understand what was happening in Gethsemane on the night that Jesus was betrayed. Jesus was asking for a different plan. He basically asked God to make it possible for us to get to heaven by some other way then Him dying a brutal and humiliating death."

"And the answer was no," said Mr. Gascon.

"Exactly," followed Miss Nelson. "Remember, the gospel of peace is brought into effect by a means that was not peaceful for Jesus, and Gethsemane is where He made Himself ready. That night He prepared Himself for the part He was going to play in bringing forth the gospel of peace."

The men again fell silent.

"We are the body of Christ, correct? Are you prepared to be the body of Christ to advance the gospel of peace? Are you ready to be broken and spilled out for the gospel of peace? Are you prepared to do what it takes to advance the good news of the kingdom of God, even if it means pain and suffering, being wronged, being humiliated, and perhaps death if it brings the gospel of peace into someone else's life? What if that death is not in one swell swoop but requires of you one drop of your blood at a time?" Miss Nelson again allowed for a pause to give silence a chance to work. "See what I mean?" Heads nodded as minds considered the implications of what she was saying.

"Please tell me the shield of faith is actually one that is pretty straightforward?" pleaded Mr. Hanson.

"Heh," snickered Miss Nelson, "I do believe it is straightforward. I think the key is in the verse that tells you what to do with it."

"'To extinguish all the flaming arrows of the evil one,'" summarized Mr. Gascon.

"Yes, the rogue stagehands will try to distract you from this spiritual perspective. They will attempt to distract you with everything from hunger to a television program. It is amazing that when the Holy Spirit begins to lead or instruct us how soon the phone rings. Or when we decide to go next door to visit the neighbor with our feet shod with the preparation of the gospel of peace, we all of a sudden hear of another pressing issue or concern that may be more urgent but not nearly as important as the leading of the Spirit. We may actually find good things to distract us from the godly thing He has put on our heart. Or perhaps the adversary will try and bring us into condemnation, or mess with our emotions, traffic in our pain, or find any other means to hinder us."

"What about the sword of the Spirit? Is that fairly straightforward also?" asked Mr. Gascon.

"Yes, as many of you know, the identity of this weapon is defined for us in Hebrews chapter four where we learned the Word of God is living and active and sharper than any double-edged sword. The Lord Himself demonstrated its usage at the time of His temptation," answered Miss Nelson.

"Isn't that where Jesus answers the temptations by quoting Scripture?" asked Mr. Williamson.

"In essence that is correct. I think we can connect this to the need for the belt of truth. Satan is trying to shape a different perspective for Jesus that is other than the one that God has defined, and it is similar to what we have seen in the Garden of Gethsemane. Satan tries to get Jesus to obtain His God-given objectives through paths God has not ordained."

"He wants Jesus to be prudent but not wise?" observed Mr. Johnson.

"Indeed," replied Miss Nelson.

"What do you mean 'paths God has not ordained'?" asked Mr. Hanson.

"Satan was challenging God's plan. In Matthew chapter four verse four, he said, 'If thou be the Son of God, command that these stones be made bread.' He was saying if You are, then do it this way. Satan was suggesting to Jesus that He could gain people's allegiance through giving them something to eat. Regardless, Satan wanted Jesus to act in a manner inconsistent with what God had ordained. Jesus says, 'It is written, Man shall not live by bread alone, but by every word that proceedeth out of the mouth of God.'"

"Isn't that what Satan was trying to do?" asked Mr. Hanson

"Well, it may have been, and I am not trying to argue against that. I was just struck by the fact that the word *Man* in the King James

Version is capitalized. And it got me thinking that the Man Jesus was referring to might have been Himself. I find it interesting that in this case Jesus could be saying something like, 'The Spirit Himself led me into this desert. The Spirit himself has ordained this fast. I am not going to break my fast by my own hand, by the expression of my own will. I am here until I hear from my Father, and that is more than food.' I think he would rather die of hunger for food than die from hunger for a Word from His Father."

"So the sword of the Spirit is the Word of God, and we are to use it to actively define the proper way to think, feel, and hold our perspectives and to defend against improper thoughts, attitudes, and perspectives that the world, flesh or Satan wants to give us?" clarified Mr. Hanson.

The other men stared at him with raised eyebrows and dropped jaws. Mr. Gascon smiled and said, "This class isn't for credit, Hanson. You don't get bonus points for being a kiss—"

"Whoa! Whoa!" said Johnson.

The men laughed. Mr. Perez said, "Oh, Gascon, you almost said a naughty word this time!"

"Shoot!" said Mr. Gascon. "And I had been doing good too."

"Do the other temptations teach us about this piece of the armor in a similar fashion?" asked Mr. Hanson, eager to understand more.

"The whole study of the temptation of Jesus in the desert yields a lot of benefits that make the study well worth the time," said Miss Nelson. "I would make mention of one other point beyond the one you have summarized for us already, which is you must be certain as to what God has told you because Satan will try to use the Word of God against you—just as he did with Jesus in His final two temptations."

"Kind of like getting shot with your own gun, or stabbed with your own knife," said Mr. Perez.

"Somewhat, yes," acknowledged Miss Nelson. "But here you can trust in the whole counsel of God. In fact, you will want to submit anything you think the Lord is telling you by testing it with this question: Does it conform with the whole counsel of God?"

"What do you mean, *whole counsel of God*?" asked Mr. Johnson.

"If you only take a few portions of Scripture, you can make them say almost anything you want them to. If you read about the Ten Commandments but don't read about the sin sacrifices, then you will get a warped understanding of God. If you read the Old Testament but not the New Testament, you will get a warped sense of who God is. This warped understanding will undo your belt of truth, causing your armor to fall apart."

"And is prayer straightforward as well?" asked Mr. Johnson.

"I don't think it is quite as straightforward. For most people, prayer is just a way to try and convince God that our will is best, or needed, or to bring God's attention to our problems. As if all God wants is to be asked. And though I do think God likes to be asked, and we are encouraged to ask for His intervention, His participation, His grace, and His mercy, I think the component we lack is the one that can have a bigger impact on our spiritual battles—His perspective. I think the outcomes of our spiritual battles are greatly impacted by our perspective. We will do much better when we enter the battle with the heavy artillery of prayer. Seeking not to let God know what is in our heart, as if He doesn't already know, but to let God reveal His heart and mind to us as we seek to understand His way."

"How do we do that?" asked Williamson.

"I find prayer is like a conversation. I learn so much when I ask why, just like a little child. Often, I think you can learn a lot when you realize things are as they must be, though perhaps not as they ought to be, and if we ask ourselves why things are playing out a certain way, the Holy Spirit begins to reveal all kinds of interesting perspectives. This is also a better application of faith. According to Hebrews chapter nine, what is in the ark of the covenant, also called the ark of testimony?"

Blank stares were all around for a few minutes until Mr. Perez closed his Bible and said, "The two tablets of stone of the ten commandments, Aaron's rod, and the jar of manna."

"You are right. Why are they there? What do they testify to, or of?" asked Miss Nelson. Mr. Perez turned in his seat and looked at Mr. Johnson as if it was his turn to answer, and everyone chuckled.

"Well, I don't know," said Mr. Johnson sheepishly.

"In my faith they symbolize or testify three important things to me. The tablets testify to God's sovereign right to define what is right and wrong. Aaron's rod testifies to God's power. It was an almond branch that budded, and only God can bring life out of death. And the jar of manna testifies to His provision. God can define by declaring He is all powerful, and He is able to provide food for the multitude, even in the desert.

Mr. Hanson attempted to see if he was following. "It sounds like you are saying He knows what is right. He is able to achieve what is right. And He is passionate enough to do something about it."

"Correct, and if that is true, then it seems like a fair question to ask what is the situation I am looking at and praying over testifying to? Why are things the way they are? Is it really because God isn't sure what to do? No, because He is all-knowing. Is it really because God isn't capable of doing what needs to be done? No, because He is all-powerful. Is it really because God doesn't care enough to do anything about it? No, because He is passionate enough to intervene. So doesn't it make sense that when we see problems or situations that aren't the way they ought to be, perhaps instead of telling God what we think He needs to do, we should quietly ask the Spirit of God for discernment into why things are as they are and begin to pray earnestly for the resolution of what needs to happen in us, or others, and not just pray for a change in the situations or circumstances? We tend to pray too much for a change in the circumstances. Remember, the winds and the waves still know who He is, and they still obey Him even to this day. The circumstances are easy to change. We should be praying for the change not just in our circumstances, but for change that needs to happen inside of us."

This again had the men thinking, and hands were cramping as they scribbled away in their notebooks.

"All right, I think that is a great place to leave it for this week, gentlemen," said Miss Nelson as she picked up her well-worn Bible. "I would recommend that before we meet again you read the book of Judges, then we can talk a bit about how that might fit into our walk.

Oh, and gentlemen, I am not sure when I last said this, but I hold you to Acts chapter seventeen verse eleven. Don't take my word for any of this. I am only sharing with you how my faith in God works. You will not be accountable for my faith. You will stand before the throne of God based on your own. Search out Scripture every day, and don't take what I have told you as anything more than advice from an old beggarly woman offering to tell you where she found the food that sustains her. Before we go, I want to pray for you."

The men stood. "Oh, Great God of the heavens, I praise Your name and lift You up asking that You would sanctify Your name. I give you recognition and all the associated glory and honor for the things I have come to treasure. Treasures I sense that have captivated the hearts and minds of these men. I come to You this day to ask a blessing. I ask that You reveal Yourself to them in accordance to their longings and may they never be the same. I pray this because I believe Your Son died for these very reasons. Amen."

"Amen," said the men.

"Attention in the institution! It's 9:45 a.m. 10:00 a.m. callouts, line movement, line movement!" said the voice over the loudspeaker.

"Goodbye, gentlemen."

"Goodbye, ma'am," each man replied, and shook her hand as he left.

• • •

An hour and a half later Miss Nelson had just sat down to enjoy a cup of tea when a knock sounded at the door.

"Come on in, Margaret!" called The Locksmith.

The door opened, and in walked Max. "Good morning, ma'am."

"Hello, Margaret. How was your trip?"

"I can say it's been uneventful since leaving Seattle. I think my heart started to beat normally around the Kelso area."

"Have you spoken with anyone yet?"

"No, not even my dad. He wasn't home when I arrived and hasn't been home since."

"Very good. I would recommend that you not speak with anyone for now. If you could do me a favor, I need you to run a package to a friend of mine in Denver."

"You want me to drive to Denver to deliver a package?" There was a touch of uncertainty that was requesting more than a simple affirmation.

"Yes, I have something for a friend, and I sense that having you deliver it for me might make it possible for you to explain your long absence from the usual social media haunts with something other than a simple trip to Seattle."

"Portland wasn't enough?"

"From what I remember, you seemed very upset after your encounter with Sandy, and it might do you good to spend plenty of time processing the whole event. Especially if you were to find out something bad had happened and were being asked lots of questions."

Max paused for a moment and realized that she had focused more on her thoughts about the passing of Sandy and what Sandy had requested her to do that next morning than she had about what happened the night before in the ceremony. That awful but necessary display Sandy had gone to extreme lengths to perform. As she was thinking she stopped for a moment and said, "It bothers me that Sandy, who seemed to be a confessing Christian, may have taken her own life."

"Is it your belief that Sandy committed suicide?" asked The Locksmith.

"It makes me wonder," Max confessed.

"Let us consider this from a more hypothetical perspective. Stick to the facts in the order they were received. In your journey of introspection, considering only the last night you saw Sandy, did she seem distraught?"

"She appeared angry and acted strangely. She said things I never thought she would ever say, especially nothing a believing Christian would say. But she did clearly explain what she said and wanted me to understand the gravity of why I should help her."

"However, that was the next morning. Given only what you … and others"—she paused only briefly enough to allow Max to grasp what was not being said—"saw that last night, if you were to find out later that she may have taken something to induce an abortion, would that surprise you?"

"If you take out that last night, then yes it would surprise me, because I now have a deeper knowledge of who she was and what she was facing. But if you suggest I only consider what happened that night with the girls as witnesses, then I am no longer certain it would surprise me."

"So, if others were considering that her horrific voodoo-style episode was an act of desperation by an unwed mother so she could escape ridicule and possibly finish school, then would suicide be a reasonable conclusion?"

"Yes, I think it would. Are you hinting that Sandy focused on generating a specific perception and you want me to keep that in mind?"

"I am. However, I believe the issue you were struggling with was the spiritual state of a young woman who may have taken her own life. Correct?"

"Yes, it bothers me."

"I actually see something different. I see a young Christian mother who sacrificed her own life to prevent a tragedy from happening to the one person she felt it her responsibility to protect with her whole life. I see a young woman who knew the life that her daughter would be facing and had come to realize that there is no greater love than to lay down your life for another. I don't think she would do anything less than everything within her power."

"Perhaps you are right. I hope you are right," said Max.

"Let's get you on your way so you can connect with your friends and find out all that has happened since you left the faux voodoo party while trying to forget the following morning," concluded Miss Nelson. Moments later Max was on her way to Denver with an envelope.

CHAPTER 13

LONGING FOR HOME

Ado-Ekiti, Nigeria
early the next week

As Christina awoke the sun was not yet up, but to say the day was already hot wasn't really being honest. It was always hot. In truth, it was either bearably hot or unbearably hot. For now, it was bearably hot. Later it might be different and likely would be.

For the past four years every day had been the same. She would arise before the sun and collect her peanuts and begin making her way, along with two other girls, to the market where they would sell as many bags of peanuts as they could. It wouldn't matter how many they sold; the amount would never satisfy their mistress. Christina would return late in the day with her companions and receive their beatings for not selling enough, then be sent to bed with what was called reduced rations of food, which never made sense as none of them had ever received full rations. Then that night the master would wander into their room and take advantage of one of them.

The next morning the mistress would speak harshly to them, berating and beating them as worthless as she tried to determine which girl her husband had been with that night and heap a double portion of tongue lashings and slaps upon that girl. Usually the mistress couldn't determine which girl had been targeted, so she ended up beating and cursing each of them in their turn.

None of that really mattered to Christina. Today was filled with hope that would overshadow the number of beatings, the amount of cursing, and whatever the temperature would end up being. The hard task of the day wasn't the selling of peanuts or avoiding the mistress, it was stuffing the hope she had inside deep down so no one would know or even suspect. If anyone got wind of what was about to happen, the mistress or master would change up the routine or accompany her all day long. If one of the other girls became suspicious, they would nag her to be allowed to come along. If they weren't allowed, they would turn on her and likely alert the mistress.

The plan was simple. At some point in the day Christina would be approached by a man on a motorcycle who wore a green bandana around his neck and a yellow cord around his right wrist. When he pulled up, she was to drop everything she had and climb on. They would then speed off into the crowd and he would later transfer her to a van for the ride toward the border with Benin. Once at the border, she would then get out and receive further instructions.

"You seem anxious, Christina," said Yolanda, one of her companions.

"What?"

"Yeah, you keep looking around. You seem jumpy. What's wrong?" asked Nicole.

Both girls had been trafficked from Togo while Christina was from Benin. Though they shared a common story, they did not know one another prior to their arrival in Nigeria.

"I keep hearing Round Roda," Christina replied. The mistress was plump and had a distinctive deep voice uncharacteristic of many women. The mention of their mistress caused the girls to immediately look around and search the crowd. "Maybe we should split up. You know how upset she gets when she sees us congregating together."

The two other girls looked at one another until Nicole spoke up. "Maybe you're right." She began to move away, but Yolanda, however, didn't move.

"I don't hear her," Yolanda said, continuing to look around. "She is such a witch. If she's not careful, one night I might stick a blade under her ribs and tickle her heart with the tip. That monster of a husband of hers isn't any better. One morning he is going to wake up missing some of his anatomy." Christina smiled at the thought and kept looking around. "What is up with you? You're planning something! I know it! What are you going to do?" whispered Yolanda.

"Nothing," said Christina, afraid her attempts at stuffing down hope hadn't worked and that she'd given away too much. Hope is hard to hide. It causes you to think different, act different, talk different. Yolanda edged closer.

"You *are* planning something! Where's Nicole?" Yolanda looked up the street in the direction Nicole had walked away and could barely see her in the distance. "Nicole!" she yelled out.

Christina struck her elbow into the ribs of the other girl. "Stop it. I'm not planning anything." Irritated, she started moving in the opposite direction that Nicole went in.

"Whoa, wait! Christina, you can't leave us," said Yolanda, grabbing Christina's arm to deter her from fleeing.

"I'm not going anywhere," she lied.

"If you're leaving, you have to take us with you." Yolanda shouted louder as she was now being torn in two by the separating girls. "Nicole! Nicole!"

Wresting her arm free, Christina moved with determination. If she got trapped between these two girls, she knew they would stick to her like glue. Remaining in this mix would likely make future transport attempts all the more difficult.

"What are you doing, Christina?" Yolanda could sense something was in the works, and she didn't want to be left behind—especially if it meant being alone with an angry mistress and her husband. The beatings would be so severe that life would feel as unbearable as the heat. Caution was imperative because if they thought any of the girls were flight risks, they might sell them off to Libya where they would be trafficked to Europe and into forced prostitution.

Christina said nothing to Yolanda but instead called out, "Peanuts!" while attempting to look as normal as possible as she walked up the street and away from Nicole. "I have peanuts for sale!" The situation had turned difficult. She could tell Yolanda still felt in the dark about what was to unfold. Also, she knew that if her rescuers were watching, they would be getting nervous. If they indeed had their eyes on her, Christina might have a chance to break away. She'd imagined her rescuers pulling up, then off she would run to try and reach the motorcycle before Yolanda did. If she and Yolanda arrived at the same time, she would not allow Christina her freedom because it would cost Yolanda and Nicole too much.

"Peanuts!" Christina called again, working her way toward a crowded area of the market. People were congregating in a grassy area in the center of town, celebrating with dancing and singing. Christina believed if she could get into that group, then she might be able to shake loose from Yolanda, who was trying to board a ship about to set sail.

"Yolanda, I have work to do, and so do you!" She again pulled free and yelled with more force than before. "Peanuts!"

Across the square on the other side of the grass sat a motorcycle with a rider wearing a green bandana and a yellow wristband, watching her.

"Yolanda! What are you doing?" said a distinctive woman's voice from about thirty feet away. "Why aren't you working?"

In that moment Christina yelled, "Peanuts!" then pulled free from Yolanda once again. Yolanda froze in place, staring at her mistress. Without another thought, Christina turned into the crowd and made her way toward the motorcycle.

"Christina! Stop! Where do you think you are going?" called out the mistress, who had finally sensed something was wrong.

Christina had no intention of paying her any heed. Once inside the mob of people, she grabbed the bags of peanuts and began ripping them open and tossing them into the air. She then reached into her pockets and pulled out the cash she had made earlier in the day and threw it into the air. The elation of the crowd seeing money sparked a melee.

"Christina, stop!" yelled the mistress, and the race was on. Christina began elbowing her way through the crowd while her mistress grabbed Yolanda, forcing her to run alongside to help stop Christina.

It wasn't much of a head start, but Christina hoped it would offer enough of an advantage. She was becoming desperate as she worked her elbows forcefully through the crowd, knocking bystanders and tripping many times. Finally, her eyes locked on the motorcycle. The rider stoked the bike to life and revved the engine to offer motivation.

Just then she could hear her mistress yell, "Michael! Michael! Christina! Stop, Christina!"

To her right she saw her master bent over near some cars, talking to a driver. When he looked up, he saw Christina running and his wife dragging poor Yolanda by the wrist with one hand, screaming. It was obvious to him a small crisis had broken out, and he immediately made a dash toward Christina.

Christina was ninety feet ahead of Yolanda and the mistress and a hundred and twenty feet from the bike, but the master was on an intercept course that would easily cut her off. This caused the mistress and Yolanda to pause briefly.

Christina turned to her left and instead of running at the bike she began running up the street in front of the motorcycle, which was revving its engine as if to continue encouraging her. The bike set off up the street on its own intercept course. Christina had turned a definite collision with her master into a foot race, and the cyclist had understood what she was trying to do.

This was the moment. It was all or nothing. If her master caught her, he would instantly put her back on the market and sell her off to European regions unknown, permanently extinguishing her chance at freedom. It was a well-known fate, and many attempts of other slaves to escape ended in such devastation, but Christina still believed trying was worth the risk because of freedom.

"Stop, Christina!" yelled her master.

She could hear his feet slapping the ground as he quickly closed the gap. She abruptly dropped to her knees, dug the toes of her right foot into the dirt, then shoved off as her left foot spun her to her right, causing her to turn and face him about waist high. The move had been so sudden that it caught him off guard. He had intended to grab her by the shoulders; instead, while trying to grab her, his balance wavered when he leaned too far forward. Christina took advantage of his moment and thrust her open palm into his groin, paralyzing him with intense pain.

He buckled with a groan while leaning forward and grasping his genitals. Christina rose to her feet and dished out more pain by driving her right knee up and into his nose. The master rolled to the ground, nose and genitals throbbing, unable to get his hands on her as he was temporarily preoccupied with properly aligning his anatomy. Christina looked at him with disdain one last time, as she turned and bolted for the motorcycle, which was now only fifteen feet away.

The mistress began yelling again, and the driver of the car squealed his tires as he pulled into traffic. The master was getting up off his knees and regaining some strength, but he was too late to do anything. When he stood, he saw Christina climb onto the motorcycle.

"Hold on tight! If you fall, I can't come back. You'll be on your own, understood?" yelled the driver. Christina nodded as she grabbed on as tight as she had ever held on to anything before. The tires spun, and smoke rose as the bike edged forward and slightly to the left until the tires grabbed hold and the bike shot forward.

The car pulled to a stop in the space just vacated by the bike, and Michael fell into the back seat as the car set out in pursuit of her.

The bike had a lead of a block and a half, which wasn't much as the people who had come to the market were flooding the streets and were slow to move out of the way. They were also just as slow to fill the space behind the riders, as if their world moved in slow-motion. The car benefited from the clearing made by the bike and didn't have as much trouble gaining speed. People weren't as shocked by the car's invasion as they had been by the bike. The distance was closing quick.

The motorcyclist started weaving through a small group of shoppers and then shot into an alleyway on the left, which wasn't as crowded, then he pulled back on the accelerator. The car didn't have quite the power of the motorcycle, but it also didn't have to avoid as many pedestrians.

A couple of quick turns allowed the bike to gain a two-hundred-yard lead. After another change in direction down another alleyway, the cyclist leaned back and said, "After a couple more turns, I am going to enter a dark, enclosed passageway and pull to a stop. You must hop off and allow another girl on. You drop back out of the light and into the shadows and wait for a brown van with a driver who has another yellow wristband like mine but on his left wrist. He will pull up where you can see him and stop. Get in and you will be safe. They will get you to the border. The people in the car should still be following us, but we will take care of them. Do you understand?"

Christina had heard what was said, but she wasn't sure her arms would let go of the body she had been clinging to. And she was certain her legs couldn't move fast enough to send her on her next mission to the van. She nodded nonetheless. The gap widened to about two hundred and fifty yards with the next turn, and by the time he slid into the passageway, it had increased to three hundred yards.

The bike screeched as it slid to a stop. "Off! Off! Off!" yelled the cyclist as another girl about her build wearing similar clothing ran out of the shadows and approached the bike. Christina knew what she needed to do but, she couldn't get her hands and legs to do what her mind was screaming for her to do.

"You have to get off now or we will all be caught, and they won't be nice!" screamed the cyclist.

The other girl grabbed her and said, "You're almost there, sister! Just get off the bike and hide!" It was something in her voice that convinced Christina that now was the time. Christina released her grip and practically fell off the bike. The other girl jumped on the bike, which then shot down the dark passageway, tires squealing. Christina was on her back and began crab-walking, pushing herself backward into the shadows as the tires of the car came screeching around the corner and shot into the passageway right past her in hot pursuit of the taillights it could see up ahead.

Christina shook uncontrollably, then started laughing and crying at the same time. She noticed the dark passageway she hid in caused the driver of the car to be unable to spot her. Thankful to be out of the bright sunlight, her heart slowed just a bit.

About three minutes later a brown van slowly came rumbling into the passageway with the driver side window rolled down. Out the window hung an arm with a yellow wristband. The side panel door slid open and a bright-eyed woman leaned out. "If you want to go home, dear one, now is the time," she said quietly.

Christina sat on the ground in the shadows with her knees pulled tight up against her chest. Tears were streaming down her cheeks. She was trembling, and not just from the coolness of the shadows. Her legs wouldn't move even if she wanted them to. She began to sniffle and then broke into a full-on cry.

The woman in the van slipped out and began to slowly work her way into the shadows in a partial squat. "Dear one, now is the time. You need to go home. You can't stay here." She bent over with her hands on her knees. As she eased into the shadows, her eyes slowly became accustomed to the darkness. The girl was wide-eyed and trembling. "Dear one, take my hand. It will be all right. But we must go."

Christina looked at the woman's eyes, then at her hands. She was strong but not forceful. She wouldn't make Christina come, but she wasn't going to leave her either. Her soft smile began to win her over.

"Come, let's get you home to your family."

"My mother has followed my father in death."

"I know, dear one, so let's find your brothers and sisters. They want to see you. In this world family needs one another to be safe, don't they? We all need that place where we can be ourselves and be accepted for who we are for no other reason than we are family."

Christina reached out and grabbed the hands of her new friend. Stumbling, she allowed the woman to help her into to the van. Once situated, the driver quickly put the van into gear and drove forward. They were just about to clear the far side of the passageway when the car that had been following the motorcycle passed them from the opposite direction. The driver of the van looked into the rearview mirror at the white eyes of the woman, who warily glanced at the car and then back at the driver. She smiled a bright, white-toothed grin as he shook his head and looked into his driver-side mirror, watching the taillights speeding out the other end.

"Michael is going back empty-handed," said the woman as she handed Christina a bottle of water and a slice of fresh papaya.

The woman sat on the opposite side of the van as Christina to give her space to let her nerves settle. She knew Christina would calm soon. They all just needed some time.

The van made its way toward the south into the wet forested lowlands of Nigeria. Upon reaching Ore, they headed west in the state of Ogun. While they traveled, the woman turned to offer Christina more water, but she had fallen asleep.

When Christina awoke, she knew quite some time had passed because the angle of the light and shadows had shifted noticeably, and the woman began preparing Christina for her trek across the border. "Dear one, you are almost home now. We can't take you across the border. None of us have the necessary paperwork. If we get caught, you will likely end up in the political system and never see your family again. But we can get you to someone who will help you cross the border and get you to your family."

Terror began to show in the eyes of the young girl. She had already been through so much. She had been betrayed by her extended family. It had actually been her uncle who came one night and took her to the slave trader. From then on, her nightmare began. The abuse came almost nonstop in one form or another; often times it came in multiple forms simultaneously. Emotional abuse was most always paired with physical abuse. Sexual abuse, unsurprisingly, seemed to entitle the abuser to inflict all three injustices at once. It was always belittling, always humiliating, and always chipped away at the mere vapors of hope that occasionally floated by until the vapors evaporated and became invisible—like air: still there but invisible and intangible, which caused her further discouragement. The thought of exposing herself to ridicule or allowing herself to be vulnerable to someone new again was almost too much to overcome.

"It will be alright, dear one." The woman seemed to sense what was going through her mind. "You will be part of a team. There will be women and men. The women are strong, and the men are there to protect you. You will be safe. No one will harm you. You must have faith, dear one. Can you do that?"

Christina shook her head no and began to pull her knees up to her chest again, her fear and trembling obvious.

"It will be fine. You will be safe. You are going home."

"I don't know what home is anymore," said Christina.

The woman looked at the driver through the rearview mirror, uncertain what to say. The driver looked back at her and then back at Christina with a heartfelt expression but no words to add. The woman addressed Christina again. "Home is anywhere that you are loved for who you are, dear one. Those who love you are your family."

"Will I see my sisters and brothers?" asked Christina.

"Yes. You are headed for the orphanage on the other side of the border where they now live. They wait for you there. Do you want to see them?" asked the woman.

"Yes," whispered Christina.

"You must walk with the team across the border, then they will transfer you to those who will take you to your family," said the woman as she reached across the van and stroked the arm of the girl.

Christina wanted to trust her. So many had used that voice to persuade her to do things, to go places, to act certain ways. They never had her best interests in mind. But they never had the softness of this lady's eyes though.

"You don't have to trust me, dear one. But you will have to eventually trust if you want to receive the blessings of home again. Those blessings never come to those who can't trust." The woman paused to allow time to have its effect. "Can you start by trusting me?" she asked.

Christina swallowed hard and looked at the hand of the woman as she held it out. The van came to a stop at the same moment the afternoon sun had gone lower in the western sky.

"You are so close, dear one. Don't give up now. Please. I need you … to find your home. I need you to love and be loved again." The woman's voice cracked, and Christina looked into her eyes and watched as the tears began to well up in the woman's eyes. Her words combined with her tears resonated with Christina and empowered her to reached out and grab hold of the woman's hands. The door slid open and the driver stepped aside.

The woman slid across the floor of the van, never letting go of Christina's hand, then stepped out of the van and guided Christina out with a gentle tug.

She turned to the driver with tears in her eyes and said, "I am going with her. She will not make it without me."

He looked at Christina and then back at the woman and knew there was nothing he could say that would change her mind. "You must be careful. This will be dangerous. The nighttime crossing of the border is risky enough, but if the Army catches you"—he nodded toward Christina—"she could go back to Michael, or more likely to the camps. You will certainly go to jail, and our daughters will be deprived of their mother."

"I can't go home to our family, to our daughters, knowing she is separated from her family."

"I know," he whispered as he bent forward and kissed her forehead. "You are in good hands, dear one," he said as he looked at Christina. He climbed into the van through the sliding door and spun round on the ball of his left foot. He pulled out a duffle bag and put in the remaining eight bottles of water, along with some fruit and nuts. Then he handed the duffle bag to his wife, who leaned in to kiss his cheek. Grabbing the door handle, the man said, "I will be back for you in four nights' time. Right here I will be waiting, for as long as it takes." He closed the door and climbed into the driver's seat and drove off.

The woman slung the bag over her shoulders and grabbed ahold of Christina's hand and headed toward the grove of trees. As they drew near, someone came out of the grove and with a whistle waved his hand. He was holding an aging AK-47. The woman began a light trot with Christina in tow, and within moments they entered the grove as the sun sank lower in the west.

The trail was barely more than a deer or rabbit trail, but the small group of fifteen slowly and silently made their way in single file. They walked for another hour until they were deep into a forested area where they stopped for the night.

They weren't allowed to make a fire out of fear it would draw attention. So the woman pulled another bottle of water and some nuts from the bag and passed them to Christina. They sat silently near one another as they chewed on nuts and drank the water.

"Go ahead and get some sleep, dear one. I will watch over you while you sleep. No harm will come. If we must go, I will wake you."

Christina looked into her eyes and then laid down as the woman rocked back on her heels and watched around the camp area. Others were clearing areas to bed down upon, and as she listened to the calming sounds of their pattering, it wasn't long before Christina drifted off to sleep. Her sleep was restless as she dreamed of Michael and the girls. Even in her dreams they persecuted her and her decision to leave. Michael felt he owned her, and the girls resented her having an escape plan when they did not. The memory of his possessiveness paired with their envy caused her to toss and turn. Once, she had to be shaken awake by the woman, who feared her verbal outbursts would disturb the others in the camp or draw attention to them from someone outside the group.

Just as the sun was coming up, the woman aroused Christina and offered her more water and nuts as well as another piece of fruit. While they were eating, a boy with an AK-47 slung over his shoulder stopped by and attempted to make small talk with Christina.

The woman rose and stood over the boy, presenting her full height. Her physical presence was imposing enough to immediately make him intimidated. She quickly began asking him questions about their trip.

"How much farther is it for my daughter and I to travel?" she asked.

He looked up at her, showing her his displeasure at being interrupted.

"Don't you know?" she said, intentionally misreading the look he was attempting to give her. She spun around and sat down in between them. "Surely you know. Or are you one of the little boys who draws the water for the men? Come on, you can tell me. How much farther? One day? Two?"

"Day and a half, ma'am. We have a full day and another half day.

But it will be very dangerous." He stood up straight, trying to cast his own emotional shadow.

"I doubt that very much," she replied. "I think if that were the case, they would have given you boys real weapons, or at least given you rounds of ammunition instead of have you carry these silly little things around."

The boy pulled the bolt back and popped out a live shell. "And I have more in my bag," said the boy, annoyed with the woman.

"Well good, then you have everything on the outside to do your job to protect us. There is only one question remaining. Do you have what you need on the inside?" said the woman.

The boy was at his limit with this nosey older woman, so he got up and let the two of them be alone.

"So a day and a half, huh? Such a short vacation," said the woman to Christina, more as a statement than a question. Her face broke into a grin as she finished.

Christina at first wasn't sure how to respond, but the moment she saw the smile she had to smile back. Smiles were no longer as easy as they were when she was a child. The smiles of innocence were gone forever. She would need new reasons to smile. *Since I no longer have a mother, it's nice to meet one who at least acts like one*, she thought. Christina nodded as she said, "Only a day and a half."

The sky was clear and the lowland forests served as cover. The heat had again moved into the unbearable range, but not because of the temperature alone; the humidity made the progress even more difficult. Christina and the woman were going through the water rather quickly, and the food was running out as well. They were trying to make their way through the shade of the forest.

The world's attention over the years had become focused on the countries of Benin and the rich and populated country to its east, Nigeria. The activity of human trafficking occurring between the two countries had been well known while the actual amount clearly hadn't. Government groups had been watching children crossing both directions, and when they deemed necessary, they moved those children into special camps and then attempted to reunite them with their families. Like many governments, they were more interested in how their solution appeared than how it really worked.

The entire day was beautiful but unremarkable. The birds were singing, the insects buzzing, and the group was substantial enough to keep the larger animals at a distance. But they weren't small enough not to draw the attention of anyone looking for a group of smugglers. As the sun was getting lower in the sky, they had stopped by a river that allowed them a chance to clean off and refresh themselves. While they were resting by the river, the woman noticed that the advanced scout had come back to the main group and was talking with the leader.

"Dear one, wait here a moment. I want to see if I can slip in close enough to hear what they are saying," said the woman as she smiled and stood to her feet. Christina looked over at the men talking and nodded as the woman washed her neck with a bandana she had dipped in the river.

She slowly made her way toward where the men were standing, all the while smiling at their traveling companions. She inched nearer and got close enough to hear them talking.

"Twenty or thirty minutes, I think," said the scout.

"Then we had better head back. We can take the trail to Idogo. I really don't want to explain why we are out here. If they start searching our bags, there will be trouble."

The woman had heard enough. She spun around as if she had forgotten something and returned to Christina.

"This is where we part ways with our companions, dear one."

"Why? What happened? What's wrong?" Christina began to panic.

"Nothing to worry us," said the woman as she began pick up her stuff and repack her duffle bag.

"What is wrong?" Christina was not comforted.

"It sounds as if the scout has found a group of people they do not want to run into. They intend to go back several miles and take a different trail. A trail that takes us the wrong way. We will slip off the trail and wait for them to leave, then wait for the other group to come through. After that, we will go on to a mission station near the border," said the woman. Seeing the fear in Christina's eyes, she added, "It will be fine. I told you I'm going to get you home. But the trail they want to take won't get you there. I will do what I have promised. Do you trust me?"

Christina looked at the group and back at the men who had grown into a small group as they began to discuss with all the men the adjustment in the plans. She signaled her agreement with a nod.

"Then we must move quickly. We must be hidden before they break up from that small discussion group because they will start to move quickly and will likely start looking for us. They will be afraid that we will give them away." The woman had finished packing and grabbed Christina's hand.

The moment she turned around, the boy who had tried to work his way close to Christina was approaching. "You need to stay with the group," he said as he thrust the barrel of his automatic rifle and his head toward the group. Just then the woman stepped awkwardly on a rock on the riverbed and stumbled into Christina, who grabbed her reflexively but was unable to keep her from falling into the water.

"Ow!" screamed the woman.

"Are you okay?" asked Christina.

"I hurt my ankle," murmured the woman. She bent down and tried to massage it. "I think I may have broken it."

The boy shook his head. He came over to where she had fallen and began to feel the ankle. The woman winced in pain. "Try to stand up!" he commanded.

The woman hobbled to her good foot and pulled Christina to her good side to help her walk. She winced with each step. The other men had begun to get the group moving back the way they had come.

"What happened?" asked the leader as he came up to the woman and Christina.

"She slipped and injured her ankle," said the boy.

The leader looked at the woman and said, "Sit down and soak your foot in the river for five minutes, then get back on the trail and catch up. If the Nigerian Police find you, you will be on your own.

When your ankle gets better, you can meet us on the trail to Iwoye. Andrew, you stay back and help them."

The boy was obviously not pleased with that instruction but said nothing. He looked at the ground, kicked a dirt clod, then looked at the girl and the woman.

The woman sat down and removed her boot, thrusting her foot and ankle deep into the water as the others set out on their journey back the way they had come.

"Five minutes, Andrew, then get them moving," said the leader. He turned and began following the main group. The boy nodded his understanding.

Within a few minutes the three were alone. A few minutes after that Andrew commanded, "Time's up! Get moving!"

"Why are we going back the way we came?" asked the woman.

"Some are out of food and we need more."

"The forest is full of food."

The boy didn't answer as they began to move out.

Ten minutes later the woman began to slow down and made like to sit down. The boy was instantly at her side to try and motivate her. He slung the rifle behind his back so he could grab the woman with both hands to force her to keep moving.

In a flash the woman grabbed his extended arm with her right hand and rolled into him like a dancer driving her left elbow into his solar plexus. As the boy doubled over, she raised his right arm and ducked backward underneath his arm so that she was now behind him. In the blink of an eye, she had mounted his back and had him in a choke hold while he was still trying to get his breath. In a matter of seconds, the young man was unconscious. The woman rolled him off of her and removed his weapon.

"Come on, dear one. We must get you home." She began running back up the trail toward where they had stopped earlier with no apparent limp at all. About fifteen yards up the trail she removed the clip and unchambered the round, tossing them into the forest to the left, then flung the rifle to the right. Fifty yards farther up the trail, she moved to the right up a slight hill away from the river and off the main trail.

Christina followed, surprised at how quickly the woman had recovered from the apparent ankle injury. "Be careful!"

"My ankle is fine. I just needed a reason to lag behind so we would be alone with Andrew. Come on! Get up here. We have to get off the trail and wait here," said the woman.

They were up the hill and off the trail, hidden by foliage, for about ten minutes when a group of thirty men could be heard coming quickly up the trail. They were talking openly with one another, and from the pieces she caught she could tell the men had spotted the footprints of the traveling companions they had just left and were trying to catch them. They were uncertain why the group had begun to double back. Regardless, it wouldn't be long, and Andrew would have company.

It took about five minutes for the group to completely pass the secluded spot where the woman and Christina had hidden themselves. Surprisingly, there were no shouts from the group when they should have stumbled upon Andrew.

The woman waited another five minutes and then began to make her way back to the trail. They continued on their way toward the border until nightfall set in, and the woman took out a torch to light their path. They walked the rest of the way to the Mission Station in silence. After making sure the station was truly abandoned, the woman and her charge slept.

The next morning they rose just ahead of the sun and were quickly on the trail. It was as abandoned as the Mission Station had been. They walked side by side, saying nothing to one another, but the woman hummed quietly to herself. Within a couple of hours, they were at the border and the woman stopped.

"Dear one, we are about to cross the border. Over the next two hills we will have crossed into Benin and will enter the village where you will meet the next group who will take you the rest of the way."

Christina looked up the trail and back down it with uncertainty.

"It will be fine, dear one. They are good people whom I have gotten to know very well, and they will take good care of you. Once you cross the border, I will have to transfer your care to them. We must part here. I have done all I can do for you."

Christina grabbed the woman and hugged her.

"We are not all that unalike, you and me," the woman whispered. "I am just twenty years further along the journey. I can tell you that the people who you are about to meet can take you to the orphanage. Trust in the Lord with all your heart, dear one, and He will help you find your way home. You will soon be with your family, but the journey home will take a longer time. But you will make it. Trust in Him."

"Thank you for everything," whispered Christina. "How can I ever repay you?"

"Do what I did. Trust in the Lord, find your way home, and then help someone else do the same." Then the woman grabbed Christina by the shoulders, spun her around, and gave her a gentle shove toward home.

CHAPTER 14

PULLING DOWN STRONGHOLDS

Ontario, Oregon
a few days later

Attention in the institution! It's 8:45 a.m. 9:00 a.m. callouts, line movement, line movement!" said the voice over the loudspeaker.

Moments later Miss Nelson was joined by Mr. Hanson, Mr. Gascon, Mr. Williamson, Mr. Perez, and Mr. Johnson. "Good morning, ma'am," said each man as he entered and took his seat.

The men were dressed in their usual blue denim jeans with the legs stamped with the orange decal labeling it the property of Malheur River Correctional Facility. Some of the men wore their dark-blue cotton T-shirts with an adherent tape attached to the left upper chest. This is where their address was marked in permanent marker identifying which housing unit, cell block, and bed that either belonged to them or they belonged to. The difference between the one or the other depended on the day, their state of mind, and, most importantly, the state of their faith.

"Good morning, gentlemen! It is good as always to see each of you. Shall we get started? Mr. Perez, would you do us the honor of opening in prayer?"

"Dear God, open our ears, and close Johnson's mouth so we can hear what You have to say to us today. Amen," prayed Mr. Perez.

"Thanks, bro," said Mr. Johnson as the others snickered.

"How is your faith today?" asked The Locksmith. It had been a while since Miss Nelson had asked them this. She really wasn't one to ask the generic, "How are you?" kinds of questions, neither was she interested in their perspectives on the weather. These questions were meaningless compared to the work she was eager to resume.

The men looked at each other and then back at her. "I feel like my faith has been doing fairly well," answered Mr. Perez. "I admit I don't feel like I understand everything we discuss. But while we talk it seems to me that we are discussin' things that have importance. And while we are talking, things feel like they make sense. I've never had that experience before. I've always been trapped in patterns of behavior and thinking that have kept me locked behind the bars of my own creating. No one ever taught me the things we are learning here, and I can feel a difference that I hope others can see."

"I feel the same way as Perez. I look in the mirror and I still see the sorry fool that came into this joint. But I don't feel like I recognize him. I feel something different on the inside. Something I never felt before I fell. I know there are people who will always see the person I used to be when they see my face," said Johnson.

"You're different, bro. I know you from way back. I knew the punk who came in here and though his face is the same, his eyes are as different—as is his heart. I wouldn't have thought twice if someone had offered me dope to shank you when you first came in here," Perez finished almost at a whisper. "But I think we are both different now."

"Ma'am, we're all different," said Mr. Williamson as he looked around the group. Then he added, "At least all of us here."

"We love to hear you explain how you see things. None of us ever heard any of this growing up. Our families..." Mr. Hanson's voice trailed off, leaving an awkward pause.

Gascon filled the space by saying, "Our families and friends were broken."

The others nodded.

Gascon attempted to be more specific. "They were all struggling to find their own way, to find meaning and purpose in life, but in their confusion and … and—"

"Lostness, they were just as hopeless as we were." Mr. Williamson filled in.

The finishing of sentences for one another left Miss Nelson with the feeling that the bond between these men had grown tight.

"Yeah, in their lostness they just showed us how to be lost," finished Mr. Gascon.

"Most of the people in my journey weren't trying to hurt me. Don't get me wrong; some were, but most weren't. They just didn't know how to guide me," Mr. Johnson said reflectively.

The Locksmith liked where the conversation was headed, but something in her spirit just wasn't sitting right.

Her mind was immediately drawn back to the discussion in front of her. "Ma'am, I think I speak for most … if not all of us," said Mr. Williamson. "We don't always understand what you are saying, and sometimes we leave this room asking more questions than were answered. But you have a way of looking at things that we have never heard before. So much of what is being said in our group here is allowing us to hear for the first time with spiritual ears. And it seems to help pull a lot of things together for us. As a result, our faith is either strengthened or encouraged because of it."

The men were nodding their agreement.

"Then my time is being well spent," Miss Nelson responded matter-of-factly. "Would it be helpful if I wrote out some of the thoughts we have discussed in greater detail so you could reflect on them when you have a bit more time? Perhaps in a journal format so that you could respond to some of the thoughts we have discussed?"

The men seemed to appreciate the offer of having some of the things discussed in written format, and they felt it would allow them to each digest the concepts at their own speed and allow them the ability to go back and reconsider some of the concepts as time went by.

"Then I will see what I can do," said The Locksmith. "In the meantime, I hope you all read the book of Judges over the past week."

The men voiced their acknowledgement in various ways, but each asserted that they had been faithful with the task they had been given. Some began opening their Bibles while others began opening their notebooks.

"Weird time," offered Mr. Gascon.

"The Judges are not the kind of Judges I am familiar with," added Mr. Perez.

"Yeah, I wasn't sure of what to make of the book. Why is it in the Bible?" asked Mr. Johnson.

"That is an excellent question, Mr. Johnson. Why is this book in the Bible?" asked The Locksmith.

There was silence for a few seconds until Mr. Perez, who felt uncomfortable with the silence, said, "Its history. It's part of the history of the children of Israel and the days before a king."

"Yes, that is true. But is that all it is?" asked Miss Nelson.

"No, it isn't. There has to be more to it," interjected Mr. Williamson.

"Why does there have to be more?" asked the elderly woman.

"The God you keep telling us about always has more. It seems He is only done feedin' when you've had enough," responded Mr. Johnson. "Like that discussion we had previously about the four different ways of interpreting Scripture. What were they?" He looked at the other guys.

"The first I remember is the literal meaning. The history is the literal meaning," pointed out Mr. Gascon.

"You're asking what other level this book is to be read at, right?" Mr. Johnson seemed to have been distracted for a moment and wanted to be sure he was back on track.

"Exactly. What other level could this be read at?" asked Miss Nelson. Her spirit was now very troubled. But the distraction of facilitating the discussion was not allowing her to focus on why. But the concern was growing, so she made a quick request of God in her heart to give her wisdom on what He wanted of her.

"Allegorical?" Mr. Williamson was checking to see if he had read Miss Nelson's signpost correctly.

"Yes." Her response was uncharacteristically simple.

Mr. Williamson rubbed his chin while Mr. Perez flicked his cheek in what looked like either a scratching of his face or the flicking of a fly. Others were opening their notebooks.

"Can someone tell me about the Principle of Expositional Constancy?"

Johnson responded, "It is the principle that says the Holy Spirit uses similitudes the same way throughout Scripture?"

"And if this is true, then what is the main similitude being used in the book of the Judges?" Miss Nelson posed the question and allowed time to tick away like a drop of water from a watering can, softening the soil with each drip. After about a minute and a half of silence, Miss Nelson asked Mr. Williamson to look up Judges chapter three and read the first two verses.

Once Mr. Williamson had found the passage, he read, "This is from the New American Standard Bible, 'Now these are the nations that the LORD left, to test Israel by them (that is, all the Israelites who had not experienced any of the wars of Canaan; only in order that the generations of the sons of Israel might be taught war, those who had not experienced it previously).'"

"Thank you."

"Yes, ma'am," said Mr. Williamson, acknowledging her gratitude.

She paused for another few seconds and asked, "Mr. Williamson, please read verse four as well, won't you?"

"Sure, 'They were to test Israel by them, to find out if they would obey the commandments of the LORD, which He had commanded their fathers through Moses.'"

"It sounds like the similitude is war," said Mr. Johnson. "Did God intentionally use these nations to test the children of Israel?"

"I am not personally convinced there is much value in determining whether God intentionally left those nations so He could use them for testing the children of Israel, or whether He used the children's inabilities, or lack of desire, to drive out these nations that resulted in them being there. I tend to think the latter is more likely."

The men stared a little blank-faced.

Miss Nelson shifted slightly in her seat. "God can remove obstacles, like a Pharaoh, or a Red Sea, or a Jericho, but if there are impediments to our journey of faith that stand as a result of our disobedience, then He often uses those results to refine us. He uses them to prove or test us."

"So the fact that the children of Israel didn't drive out or destroy all the nations in the land not only required that they be refined, it also became the means by which that refinement happened," summarized Mr. Williamson.

"And He is using the similitude of war to do it?" asked Mr. Johnson.

"He used the historical reality of war to refine the children of Israel to conform to the perspectives outlined by Moses, and He uses this historical reality as an allegory to show us many of the attributes in our own lives." The Locksmith was trying to focus in on the point she was trying to make.

"So how does this apply to us?" asked Mr. Williamson.

"There are perspectives, longings, worldly and fleshly traits that reside in each of us that remain after we have come to know the Lord, much like these other nations, and we need to war against them. I think this is why many of the problems, pet sins, and unrighteous perspectives aren't removed. They remain so that God can use them to test, prove, or, more accurately, refine us. The point is that many of the things we struggle with are not going to be removed even when we ask. It is the reason many of our prayers for removal are not answered quickly, or in the way we might like. The presence of struggles in our life results in a spiritual tension that God can use to refine His image in us, an image described by God through Moses in the Torah—or as the Greeks called it, the Pentateuch."

Some of the men were scribbling away in their notebooks while Mr. Perez was looking for another pen.

"So how does this tie into the role of the judges?" asked Mr. Williamson.

"Interesting question, isn't it? What is it exactly that the judges are actually doing?" asked the woman.

"Like I said, they ain't like any of the judges I've ever met," said Mr. Perez, still looking for a pen.

"They sound more like warriors." Mr. Williamson had his Bible open and sounded like he was talking to himself rather than the group.

The answer to the trouble she had in her spirit came to her all of a sudden. It was Mr. Hanson. He hadn't said a word since his voice trailed off and his sentence was finished by Mr. Gascon. "What was that, Mr. Williamson?"

"They don't sound like judges. They sound like warriors."

"So if they sound like warriors, but the Bible calls them judges, why is that?" asked The Locksmith.

"Because they are being *tried*," said Mr. Perez as he elbowed Johnson. "Get it, the judges are trying—" Mr. Perez stopped midsentence and sat up straight. "Now come on, man, that was a good one." He was looking at Johnson, who was still ignoring him. "Really, ya gonna do me like that?"

Then he looked at Miss Nelson. She was looking at him with her head slightly cocked to the right and her eyebrows raised.

"Wait, I'm on to sumpthin!" A smile returned to his face, and he turned back to address Johnson. "Quick, bro, what I just say?"

"The judges are trying the children of Israel because they are refining them. They are bringing them back to God."

"Very good, Mr. Williamson," said Miss Nelson.

"Wait! Is that what I said?" asked Mr. Perez.

"And driving out the competition," said Mr. Gascon, completely ignoring Mr. Perez' shameful attempt at glory.

"True, Mr. Gascon, very true." Miss Nelson paused to allow the thought to sink in a bit. "Do you have judges in your life?"

"You mean, do we have people in our lives who are calling us back to God and who are chasing away the voices, the perspectives, and the longings that keep us away from Him?" asked Mr. Williamson.

"I do."

"Well, Perez is a judge to me," stated Mr. Johnson. This made Mr. Perez sit up and look at Johnson. "It's true. You remind me of the people Gideon called out and separated because they were afraid. The way you share your faith with the guys in the unit. You're fearless. There have been many times where God has convicted me of the way fear has caused me to be hesitant in sharing my faith, and you could say I am being tried, and God is using you as an example to refine me and make me stronger in my faith."

"Very interesting," said Miss Nelson. "I think you are on the right track. God uses other people's ability or willingness to shape and fashion us into His image. As a side note, I do not know that there is much difference between the willing and the able when it comes to God."

"Because 'those He calls He also equips'?" asked Mr. Williamson.

"Yes, I think the only question is whether you have been called or not. If you are called and are willing, then you will be enabled. I wonder if that's part of the meaning behind the selection process for Gideon's army."

"You mean to say a judge ends up being someone who, by their actions, continues to cling to God's directives and inspires us to do the same?" said Mr. Johnson.

"Yes, in essence that is true. I remember a particular judge in my life."

The men stopped looking at their Bibles and notebooks and put their attention on The Locksmith.

"There was a young family in our church who were undergoing a pregnancy and were all excited about what the future held for their young family. Excited, that is, until one day they received troubling tests results. Those tests were followed by more tests and ultrasounds, and then more tests, until one day the doctors took the young father and mother aside and told them there were serious concerns with the unborn son growing in her womb.

"There were questions of viability, and it led the team of doctors to recommend that the pregnancy be aborted. They said it was likely that the baby boy would not survive but for a couple of hours. The parents decided to return home and pray about their pregnancy. They asked their church to pray. They asked their family to pray. When a week had passed, the parents felt it was clear what God was calling them to do. So, they returned to the next appointment with the team of doctors and said they were prepared to bring the child into the world and attend to whatever needs he would have for as long as he had them. They determined to love him for who he was—a gift from God—even if he was broken, according to worldly standards.

"As the pregnancy progressed, ignorant and immature fellow believers would comment behind the young parents' backs, wondering if this was some kind of punishment for sin in their lives. Some even felt they were being spiritually arrogant.

"Months later, the ultrasound picture remained much the same, and the young family was encouraged on numerous occasions to consider the expense of delivering a nonviable fetus into the world. To consider the emotional difficulties it would present to the care providers attending the delivery, watching a newborn suffer as it died. And to reconsider terminating the pregnancy, which was the doctor's recommendation. The pressure was immense, and the family kept having to go back to the Lord to reassure themselves that they were not being irresponsible, as the physicians had implied. And that they were not being arrogant, as some people within their spiritual family had accused.

"They remained steadfast throughout the pregnancy, and the day finally arrived. The thin and seemingly frail young woman began having labor pains, and they knew the delivery was only hours away. The young parents were tearful and afraid because they'd spent the past nine months constantly second-guessing themselves and wondering how this whole event would unfold. But they were confident in what they were called to do. They were confident that regardless of what happened, anyone who cared to watch would see God at work, supplying grace and joy to a family even amidst their brokenness.

"Upon delivery, the team was fully expecting an infant who was destined for a momentary existence. To everyone's surprise, it became apparent that even though the child had obvious abnormalities, he wasn't in any distress. The nurses who were prepared for comfort measures shifted gears and provided the usual kind of care following delivery—more out of habit than any planned procedure. They stated that though he looked good initially, he would never walk, he would never talk, and he would die at an early age.

"But God had a plan in that young man's life. As the hours became days, and days became months, and months became years, the experts kept adjusting their expectations. What had been an 'upon birth' death prediction became a prognosis of a vegetative state for a few days until his inability to feed resulted in death. Then, when the child began to feed, the prognosis was changed, declaring that he would never leave the hospital. But as the infant grew stronger, the expectation changed: he would need permanent care in a convalescent center. Then they claimed that he would never walk or talk.

"Today, this young man walks … with braces. He doesn't talk … but he uses sign language. The young family will tell you how their lives have been blessed by the strength they see and the joy they find in his life as God continues to prove the experts wrong. The beauty is not because it is so easy, the beauty is because it is so obviously difficult. Yet they remain true, and God continuously blesses them.

"The moment this young mother became a judge in my life was the morning she stood up in church and sang with a loud, strong voice—a voice that did not fit her tiny frame and stature. It was a Sandi Patti song popular in the time called "In Heaven's Eyes." It is a beautiful song about how the world sees and values people and how heaven sees and values people. It becomes clear in the lyrics that the two types of seeing are not the same.

"I remember the day like it was yesterday. And the days after these events happened have never been the same as the ones before. God has used that young woman in my life as a judge. I have not been able to overlook any student of mine because of what others say has happened or will happen. I keep looking for the mercy and grace I know my God loves to lavish on those who are willing to believe."

The men sat silently as a few brushed away the tears welling up in their eyes, including Mr. Hanson. She whispered in her heart, "Lord, help him."

"It's why you're here, isn't it, ma'am?" asked Mr. Gascon.

The woman smiled as she repeated the refrain looking at Mr. Hanson, "'In heaven's eyes there are no losers. In heaven's eyes no hopeless cause. Only people like you with feelings like me, amazed by the grace we can find, in heaven's eyes.' Grace is alive and well in Malheur River Correctional Facility, and I know it."

The men sat, reflecting on what they just heard and the value she had just validated them with.

"Do you have other judges?" asked Mr. Gascon quietly.

"I do. I know a young woman who lives in a broken relationship with her husband who does not know the Lord. She could leave him, and many around her know of his unfaithfulness toward her. They know the names he refers to her as. They see the depths of loneliness she experiences in what was meant to be the richest of human relationships. A scientist I know used to be a defiant atheist who couldn't see anything beyond the lies of evolution. I witnessed his transformation into a wide-eyed fanatic for the design he now sees everywhere in creation." She looked at her hands folded in her lap. "I have many judges in my life, and I thank God for at least one of them nearly every day at some point or another." She smiled as she looked up at the men who were staring back at her.

It was Mr. Williamson who spoke up first. "Are you sure these judges aren't any different than the others? I feel kind of convicted. I'm not like them."

"Then you need to adjust your helmet and breastplate, and you need to tighten your belt of truth, Mr. Williamson, because Satan has come to do battle with you in this moment, in this place." Miss Nelson paused, then said, "The truth is that God has saved you with His righteousness, and even though you don't deserve it any more than the rest of us, you definitely do not deserve it any less either."

"'There is therefore now no condemnation to them which are in Christ Jesus, who walk not after the flesh, but after the Spirit,'" quoted Mr. Perez.

"Nice use of the sword of the Spirit by a faithful judge." Miss Nelson smiled with a nod.

"So the judges aren't there to condemn us but to inspire us to be who we were called to be?" asked Mr. Williamson. Miss Nelson gave a half nod, half shrug of the man's uncommitted offering of an opinion.

"Perhaps it is not about us but about the perceptions surrounding our circumstances that they are judging. Even people who do not intend to can be an inspiration. Look at Samson," Miss Nelson said.

"I was gonna ask 'bout that guy," commented Mr. Perez. "Seems like a strange judge."

"Strange, yes, but still a judge in my eyes," said Miss Nelson. "I find it interesting that Samson took a vow to be different, set apart, holy, which is the essence of the Nazarite vow. He was also living in a region called the Shephelah. It was the region between the Judaean Mountains and the coastal plains, home to some of the tribes of the people of God and future home of the Temple, home to the Philistine people—or the worldly people of that day. In essence, he lived as a judge between the people of God and the people of the world. Yet despite his calling, he chose for much of his life to live in the coastal plains among the people of the world. And even though he had been given strength to make a difference, he rarely used it for that purpose.

"Samson's story is a tragic story of potential, wasted by one gifted and called, who instead chose to live in the world. Nonetheless, he is still considered a judge, and he inspires me to action. He cautions me from out of history, and by allegory, to not live a life of leisure, or for myself, but one that points to God and remains true to the commitments I have been called to.

"I think you might also be interested to know that Samson's father's name was Manoah, which means 'rest' or 'quiet.' I find that I was challenged by that name. Given our discussion of why the book of Judges was written, showing God was not going to give the children of Israel peace, but used war instead, it makes me wonder if there is a little insight into what would have happened to the children of Israel, after the death of Joshua, if God had given them rest. Would their offspring have been careless like Samson?"

"Hmm," said Mr. Gascon.

"I think it is also interesting Samson was also of the tribe of Dan," said Miss Nelson.

"Why is that interesting?" asked Mr. Gascon.

"Do a study on the tribe of Dan and focus on the fact that they lived in this area at this point in history and later ended up elsewhere. Watch the circumstances around them leaving and where they end up as a tribe. I think it also ties in interestingly in another way. How many tribes of Israel are there?" The Locksmith smiled.

"Twelve, right? The twelve tribes of Israel?" said Mr. Gascon.

"Is there?" asked Miss Nelson.

"No, there are thirteen," corrected Mr. Williamson.

"That is correct. As part of your study, look at when the tribes get listed, who is listed and who is not listed and when. I think you will find something very interesting." The Locksmith smiled again as she threw down the proverbial gauntlet.

The men scurried to write the challenge in their notebooks. Mr. Perez needed to look off Mr. Johnson's notes, who obliged him with a look that said, "*Really?*"

"Well, I think that is a great place to leave it for this week, gentlemen," said Miss Nelson as she picked up her well-worn Bible. "I think I would have you reflect a bit more on what we have been talking about the past couple of weeks."

"Chew the cud a bit?" asked Mr. Perez.

"Indeed, Mr. Perez. I think that would be appropriate. Before we go, I want to pray for you."

As was their routine, the men stood and awkwardly held hands. "Oh, Mighty Father, I praise Your name and lift You up, asking that You would sanctify Your name in the midst of these men. I give You the recognition You deserve and all the associated glory and honor for the things we are coming to treasure so greatly. Your name, Your perspective, Your grace, Your mercy, all the great gifts created by You when You created light. Let Your light so shine in our lives, and may we seek You daily that we might live in Your light. And may we long to share it as Mr. Perez does. I ask that You continue to reveal Yourself to them in accordance with their longings, and may they never be the same. I ask this because I believe Your Son died for these very reasons. Amen."

"Amen," said all the men.

"Attention in the institution! It's 9:45 a.m. 10:00 a.m. callouts, line movement, line movement!" said the voice over the loudspeaker.

"Goodbye, gentlemen."

"Goodbye, ma'am," said each of the men as they shook her hand.

"Mr. Hanson, just a few more moments if you please," asked The Locksmith. She looked at the correctional officer to confirm she was okay to have him stay. The CO nodded an apparent understanding as the others left the room, each glancing at Hanson.

"Mr. Hanson, I could not help but notice you were not yourself this morning."

He watched the men leave and then glanced at the CO. The moment the room was empty, he said, "I'm getting out!"

The elderly woman stared at him, not quite sure what was being said.

"I'm being released."

Her face relaxed a bit.

"I've been here over thirty years." He paused and glanced at the CO. "I knew it was coming, but I got confirmation yesterday."

"So it will be soon then." This came out not as a question but more as a statement.

The man nodded. He looked the elderly woman in the eyes, looking for something, anything that would reassure him.

The woman smiled. "It will be just fine, Mr. Hanson. In fact, it will be better than fine."

"Let's go, Hanson!" bellowed the CO.

The man looked at the CO and then glanced back at The Locksmith, who took his hand and patted it. "I will be in touch."

And with that, Mr. Hanson left Religious Services and headed to what had been his home for more than thirty years. Miss Nelson realized the tension that must be felt in the heart of a man for whom going home held fear, not peace; uncertainty, not confidence; pain, not joy. Her friend was not feeling any of the emotions home ought to have brought. And she felt a lump forming in her throat.

• • •

An hour and a half later, Miss Nelson was putting a pot of tea on to boil when there was a knock at the door.

"Come on in, Margaret!" called The Locksmith.

The door opened with a gentle nudge, and in walked Margaret Smithson. "Good morning, ma'am," greeted Max.

"Oh Margaret, it is so good of you to come. Your father had said he thought you would be back the night before last."

"Yes, ma'am, but it was rather late. I really didn't want to deal with what I might find if I got home too early."

"What did you find when you got up yesterday morning?"

"When I turned on my phone, I had a lot of voice mails and text messages from the gang. And a phone call from the Caldwell Police Department. They want to interview me later this afternoon."

"And…?" asked Miss Nelson, wondering just how much of her counsel had been heeded since their last visit.

"And…I am in shock to hear of what happened since I checked out."

"What happened?" asked Miss Nelson, testing her young friend.

"I don't know exactly. Apparently, Sandy had been pregnant, and no one really knew it. I had no idea even that night she came over for the verbal dressing down she gave me after the voodoo ceremony. If you had asked me if she was pregnant, I would have asked if you were talking about Jaz. Then somehow, at some time, at some place, she delivered that baby."

"Did she seem depressed to you?"

"No, not prior to that night. She had seemed engaged and eager to learn more about God. But that night she did seem different. I really have no idea if she was depressed, despondent, or just losing it. It was all very strange."

"Where were you later that night?"

"I was up a good part of the night, crying off and on at how she treated me."

"Can anyone confirm your presence at home through the night?"

"No, I live alone. Do I need someone to?"

"Just curious. They tried to reach you later the next day. Why did not you respond to their calls?"

"I was so upset, and I knew the girls in our group would be checking on me, and I just wasn't ready to talk about what had happened. At least not until I had a chance to think about it a bit."

"They tried to come see you and you were not at home. Where did you go?"

"I had planned to leave on Tuesday, but after Sunday night's face-off, I didn't sleep at all. So before the sun was up on Monday, I got out of bed, packed my stuff, and headed home."

"What time was that?"

"It was still on the early side, about six a.m."

"What time did you get home?"

"I made some stops along the way, so it was later."

"Where did you stop that early in the morning?"

"I headed to Emmett, through Middleton, and took the back roads through New Plymouth and Payette, then on home to Weiser. I stopped at some of the high schools where I had played sports."

"Did you attend all of those schools?"

"No, I attended Weiser High School and played soccer, basketball, and ran track. I spent a lot of good times at those schools and ..." Max inhaled deeply and shrugged her shoulders as if there were no better words. "I just needed to have a sense of good times."

"What did you do when you got home?"

"I got home before my dad, and we talked about what had happened. The next morning I was still pretty upset, so I decided to take several days and go on a road trip. I've been to Denver, Portland, and Seattle"

"By yourself?"

"No one to talk with except myself."

"No friends to take the trip with?"

"Again, I didn't feel like answering questions of my friends or reassuring them that I was fine until I had a chance to process the whole experience."

"And have you?"

"Processed it?"

"Yes."

"I think so. I don't know what happened with Sandy. My plan was to get in touch with my friends after returning and see if they had talked with her. I wanted to be sure she was alright—"

"Why? Do you feel she was in some kind of trouble?" The Locksmith interrupted.

"I knew something was wrong, but I didn't want the discussion to be about me and my feelings. I consider ... considered Sandy a friend. I didn't think she would do something like this. But now I don't know if I knew her at all."

"Have you spoken to your friends?"

"Yes, I spoke with each of them, starting with Jasmine D'Silva."

"What did she say?"

"She is the one who broke the news. Like the others, she had more questions than answers."

"Did you not get our message to call us immediately?"

"Yes, and that troubled me enough to want to return all the voice mails and text messages to find out what the blazes was going on."

The Locksmith sat there looking at Max. "How much is a lie?"

"It's all true. I stopped by the schools today, though not the morning I came home. The fears and concerns are true. Every place I went and stopped is true."

"It is the truth and nothing but the truth?" asked Miss Nelson.

"Yes, ma'am, it just isn't the whole truth. I left some things out. Things that if they don't ask, I don't feel the need to tell. I have done some of this work with the military. And if they don't ask the right questions, they won't get the right answers. But I won't lie to them."

"What if they do ask the right questions?" asked the older woman.

"Then I will tell them the truth, the whole truth, and nothing but the truth. And then trust God with the truth."

The Locksmith patted Max's hand. "I think I shall fast and pray until I hear back from you after your interview." She picked up her tea and with a second thought set it aside. Max got up to leave. "Oh, and Margaret? I would like to have you see if your father will let you drive his Buick to your interview. I think your Jeep could use an oil change after your long road trip."

CHAPTER 15

TRUTH ON TRIAL

Caldwell, Idaho
later that same afternoon

Good morning, Miss Smithson. Thank you for taking the time to meet with us. I'm Officer Gregory Thornson, and this is Lieutenant James Knight. We are the detectives who have been assigned to look into the death of Miss Santana D'Souza."

"I'm sorry, who?" Max squinted her eyes and shook his head. "I didn't know a Santana. I thought this was about my friend Sandy."

"I'm sorry, Miss Smithson. We will get to that. But let's start at the beginning, can we?" asked Lt. Knight.

"Sure," said Max, who was obviously uncomfortable but now felt she at least had a reason to be.

"Thornson, why don't you get started for us," said Lt. Knight.

"Alright, miss, could you please state your full name for us?" requested Officer Thornson.

"Margaret Anne Smithson."

"Can you state your age and profession for our notes?"

"I am twenty-five and currently a student at Pacific Northwest Christian University."

"Kind of a late bloomer, aren't you, miss?" asked Lt. Knight.

"The boys at school didn't think so." Max could already sense they had defaulted to the good cop, bad cop routine. At least now she could tell who from whom.

"He means school, miss," clarified Officer Thornson. "Shouldn't you have already graduated from the university?"

"I served five years in the military before I went to the university. My father is in law enforcement, and on his salary, I needed the GI bill to pay for the school I wanted to attend."

"Which branch, miss?"

"Army."

"What was your rank?"

"E-5"

"Are you Reserves now?"

"Yes."

"What are you studying at the university?"

"Criminal justice."

Officer Thornson glanced at the lieutenant, who had moved behind Max. Knight, shrugged his shoulders, and cocked his head as if to say, "*So what? Keep going?*"

"Miss Smithson, could you tell us about the small group that was meeting at your house a couple of weeks ago?"

"I joined the group my first year at the university and have been a part of the group for the past two years. Girls graduate and leave, and others can join as early as their freshman year. We meet to study the Bible and support one another."

"How does someone join the group. Do they apply?"

"There isn't any formal application. It is mostly by referral from the other girls in the group."

"When did you meet Santana D'Souza?" asked Officer Thornson.

"Sandra Acedia," corrected Lt. Knight, who had given up trying to disrupt Max's train of thought for the moment and had moved over to the corner where he could lean with his back against the wall and listen.

"Oh yeah, when did you meet Sandra Acedia?"

"Are you saying Sandy wasn't her real name?" asked Max.

There was a buzz, and Knight took out his phone.

"Are you saying you didn't know her real name?"

"Toxicology report is in?" interrupted Knight.

Thornson looked at Knight.

"Was she poisoned?" Max interjected.

"Not to our knowledge. Do you know of any reason someone would want to hurt your friend?"

"None of the people I know. But apparently, I didn't really know her," said Max truthfully.

"How would you categorize your friendship with the deceased?" asked Knight.

"I thought of her as my friend."

"Weird way for a young woman to treat her friend?"

"You're talking about the last night I saw her?" Thornson nodded the affirmative. "It was strange. But again, I'm beginning to think I may not have really known the real Sandy Acedia."

"What did she do and say that night?"

"The last night I saw her, you mean?"

"Yes."

Max gave a shallow shrug. "The group met for our Bible study at the house I have been renting the past two years. Nothing seemed out of the ordinary. We met at the agreed-upon time."

"What time was that?"

"We met about seven p.m."

"Was everyone there?"

"Everyone except Sandy, or Santana, or whatever her name was. Uber, I mean Erica Uberis, and Lindsey Avaritia were late. They were Sandy's usual ride to the group, and they had been waiting for her on campus at Ribley's College, but she never showed."

"Didn't that tip anyone off that something was wrong?"

"It was unusual, but Sandy had been the one who had spotted the guys after Jaz, and she—"

"What guys?" Lt. Knight interrupted.

Max went back and explained the excitement of Jasmine's family and the concern they as a group all had for her safety after seeing the two guys that Jaz said were men working for her grandmother.

She also informed them of Sandy's willingness to stay at Jaz's house to make it clear that the house was neither empty nor was Jaz alone. The hope was to dissuade anyone from entering the house and to keep them confused about where Jaz was through the night.

"What do you mean, 'confused about where Jaz was'?" asked the lieutenant.

"Because of the fear and uncertainty of the day, we all decided that it was best for Jaz not to go home by herself. Instead, my house seemed the safest and least likely place for them to look for her," replied Max.

"Why was Jaz so concerned about these men?" asked Officer Thornson.

"She left me with the impression that her grandmother was some kind of force to be reckoned with in her family. If her grandmother didn't like something, she had people in her employ who would send a message."

"Is that her maternal or paternal grandmother?"

"I don't recall her ever saying, specifically. But I think it was her maternal grandmother."

"Did she see her grandmother like some kind of crime boss?"

"Maybe," said Max. "Like I said, it was an impression."

"Did you ever see these guys?"

"Yes! First, Jasmine flew past us at The Oasis, then Brook told us what was going on. So Lindsey and I went back to the place Brook had said Sandy spotted them. When we got there, we found two big guys dressed in expensive-looking suits. They would have fit right in with most city crowds here in the United States, but they stood out in our little setting. They reminded me of football players."

"Why, because they were Black?" asked Knight.

"No, because they were big and fit. Men with size and athleticism have the ability make a lot of money. Women tend to be ridiculed for it," responded Max.

"Are you racist, Miss Smithson?" asked Knight.

"I don't think so. Nor do I think it takes a racist to play the game 'One of These Things Is Not Like the Others' that we were all taught on *Sesame Street*," reported Max with a smile.

"Do you resent men being bigger and stronger, Miss Smithson?"

"I resent it when it makes them think they are more valuable because of it," Max stated matter-of-factly. "I guess it shows."

Knight could tell his tactic wasn't having the effect he was looking for.

Officer Thornson was reviewing his notes. He looked up and asked, "Anything unusual about the Bible study that night?"

"No, it actually went rather well. I do remember being disappointed that Sandy hadn't been there for the group."

"Why was that?"

"None of us knew why she wasn't there."

"No, I mean why were you disappointed?"

"Oh, Sandy and I had a very good talk the day before, just prior to her seeing the guys and freaking out Jasmine."

"What was that about? Your topic of conversation?" Lt. Knight emphasized.

"The whole idea of the day was to spend time together before the end of the year. So Lindsey, being the official leader, came up with the idea of our group dividing into threes and spending time talking casually in a more intimate setting."

"What did you talk about?"

"The instructions were to have each person discuss their plans for the summer, then we'd spend some time praying for one another."

"And you and Sandy had some time to talk?"

"Yes, it was during that time that Sandy and I talked about how our self-perception takes three forms: the way we perceive ourselves, the way we think other people perceive us, and the way we want to be perceived." She recounted the tale of the photographer.

Officer Thornson's cell phone buzzed this time.

"Which face are you showing us now? A true one or a fake one?" asked Lt. Knight.

Thornson handed the phone to Knight, who took it and read it. Knight seemed distracted. "Do you know what an abortifacient is, Miss Smithson?"

"Yes."

"Can you think of a reason why someone would want to take one?" asked Officer Thornson.

"To induce an abortion," said Max matter-of-factly.

"Do you know what a tocolytic is?" asked Mr. Knight in follow-up.

"Yes."

"Can you think of a reason why someone would want take one?" asked Mr. Knight again.

"To stop contractions," answered Max unaffectedly.

"Can you think of why we would find herbs belonging to each class in Miss D'Souza's house?" asked Officer Thornson.

"Not really," said Max. "But both of those substances seem like crude tools for obstetrical care in one's home. Perhaps one would attempt to use them against one another to balance out their effects. Why?" Max forced the vision of Sandy "rehydrating" when she got out of the Jeep and headed for home out of her mind.

"That's just it. We now know *what* was used, just not *why* they were used," said Thornson.

"Do you know any of Miss D'Souza's family, Miss Smithson?" asked the lieutenant.

"No, I've never had the pleasure."

"Miss D'Souza's grandmother is convinced that Miss D'Souza delivered the baby and gave her to someone for safekeeping."

"Do you know anyone Miss D'Souza would trust enough with a baby?"

"Given she didn't even trust our group with the fact that she was pregnant makes it seem unlikely that she would trust any of them with the baby."

There was a knock at the door. Knight went to answer it.

Just as he opened the door, Officer Thornson asked, "Could she have trusted you with the baby?" Casually, he leaned back to see who had knocked. Both men were all of a sudden more interested in what the person at the door was saying than in listening to what Max's response was, so she showed them the courtesy of not interrupting or derailing their train of thoughts.

She couldn't help but see a woman whisper into Lt. Knight's ear.

Simultaneously, in her mind's eye, she saw an elderly woman sitting at her breakfast table, hands folded in prayer. She also noticed that each time she had difficulty answering questions, the officers were distracted, and neither of them seemed to be tracking the question in their note pads. As a result, every time they reviewed their notes, there wasn't anything to remind them that she had never answered those trickier questions. She couldn't help but sense the investigators were going through their routine, but they didn't really feel she was a suspect in anything. If they did, they would never have allowed the distractions.

"Miss Smithson, what make, model, and color is your vehicle?" asked Lt. Knight.

"It is a four door Jeep Wrangler, orange colored," replied Max.

"Have you seen a black late-model Mercedes in any of the neighborhoods you have been in lately?"

"No, I haven't. Not that I remember at least. Why?"

"It keeps showing up in some of the video camera feeds. It shows up in a parking lot feed at The Oasis on the day you and your friends were there. And it shows up again on some of the feeds in Caldwell on the morning Miss D'Souza's body was found."

"Really?" asked Max, who was not only surprised but thankful they hadn't asked about her Jeep showing up in any camera feeds. All the credit for that planning detail went to a diligent Santana.

"It also shows up in some of the feeds in Weiser," commented the Lieutenant.

"Where in Weiser?" she asked.

"That's what we were hoping you could answer for us."

"As you know, I live in Weiser, but I don't remember seeing a late-model Mercedes over the past couple of weeks."

"I suppose they aren't all that common in Weiser," commented the officer.

"Well, Mrs. Grayson has one. But like I said, I haven't seen one at all over the past couple of weeks."

Officer Thornson was reviewing his notes. "Let's go back to the Bible study the night before Miss D'Souza's death." He flipped back and forth between a couple of pages. "What did you guys talk about?"

"We spoke about how God communicates with humanity."

The men glanced at one another.

"Oh, and how is that?" asked the Lieutenant.

"Let's just say it isn't usually as direct as you guys are."

"And what does that mean?"

"He speaks in similitudes."

"He speaks in what?"

"Similitudes."

"And what is a similitude?"

"A similitude is a manner of speaking, a way of communicating ideas. Like the book *The Wonderful Wizard of Oz*. Some people have believed the book contained a similitude regarding a debate of using two metals as the basis of monetary policy in the late eighteen hundreds. Or the spiritual attributes of movies like *Shawshank Redemption* or *The Matrix*."

Officer Thornson looked at Lt. Knight, whose squinting eyes signaled he likely doubted the value of higher education. There was an awkward pause as Thornson flipped through his notes.

"I thought you said the talk you and Sandy had the day before was related. That you had been disappointed she hadn't been part of the gathering that night. How does philosophizing about the three perceptions a person has tie into a talk of similitudes?" asked Thornson.

"The discussion on the three perceptions was a way of discussing who we have been, who we are, and who we want to become. The person who each of us sees from the inside is different than the person God sees, or even who others see. We are all on a journey of becoming either who God wants us to be, or what others want us to be. That was the discussion with Sandy. God directs us along the path He wants us to grow by the use of His similitudes."

Officer Thornson looked at Lt. Knight. "Are you getting any of this?"

The lieutenant bounced himself off the wall he had returned to leaning against as he shrugged and put his hands in his pockets.

"Perhaps you should join a Bible study class," suggested Max.

Thornson smiled as he again flipped through his notes.

"What happened later? Was there any more discussion about Miss D'Souza?" asked the officer.

"Sometime later, the discussion wrapped up without any further mention of Sandy until we went into the kitchen to get some refreshments."

"How did her name come up?"

"Brook saw some unusual activity in my backyard, and then we all heard distant drum beats."

Officer Thornson looked up from his notes. "Drum beats?"

"Yes, like distant drum beats."

"What was the unusual activity?"

"There was what looked like a haystack in the yard that began to twirl and spin and move. While I was gone, I googled 'voodoo haystack' and found a site discussing Zangbeto of West Africa." Knight was thumbing away on his phone, which he showed to Thornson, while Max kept talking. "This haystack, or Zangbeto mask, was spinning and whirling to the beat of the drums, dancing around a pole in the middle of my yard. At the base of the pole was a dead cat on a rope and an assortment of jars. The whole thing was just weird, so I went and approached the haystack, figuring that there must be someone under it."

"And was there?" asked Lt. Knight.

"Sandy," replied Max. "As I approached the mask, the drums stopped, and the stack tipped over. When I gathered my senses, I realized it was Sandy."

"Weird," said Thornson.

"No, finding Sandy under the haystack made sense. The weird part was all the yelling she did in a foreign language and the voodoo activities she started acting out. She drew pictures with some kind of flour and threw the dead cat at one of the designs." Then Max grew silent and started to tear up as she looked at her feet, "That's when she went off on me. I really don't even remember what she said. Then … my friend … slapped me."

"What did you do? Did you strike her back?" asked the lieutenant.

Max looked up with tears in her eyes. "I told her that I loved her and always would, and she slapped me again."

"Yeah, and what then?"

Max paused and collected herself. "Then I turned and went inside."

"And no one noticed she was pregnant?"

"I didn't. If the others noticed, they didn't say anything to me. She always wore baggy, ill-fitting clothing. I thought it was just her style. She wasn't someone to make herself stand out."

Officer Thornson's phone chirped the receiving of a text, and there was another knock at the door that the lieutenant went to open. Thornson was looking at his text message while asking, "Did you ever see Miss D'Souza again after that?" Max sat there quietly, allowing them time to address their mutual interruptions before she answered.

But before she could answer, Lt. Knight closed the door. "They have the forensics back on the rental car. They have a blood match with the deceased from both driver and passenger floor mats and base of the seats. They want us to look through everything else and see if there is anything that strikes us as useful."

"I can later, but I need to call my wife first. Trouble at home. I usually don't bring my phone into interviews, and now I remember why. They can be so distracting."

"Give us a few minutes, Miss Smithson, and we will be back to ask you more questions or let you go. Okay?"

"Sure."

With that, the men left the room, and Max was left to her own thoughts.

A few minutes later the captain walked up to the officers. Thornson hung up the phone and all three men sat around his desk.

"All good?" asked Knight.

"Yep, I just need to have things wrapped up on time tonight. I forgot about a dance recital, and I don't want to miss it."

"Where are we at, gentlemen?" asked the captain.

"What do you think?" Knight asked Thornson as he nodded toward the interview room.

"Capt'n, her story checks out with the others and with what we found in the backyard of Smithson's rental. I don't see any evidence that any of the girls knew she was pregnant. No evidence that any of them were involved in the delivery. The scene at D'Souza'a suggests someone else was there, and now it appears to have been whomever rented the car."

"But we haven't been able to trace the names on the rental car agreement, though they do give a Louisiana address. Likely some thugs related to this grandmother Madame D'Souza lady in New Orleans. She seems to know and suspect a lot from such a distance," added Knight.

"Yeah, but if they were there in the house when she delivered, why did the grandmother come to us about a baby? She could have kept quiet and we would never have tracked her down. If they caused the girl to miscarriage, then they should have disposed of the infant's body and stayed hidden. 'Cuz now we are looking at manslaughter, and possibly murder."

"If the infant is dead, why would the grandmother risk being connected to manslaughter or murder charges? Unless she really thinks the baby is alive for some reason," said the captain.

"No infant has been found anywhere—alive or dead," added Thornson.

"There is also that drop of blood and the bloody footprint out on the back porch, but it is hard to say how it got there. Given the body of the mother was found inside, one can't say whether it was the blood from her coming in, or from the person who made the footprint going out."

The men sat there a few minutes.

"Either way, I don't see these co-eds involved in any meaningful way. We processed their vehicles and their rooms, except Miss Smithson here." It was Thornson who nodded toward the interview room this time.

"Have you had her vehicle processed?" asked the captain.

"Not yet, but we were going to go back and ask her," reported Officer Thornson.

"Let's see if we can get her permission to process her Jeep. You have already tried to have forensics process her rental house, right?"

"Yes, but Miss Smithson has been gone, and the landlady said she liked Miss Smithson and was going to require a warrant," said Knight in summary fashion. "If we were more suspicious, and had more to go on, then I'd take the PR risk."

"If we were more suspicious, I would make you," said the captain.

"I'm with Thornson. I don't see these co-eds involved in anything sneaky with a baby. I'm thinking there is more to the guys at The Oasis, and I'm betting they are the guys in the rental car, which puts them in the house," said Knight.

"You might be able to lean on them a bit to learn something new. I would see if you can get an image of these guys from the video surveillance footage at The Oasis, then see if you can locate them in Louisiana for an interview. Keep the image in your packet while you interview. See what they deny and what they confirm during the interview. You might learn something interesting," instructed the captain. "I just don't feel right about these guys. They're hiding something, and these co-eds don't seem to be hiding anything. And since there isn't any money to follow—"

"Follow the liars," they all three interrupted together.

"Ask if you can process the Jeep. If she says yes, then great; if she says no, then maybe she is hiding something. Either way, get the picture from the IT guys and get to Louisiana. Got it?"

"Yep," said Thornson.

"Sounds like a plan," added Knight.

The captain left as Knight said, "I will talk with IT and see if they can get us a still-frame image of the guys. If they can, then as soon as we get it, we are off to Louisiana."

"I will check with the co-ed regarding her Jeep."

Thornson got up and turned around. "Can you think of any other questions for Smithson while we have her other than asking to process the Jeep?"

Knight looked up and paused to think for a second. "No, I don't think so." He dialed the IT guys. While it was ringing he said, "Ask her about where she went Monday." He stepped away from the desk as the other end of the line picked up.

"Okay," said Thornson as he turned and headed off to the interview room.

"Miss Smithson, I am sorry to keep you waiting. We appreciate your cooperation today."

"Sure, I hope I have been helpful."

"Yes, miss, you have. Thank you so much. We do have a question and a request to ask though."

"Yes, how can I help, Officer?"

"Where did you go when you left for your road trip?"

Max relayed the various destinations in no specific order.

"Did you meet with anyone while you were gone?"

"Only my dad and a close friend. Sorry, Officer, I intentionally avoided being seen."

"Okay." Thornson was scribbling down her response.

"Was there a request as well, sir?"

"Um, yes, we would like to have forensics go over your vehicle. Could we do that?"

"Yes, certainly you can. But I don't have it with me today. I have my father's Buick. My Jeep is getting an oil change after all the miles I put on it."

There was a knock at the door as Lt. Knight entered. "IT already had an image in their evidence. It's the guys. Is the Jeep available?"

"It's being serviced. We could probably get it scheduled with forensics while we are gone."

"Forget it. Let's get to Louisiana. Thank you for your time, miss. You're free to go," said Lt. Knight.

"Are you sure, sir? I could come back here next week," offered Max, having the sense that heaven was making sure there was no way these guys were going to get any information out of the Jeep that would change the destiny of the little Mulatto baby girl in the Seattle area.

"No, that won't be necessary at this time. We will let you know if anything changes. Thornson, let's get flights scheduled, then you have a recital to get to and I have a date."

• • •

It was late afternoon, and Max had an hour drive ahead of her, so before leaving the Caldwell Police Department, Max called up Miss Nelson to invite her over for dinner with she and her father. By the time she arrived home, the table was set, and her dad was getting the food to the table. Miss Nelson was already sitting at her place.

"Hello, honey. Glad you're home. Are you hungry?" asked the deputy.

"Not super hungry. I ate just before I went to the station. I know how important it is in an interview like that to not have your own thoughts being bounced around by the sound your stomach is making as it is churning away. But I could eat. Looks good." Max went over to her dad and kissed him on both cheeks, as was her tradition.

"Hello, Margaret."

"Hello, Miss Nelson. Thanks for coming over. I thought it would be easier to tell this thing once and have each of you quiz me. This way I don't have to tell it twice nor tell the one what the other said." She bounced her eyebrows as she smiled, giving her special kiss to The Locksmith as well.

"Fair enough," said her father. "Let me say a prayer, and then you can fill us in. Father in heaven, we are thankful for so many things tonight. It just wouldn't be right if we did not stop and give You thanks for the way You love us and provide for us. Please bless this food as we ask that our bodies might continue growing strong and being healthy. Please be with us as we hear of how You were in the events of this day. Amen."

"Amen," said the ladies, and then they all began dishing items from the service platters and passing them round.

"Let us have it. We've been praying all day and some have been fasting. How did it go, honey?"

"It went amazingly well."

"Were they thorough?" asked the deputy.

"Fairly thorough."

"Who interviewed you?" asked her father.

"It was an Officer Thornson and a Lieutenant Knight. Do you know either of them, Daddy?"

"I have heard of them. Good guys from what I know."

"The lieutenant tried to play tough cop with me. I think it probably works on people most of the time."

"Saw it coming, huh?" asked her father.

"He accused me of being a late bloomer for being twenty-five and currently enrolled in college," said Max, smiling. "I told him the boys in school didn't think so!"

"Ha! I bet he didn't know what to say!"

"Nope, he didn't."

"Did God show up?" asked The Locksmith.

"Oh yeah! You can say that for sure."

"Well, then tell us about it." The Locksmith wanted to learn how God answered their prayers that day.

"When a question was asked or they were trying to form a question—one whose answer would open the door to finding Abomey—there was always an interruption: a text, a phone call, a knock at the door. They asked me if I knew her real name was Santana but never waited for my answer.

"We got to talking about your photographer friend and the three perspectives he tries to create by adjusting how the subject perceives themselves. I briefly explained how it works. You know … how we perceive ourselves, how others perceive us, and how we want others to perceive us. The lieutenant took that to mean a person was either being truthful or lying, and he asked if I was being truthful or hiding something. Just before he did, thankfully, there was an interruption. It was like he forgot he had asked the question. Then we got to talking about the fact that no one knew Sandy was pregnant, and one of them asked if she might have trusted anyone to give them her baby. I pointed out that she didn't trust anyone in the group to know that she was pregnant, which caused me to doubt if she would trust anyone in the group to take her baby. Just as I was being asked if she could have trusted me with the baby—"

"There was an interruption," Miss Nelson finished her sentence.

"Exactly," said Max. "It was crazy. I got to where I could almost predict when they were going to ask a direct question that I couldn't get around, because just before those questions were asked there would always be an interruption."

"Prayer doesn't always work like that, Margaret."

"I know it doesn't for me. Why is that?" Max looked first at her father, then at The Locksmith. Her father shrugged as if it was a great question to which he didn't have a great answer.

"Sometimes God acts in blatantly obvious ways just like He did today. Other times, He does not act as obvious."

"Why the difference?" asked the deputy.

"I think sometimes God's will is in an outcome. But most of the time His will is in the transformation. He uses the difficult, undesirable, or painful outcomes to refine us."

"It's like we've talked about before. He seems more interested in the journey *toward* an outcome and not the journey *to* the outcome," summarized Max.

"Yes, I believe so," confirmed The Locksmith. "Today we saw Him invested in an outcome in a rather large way. It makes me wonder if He has special plans for little Miss Abomey."

"It was weird. I got to where I felt there wasn't anything they could do that would help them find that baby. I certainly feel He is protecting Abomey in ways that her mother never could have."

"I'm glad it's over," said the deputy. "I mean it is over, right?"

"It seems so. Oh, and good call on the oil change for the Jeep. They wanted to have forensics process the Jeep. But I think they are more interested in talking to Henrí and François at this point. It feels like the attention on me and the other girls in the group is lessening."

"Why do you say that?" asked Miss Nelson.

"They were in the process of asking me for permission to process the Jeep when they got a still image of both of the guys from surveillance footage from The Oasis in Meridian. Once that photo surfaced, they dropped me like last month's stew. In fact, the lieutenant basically told Thornson to forget the processing of the Jeep because they had to get plane reservations for Louisiana. Thornson was even going to schedule forensics to take my Jeep later, but Knight told him to let it go. I think if the Jeep had been there, it would have been scheduled for processing right then and there."

"Deputy, do you have any Luminol that Margaret could use to search her Jeep for trace blood?"

"Yes."

"Margaret, it might be a good idea to go over the Jeep everywhere Santana has been. And I would get that area cleaned out, but only that area. It would be strange to not find any blood on the Jeep. You just don't want them finding her blood."

"Is that necessary? I mean, it was pretty clear in the way He moved today that He wasn't going to let them get anywhere near the baby. Wouldn't this be a break in trusting Him, like a lack of faith or something?" asked the Deputy.

"When the children of Israel were up against Jericho, it wasn't their fighting skills that brought down the walls. It was God Himself. But He still had them participate. God had said He would fight their battles, but He still sent them to the battlefield. In my mind, it really isn't a question of whether it is necessary or not. I think it is clear He doesn't want the baby found, and I want to be a part of keeping her safe. I think anytime we put our effort in the direction we know He is working in, it isn't because He needs our help. It's just another way we can affirm that we see His hand and we trust His heart. I am adding some prudence to the wisdom He has shown. It would be a break of faith to take the Jeep to Caldwell and point out the blood; it would not be wise or prudent."

CHAPTER 16

LOST LAMB

Ontario, Oregon
a few days later

"Miss Nelson, please enter visitation through door A," said the voice over the loudspeaker.

About twenty minutes earlier, The Locksmith had arrived at MRCF in the usual fashion. But instead of heading through Master Control as had been her routine for the past seven years, she headed through Visiting Control at the northeast corner of the facility. She was buzzed into the large waiting room where she then sat down and began collecting her thoughts.

The older woman stood to her feet and could hear the familiar click and hiss as she began moving toward the door that was sliding open. As she passed through the portal there was another click, and the door began to slide shut. She was met on the other side by a young female CO, who smiled as she said, "Good morning, Miss Nelson. Would you please hold your arms out from your sides with your feet shoulder-width apart?"

The Locksmith did as she was asked, and the younger woman gently but firmly patted her down in a manner that not only confirmed no contraband, but made a clear statement that no breech of protocol would be tolerated.

The CO directed The Locksmith's attention to a placard and said, "Ma'am, after reading this sign would you confirm that you are aware of these expectations and that it is your intention to visit with your adult in custody and that during your visit you will adhere to all of these expectations."

"I believe this is the same sign as in the waiting room. I have read it, and I will adhere to these expectations."

The young woman smiled and said, "Thank you, ma'am. Would you please sign here to document your verbal confirmation?"

The elder woman smiled and said, "Yes, indeed." She bent over the desk to her right, picked up the pen, then signed and dated the paper.

The CO stepped aside to The Locksmith's left and, with a quarter turn to her left, extended her left arm toward the door as it clicked and opened with a hiss. "Enjoy your visit, ma'am."

"Thank you. I think I shall."

The Locksmith moved through the final portal and into the visitation room. She was met by a second uniformed CO, who smiled and gestured to a table near the glass windows. She nodded her appreciation, walked over to the round table, and took her seat.

Moments later, a buzz and click sounded across the room and lasted until the door opened and in walked Mr. Hanson. He was wearing his long-sleeved denim shirt, and his hair was nicely groomed. Walking across the room, he nodded and smiled toward the COs congregating at the center behind the desks. "Hanson," they said, with returning nods of recognition. Mr. Hanson pursed his lips with his head bowed and his eyes locked on The Locksmith's. They both smiled and she arose from her seat as he approached. They shook hands and then each took their seat. "It is very nice of you to visit me, ma'am," said Mr. Hanson.

They continued to smile at each other, and she waited. He glanced out the window, unsure of what to say. The Locksmith decided that for a change she would start. She joined him in his gaze out the window.

"Do you remember our previous discussions about salvation?"

He turned his face back from the window and looked directly at her. "You mean the fact that salvation is a messy, vague term that is often easily misunderstood?"

The mentor nodded, still looking out the window.

He nodded back. "From what I remember, salvation has a past tense, present tense, and a future tense that if you are not careful can be very confusing. There is a past tense in which we *are saved* from the penalty of sin, a present tense of *being saved* from the power of sin, and a future tense of *going to be saved* from the presence of sin."

She turned her face back from the window, then looked into her lap as she folded her hands and remained silent.

"To be honest"—he looked around the room and gently gestured— "in prison it has been hard to feel saved from the penalty of sin." He dropped his hands as he paused. "For the longest time, I was constantly being reminded of the penalty of my sin, and those bonds were just as tight, just as dense, just as real as…" He paused and shifted his voice so it got quieter and more serious. "Well, just as real as any I've seen or experienced here." He went silent as his mind replayed the memories of his early days at MRCF.

The Locksmith waited patiently.

"In the past I've been so angry… so hurt, so ashamed… so full of guilt." He looked out the window again as he paused. "I was convicted of crimes I committed. They just weren't done in the manner it was said to have happened."

She continued to watch him carefully, looking for a lock that needed picking. But he seemed to be doing just fine without her help at this point.

He shrugged his shoulders and with a stifled, forced exhalation said, "Not that it matters." He rubbed his head, and his hair lost its grooming. "For the wages of sin is death, right?" A faint, knowing smile formed on his face.

She gave a brief but firm nod back.

"Sin is sin. It took me a while, but I think that was one of the first lesson to have sunk in." He leaned forward just enough to facilitate the interlacing of his fingers that he used to pull up his right knee, allowing him to cross his leg upon his left knee. "For quite some time

I was bitter with what appeared to be an injustice … But it wasn't." He looked from her to his knee to back to her. He was smiling the smile of satisfaction of having learned something valuable and meaningful. "The Sermon on the Mount taught me that."

The Locksmith gave another brief but knowing nod. "One can be just as guilty thinking about it as they can be from doing it."

It was his turn to nod knowingly.

"Honestly, my friend, I am not here to preach salvation from the penalty of past sins. Suffice it to say that though we may not all end up in prison, we all deserve the death penalty before the Great White Throne."

It was his turn to be silent, and he was pleased for a change.

The Locksmith looked out the window again as if looking across the parking lot and out onto the distant fields would bring the words she felt directed to share.

"Do you remember when Israel was sent into captivity as a penalty for their disobedience?"

The man nodded and said, "We learn from Jeremiah that it was determined to be a penalty of seventy years. One year for every sabbatical year that they did not leave the ground untilled."

"Correct. Basically, God said, 'You did not honor me in the sabbath year of the land, and you owe me seventy.' But as I said, I am not here to review lessons of the penalty of sin." The smile had left her face and was replaced by a solemn countenance that reflected the gravity of the moment, yet it was just as loving. "I do not believe you are in need of salvation of the penalty of sin."

His eyes began to moisten.

"It is not the penalty that has you bound at this time, is it?" She paused to give him a moment to ponder the alternatives. "Before you can truly go home, there is one more lesson to learn. You have to be free from the bondage of a certain fear. A fear that comes from having to learn to live a life that is not directed by the power of sin."

The tears began to well up in his lower eye lids. "I don't know what I am going to do." He shook his head and gave a shallow shrug. "Where will I go? It has been thirty years of captivity. I don't know anyone who can help, nor anyone who would if they could."

"Do the others know?"

"You mean Williamson and them?" He sniffled.

She nodded.

"Yeah, I've told them." He looked back at his knee as he grasped it and slid his haunches forward in the chair, sliding his back into a slouch. "They say they've committed to one another to be praying for me."

"Good. That is as it should be," responded the older woman. "They have been quite a support, have they not?"

"Oh yeah. For sure. They have really been there for me. And I think that is part of the fear." He looked back into her eyes. "Here, I have them. Out there, I have no one. At least no one who will help." He let go of his knee and once again sat more upright in his chair. But his discomfort resulted in him bouncing his heel off the ground with the thrust of his toes. "My victims still live in the area I will be released into. I am also unsure what will happen when they find out I have been released. But most of all, I'm unsure of how to live my life above the power of sin. I know I am forgiven. I just don't want to go back to the way I was."

"Perhaps that is where this thought I have for you might help." This time it was The Locksmith who adjusted herself in her seat. "At the end of the Israelites' seventy years of captivity, do you remember what happened?"

"They were released, and some returned to the promised land, right?"

"Indeed. Darius released them and about fifty thousand returned. Do you know what happened when they got back to the promised land?"

Mr. Hanson stuck out his lower lip, shrugged his shoulders, and said, "They were no longer captives. I would think they went back and had a good life."

The Locksmith smiled and stifled a single chortle. She gave a quick shake of her head and said, "No ... not quite. Nehemiah tells us that years later men came to him in Persia and told him that the city remained in ruins while the people remained in great affliction and reproach."

The words *ruin*, *affliction*, and *reproach* caught the adult in custody's attention, and he looked intensely at The Locksmith, confident that she wouldn't stop the story there.

"Scripture says that when Nehemiah heard those words, he sat down and wept and mourned certain days." The Locksmith paused, watching the younger man. "He knew things were not as they ought to have been, so he began to fast and pray."

Mr. Hanson continued to watch her intently as he began to stroke his chin. "What did he pray?"

"He called out to the God of heaven, recognizing His power and the grandeur of His greatness. He recognized that God was a God who keeps His promises. In essence, he expressed his belief that God could be counted on to keep His promises and was merciful to those who loved Him and observed his commandments."

"Interesting," said Mr. Hanson.

"What is interesting?"

"That Nehemiah recognized God as one who was merciful to those who loved Him and observed his commandments."

"How so?"

"It just reminds me of one of our studies when we were looking at John fourteen where it says, 'If ye love me, keep my commandments.'"

The Locksmith smiled as she remembered.

"You were teaching us of Dr. Chapman's work that said we each have a love language. Our preferred language is the way we tend to communicate love. More accurately, it is the manner in which we feel loved. The problem is that we often try to communicate using our own love language and not the language of the one who is the object of our affection."

"And what happens?"

"That miscommunication leads to that person not experiencing the love we are trying to express."

"And what are some of the different love languages?"

He looked up at the ceiling, trying to remember the past more distinctly. "For some it is words of affirmation; for others it is touch. Others value acts of service, quality time, or receiving gifts. At least that is what I think I remember."

"But for God? What is His love language?"

"You said God's love language is obedience." He looked back at The Locksmith. "If you want God to feel your love, then you have to obey."

The Locksmith had a look of pleasure as she realized just how far this gentleman had come through the time they had spent together. "So, you find it interesting that Nehemiah would connect loving God with obeying His commandments?"

The man exhaled a stifled snort of laughter as he shook his head. "No. I meant how he connected God's mercy to those who love Him."

"Then you will not be surprised when you learn what Nehemiah did when he got to Jerusalem," said The Locksmith, pleased to see him picking one of his own locks. She had a feeling that with prayer and a little bit of guidance, Mr. Hanson was going to do just fine on the street upon his release.

"But go on. You were talking about Nehemiah's prayer." He sat upright in his chair, somewhat afraid he might have distracted his teacher from her lesson.

"Oh yes, let me continue." She again adjusted herself in her seat. "After recognizing His awesomeness and His mercy, he asked that God would be attentive to his prayer as he then confessed not only the sin of the people, but the sins of himself and his family." The woman paused, distracted as a thought popped into her head. It reminded her of Daniel's prayer where he, too, confessed the sins of himself and the people. She shook off the distraction and returned to her thought. "He reminded himself before God of not only the commandments of Moses that had instructed them that if they transgressed, they would be scattered among the nations, but also of the promise that if they returned to Him and kept his commandments, He would gather them back. In essence, Nehemiah trusted that God could be counted on to be merciful and change their condition of affliction and reproach."

Hanson placed his elbows on the table and he rested his chin on his folded hands. He was momentarily distracted as a CO passed by to check on their visit. Being reassured that all was well, the CO moved on, and Mr. Hanson's attention returned to the thoughts that had been circulating through his mind. The Locksmith observed him looking about the room, out the window, and then back to the room, pondering the thoughts that were presented for his consideration.

"How has this passage helped you in the past?"

"Me?" asked The Locksmith.

"Sure. I have often felt that the things you share must come from some personal experience at some time." He looked at her again with curiosity.

"I tend to believe there are phases of growth in a believer's life."

"Like Paul's teaching of the milk and the meat of the gospel?"

"Are you referring to the beginning of First Corinthians chapter three?"

The man nodded his affirmation. "Sure."

"Well, kind of. But I was thinking more along the lines of how we started." The man gave a confused expression. "The tenses of salvation," she said, trying to jog his memory.

"Oh yeah, salvation from the penalty, the power, and the presence of sin," he recollected.

"Correct. In the early stages of a believer's life, they are focused on dealing with the penalty of sin in their life. They are struggling to come to terms with how God could forgive them. They are constantly trying to deal with their guilt and shame because of the effects of their sin. They focus on being holy, yet frustrated that they aren't perfect."

"Constantly asking forgiveness for every little slipup?"

"Yes, in some degree. But more because they believe that the change God has done is one that should be fully realized now. And they tend to be legalistic, which leads to a lot of guilt and shame."

He smiled. "They are freed from the penalty but are still under great affliction and reproach."

"Yes, but not just from others. From themselves as well. They get stuck constantly having to deal with a sense of guilt under the penalty of sin because they have not experienced the salvation from the power of sin. They have experienced justification, salvation from the penalty of sin, but they have not yet experienced sanctification—salvation from the power of sin."

"I'm not sure I'm following you."

"Early in the life of most Christians, their focus is on becoming used to the fact that their sins are forgiven. It takes a while to let go of the shame and the guilt, even though it has already been forgiven. Their spirit is sensitive to the consequences of sin, the penalty of sin. So, they work hard to do the right, avoid the wrong. And for a while it seems to work."

"But no one can be perfect," interjected the man.

"Indeed, not."

"So they become legalistic?"

"Yes. Sometimes it affects how they interact with others. They act in opposition to Paul's teaching in Romans chapter fourteen."

The student squirmed a bit from being unfamiliar with what she was sharing. "I am not familiar with that teaching."

"In the fourteenth chapter of Romans, Paul teaches us about how one person's faith causes them to avoid eating certain things because the law tells them they shouldn't, which is fine. But they go beyond that and begin to tell other people they also shouldn't eat those things. In essence, they begin to judge others based on what God is doing in their lives. Often in things that really don't matter."

"They don't matter? How can things in the law no longer matter?"

The woman tried to illustrate. "God has told me not to eat bacon, but for you He hasn't made that a big deal. God has told me not to smoke tobacco, but for you He hasn't. I treat Saturday as the Sabbath, while for you it is Sunday."

"Are you saying that while murder might be wrong for me, it might be all right for you?" asked the man, a bit concerned with where this might be heading.

"I think the question you are asking will fantastically illustrate my point."

The man gave her a sideways glance as if to say, "*Oh, yeah?*"

"What have we been talking about?" she asked.

"Salvation," he replied.

"And more specifically?"

The man briefly reflected on the question and replied, "Justification, salvation from the penalty of sin."

"Indeed. Let me ask you this. Do people go to hell and miss out on heaven because they sin?"

"Of course," he responded indignantly.

"Do they?" she quipped. "Have you sinned?"

"Yes," he said cautiously. He sensed there was an important point she was about to make, and he wasn't sure he wanted to be on the wrong side of the lesson.

"I know I have sinned," the woman continued. "Are we both going to hell?"

"Well, no …" Now he had his first glimpse of where this lesson was headed. "We have confessed our sins, repented, and been forgiven."

"Perhaps you could say we have seen the desperate situation we were in and have accepted the salvation that has been offered through forgiveness. A forgiveness that has only one condition: we admit He is right and we are wrong."

"I thought God's forgiveness was unconditional."

"Oh? I thought it was God's love that was unconditional. I can agree that forgiveness is available to everyone, but it does have terms," qualified the elderly woman.

The younger man was silent but his focus on her was intense.

"The Old Testament uses two Hebrew words a combined twenty-two times to reflect one of two possible thoughts: changing a course of direction, or going back to the beginning to make that change. Every one of those twenty-two times, those two words are translated into English with the same word—*repent*. And in the New Testament we are told that the only sin that is unforgiveable is blasphemy against the Holy Spirit. Why is that?"

"Because the Holy Spirit is the one who convicts us of sin, and if we don't listen, then we won't repent."

"And if you don't repent?"

"I can't be forgiven?"

"Exactly," the woman said quietly. "If we want to be forgiven, we have to leave the fruit of the Tree of Knowledge of Good and Evil alone. God alone is the determiner of what is good and what is evil, of what is right and what is wrong."

"But that sounds like we are back to saying that sin is what sends us to hell."

"You can quickly see how desperate Paul felt in middle chapters of Romans that lead up to the powerful chapter eight. This is the downside to the law. It can only tell you what is broken. It cannot fix what is broken. And when your life is centered around this, you are constantly dealing with the penalty of sin, causing your spiritual growth to become stunted.

"In fact, this is a good place to take us back to Nehemiah. When Nehemiah was at the work of rebuilding the walls of the city, his adversaries—Sanballat, Tobiah, Geshem, and their people—conspired against the project. They had no desire to see the people of God safe behind walls, with a palace for their King, a temple for their God, and storehouses for the treasures they would receive when their King sat on His throne, and their God was in His temple. So they planned to 'come in the midst among them, and slay them, and cause the work to cease.'

"Notice their goal was not just to slay them. That was the means to the end. They wanted the work to stop. And so it is in our life. Our adversaries want our spiritual lives to come to an end and for the work that is being accomplished in us to come to an end, or at least be hindered.

"Once the breaches in the walls are closed, the walls are up and the beams, doors, bars, and locks of the doors of the gates are in place. Then our lives become Jerusalem as it was meant to be. Do you know what the name Jerusalem means?"

Then man shook his head but was all ears.

"It can be interpreted as 'they will see the wholeness', or 'they will feel the awe of the completeness,'" she said with a smile.

"It sounds like home," the man said.

"Home as it ought to be."

"So how does one do that?" He shrugged his shoulders. "Rebuild the walls."

"I think we look at these 'brethren' of Nehemiah, who had a right to be free. They had a right to have a temple. They had a right to live in the land. It had been granted by Cyrus, but it was not a reality they were enjoying."

"They were living under affliction and reproach," whispered Mr. Hanson.

"Indeed."

"Again, how does one rebuild the walls?"

"I think one needs to move beyond the milk and move on to the meat."

"Move beyond the milk of justification and onto the meat of sanctification?" asked the man, trying to get to the main point.

"In essence, yes." The woman paused and leaned forward a bit in her chair. "There comes a point in time in a believer's life, and this is what I was mentioning earlier, when one moves from justification to sanctification. One moves on from the place where they are focused on avoiding the penalty of breaking a sin, then walks into sanctification, where the freedom from the power of sin becomes not an issue of breaking a law but instead an issue of breaking a heart—God's heart."

The man sat there for a moment as the thought began to sink in.

"It is at this point that the law becomes not a broken commandment but a guidebook into the heart and mind of God."

Hanson was still processing.

"In fact, most people interpret the word *Torah* as 'the Law,' as in the first sense of a commandment to avoid breaking. But the word also means 'teaching, direction, guidance,' as in the second sense of a guidebook."

"So justification frees me from the first sense, then allows me to move on to the second."

"And until you do, you will have never secured the proper foundation to rebuilding the walls."

The CO had made his way toward their table and addressed the adult in custody. "It's time to begin wrapping it up, Hanson." He turned toward The Locksmith with a nod and acknowledged her kindly. "Ma'am."

Hanson's eyes were welling up. "I think I have been wisely following you. But how am I ever going to make the transition without your continued guidance?"

The woman smiled as they both stood up. "God never leaves his children alone. He is preparing someone for you. Someone to encourage you and support you. I have a feeling you are headed home to a family you never knew you had before you came here."

The man looked into her eyes and smiled.

"Where are you being released?"

"My jurisdiction is in Salem, so I will head there."

The woman squinted her eyes as if an idea had just popped into her head that was brimming with wonderous possibilities. "All will be well, my friend. All will be well."

And with that, they each turned to leave. He hadn't gotten but two steps away when he turned around. "I'm thinking of changing my name."

"Oh?" said the elderly woman, more as a way to ensure him that she was listening.

"Yeah, many guys do it in order to hide in the community they move back to. But for me … I don't know. It's more of a way to get a new start. Kind of a Saul to Paul kind of thing. I was adopted after my parents gave me up, and my adoptive parents were distant family on my mother's side who didn't really want me as a responsibility but weren't able to shirk the sense of obligation."

The woman was looking at the floor, thinking, listening to him speak.

"Because they were family, I learned later in life what my real last name was."

The woman looked up into the eyes of the man, truly interested in his real name.

"But I have decided not to take it."

The elderly woman appeared startled with surprise.

"I thought about taking the name Nelson. Many times, I have wondered what might have been if you and me had been family. But that just seemed too weird."

The woman smiled and waited for him to continue.

"I have decided on Christianson." The smile he gave showed he was filled with pride and a renewed sense of self.

"Mr. Christianson!" He looked back at her while he was making his way to the door. "None of my children carry my name. But I carry each of theirs right here." She set her hand firmly across her chest.

"Well, I hope for once I can make all of my parents proud."

The woman smiled broadly. "I am confident your Father is very proud. I know I am."

Both were filled with a knowingness that a new and brighter chapter lay ahead for Mr. Christianson. And with that peace, they both went their separate ways. She to a door that led to the world outside. But before she reached that door, she heard his door click and buzz. She glanced over her shoulder to see him enter a door that only *appeared* to be leading back into the heart of a prison. This made her chuckle in pleasure at the wonder of the redeeming love of God.

CHAPTER 17

THE STAGE SETTER

Ontario, Oregon
moments later

The sun was well on its rise when Miss Annabelle Nelson passed out of the visitation doors. She turned right and began heading toward the parking lot.

The warmth of the sun was delightful as it struck her full face countering the cool breeze also coming from the east. She could faintly hear it whistle as the breeze raced past the razor wire and across the compound, ignoring the entrance, ignoring the presentation of ID, ignoring the sally port doors, ignoring all protocol and procedures.

She smiled at the thought.

She was about twenty paces down the sidewalk when she was hailed from behind.

"Miss Nelson! Miss Nelson!"

She stopped and turned partway to get a look at the caller. "Good morning, Captain Stiles," she said as the officer in charge trotted closer to within earshot.

"Good morning, ma'am. Could I have a moment of your time?"

She paused just briefly as she tried to discern any urgency in his tone or demeanor.

"How can I help?" She resumed her slow and measured pace, assuming that in the absence of urgency this would likely be a brief request.

"I want to ask you about your special sauce," the captain stated matter-of-factly.

The elderly woman came up short in her stride, somewhat taken aback by the unexpected term. "I am sorry Captain. You are asking about what special sauce?"

The captain, through years of experience, had easily been able to respond to her stride by adjusting his, so much so that when she came up short, he was able, with that same experience, to come up short himself, then with ease directly position himself in a manner to address her. "I am sorry, ma'am. It is a term that we have come to use here at the facility to signify whatever it is you do, or say … or add to the lives of the men you work with here."

She paused again to look into his eyes to discern just what kind of conversation this was going to be. It wasn't the eyes that revealed the importance of this conversation. It was the fact that the captain had left his busy desk, broken his routine of the day, and rushed out the front in an obvious attempt to catch her right here at this moment that revealed this wasn't just a brief request. "Would it be all right with you if we walk up the pavement to the bench, sir?" She broke off her gaze and glanced up the cement walkway to bench just fifteen feet away.

The captain followed her gaze with his own, bowed at the waist, and extended his arm as if to say, "*Lead on.*"

Seconds later they were both seated on the bench. The Locksmith sat with her hands folded in her lap, and the captain sat to her left, sideways, with his right arm across the back of the bench.

"*Secret sauce* I believe you said." She offered this statement as a way to restart to their conversation.

"Yes, ma'am. To be honest, no one really knows what to call it. Through the years the entire staff has come to see the benefits of the time you spend with the men. They are the ones who talk far less about the change that is happening, but they are also the ones in whom we see the greatest transformation when they don't realize they are being watched." The captain paused and looked back toward the armory. "We have all kinds of programming here designed to bring about the effects that you are getting." He looked back at The Locksmith. "Don't get me wrong. The programs work. They make a difference. They are not useless. They have been studied and adjusted and validated. We know precisely what our outcomes are and what to expect."

The woman smiled. "That is very prudent of you."

"And so do they." He nodded back over his right shoulder toward the compound. There was the difficulty. "The programming in many ways is designed to bring about a result, and when the adult in custody knows what that result is, then they can adjust their behavior for a while to provide the *appearance* of the expected outcome."

"And the transformation is not present as you observe them *when they don't realize they are being watched*," the older woman completed his thought.

"Exactly."

The woman turned her face to the rising sun and closed her eyes in a brief but silent prayer. She did a quick assessment of the path that lay before her and the potential for landmines she might encounter. She understood the risks. She understood the dangers. She understood what was and what wasn't being asked. She understood that the one asking her these questions was a state officer. She understood it wasn't just this man in the uniform asking her these questions. Her response would be reported all the way up the chain of command. It would ultimately sit on a desk somewhere in Salem where it, too, would receive a quick assessment.

There was a facility full of people who had witnessed the transforming power of the kingdom of God at work, and they were aware that there was something more going on here than a sling and five small stones in a shepherd's pouch. There was a statewide department being represented by this uniform. There was an army who had studied their war, knew their instruments of warfare, and had thoroughly evaluated and knew their opponent. They knew their objectives, they knew their strategies, and their tactics were tested and validated. They were the best in the country. So how was it that an elderly woman with bluish-gray hair could meet weekly with these guys for an hour and shatter every expectation with such undeniable results? It wasn't just some friends and former students who were wanting to know. Many of them already understood the secret sauce. It was the state wanting the recipe to her secret sauce.

Her spirit was calm as she sensed the apparent danger, the importance of the circumstances they were engineering. She was aware of the risks associated with the questions she was being asked and how they could truly harm the work she was a part of. She knew the Enemy was near, but she also knew that He was on the warpath. It was this awareness that assured her to move forward.

The prayer she prayed was more of a groan, sigh in her spirit as the gravity of the entire situation sunk in, but it only lasted about four seconds. She turned to face the captain. Her smile had faded and was replaced with a look of grave uncertainty. The eyes were The Locksmith's favorite point of contact. She held his gaze for several moments.

"You may speak freely, ma'am. It's just me."

"Yes, James, I know it's you. I have known you for some time, and I have known your wife even longer. I have no problem answering the question for the man in the uniform. However, I am uncertain of how those up the chain of command will perceive the answers I would give. There are those in Salem who are not interested in the outcomes of which you speak, if they are forced to face a means they cannot accept."

"You don't work for the state, ma'am. You are here as a volunteer for religious education. Your purpose here has already been declared. You are not being held to a policy grounded in the separation of church and state."

"Yes. I understand that. I have worked for the state before, and the dangers were similar then. There were those who knew the outcomes of my means and were pleased with it. But even in Idaho there were those who felt threatened by those means and tried to enforce a policy grounded in the separation of church and state but were unsuccessful."

"Will you not share the secret of the sauce?"

She smiled and again turned her face to the sun for a moment.

With her eyes still closed and her face soaking up the warmth, she calmly stated, "It's less like a recipe and more like arranging a room." The Locksmith paused and the captain waited. "It isn't like two cups of flour, two cups of milk, and half a stick of butter. It's more like preparing to receive guests. The thermostat may need to be turned up or down, the curtains drawn or opened. There may be a need to move a chair, or perhaps adjust the entire layout of the room. There may be views that need to be avoided, or pictures taken down. We may need to sit on the porch, or at the dining room table. There may need to be some faint music playing, or just the ticking of the clock on the wall."

"That's it?" the captain asked as he gave a brief nod to a passing officer headed toward Master Control. There was a sense of disappointment in his voice. "You just set the stage?" The Locksmith smiled but kept her face toward the sun and her eyes closed.

"Oh yes, at least the start," she whispered. "That is the start of the sauce. I set the stage."

The captain smiled. He knew The Locksmith well enough to know to listen to her words carefully. She had said, "That is the start of the sauce." He also knew to pay attention to what she hadn't said. She said nothing about the part that made the secret sauce secret. "But ma'am, what's the secret in the secret sauce?"

She opened her eyes and rotated to face the captain. "The secret is for whom the setting is set," she stated simply. "Most think the setting is for the adult in custody. They think if the right piece of furniture is rotated, or the right picture is placed, then the adult in custody will come to their senses and transformation will occur."

"That isn't how it works."

"No. The setting is set for the one who comes later." She was again looking into the eyes of the captain.

The captain smiled and gave her an understanding nod. "The Lord," he surmised.

"Indeed, it is the Lord." She smiled back with an agreeing nod. "I cannot transform them. In fact, they cannot transform themselves. And that is where your system breaks down."

"How is it then that we see some of them changing?"

"You see a choice made differently, and it can be done—for a while. But only the Lord can give a person a new heart."

"You're telling me you set the stage for the Lord?" clarified the captain.

The older woman blinked her eyes as she shrugged her shoulders, giving a small shake of her head while rolling her hands into supination as if to say, *Yes, that's it.*

"I really don't do anything. It is more of an introduction," she said humbly.

"No need to be coy, ma'am. We all know that it isn't as simple as you make it sound." This time he closed his eyes as the warmth of the sun fell against his face. "Nonetheless, I think I understand. You facilitate a meeting. You declare His greatness. You celebrate His achievements. You give the glory and honor and praise where it belongs. You recite His truths, His judgement, His promises. As they begin to sense His presence, they glimpse a reality, or perception, they never had before." At this point the captain opened his eyes and added, "And they like it!"

"I introduce people to the things of God, and He not only helps them apply it to their lives, but He helps them to want it, to need it, to crave it. His Word touches needs they never knew they had. Hopes they never dreamed of. He clarifies things they thought they already understood. I set the stage and walk them through the setting and watch for what resonates." Miss Nelson paused and then asked, "Is that what you were wanting, Captain?"

He squinted against the sun and took a deep breath as he nodded, thinking about all the men who had come through this facility under his watch. He recalled faces and names. Many had left. Some were still there. Some had changed. Some hadn't. But he still wasn't sure he could tell where, when, or how that change happened. Just as importantly, he couldn't tell who, where, when, or how others would change. That was what was really bothering him. Who would change? How does someone find the ones who had the desire to change? Who gets invited into the special room? The Locksmith sat silently with a faint smile and hands still folded in her lap. "I think that will do just fine, Miss Nelson. That will do … at least for now." The captain stood and smiled. "Thank you, ma'am. Have a good day."

"Thank you, Captain. I think I shall," stated the elderly woman. He turned to reenter the facility. After a few strides, she called out, "Oh, Captain?"

The senior officer turned back to face her. "Yes, ma'am?"

"How well do you remember your Bible?"

The officer squinted again as he shrugged and tilted his head.

"Do you remember what happened to Adam and Eve after the fall?"

"I think they were kicked out of the garden, weren't they?"

"Yes, 'and he placed at the east of the garden of Eden Cherubims, and a flaming sword, which turned every way, to keep the way of the tree of life.'"

The officer squished up his lips and asked, "Cherubim?"

"A cherub is a supernatural being many call an angel. The 'im' ending makes it a plural, but that is beyond the point at hand."

"Why do you say 'many call an angel'?"

"I think the word *angel* is misleading."

"Oh?"

"The term dates back to old Latin language and simply means *messenger*. And it doesn't just mean supernatural beings. It can be any being, natural or supernatural, who acts as a messenger. It is more of a job title than a type of being."

"But cherub—"

The older woman smiled. "Yes. Cherubim are supernatural beings. But as I said, that is beyond the point."

"Okay," conceded the captain with a shrug, "then what is your point."

"Why were cherubim placed at the east of the garden of Eden?"

The captain squinted again as he thought. Then he responded, "To enforce the banishment. To enforce the punishment?"

"Perhaps," Miss Nelson smiled. "That response makes sense coming from a correctional officer."

"But you don't think so?"

"No, I don't." The woman smiled as she stood and faced him. "Scripture says, it was done 'to keep the way of the tree of life.' Why does it have to be that they are keeping humans out of the garden? Why can't it be that they are keeping the way open for humans to return to it?"

The captain was taken back a bit.

"Captain, how does your job change if you begin to see it not only as enforcing their prison stay but also as protecting their ability to return to this path and to their lives and their families?"

The captain looked back at the doors that he had always seen as the entrance into the prison. He hadn't ever really thought of it as a path out. Most adults in custody leave the facility through a different path, one that leads them back to their county of jurisdiction. But the comparison had captured his imagination. "Why do I have the feeling you are setting a stage for me?"

The woman smiled. "Perhaps we are all messengers who spend our lives either passing judgment on our fellow humans or joining God in keeping the path open to the Tree of Life for those who long to find it. I cannot be trusted to be correct on every topic. I am sure some of my beliefs are likely heretical. I try to guard my life and doctrines carefully, and I can only share what I believe God has shown me. Make no mistake. I do not change anyone. Only the Spirit of God can do that. I just set the stage and make the introductions."

The captain returned the smile. "Perhaps you are right, Miss Nelson. Perhaps you are right." He paused before saying, "Thank you for your time, ma'am."

"Have a good rest of your day, Captain." The two parted ways as he headed back toward the entrance.

* * *

Later that afternoon upon returning home, the elderly woman was about to place a call when she thought first to check her watch. Once she did a quick mental calculation, she decided instead to send a simple email. It stated, "If I understood our conversation of last month correctly, I think you might be able to help me with a small project. Give me a call when you get this. I would be very appreciative of a chance to discuss it with you."

CHAPTER 18

A GREAT LIGHT

*The Orphanage, Benin, West Africa
a few days later*

Good afternoon, ma'am. Or should I say good morning?" asked Jaker.

"Either way works for me, Mr. O'Malley. How have things been at the orphanage the past few days?"

"We have been having fun." His voice altered direction. "*Hé, regarde toi!*" said Jaker, obviously not to Miss Nelson

"Who was that?"

"It was little Lizbet. She loves to sneak up behind me and try to tickle me. Let's see, where was I? Oh yeah, we have been having fun playing games in the evening. The kids are still in school, so during the day we have been talking about the crusade."

"Anything new with Solomon?"

"He is discouraged. But I think he is coming to the place where he isn't seeing God's hand in it, so he isn't sure what to do."

"Has there been any gathering around a central agenda by the other pastors?"

"Well, that's what I mean. He and I can now both see that there is a common ground in evangelism. All the pastors are interested in it. But they can't agree where to focus their energy. I think he sees such a need in his people, and he expects others to not only see the same need in their people as well but to also join him in the way he feels God has called him to address this issue. He is interpreting the solution to the problem in his flock as the same solution to the same problem that other flocks also have. However, his pastor friends are going after the same problem by different means."

"They all see the need for evangelism but can't agree on how to address it together, correct?"

"That is what it appears to me. They are all good, loving, well-meaning pastors. But I think it is hard for some pastors to allow another to define the solution for each of their individual flocks."

"Try to encourage him to be patient, and postpone the larger crusade if need be. Instead, have him focus on what God has called for him to personally do in his flock, unless he can see clear direction from the Lord to do otherwise. It may not be God saying, 'No, do not do that.' But it may be Him saying, 'No, do not do that right now.' As you yourself are aware, God's will is not only about what to do; it is also about when to do it. If he keeps pursuing in a direction God is not leading, then he will not only continue to be disappointed, but he will also miss out on seeing God at work somewhere else."

Jaker raised his eyebrows as he considered what was being said. "Agreed. I will let him know we talked, and your counsel is to consider waiting on the cooperative effort. I'll make it clear you encourage him to move forward on what God has shown him for his own flock."

"Yes, I think that will cover it," Miss Nelson said in confirmation. "How are the Truesdales?"

Jaker smiled to himself at the thought. "Michael is having a blast. The lack of progress on the crusade has granted him more time with the children, many of whom are the age Lacy would have been if cancer hadn't cut her life with her family short. I see him tearing up at times. But he sure loves these kids. It has been fun."

"How about Cherish? Is there anything new with her?"

"It is pretty much the same. It continues as we have seen. However, … " Jaker paused to put his thoughts into words.

"However, what?"

"However, I have noticed something interesting."

"Yes?"

"I think the joyfulness of the children in the midst of their brokenness is breaking through to her."

"Is it challenging her perspectives on what is truly valuable?"

"I think that's it. In some ways she is reliving her Mexico mission trip, and seeds planted in Mexico maybe bearing fruit in Benin."

"Perhaps she is missing the strength those older, more nutritious home-cooked meals provided, compared to her steady diet of cake, huh?" asked Miss Nelson, returning to her previous analogy.

"I think she is becoming envious of the joy they have despite their brokenness and their humble environment. Perhaps this will be the start of a turnaround for her." Jaker sounded hopeful.

"Perhaps, but I have seen a lot of children in my days, and it seems to me that children who like cake don't easily go back to their green beans." Jaker could tell The Locksmith was pondering how best to address the locks binding this young lady, so he remained quiet. "Let's keep praying for her for now. I do not sense the Lord has revealed a direction for us to be moving yet. How is the newest addition to the orphanage?"

"She is a tough nut!"

"Oh?"

"Yes, she spends a lot of time off by herself. She appears sullen at times, tearful often, and sometimes just plan angry."

"Hmm."

"At first she seemed pleased to see her siblings. After being here for a bit, she seems to be more resentful."

"Aww, she still needs prayer as well. See if Deborah can teach her to sing and dance."

Jaker raised his eyebrows and puckered his lips as if he hadn't seen that piece of advice coming but could see the potential value in it. "Okay, I will get to work on it. What about Max?"

Miss Nelson spent the next several minutes retelling the tale of the interview and current state of the investigation. "The police have become completely distracted away from Max and her Bible study group. They were directed to Louisiana to investigate the Madame's henchmen. I think the pressure of having the police snoop around is having an effect on the grandmother, putting more distance between her and Abomey."

"All the better," said Jaker.

"Agreed," said Miss Nelson. "Good afternoon to you, Mr. O'Malley."

"Good morning to you, ma'am." Just before the connection went dead, Miss Nelson could hear Jaker say, "Come here, you!"

After dinner, Jaker went looking for Deborah and found her in the kitchen washing pots and pans. As she washed, she and Solomon were deep in a discussion.

"I know, Pastor. It still seems strange to me," said Deborah.

"What seems strange to you?" asked Jaker.

"Aww, my friend, perhaps you can help us," said the pastor as Jaker entered the kitchen.

"I can try. How can I help?"

Deborah looked at the pastor with incredulity as if saying, *"Are you really going to try and get this White man to explain this to us?"*

"What's up?" asked Jaker.

"While you have been here in our country, there have been protests in your country. We are not exactly sure what is happening, and we are hoping you can explain it to us. There are some strange things with your people that we do not understand," said Deborah.

"Strange things like what?"

"There have been protests in Birmingham, Alabama, these past weeks," said the pastor.

"Oh, I wasn't aware of any protests. What have they been protesting?"

"A statue," they said together.

"A what?" asked Jaker.

"They are protesting a statue of a man who lived one hundred fifty years ago," said Deborah as she was drying some pans with a towel. "Why?"

They were both looking at him as if it was the stupidest thing they had ever heard of.

"You're asking why they are protesting the statue?"

"Yes, that is what we are asking," said the pastor.

"Well, I obviously don't know all the details. I've been here the whole time."

"Yes."

Jaker could see his response wasn't satisfying their curiosity, so he tried again. "I believe they are protesting what the statue stands for, what it symbolizes," said Jaker as both Black people just stared at him. Jaker squished up his face, uncertain of what else to say.

"What is it a symbol of?" asked Deborah.

"Well, the … uh … The Southern States back home were the agrarian South, and many of the people of the South bought slaves and used them to farm their fields and keep their homes," said Jaker as he tried to explain. He couldn't help feeling more than a bit awkward trying to explain the topic of slavery to the Black people of West Africa.

"Is his family still buying slaves?" asked the pastor.

"Not that I know of."

"Does his family still have land that requires slaves to work it?" asked Deborah.

"I very much doubt that, given the fact that it is so much easier with modern farm equipment we have today."

"Why did they select him for their protest?" asked Deborah, still drying pans, which, given the topic, made Jaker feel a bit more uncomfortable. So he grabbed a towel and began helping her.

"Because he has become a symbol of all the bad things in the past, and there are those who feel he represents many of the reasons some people of today are struggling now. The history of slavery in the South represents a very dark time in American history, and one that many people are still very sensitive over. There remains a natural connection between the current injustices that many still see in the world today, and those symbols still represent the values of the people of the past that led to those injustices. All this history, fueled with frustrating injustices, makes them angry."

"They are symbols?" asked the pastor, who seemed to still be struggling.

"Yes. But symbols are powerful things. People rally to a flag, or a cause, or stand for a song, or a pledge. Symbols are important because … because … Well, because they're symbolic." Jaker was beginning to wonder how he got into this.

"Aww, because they are symbolic," parroted Deborah with a smile as she looked at the pastor, who simply smiled back at her while looking through the corners of his eyes just beginning to realize how much fun this was becoming. Jaker shook his head, sensing the futility and inappropriateness, if not foolishness, of even being in a position of trying to explain slavery to a Black person. As well as the fact that he felt he was being played with.

"Symbols, huh?" asked the pastor.

Jaker just nodded and kept his mouth shut.

"Is there any slavery today in your country?" asked the pastor.

"Sure," reported Jaker. "One of the biggest human trafficking events surround the huge sporting events like the Super Bowl."

"Where do they hold the protest for those slavery events?" asked the pastor.

"If they are spending so much time protesting symbols, it must be because you do not have any forced marriages in your country, where women or children are forced against their will to marry," pointed out Deborah.

"Or coerced into fraudulent domestic servitude," added the pastor.

"You must not have any illegal immigrants who were smuggled into the country under the promise of freedom, only to find themselves compelled to work in order to pay back the debt of being brought into your country," Deborah added.

"That is one of the most common forms of modern slavery, and if your country is out protesting symbols of men who held slaves one hundred fifty years ago and more, then it must be because you don't have any of these other forms of slavery the rest of us in the world deal with," summarized the pastor. "Just symbols. That is all that is left?" The two were smiling at one another.

Jaker saw his chance. "Well, that reminds me of why I am not only here in West Africa, but more to the point, why I am in this kitchen with a pair of interrogators?"

Jaker laid down his towel as he finished drying the last pot. "Thank you for your help, my friend," said Deborah.

"Miss Nelson wanted me to talk to each of you about something."

"Yes?" asked the pastor.

"Pastor, Miss Nelson is wondering if you might consider that one of the reasons the crusade isn't moving forward as you had hoped is because the other pastors are so fixated on the individual solutions they feel God has shared with them. They may not see the same benefits to the solution God has given you, or don't feel released from what God has shown them, to pursue the solution God has shown you. Perhaps this has caused God to not yet be able to move forward in the manner you have envisioned. Perhaps God is asking you to be faithful to the wisdom He has shown you while He is asking them to do the same? Maybe you are being asked to enter into a season of waiting upon Him?"

"I have begun to believe much the same thing. I believe her advice is confirmation of what I have been sensing in my own spirit. Tell her I will take that under advisement as I continue to pray," said the pastor. "Thank you, my friend, for being open with me. I treasure your contribution."

"I am sure Miss Nelson will want to know if there is anything she can do to support you in your ministry here. I know you mean a lot to her. She is pleased if she can be a part of the wonderful work you are doing and the love you are showing your people." The pastor nodded his appreciation.

"And Miss Deborah." Jaker stuck out his lower lip and drew it tight against his upper lip before taking a deep breath and continuing. "She has a very special request of you. To be honest, I am not sure what she means, but I am sure you will understand."

"Yes?" asked the cook.

"She would like to ask if you would teach our newest member here at the orphanage how to sing and dance," he said with a smile.

Deborah looked seriously at the pastor, her smile now gone. The pastor looked back solemnly, not wanting to persuade his parishioner one way or the other. She was fiddling with the towel.

"Pastor, this is something very private."

He nodded his agreement.

"It is very personal," she said. "It has been so critical and pivotal to my own healing. It helped me to trust and helped me to find a reason to love again." She looked at her towel. "I am not sure something so personal can ever be used by someone else. How can you help someone feel beautiful again by having them wear a dress that fits yourself so perfectly but looks ill-fitting on anyone else?"

The men just sat quietly.

"Jaker, I am not sure this will work. I am not sure it is healthy for me either. I don't think she knows what she is asking," said Deborah.

"Dear one, we all three know why she is asking you," said the pastor. "What if she had said the same to you?"

"My wounds are scars now. But I am not sure I can show them to anyone else. I still remember them being open, raw, bleeding, infected, and so very painful. I was not a nice person back then."

The pastor reached across the table and placed a hand on hers. "Which is exactly why she is asking you," he said, tears welling up in his eyes. "But all three of us will support you. She is only asking. She would never presume to command you."

Jaker remained silent as he watched the two begin to talk in Fon. As they talked the tears began to well up in her eyes as if she was recalling some deeply painful memories. When they had finished talking, she looked at Jaker with a small smile on her face and said, "If my suffering can allow me to be a blessing to someone else who is suffering, then it will be my pleasure to offer them a look at what God has used to help me to heal."

Jaker smiled and nodded his understanding and his appreciation. Once she accepted her assignment, Deborah laid down her towel and walked out.

Two nights later Jaker was having a hard time sleeping, which usually meant the Lord had some reason for him to be awake. He tossed and turned and prayed through his flock until he felt he had covered them all and released every concern and care he could think of to the Lord, finally ending in praise. He felt the familiar sense of

Sabbath peace move across his soul, leaving him with the sense that regardless of what might happen, all would be well.

Moments later, he heard the soft rubbing and slapping of sandals against the concrete outside his room and the subtle scraping of a chair being pulled into position. He got up and quickly dressed, slipped out the door, and found Solomon sitting in a chair in the darkness of a new moon.

"Good morning," whispered Solomon.

"Good morning. What time is it?" asked Jaker.

"It is about two o'clock in the morning."

"What are you doing here?" asked Jaker as he took the chair next to Solomon.

"I couldn't sleep and was wondering why the Lord had me awake."

"And He told you why?"

"Heh!" The pastor laughed. "He did." He pointed across the campus toward a shadowy figure moving in the light of security lamps on the water tower.

"Who is that?"

"Deborah," responded the pastor. "When I realized what time it was, I instantly knew why I was awake. This is the time Deborah would always have her appointment with her Lord."

He nodded toward the figure as it made its way into the girls' dormitory.

There was the additional scrapping of sandals as the night guard approached the two men.

"Good morning, Pastor. Good morning, Jaker."

"Good morning, Timothy," said the pastor. "So now is the time, huh?"

"Yes, she spoke to me this past evening and asked if I would lock up the dogs so they wouldn't disturb them if they danced. I told her I would and that I would be praying."

Then it began to click in Jaker's mind just what he was watching, and he smiled. The guard noticed and asked, "Do you know what you are watching?"

"I think so," said Jaker with a smile. "I bet she has been doing this for at least ten or fifteen years."

"Over twenty. How did you know?" asked the pastor.

"Something Miss Nelson told me when I was much younger."

"Did she tell you the story?" asked the pastor in surprise.

"No, just that she had a friend who had suffered great trauma, who eventually found 'a language of hope that led to healing and purpose' while learning to sing and dance in the moonlight as a young girl," explained Jaker.

"That's the one," stated the pastor with a smile.

"Are there details to that story?" asked Jaker.

"I am sure that as with every story there are details. But what they are none of us know, nor have we been willing to ask," said the pastor.

"Apparently, there have only been two people who have known the details of that story," added the guard. "But I think tonight a third will learn. Sorry, my friends, I must pray as I was asked." The guard slipped out of his chair and moved off several yards away and hid in the shadows of a great tree in the middle of the campus.

"I think that is what we should all be doing," shared the pastor, and he slipped out of his chair and off into the shadows of the boys' dormitory.

Jaker shifted his chair into the darker shadows of his building feeling that the Lord had invited him to be a part of the dance through prayer by waking him up.

Just then the door to the girl's dormitory creaked opened, and out stepped two shadowy figures holding hands. They crossed the center of the quad of the campus and sat at a picnic bench together, where they sat for the next hour and a half talking with one another. At the end of their time together, the older woman stood up and embraced the younger one. Then she moved off from the table and began to sway in the darkness. As the memories returned, you could hear her begin to sniffle, moan, and groan, which ultimately turned into a humming sound as she swayed. The older woman danced while the younger woman fought off sleep until she was no longer able. She lay her head down on the table and drifted off while Deborah watched over her. The men left their seclusion and returned to their respective quarters.

Later that morning as the sun was coming up, Jaker arose, groomed, and joined the children playing about the quad. Later, he found his way to the kitchen and saw Deborah busy at work with a new helper.

"I see you have some new help!"

"I have," replied Deborah. "My previous pot and pan drier just wasn't going to work out."

"That's too bad. I hear he was cheap labor," said Jaker with a smile.

"And too expensive, even free," smile Deborah back. "Besides, I think my new helper may be better company during the hard times."

"You are probably right," bemoaned Jaker.

"Good morning, Christina. How are you today?" he asked.

"I am fine, thank you," replied the young woman.

"You look rested," offered Jaker.

"I haven't slept well in years—until last night." Christina did look different this morning, and though the sleep likely helped, it was more likely due to her new companion.

"What's on the agenda for today?" asked Jaker.

"You will have to ask the pastor." Deborah smiled and greeted Pastor Nosakhere as he walked into the kitchen.

"Good morning, Pastor," said Deborah.

"Good morning," said Solomon. "How is everyone today?" he asked, sitting at the center of the prep table.

"I am fine," said Christina.

"I am well," said Jaker. "What do we have planned for today."

"I know what I had planned. Now we will begin to see if it is what the Lord has planned."

"What do you mean?"

"We recently took the crusade off the table for the regional pastors—"

"For now," interrupted Jaker.

"For now," the pastor agreed with a smile.

"But we have recently decided that we shall move forward as planned and use the *Jesus Movie* to spread the gospel to the areas of our parish instead of the whole country."

"Yet?" prompted Jaker.

"Yet." parroted the pastor.

"So how do we do that?" asked Jaker.

The pastor led Jaker, Deborah, and Christina to one of the classrooms in another building where Mike and Cherish Truesdale, as well as a small group of the pastor's parishioners, had gathered around a table on which sat a large backpack.

As he entered the pastor spoke in Fon. "All right, brothers and sisters, let us pray and then begin." The small group gathered and bowed their heads. "Great God of heaven. Thank You for these people. Thank You for their willingness to lock arms and march toward the gates of hell to reach those who are lost and confused. We humbly ask that as we move, You will bless our efforts not for our glory, not for our pride, not for pleasure, not for our arrogance. We ask because there are sheep lost in the thickets of our neighborhoods who need to meet the Good Shepherd." Whispered prayers were being interrupted with "Amen" and "Help us, Jesus."

"They are our neighbors. They are our friends. They are our families. Today we confess that we are a broken people. We realize that pride and arrogance run in us as do other iniquities. Forgive us, we pray. We come to You as damaged vessels and ask that You fill us with Your Holy Spirit and give us the grace we will need to face the challenges that will be put before us. Protect us, we pray, through the power of Your Holy Spirit, so that the Enemy who considers this his home turf cannot distract or dissuade us from the task You have appointed for us to do.

"As we do our best, we realize it is only a few loaves of bread and a few fish. Please be gracious and do what only You can do. We ask this because we know that Your Son shed His blood for even us in this dark region of the world. And we know His blood cries out from the ground on behalf of the lost and broken in our neighborhoods. Amen and amen."

The congregated body of believers all said, "Amen."

"Brothers and sisters, let me share with you what the Lord has put on my heart. About eighteen months ago I was made aware of a group who were using a movie about Jesus to introduce the gospel to the lost and broken of the world. What they were doing captivated my imagination, and I began researching what they were doing. They have been working for over twenty years presenting the film to the various regions of the world, then they follow it up with discipleship and the start of new churches

"Over those twenty years, they have made it possible for the movie to be shown over eighty-million times. There have been nearly sixteen-million decisions for Christ. There have been seven million initial discipleship follow-ups, and over seventy-five thousand new preaching points have been established. They report that for every three American dollars invested, one person comes to know the Lord. I want our friends, neighbors, and family—who live one yard from the gates of hell in the heart of Vodun—to have had every opportunity to know Jesus.

"I looked into their equipment, and we have secured one of their packs for our own, thanks to the generous contribution of our brother, Michael Truesdale." The pastor motioned for Mike to come forward and open the backpack.

For the next twenty minutes, with the assistance of the pastor as translator, Michael Truesdale opened, removed, and explained the various components of the *Jesus Movie* backpack. He showed them the evangelism soccer ball of different colors and explained how they could use it to draw the attention of children who love games and share with them by using the different colors that form the basics of salvation. He showed them the cubes hinged together in the manner that could be unfolded, displaying pictures with which they could tell the gospel story. They had evangelism pencils and evangelism hats, and he explained how all of these could be used to raise interest in the children.

Then he unpacked the projector and the screen and showed how they were assembled and how the sound system worked. When all the contents of the backpack had been revealed, he showed them how it was all repacked into the easy-to-transport backpack.

Many of the parishioners were excited and began to ask the pastor what they were going to do with this wonderful gift.

"That is why we are here today. I have some thoughts on where we go from here, but I want to hear from you as to what you think can be done with such tools as these," stated the pastor.

Jaker smiled at how easily it transitioned from the faithful step of a pastor to the faithful step of a people, as if it were meant to be. For the next forty-five minutes the group discussed the various who, what, where, when, how, and why of their new project. Within another forty-five minutes, a plan was in place for the coming month, and the people and their pastor were already sensing the power and presence of God at work in their midst. All felt well.

Later that night after dinner, Jaker entered the kitchen and found Deborah and Christina drying pots and pans while the pastor sat at the preparation table sharing his excitement for the upcoming evangelistic event.

"…And then we will invite them into the church and show the movie. At the end of the movie, we will have an opportunity for those who would like to accept Christ to come forward, then we will have them move to a place where we can get their name and contact information so we can follow up and invite them to our small Bible study group for discipleship training."

"People are hungry, Pastor. Now is the time of their salvation," said Deborah.

"Amen," said the pastor.

"What are you going to do for the prayer cover? The mambos and houngans won't be pleased, and they will respond," challenged Deborah. Jaker sat down completely interested in the answer to the question he and Miss Nelson had been asking themselves.

"We have already developed a prayer time. They meet every day through our mini-crusade and will be praying for me, our church, the workers, the equipment, those who will come, the weather, and anything else the Lord brings to mind. Then they have committed to praying for the twenty-four hours before, the whole time of, and then the twenty-four hours after the showing of the movie."

"It sounds like you have the right team in place," commented Jaker.

"I believe we have done all we can do. The rest is up to the Lord.

I think it was His plan anyway. What will be, will be. I think we can live or die by that," shared the pastor.

Over the next several nights, the Lord woke up Jaker every morning a little before 2:00 a.m. Feeling invited by the Lord of the universe to watch, he would get up, dress, and slip out on the concrete porch outside his room. Then he would relax into the chair and watch with interest as the two women danced and hummed. Each morning started with the older one talking to the younger one. He could never hear what they were saying, which wouldn't have helped anyway as he was certain they were speaking Fon.

After talking for several minutes, the older one would stand up, move away from the picnic table, and begin to sway. For the first couple of nights, she was doing all the humming and dancing. The melodies were very similar every time. They were slow, sad, haunting melodies that at times were punctuated by groans and sniffles. It was only a couple of mornings later when one could easily tell the younger one was crying as well. After about the fourth morning, the younger one began to stand at the table and sway as she hummed to herself. Jaker never approached either the older or the younger to ask them anything of their personal time of communion.

Around 1:30 the next morning on the day of departure, Jaker was again awakened, and as usual he knew the way. He quickly dressed, exited his room, and sat quietly, waiting in the shadows.

"What are you doing up at this hour?" said a female voice in English. Jaker jumped.

"Cherish? I could ask you the same."

"Yeah … Well, I couldn't sleep."

"Same here. Since we are both up at the same time—"

"Yeah, kind of weird, isn't it? What are the chances?" interrupted Cherish.

"I have a mentor who quotes Rabbis as saying, 'Chance, isn't a Kosher word,'" concluded Jaker.

"You like doing that, don't you?"

"Doing what?"

"Throwing out little tidbits like, 'Rabbis say chance isn't a Kosher word.'"

"Oh, does that bother you?"

"No, not really. I think it helps make harder thoughts simpler and easier to understand. But it's definitely not normal," confessed the girl.

"Not normal or not common?"

"I don't know yet."

"So, what are you doing out here?" asked Jaker.

"Thinking."

"Thinking about what?"

"I wish I knew."

"You've seen a lot this week."

"Yep."

"Do you find yourself thinking about any one thing over and over?"

"Well, kind of."

"Does it remind you of Mexico"

"Yeah, how did you know?"

Jaker paused to see if the girl had formulated any thoughts beyond *kind of.*

"Both places are poor and yet..." Cherished paused, unable to find the right word.

"And yet so rich in the things that matter?"

"Yeah, I think so. The first time I traveled outside the US, I thought everyone was living life weirdly. But the more I travel, the more I feel the way I live at home is kinda strange. They all have something I want but have trouble finding."

"I think you are on to something the Lord is trying to teach you," explained Jaker.

"Is that why I can't sleep?" asked Cherish.

"I don't think so." There was a slight creak across the quad. Jaker pointed his finger at the girls' dormitory. "Shh, I think *that* is."

CHAPTER 19

RETURNING HOME

Benin, West Africa
later that evening

Jaker fell back to sleep sometime after 3:00 a.m. and rested peacefully until about 6:30 a.m. when he awoke to the sound of children playing in the quad. He arose and finished packing his luggage, and an hour later he had stripped the bed, cleaned the room that served as his water closet, and was ready for the early afternoon departure.

He left his belongings in the room and went to play with the children one last time before they left for school. There were hugs and tears, as many came to realize they would not be seeing the young White man again unless the Lord had reason to intervene. He was struck by how easily he had come to love these children and how easily they gave away more love than he ever could. After breakfast, they were gone.

The rest of the morning was a kind of debriefing time with Pastor Nosakhere and the orphanage staff. It was clear to Jaker that the orphanage, home to just a few of the broken, bruised, and hurting children of West Africa, was in capable and loving hands. He knew that nearly a quarter of a million children are reportedly trafficked into realms of the kingdom of darkness, and so few ever escaped. He knew that if his trust was based on God only meeting them here, in this orphanage or another one, then he would despair. But he trusted in a God who knew how to find the broken, bruised, and hurting and move them to the gates of heaven that were within one yard of where they lived.

The crusade was off to a great start, and there was optimism in the young pastor and his parishioners. The showing of the movie was still a few weeks off, but the small group was meeting daily to pray, to plan, and to participate in whatever it was that God was doing. Their passion showed they believed in a big God.

By late afternoon, just before the children were to return, the team of three decided to begin their trek back to Cotonou to catch their flight home by way of Paris. Given the time difference, and the fact he still had a little time before they were scheduled to depart, Jaker decided to make his final call to The Locksmith.

"Good morning, ma'am," said Jaker.

"Good afternoon to you, Mr. O'Malley," responded Miss Nelson. "What has the Lord shown you of what He is doing in West Africa?"

"It appears the body of Christ is going out to collect lost sheep in about two weeks."

"Fantastic! Isn't that what Solomon wanted to do?"

"Yes! Exactly! However, he has had to trim back his activity to fit the vision. The conflict between his faith and the faith of his fellow pastors does not appear to have been in conflict against the dream, only the scope of that dream."

"I believe Solomon's heart is so big for his people, and his belief in his God is so complete, he probably overstepped the vision God was presenting."

"Agreed, but I can't fault him for the error. He erred on the side of big, not small."

"Yes, it is too often that we see people who just do not believe enough in what their God can do. As a result, they miss seeing all the places He is at work."

"Then they miss all the places they could be joining Him."

"Very true, Mr. O'Malley. So how are Cherish and Christina doing?"

"Interesting you should ask about them together. The past several nights the Lord has awoken me just before the hour of Christina's time with Deborah," relayed Jaker.

"Oh?"

"The first night Christina fell asleep in the middle of the lesson. But Deborah has been patient, and they continue to meet each morning."

"Can you see a difference in her level of interest or participation in the early morning lessons?"

"Yes, but the greatest difference is that Christina has begun to hang around Deborah more in the kitchen. In the process, she has become less sullen, less resentful, and though she is still withdrawn, she isn't as snappy."

"She appears less tortured inside of her own skin?"

"Yes! However, this has generated an interesting problem," said Jaker.

"What to do with a girl too old, and academically delayed, to be in school yet too vulnerable to be in an internship for vocation training."

"*Exactement!*"

"She will need a place to live because she can't stay in the orphanage."

"Yes."

"She will need someone to teach her a trade so she can support herself and potentially a family."

"Yes."

"Regardless, I prefer her in the proverbial frying pan instead of the fire."

"Agreed."

"Perhaps, if the lessons continue, there may be mutual benefit."

"Like the childless helps the motherless?"

"Something like that. It might be that mother needs the child as much as that child needs the mother. It won't solve the internship issue, but it might solve the vulnerability issue. We will have to see where this relationship leads. At least—"

"We can pray," finished Jaker. "Agreed. And then there is Cherish."

"Yes?"

"Guess who else the Lord woke up a little before the dancing and singing lessons this morning?"

"Oh my, I confess. That shouldn't surprise me, but it does."

"Uh-huh."

"Well then, once you get to Paris, see if you can find a way to get a seat next to Cherish, or she and her father, but at least get close to her. Then call me regardless of the time difference. I have some praying to do and another call to make before we talk again."

"Very good. Enjoy the rest of your day, ma'am. I will talk to you in about seven to eight hours," said Jaker.

"Good afternoon, Mr. O'Malley. *Bon voyage*," replied The Locksmith.

• • •

The flight from Cotonou to Paris was one that flew through the night, beginning about 11:00 p.m., and arrived early the next morning. Jaker was not able to switch his seat to where Cherish and her father were sitting, but he was able to learn that the person occupying the seat next to them was a single businesswoman flying alone. Jaker was able to upgrade his seat to first class, and the woman was more than willing, pleased actually, to trade seats so he could be near his friends. He contacted Miss Nelson, who answered on the first ring. She informed him that she had spoken to Deborah and received permission to tell the background story of what occurs in the sessions of singing and dancing with the moon. Then she proceeded to tell the story in enough detail that Jaker would be able to relay it to Cherish. Both Deborah and The Locksmith felt now was the time to allow the story to be told.

• • •

Hours later, the flight to SeaTac left Charles de Gaulle, and Jaker was in his seat next to Cherish.

"Have you told your father about what you and I witnessed this morning?"

Cherish chewed the inside of her lip. "No."

"You haven't? Why not?"

"It didn't seem right. There seemed to be a reason for why they were there alone last night."

Jaker gave a shallow sigh. "Ah, yes. I would agree. That is very insightful of you."

"Well, I'm thirteen. I'm not an idiot."

"Heh, true. What if I told you I had permission to tell you some of the details of what we saw and why it was happening?"

Cherished looked at her dad, who sat silently looking out the window with a tear in one eye as he silently prayed. Cherished looked back at Jaker, making intentional eye contact. He realized she wasn't playing with her phone.

"Do I want to hear it?"

Jaker broke eye contact and looked up the aisle toward the front for several seconds, then looked back into the eyes of his friend. "I can't answer that for you. But I can tell you two things." Jaker paused to select his words carefully. "The first is this: There are stories that are not worth hearing; therefore they are not worth being told. There are some stories that need to be told and never are. There are stories that are told over and over and over again, yet they are never heard. Then there are those special stories that once heard, the person listening is never the same."

"And this is one of those stories?"

"Yes."

Cherish looked at her dad, whose eyes were closed and cheeks were moist from the tears. He could only bring her so far. She was becoming a woman, and the spiritual war was being fought on multiple fronts. And the world and the flesh were having their effects. But the choice she made here and now was one that could turn the tide of the war in her life. He knew she alone would decide what direction her life would take. He and his wife had done all they could do to prepare her for this moment. Now he was praying like a man who believed a life depended on it. Because it did.

"What is the other thing? You said there were two things you could tell me."

"Once I tell the story, you will be responsible for what you do with the story."

"What do you mean?"

"Billions of people will never hear this story. Thousands can hear it, and nothing will change. But for the fortunate few, they will hear it, and as I said, their life will never be the same. Once I tell you the story, you will no longer be one of the billions. You will either be one of the thousands or one of the fortunate few. But you will only hear the story once."

Cherish was looking intently, trying to decide if she really wanted to hear the story.

"Cherish, your dad is a pastor, right?"

"Yeah."

"He and I have a common purpose in life. We share stories like these with people and hope that God can use them to help people find their way to Him. You could say it's in the family blood. You have to decide if you are ready to hear the story now or not."

She looked again at her father, then back at Jaker, and said, "I want to hear the story."

Jaker smiled. "I figured you would. The woman you saw dancing was Deborah from the kitchen. Nearly thirty years ago when Deborah's mother was pregnant with Deborah, her older brother by four years died under suspicious circumstances. Many people believed it was her father, who had sacrificed the boy in a voodoo ceremony to obtain a blessing of strength and power on his next-born son. But no one felt strong enough to say anything. No one felt it was their place to say anything because many other people in the region were doing the same thing.

"On the day that Deborah was born, the mother and village were ecstatic, but the expectant father became sullen. Over the following three years, he began to withdraw from the family. But not completely, as in time his wife became pregnant again, and the father slowly began to reengage. Until on the night when the mother once again gave birth to another beautiful baby girl, and her father became enraged, leaving the family.

"Over the next ten years, the mother and daughters struggled to survive. Times were desperate, but they had one another—until one dark night. When Deborah was almost thirteen, her father burst into their hut unannounced and moved back in as if nothing had ever happened. From that night on, fear reigned in that home again. He drank, he cursed, he berated, and he beat each of them mercilessly in his fits of intoxication.

"This continued for a couple of months until the day Deborah began her menstrual cycles. That night her fear transformed into something worse—terror. During the nighttime, her father came into her room and sexually abused her in a manner that is unspeakable. Then he began to 'loan' her out to his male friends. When her mother found out, she was furious and confronted her so-called husband. Once again, he became enraged, blaming her for the loss of a son. She said she had nothing to do with the loss of their son. He said not the oldest boy; he was sacrificed for strength and blessing on the next son. He blamed her for the loss of the second son, whom she never provided. But the secret was out about the murder of the firstborn. The two younger girls shrank into the corner of their hut as their mother flew into her husband and attacked him with a pan.

"The fight overflowed into the street where witnesses watched the mother, mad with rage, clawing and screaming. In front of witnesses, the father picked up a stick and in 'self-defense'—but really untamed rage—struck their mother. She fell with one blow and never stood back up again. Because of the testimony of the community, he was set free, and both of the girls entered into bondage.

"The rapes continued on Deborah until one day her father sold her off to an elderly man in Nigeria as a wife, his sixth. Her sister was sold off to a man also in Nigeria, who ended up being a fairly good husband to her. Over time, Deborah's sister gave birth to a daughter.

"In the months that followed, Deborah lived a nightmare. She was beaten and raped by her 'husband' while one of his other wives sat on her chest. Through it all she developed repeated severe pelvic infections, as well as scars on her body from the beatings and emotional scars from the trauma she endured.

"One night she begged the others in the house to let her go out and pick some papaya from the tree in the front of the hut to assist with her menstrual pains. For months she had been timid and compliant, which led them to believe she was not a flight risk. They were wrong. The moment she was out of the hut, she ran, and ran, and ran. She ultimately found a church that took her in, providing food and shelter. Over the following months, she found her way back to Benin and into the home of an elderly pastor and his wife, who without question cared for her as their own.

"One summer a friend of mine came to visit and got to know the young woman, who was having a hard time adjusting to life in the home of a pastor. During the day she was bitter, unable to contain her outbursts of rage and hysterical weeping.

"My friend noticed that Deborah liked to sit outside by the hut in the cool of the night, away from the moonlight, and look at the stars. During these times Deborah was more peaceful. The second night my friend felt inspired to hum hymns as she went out and ballet danced in the moonlight. She allowed the girl to watch as they both continued to say nothing to one another for a week or two.

"When the moon was full, my friend felt the Lord speak to her. That same night the young woman asked, "What are you doing?"

"I'm singing praise songs in the moonlight."

"That's stupid. You should sing songs of pain and suffering," said the girl, who thought she was being smart and wanted to teach the White woman about the real truths of life.

"No, I start to sing those songs in about two weeks."

"What?"

"I will not sing of pain, suffering, despair, or death for another two weeks. Tonight, I sing of the light."

"You are a crazy White woman."

"And you are an angry Black woman."

"The girl went inside, and my friend wasn't sure if they would see one another again. But as was their routine, Deborah was outside when my friend went out and began to hum and sway. Each night was the same for another two weeks except that as the moon was waning toward a sliver of light, my friend's tone of music and dancing began to change. As the moon waned her music become sadder, expressed more pain, until in the new moon she sang about her darkest days of her life, and all she could do was sway. During these times the younger woman began to hear of all the pain, suffering, and loss, my friend had experienced. After that, for another two weeks, she learned of the joys and heard the laughter. That summer, night after night after night, the two women met outside; one sang and danced while the other watched and learned.

"By the time they were into their second month, the younger had learned a lot about the older. It wasn't much longer after that the younger began to join the older and learned to sing and dance her own story in the moonlight."

"Wait, I don't get it. How does the moonlight figure into this?" asked Cherish.

"Deborah asked my friend the same thing. The answer is in the story of creation. On day one, God made the light and separated it from the darkness. The light is God's symbolism for all the good things that ought to be. He made all the fruit of the Spirit on the first day. With the light he made all the things symbolized by the light: love, joy, peace, patience, kindness, goodness, gentleness, faithfulness, and self-control—not to mention wisdom, mercy, grace, justice, righteous, and anything else that isn't physical. Things you can say are of the light were made on that day. All the good that ought to be was made on the first day of creation.

"Then He separated the light and all these wonderful things from the darkness, which symbolizes all the things that ought not to be. That's why good and bad things feel different. They don't feel the same. They aren't experienced the same. You can't experience hate and feel the benefits of love. That is why some people search for joy in happiness, but it isn't the same. You can't be impatient and experience the wonder and beauty of patience. You can't live a life of unfaithfulness and enjoy the experience of faithfulness.

"God gave two sources of this light to world. One that is radiating and is the source of all light. The other is simply a reflector of the first. In every life lived on the planet, there are both sources of light. The greater source is the sun, and there is only one Son. The other source is the moon, and on this planet the source of light is either the one generating or the one reflecting. In the dark places of this world, in the dark side of the world we live in, where the sun does not shine, all the beautiful things of the light are provided through the reflection of the moon. In the early days of creation, the moon was always full as it radiated from Adam to Eve, and from Eve to Adam, and they walked in the light of God every evening in the cool of the day.

"But with the fall of man, the moon was no longer full in the dark places of the world, and the world began to be filled with pain, suffering, loss, and despair because when He separated the two, the benefits of the light are never felt in dark places by any means other than the sun giving it or the moon reflecting it."

"That sounds awful!" said Cherish.

"That is because it is supposed to be awful," corrected Jaker. "One of the purposes of the dark is to make you appreciate the light."

"So why the dancing?" asked Cherish.

"The cycle of dancing and singing honors the fact that there are days in our lives when we, or others, are acting like the full moon," said Jaker.

"Like my father," interrupted Cherish.

"Like your father," confirmed Jaker.

"And days when we, or others, are not acting like the full moon—"

"Like when the moon is dark," interrupted Cherish, who was obviously tracking now.

"Like when the moon is new and dark," parroted Jaker.

"Like her father."

Jaker paused to steady his voice. "Yes, like her father. And the truth for humanity is that we are all currently living in the night, on the dark side of the planet, waiting for our glorious King to return and live in the presence of the true source of light, not the symbol, as it says in Revelation chapter twenty-two.

"And she dances to remind herself, on mornings when the moon is waxing—or full—that God puts people in our lives who reflect the good things of heaven. She dances to remind herself on mornings when the moon is waning, or new, that there are people in the world who are not good reflectors, or imitators, of His goodness. It is in these times she prays to be a better reflector of His light. She prays for those who live in darkness and need to see a great light. She prays to be refined. She prays that she never forgets the Son. She spends her mornings dancing to remind herself of all these things.

"Through this process she demonstrated a way for Deborah to live in the light and be able to embrace the reality of the darkness she has lived in, and that others are currently living in."

"Is that why she taught Christina to dance and sing in the moonlight?" asked Cherish, tears now welling up in her eyes.

"Like every true believer, she is willing to offer those in darkness a chance to see and live in the light. And Christina, like Deborah, has seen great darkness in her life. Did you see how she behaved in the early days she was at the orphanage?"

"Yes, she was not a nice person."

"No, nor was Deborah when she first came to live in the light. But did you see her soften in the few days following when she was being taught to sing and dance?"

"Yes, there was the beginning of a change."

"Deborah is using her story of light and darkness to lead Christina out of her own darkness and into the light so that one day she will be able to reflect that light to others—"

"So that they can find their way into the light."

"Yes! I would not tell that story to just anyone, nor can you."

"It's not my story to tell."

"Correct, but I think the Lord woke you up early yesterday morning so you could not only see, but learn about what was happening in the quad."

"Now I am no longer one of the billions who hasn't heard the story."

"Correct again."

"And I must decide what to do with the story. Do I let it just fade like a waning moon, or do I let it sink in and transform me into a full moon?"

"Remembering that we aren't perfect yet, but we can always do a better job tomorrow than we did today," said her dad.

"And on the bad days, remember that the sun still shines. Then confess we are not the light. We can only testify to the light," added Jaker.

"I don't think I ever can be the same person I have been with all that I have seen. Still, I'm not sure I know how to be different," confessed Cherish.

"None of us are on this road alone," said Jaker as he grabbed her phone and began typing away. "There! I have entered in my contact info. If you need a friend or have concerns you want a friend to pray for, or you have questions, then I want you to call me. To not call me when you are in need will be offensive to me.

"I will give it some thought. One thing is for certain though. Things can never be the same," Cherish admitted.

● ● ●

"Attention in the institution! It's 8:45 a.m. 9:00 a.m. callouts, line movement, line movement!"

Within minutes, the 9:00 callout small group with Miss Anna Belle Nelson had gathered, and everyone was in their spot.

"Mr. Williamson, would you do us the honor of opening in prayer?"

"Sure! Heavenly Father, we have come together again today to learn more about You. Please open our hearts and minds that we might hear all that You have to say to us today. Amen."

"Amen," replied the group.

"The last time we met, we talked about having something you could use as a study guide to help you process some of the things we have been discussing. If I remember correctly, there have been times in the past where, as Mr. Hanson said, you left asking more questions than were being answered."

"Yeah," said Mr. Hanson.

"I think that those of you who have been with me the longest can attest to the fact that in time, I often repeat myself and come back to concepts I have previously presented. Have I not?"

"Yes, ma'am," interjected Mr. Johnson. "Some of the things I understand better the next time I hear it."

"Then let us try and modify a concept I call the third book rule," said the elderly woman.

"The third book rule?" asked Mr. Perez, who wasn't sure if this was something he should be writing down or not.

"Yes, the third book rule. The father of a friend of mine taught me the rule as something he had learned in medical school. The third book rule was born out of an observation of professors at his school who noted something interesting on the end of semester evaluations they received from students. The students noted that there were three reading lists presented for the class each term.

"The first list was the required reading list, the second list was the recommended reading list, and the third list was the optional reading list. At the end of the semester evaluations, students would, with great frequency, note that they didn't feel the required reading texts were of any value. They felt the recommended texts were of some benefit, but the optional reading lists were often the most helpful. So the next year the professors would adjust the columns by shifting the optional to required, but the same response was noted on the end of that semester's evaluations. The professors soon noticed that it did not matter which column they listed the texts in; it was always the third book the students read that made sense."

"What?" asked Mr. Perez in an unconvinced tone.

"I admit, I think the story was fabricated by the professors. But I think it was to point out a simple truth. The longer you ponder something, the more sense it will make as you move through life."

"You're saying that the third book rule simply means don't give up. It means keep chewing the cud," summarized Mr. Williamson.

The Locksmith just smiled.

"So what does this have to do with the study guide?" asked Mr. Gascon.

"I pledge to you that I will write out some of the concepts we have previously discussed, essentially trying to restate them so that you can have another round of chewing the cud. Or, if you like, hear it a second time."

"Then when we hear it again, it will have been for the third time, or more," pointed out Mr. Johnson.

"And perhaps it will begin to stick a bit better," added Mr. Gascon.

"That would be the plan I am proposing," stated Miss Nelson.

"What will go in it?" asked Mr. Perez.

"That is my next question. What topics do you want me to bring up for review?"

"I don't know about the others, but I would like to review the thoughts you shared a few months ago on the first chapter of Genesis," said Mr. Johnson.

"Yeah, and start with an introduction on similitudes. I don't think I had any foothold on those Genesis topics until you went over the similitude talk again," requested Mr. Williamson.

"Ah, so an introduction to the principle of first mention and the principle of expositional constancy as two underlying principles for similitudes?" asked Miss Nelson, looking for confirmation.

"Yeah, I'm lost already," said Mr. Perez.

"Sounds like the perfect place to start then," said Mr. Johnson.

"Then you can review the first chapter of Genesis," directed Mr. Williamson.

"Then while we are in Genesis, a review of chapter three with the fall of man being a pattern of all sin. I remember us talking about that before, and I could use a refresher," Mr. Gascon added.

"What else do you want to review?" requested Miss Nelson.

"I know we were just talking about it, but can we go back over the armor of God?" asked Mr. Perez. "I think there were some things I missed."

"Okay. How about one more topic?"

"I remember you telling us how you pray the Lord's Prayer every day as a way to dedicate the day. Can you review that as well?" asked Mr. Johnson.

"Okay," said Miss Nelson. "I think we have a great starting place for our review, or study guide. I will get to work on that and hopefully have it out to you before long. For the rest of our time today, can we pray for one another?"

"Especially for Hanson. He will be leaving soon," said Perez.

"Thanks, bro," replied Mr. Hanson.

Miss Nelson asked and received prayer requests, for which they each took a moment and prayed. It didn't seem long, and their session was interrupted by the loudspeaker.

"Attention in the institution! It's 9:45 a.m. 10:00 a.m. callouts, line movement, line movement!" And each man stood up, shook Miss Nelson's hand, and with words of appreciation, left the room.

* * *

An hour and a half later she was sitting at her breakfast table with Max, sharing a pot of tea.

"When does Jaker get home?" asked Max.

"He is in route as we speak. He called me early this morning, or was it late last night? Heh!" Miss Nelson chuckled to herself. "You know, right now I don't rightly remember what time it was. Regardless, it was before he left Paris. He has a stop in Seattle, then he catches a flight back to Boise. I expect we will see him tomorrow."

"Have you heard any more of Madame D'Souza through your sources?" asked Max, sounding rather sinister.

"Ha! Margaret, you make it sound so nefarious." Miss Nelson seemed to be in a happy mood as she let a little laugh slip out. "Yes, as a matter of fact, I have."

"What's the word?"

"According to sources in the New Orleans area, when the Caldwell Police showed up and started asking questions, even the Feds became interested."

"Oh?"

"Apparently, the possibility that a different jurisdiction might have a claim on the two henchmen caused everyone to start turning up the heat and jockeying for position."

"Everyone was afraid their case would get bumped, or at least messed up."

"It appears that may be what is happening. Nonetheless, Madame has ceased her inquiries and is trying to lay low. There is no more word of her in Denver, according to our local agencies, and she never began making inquiries in the Seattle area. She appears to have at least put her search on hold, and every day of respite gives another day for Abomey to find a home."

"Any word on a home? Any home situated one yard from the gates of heaven as her mom requested?"

"A couple of people have expressed interest, but for one reason or another their requests cease. They are even having trouble finding a foster family placement."

"That seems strange to me," said Max

"Indeed, Miss Smithson. It does to me as well."

"Well, at least we can pray," they said together with another chuckle.

CHAPTER 20

ARRIVING HOME

Weiser, Idaho
the next week

It was a beautiful Wednesday morning in the upper end of the Treasure Valley. Even though the air was cool and the sun bright, the weatherman had promised it was going to get hot.

Miss Nelson was at her breakfast table with Max, Jaker, and, as usual, a pot of tea. The events of the preceding weeks had quieted down significantly. Thus, the three of them believed now was the time to reflect on those events and gather for their usual debriefing.

"Do you feel your internal clock is back on schedule, Mr. O'Malley, or are you still out of synch with our Idaho time schedule?" asked Miss Nelson.

"I'm not quite back to my normal, ma'am."

"I don't know. You look as sharp as ever to me. Wouldn't you agree, Margaret?"

"Yes, ma'am. I would call it baseline for the capable Mr. O'Malley," replied Max. "How was the flight back, Jaker?"

"As you know I had to adjust seats, but I think the change will likely bear fruit."

"How so, Mr. O'Malley?" The Locksmith hadn't had a chance to speak to him much over the past week, and she was curious as to how the discussion with Cherish went.

"I shared with Cherish and her father the basics of Deborah's story, which I think was an eye-opener for them both. I really don't think there are many within the church, or body of Christ, who have had much experience with the types of horrors so many live with in West Africa, or throughout the rest of the world for that matter."

"Did she say anything specific about her thoughts?" asked Max.

"No, I wouldn't say she harvested any fruit from that experience while on the plane. However ... " Jaker smiled as he took a sip of tea. "It was easy to see the soil was well tilled and seeds were planted. I have been praying for her daily."

"What about you, Max? Are you still a suspect in a murder investigation?" asked Jaker, still smiling as he lowered his cup.

"Hardly! Murder, sir? Please!" cautioned Miss Nelson. "Our Margaret Smithson is an upstanding citizen, I will have you know!"

Max raised her eyebrows at Jaker and cocked her head as if to say, "*So there.*"

"What's the news on what the Caldwell PD is up to?" asked Jaker.

"The word I hear is that they continue to attempt to put pressure on the Louisiana Henchmen. However, because other jurisdictions have been watching them, the Caldwell PD has kicked up a hornet's nest. The South just got a lot warmer, and Madame and her lieutenants are trying to lay low. As a result, there has been pressure on the Caldwell PD to stand down and not interfere with the game the big boys are trying to play," stated Miss Nelson.

"So what are they doing?" asked Max.

"They are still trying to get interviews, but the Feds are edging them out. The PD feels these guys are central to knowing what really happened in the hours leading to Santana's death, and they want to pursue it. So much so that they have ignored all other angles."

"Is the great-grandmother still trying to find Abomey?" asked the young woman.

"No, I think the noise this whole thing is causing through law enforcement has her trying to not draw attention to her herself. I do not hear of any questions being asked or searches being performed in our area of the Treasure Valley, The Front Range Urban

Corridor of Denver, nor throughout any of the Puget Sound region of Seattle."

"What about getting Abomey adopted, or at least into foster care? Is there any news there yet?" asked Jaker.

"No, that is the one piece that still seems to be unresolved. It sure would be nice to get her in with a family that could shelter and care for her. All the foster situations she has been in so far have been very temporary."

"That doesn't seem to be a very good scenario for a vulnerable new-born," commented Max.

"No, it doesn't. But I still just see God's fingerprints all over the events leading up to where we are. I am confident it will all turn out well," summarized The Locksmith.

"Ma'am, have you heard from Solomon?" asked Jaker.

"Yes, two days ago I called him, and he said they are moving forward on the crusade with the movie. They have been making new contacts in the villages surrounding the church, and excitement is building. They are concerned that they may have to move the showing outside."

"Well, that is something to be praying for. That region has so much history of pain and sorrow, and these people need the Lord. While I was there, Deborah had said the people of the area were hungry, and I think she was right," shared Jaker.

"It is a very dark place, habits and traditions that are generations old are strongholds that the enemy won't want them messing with," pointed out Miss Nelson.

"At least we can pray," they all said together.

"And speaking of Deborah…" continued Miss Nelson between sips of tea.

"Yes?" asked Jaker in an attempt to coax more information.

"It seems that she will be a foster mother for Christina, who will be moving in with Deborah near the orphanage, then she will begin a cooking internship."

"How are the dancing and singing lessons coming?" This was a question Jaker had been wondering about since arriving back home.

He found himself naturally praying for them and was pleased to realize it was about 2:00 a.m. in Benin when he did.

"Christina has quite nearly had a half cycle of the moon with which she could explore and consider her relationship with the Lord. Deborah has reported that the clam has begun to open her mouth and reveal the pearl that has been growing inside her through the process. Deborah feels the fact that they can now speak, at least in generalities, about their similarities in the past has brought Christina to a safe place to begin discussing her trauma without reproach from others, or herself."

The threesome sat for a few seconds either sipping their tea or playing with their cups and saucers.

"I guess that puts us in the best place to begin debriefing on what we have experienced so far this summer," offered The Locksmith.

"You want to start, Max?" asked Jaker.

"Yeah, I think that there have been several major themes for me this summer," shared Max.

"The amount and diversity of pain and suffering that I have experienced within my small group has amazed me."

"How so?" asked Jaker as Miss Nelson sat and sipped her tea, listening to the two young people process their thoughts.

"Sandy's family is a mess, and to hear her discuss her experiences within her family was hard to hear. Jaz's family isn't much better. Several of the girls have parents, or families, that are variously engaged presenting their own problems. Then there is Lindsey, who has never known some members of her family. And now as I think about Abomey, I can't help but hurt for a girl who won't have a blood relative that she either can't know or shouldn't know."

"Sounds much like what I experienced in West Africa. The orphanage was full of children who were either separated from their families through death or separated from their families in order to protect them from being abused. I often went to bed in tears, marveling at how they have once again come to trust, laugh, and love."

"Pain is a problem, isn't it?" remarked Max, stating more than asking. "How does someone who believes in a loving, all-powerful God address the issue of pain?"

"That has been a question of sages throughout the ages," said Jaker with raised eyebrows as if to show his acknowledgement that he was saying something that likely didn't need to be said.

"Ma'am, any thoughts for us?" asked Max.

"Margaret, that question of pain, probably more than any other, has had the greatest impact on how people see God and interact with Him."

This time the two younger people were silent and allowed the silence to work on The Locksmith.

"First, do not forget every person you meet is a person who experiences pain and suffering to some degree or another. Each of them is caught up in the cosmic chess match." The Locksmith took a sip of her tea.

"A pawn to be sacrificed, or advanced to be made a queen," added Jaker as The Locksmith set down her tea.

"In addition, I believe there are at least two other things of which I am certain," started The Locksmith.

"There is a God, and you aren't Him?" asked Jaker jokingly.

"That is true. However, the two things I was thinking are slightly different: there is a God, and there is pain."

"Hard to argue with that." Max looked at Jaker and smiled. He gave a nod. "How are those two facts impacting how people see and interact with God?"

"For me, the fact that most people are more intimate in their knowledge and perception of pain than they are of their knowledge and perception of God puts God at a huge disadvantage in how people see and interact with Him when they deal with their pain."

"Okay," offered Max as Jaker watched the elder woman formulate her thoughts.

"When pain is severe, intense, or of long duration, it begins to seem like an injustice. How can that be the will of God, or an action consistent with a loving God?"

"One feels like a pawn being sacrificed," said Max, making sure she was following.

"People end up questioning either the character or power of God."

"Correct, Mr. O'Malley. If God allows, or condones, the circumstances leading to pain, then He either isn't all-loving, or He isn't all-powerful."

"Because God either can't, or won't, stop the suffering of painful circumstances or perspectives."

"Correct, Margaret. That appears to be the dilemma. He either has insufficient power and can't save people from suffering, or His character is flawed, and He won't save from suffering."

"Ma'am, how do you approach the issue of pain and suffering in your life so that you can believe and embrace a God who either can't, or won't, intervene to prevent or resolve suffering?" asked Jaker.

Miss Nelson looked her young protégé in the eyes and said, "I believe you know as well as I do how to embrace a God who either can't, or won't, intervene to prevent or resolve suffering. Don't you, my friend?" Max looked into the eyes of Jaker as he blinked and looked out the back door into Miss Nelson's backyard.

Shortly after moving to Weiser, Jaker's younger sister was struck and killed by a farm truck while she was crossing the street walking home from school. It had been the first year Jaker and his sister didn't walk home from school together, and it caused the young boy great guilt. His mother had witnessed the accident and blamed herself for not parking closer, not walking her daughter back from the building to their vehicle. His father was on call for the emergency department when she came in and felt guilt at not being able to save his little girl.

"You cannot tell me there wasn't pain and suffering living within the walls of the O'Malley home in those days," whispered The Locksmith.

Jaker sighed deeply. "I remember guilt … anger. I remember wandering into her room to find her, to see her, to tease her. I remember expecting her to be a part of my daily activities, as she always had, only to have to shake and scold myself with the reality that she was no longer there. So many times, I felt a sense of apprehension of being unable to find my sister. I would realize she wasn't near me and fear that she was lost and in danger, and I couldn't find her. Other times I would feel guilty for not remembering her. For a very long time, I no longer knew who I was anymore." Tears were slowly forming in his eyes as he recalled not only the events but the feelings also.

"I think all of the O'Malleys felt that way," said Max with tears in her eyes as well. "How did you cope and come to embrace God through your pain?"

Jaker took a deep, cleansing breath and exhaled slowly. "The healing started with something Miss Nelson said." He looked at his aging friend and mentor. "She told me, 'Pain is a shadow, the dark spot where light ought to be.'"

"And you understood that?" asked Max mockingly.

"I came to."

"That's when we began discussing the first day of creation," said Miss Nelson, smiling at the memory of the boy who sat in front of her as a man.

"I think what finally helped me to begin to grasp what she was trying to teach me was when I realized I could be angry at the God who took my sister, or I could choose to love the God who had given her to us in the first place." There was a slight pause in the conversation as each pondered what that meant to them.

"Where did it go from there?" asked Max.

"Once I realized I had a choice in how I interacted with God, then I began to get the footing I needed to understand our creation theology. Once we had a common language for good and bad, light and darkness, right and wrong, day and night, I began to accept a God who allowed the darkness because it enriches and validates the light. I began to realize the connection, then anytime I found the darkness, I immediately began searching for the light the darkness was a testament to," explained Jaker.

"Darkness is evidence of missing light," said Max with a smile.

"Those who walk around in the dark, suffering, only sense injustice because it *ought* to be different, and they know it deep inside," summarized Miss Nelson. "The pawn that is sacrificed is the one who has been overcome by the darkness in their life. They sense life ought to be different and isn't, which is why they suffer. The pawn that advances to become a queen is the one who experiences the darkness and refuses to be overcome by it; instead, they search for the light. Even if they don't find it, they keep searching for it anyway."

"'And ye shall seek me, and find me, when ye shall search for me with all your heart,'" quoted Max.

"Which is the essence of spiritual warfare, isn't it?" asked Jaker.

"It is for me," said Miss Nelson. "Helping those in darkness to see a great light."

"It is the business of making queens out of pawns," said Jaker.

"It is realizing that the fight is for the perspective of a funeral dirge or a coronation march," followed up Miss Nelson.

"How much of this do you think Jesus was talking about when He said He had overcome the world?" asked Max.

"Everything," whispered Miss Nelson. "'These things I have spoken unto you, so that in me you may have peace. In the world you have tribulation but take courage; I have overcome the world.' He has told us that even though we will have tribulation, we can have peace. I think the tribulation He was talking of is the pain and suffering caused by the darkness that has spilled over into the lives of humanity since the fall, not just persecution from unbelievers."

"'My brethren count it all joy when ye fall into divers temptations. Knowing this, that the trying of your faith worketh patience. But let patience have her perfect work, that ye may be perfect and entire, wanting nothing.' I think that expresses the spiritual warring that we experience," added Jaker.

"Isn't it a few verses later where the passage says, 'Blessed is the man that endured temptation: for when he is tried, he shall receive the crown of life, which the Lord hath promised to them that love him'?" pointed out Max.

"I like how it is stated in second Corinthians: 'But if our gospel be hid, it is hid to them that are lost: In whom the god of this world hath blinded the minds of them which believe not, lest the light of the glorious gospel of Christ, who is the image of God, should shine unto them. For we preach not ourselves, but Christ Jesus the Lord; and ourselves your servants for Jesus' sake. For God, who commanded the light to shine out of darkness, hath shined in our hearts, to give the light of the knowledge of the glory of God in the face of Jesus Christ. But we have this treasure in earthen vessels, that the excellency of the power may be of God, and not of us. We are troubled on every side, yet not distressed; we are perplexed, but not in despair; Persecuted but not forsaken; cast down, but not destroyed; Always bearing about in the body the dying of the Lord Jesus, that the life also of Jesus might be made manifest in our body. For we which live are alway delivered unto death for Jesus' sake, that the life also of Jesus might be made manifest in our mortal flesh. So, then death worketh in us, but life in you. We having the same spirit of faith, according as it is written, I believed, and therefore have I spoken; we also believe, and therefore speak; Knowing that he which raised up the Lord Jesus shall raise up us also by Jesus, and shall present us with you. For all things are for your sakes, that the abundant grace might through the thanksgiving of many rebound to the glory of God. For which cause we faint not; but though our outward man perish, yet the inward man is renewed day by day. For our light affliction, which is but for a moment, worketh for us a far more exceeding and eternal weight of glory; While we look not at the things which are seen, but at the things which are not seen: for the things which are seen are temporal; but the things which are not seen are eternal.'"

The two younger people sat there for just a few moments, sipping their tea and reflecting on what they had just heard from the elderly woman.

"And we fight these spiritual battles which are 'not against flesh and blood,' as we are told in Ephesians chapter six verse twelve, by first realizing we are in a battle, the cosmic chess match, then by wearing the armor of God?" Max asked.

"Right. We put on the belt of truth by choosing to believe what God has said and selecting it as our chosen perspective on life," said Jaker.

"We choose to believe that 'if we confess our sins, He is faithful and just to forgive our sins and cleanse us from all unrighteousness,' and this allows us to wear the breastplate of righteousness," added Miss Nelson.

"And in a similar manner, our salvation comes from the Lord, and we can wear the helmet of salvation," contributed Max.

"Our willingness to be the broken body of Christ allows us to be prepared to suffer for the benefit of others. This may be in the form of forgiveness for wrongs done to us, or sacrificing our will, our hopes, our dreams, and our expectations so that someone else might advance in the kingdom is the way we shod our feet with the preparation of the gospel of peace," said Miss Nelson.

"And when we choose to believe these truths over what the world, the flesh, or Satan tries to tell us, we are using the shield of faith," pointed out Jaker.

"The sword of the Spirit is used effectively when we learn His Word and gain the truths we need for all this to happen," said Max.

"And then ... " said Miss Nelson, looking at each of them in turn.

"We pray," all three said in unison.

"Finally, don't forget the role of judges we have in our lives, and that we become judges for others," said Miss Nelson as she began to wrap up their debrief. "They are not the types of judges we are used to. These judges don't condemn; they inspire. They don't judge; they discern. And how do you distinguish between judging and discerning?"

"Judgement is a declaration while discernment is a question," stated Max. The Locksmith smiled.

"Being the inspiration to others in their battles through testifying to the light of God in our own," stated Jaker. "Boy, have we seen that play out this summer. Max being a judge for Sandy, and Deborah being a judge for Christina."

"And perhaps for Cherish as well," noted Miss Nelson.

"Yeah, you may be right. I haven't heard from her. Have you, ma'am?" asked Jaker.

"I have spoken to Michael and Catherine, and they have been impressed with the change they have seen in Cherish. In fact, she has been pushing to make some changes in the family, and they are excited to see her being proactive and engaged in where the Lord is leading them as a family."

"It was a delight to see her face no longer reflecting the world as she looked at her phone. Instead, I saw her truly desiring to reflect the light of God," recognized Jaker.

"I think you have picked some nice locks there, Mr. O'Malley," said Miss Nelson. "I am very proud of you. Proud of you both," she said as got up from the table and set her cup and saucer in the sink. Then she opened the drawer next to the sink and pulled out two keys. She gave one to Jaker and the other to Max. "Very proud, indeed."

Miss Nelson often presented her two pupils with a key when she thought they had grasped some important principles that would be helpful in their own journey as locksmiths. It was an act between them that was more valuable in the gesture than it was in the metal. The key no longer opened anything that any of them were aware of, but its symbolism suggested the ability to unlock something of greater value than just some old door. Through the years the gifting of the key after a recitation of truths had become one of their most treasured moments together. Jaker still had the first key she ever gave him. She had told him to keep it and never lose it.

● ● ●

Months later as August was ending, another year of school was on the horizon for Max, her next to last. Jaker had just arrived from a quick trip to Washington, DC, and had another one planned for the week Max returned to her apartment in Nampa. The days had become intolerably hot, so the two friends met every morning they were both in town to spend time together. Today, Max was playing Jaker a game of twenty-one on the basketball court, using her left hand to give him a sporting chance. Of course, she beat him three out of three games. He was used to it.

Ding! "Wait, that's my phone." *Ding!* "And that's yours," said Jaker.

They both picked up their phones to see a message from The Locksmith. "I have someone I want you to meet."

"I wonder when—" *Ding!* Max was unable to finish her question as the notification came through.

"Before lunch," it read.

"Sometimes she's cryptic," said Jaker.

"And sometimes she's creepy," added Max as they chuckled.

"I need to shower first. How about I wait for you at my house, and we can walk over together?" recommended Jaker.

"Okay, see you in a few," confirmed Max as they each responded to The Locksmith.

About twenty minutes later Max was at Jaker's front door, ready to knock, when his mother opened and greeted her.

"Oh! Hi, Mrs. O'Malley."

"Hello, Margaret. You are as lovely as ever. When are you going to join my family?"

"Yeah, thanks, Mom," interrupted Jaker.

"Jaker, don't be rude, Max and I were having—" said Cokie O'Malley, who had on several occasions expressed her desire to see her son officially date his best friend.

"Mom! Miss Nelson said to meet her before lunch, so we have to go," interrupted Jaker as he bustled Max off the porch.

"We still need to talk, my dear," said Cokie.

"Okay, we will," said both Jaker and Max together as they cut through the lawn to the house next door.

"Whose van is that?" Max nodded toward the silver-colored, late-model Toyota minivan.

"Not sure. I saw it when I got home. I saw it had Oregon plates though. I started trying to think of who of Miss Nelson's Oregon contacts that might be. But I quickly gave up."

"Because why would she call you over to introduce you to someone you already know?" said Max with a bobbing of her head from side to side and her notorious, *Well, aren't you Mr. Know-It-All* voice.

Jaker just smiled and shrugged his shoulders, implying, "*Well, yeah.*"

The two mounted the porch and could hear several voices. "Come on! Come on! You can do it!"

"What in the world?" snorted Max.

Jaker rang the doorbell.

"Keep going! Keep going!"

"Ahh Nooo!" was the universal cry of defeat.

Miss Nelson answered the door. "Come in, come in. You two you are about to miss it!" she said, waving them in.

Jaker opened the door and let Max enter, then followed close behind.

"John Quinton Riley, I believe you know father and daughter Truesdale," began the elderly woman.

"Hi, Jaker!" said Cherish, who was sitting on her knees in the middle of the floor.

"Hi, Cherish," said Jaker with a smile as he moved over and gave her a high five.

"And this is Mrs. Catherine Truesdale," introduced Miss Nelson. The woman put her hands on the floor as if to push up.

The woman looked up with a smile and said, "Cathy, please."

"How do you do, ma'am? Please don't get up," said Jaker, who leaned forward to shake her hand. She, too, was on her knees in the middle of the floor. "Hi, Mike! How are you doing?" He shook hands with Mr. Truesdale. "I thought you guys were from Washington."

"We were, but shortly after adopting this little one, we transitioned to our new pastorate in Salem, Oregon."

Miss Nelson made the introductions to Max as well. "And this is Miss Margaret Smithson. Margaret, this is Michael, Catherine, and Cherish Truesdale."

Max shook everyone's hand, and as she finished, she knelt down on the blanket that had been spread out. In the middle of the floor, laying on her stomach, was an infant about four months old who had mulatto skin and a pink bow that held back her curly black hair from her face.

"The Truesdales have a new baby that I believe needs to be introduced," stated Miss Nelson. Tears began to well up in Max's eyes.

"When we got back from Africa, Cherish thought it was time that we as a family started being the moon for someone less fortunate. We talked about it and decided to become a foster family. We had given thought to it before in the past, and the paperwork was already in the works. Which allowed the whole process to rapidly advanced to adoptive parents," said Mike.

"How has it gone so far?" asked Max in little more than a whisper.

"It has gone really well," said Cathy.

"It has gone very well. It happened faster than anyone thought it could," finished Cherish.

Miss Nelson couldn't help but smile at how with God, decades could pass where nothing happens, then there could be weeks where what one thought would take decades could happen in weeks.

"What are you going to call her?" asked Max.

"We decided to keep the name her birth mother gave her. We will call her Abomey," said Cathy.

"Fascinating, considering where we were earlier this year, don't you think?" said Pastor Truesdale as he elbowed Jaker with a smile.

Max wiped away a tear with the back of her arm as she chortled a laugh.

Jaker couldn't help but smile.

"Pastor, have you seen my friend in Salem?" asked Miss Nelson.

"Indeed, I have, Anna Belle. I met him as he stepped out of the gate. He has been well taught."

The Locksmith smiled.

"We have communicated daily, and we meet at least once a week. We were able to find him a job, and he is well established in our fellowship." The Locksmith was nodding not only her understanding but her appreciation as well. "He is soaking up our Nehemiah discussions."

"I believe he is in good hands," replied the elderly woman.

The pastor smiled, knowing she meant not only the "hands" of the Holy Spirit, but his as well. "He is in the Best of Hands. And I will do my best as well."

"I have no doubt," said The Locksmith, "in either of your hands."

"Oh! She's trying again! She's trying again! Come one, Abbey! You can do it," said Cherish with a clap of her hands. All three Truesdales began their encouraging words: "Come on! You can do it! Come on, Abbey!" With their happy intonations and claps, the baby began to arch her back and push up with her arms. The closer she got the more excited they became, and before long everyone was cheering, laughing, and encouraging.

With one last burst of effort, the baby rolled over onto her back, offering those who loved her the biggest smile she'd given. As Abomey looked up into the loving faces that were one yard away, the baby with bluish-gray eyes saw reflected in those faces the light of God, and she giggled as through the gates of heaven she was filled with peace, joy, and the feeling of safety only a well-protected and well-loved baby understands.

VALUED PARTNERS

To learn how you can actively participate in combating human trafficking and commercial exploitation around the world please review the following sites and consider joining them in their mission.

ORPHAN RELIEF AND RESCUE

(focusing on the children of West Africa)

"Following the model of Jesus, we believe that every child is valuable and has a name, dream and destiny. We are working hard to ensure that they are given a voice and hope for the future."

www.orphanreliefandrescue.org

EUROPEAN FREEDOM NETWORK

(focusing on Europe)

"Modern day slavery is a human rights violation and heinous crime that robs people of their freedom, dignity, and ability to flourish. It still exists today, even if you can't see it. Right now, it is estimated that over 40 million people are trapped in modern day slavery."

www.europeanfreedomnetwork.org

To learn how you can actively participate in sharing the good news of Jesus Christ around the world please review the following site and consider joining them in their mission.

JESUS FILM HARVEST PARTNERS

(focusing on nearly every region of the world)

"JESUS Film Harvest Partners (JFHP) is a Kingdom-building ministry devoted to world evangelism through the JESUS film and other tools. JFHP equips and supports JESUS Film teams of local people to do evangelism, discipleship, and church planting."

www.jfhp.org

For more about Abomey and its author go to:

WWW.RANSOMSPLACE.COM